Margaret Garth was born in Manchester. Despite an early desire to write novels, she studied Chemistry and Maths. Marriage resulted in a move to the Midlands and later to Norfolk. She now resides in Bedfordshire with her husband.

Her imagination was kept lively by the demands of her children for stories. Interests are gardening and dressmaking.

This book is dedicated to my husband Alan in recognition of his unfailing support.

Margaret Garth

THE WITCH OF BELLUE

A TALE OF SALIMA

AUSTIN MACAULEY
PUBLISHERS LTD.

A CIP catalogue record for this title is available from the British Library.

ISBN 978 1 78455 209 1 (paperback)
ISBN 978 1 78455 211 4 (hardback)

www.austinmacauley.com

First Published (2014)
Austin Macauley Publishers Ltd.
25 Canada Square
Canary Wharf
London
E14 5LB

Printed and bound in Great Britain

Acknowledgments

Acknowledgement to Mr John Barnett who wrote the melody for Margren's song.

Pronunciation

Coan – cone
Frelius – Fraylius, accent on first syllable
Gery – Gairy, to rhyme with fairy, hard 'g'. Short form of Gerharst

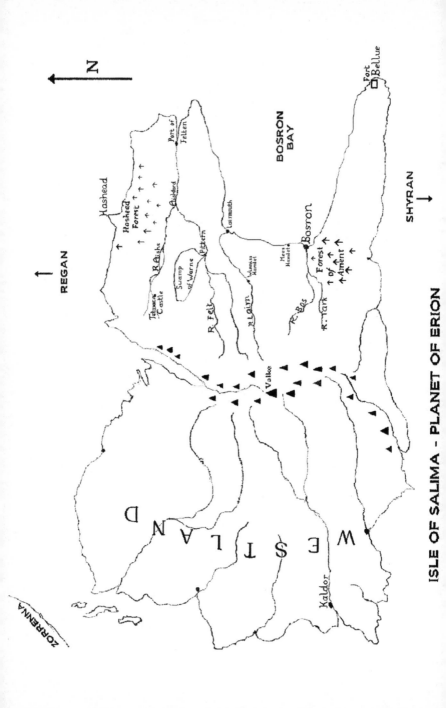

ISLE OF SALIMA - PLANET OF ERION

Chapter 1

Morrell rowed slowly. He had rowed far since leaving Tullen in the early morning. He was sure that no one had seen him retrieve his boat from its hiding place, but he still put a good distance between himself and the village before considering himself safe. By then he was in waters that he did not know. He had found a landing place and had surveyed the coast carefully from the cliff. He had noted the rocks, above and below the water and, some distance further on, he spied a likely cove with a tiny stretch of sand where he could land. There was a village near that cove. It had seemed ideal. It had *been* ideal.

He cursed the boy again. The dark pains of Hadron were too good for him. He ought to have been cleaning fish, or working in the fields or cutting wood for fires or even attending school if the village boasted such an establishment. He certainly ought not to have been idling in one of the caves by the shore.

He had been quite hidden. Morrell's careful scan of the cove had revealed no trace of any human activity; no scrap of cloth, no pail nor fishnet, no footprints in the smooth sand. It had seemed safe to land.

The boy had appeared as he was struggling to pull the boat out of the water. He had taken off boots and cloak – salt water ruined both leather and wool – and hitched his long tunic round his waist with a cord. There was sand under his feet when he had first stepped out of the boat, but he discovered painfully that there were hidden rocks just beneath its surface. He stubbed his toe against a particularly sharp one and was cursing loudly when he saw the boy.

He cursed again. No chance of rising from the waters at Namier's command when one had been seen hauling a boat out of the sea! He was considering other approaches when the lad had laughed.

"Trod on a poison-spine did you? Good. There are enough old men in Fabbae without you a-joining them."

He spoke with such a guttural accent that Morrell had trouble understanding him, but there was no mistaking the mocking laugh, or the stone that was thrown. The first fell short, but the boy picked up others and aimed more carefully.

Morrell had pushed the boat out again and scrambled into it as fast he was able. It was an undignified and painful retreat. Several stones had found their target, he had grazed one foot on a rock and something seemed to be embedded in the sole of the other. He left the cove as fast as possible and continued eastward.

Now he rowed slowly. For one thing, his arm hurt, to say nothing of his feet, and for another he did not know these waters. He had surveyed no farther than the cove. The last thing he needed was an encounter with an unseen rock. His boat and its contents represented all his worldly goods and he had no wish to lose any of them to the sea.

To be sure the most valuable, a heavy silver chain and a gold pin with a fine stone, were fastened firmly round his body beneath his tunic, but he needed to keep everything, even the meagre haul he collected in his two years in Tullen.

His keep had been provided there – food in plenty, though rather more of the strongly flavoured barfish than he would have chosen, and a comfortable pallet in the stone church. It had been warm enough when he had persuaded the population that a heavy curtain would protect the holy area, where he performed the sacrifices, from the wind. When it blew, it either fanned the flames of holy fire to unmanageable heights or scattered the hot ashes over his clothes.

He had no complaint about the living; it was the value of the gifts when he had left that had been disappointing. They had not rated him highly enough to give silver or gold or purchased goods. They gave him what they had made and what they themselves used – a carved wooden cup, a coarse wool blanket, a single loaf of bread.

Even his most devoted worshipper had produced only an embroidered coat. True it had been of the finest wool that the village produced, but the embroidery was crude and dominated by symbols of Namier – the sun, the crescent moon, the flower of Krundel, the dagger of Gerharst, the tree of snakes. That limited its value, and even the finest of Tullen wool would not be highly rated in a more sophisticated market.

The gifts, he thought bitterly, were entirely appropriate for a holy man. They were near useless to him.

They could, he thought grimly, be displayed to his next congregation. If he admired their lasting quality, praised the devotion that had inspired their making and stressed the small needs of a wandering holy man, perhaps, at the end of his stay, they would give him coin instead. He must not stress his unworldly life too much though. A fine balance between his self-sacrifice and their duty to support the Chosen of Namier was required; else he would be given nothing but prayer when he left. All this was supposing that he found somewhere suitable to stay.

He rowed on. He rejected the next inlet. It was a fine natural bay with several large fishing boats and a busy quay. Deep enough for trading ships to call, he thought. He wanted to avoid trading ships and those who dealt with them. Too much knowledge of the wider world rubbed off on the locals and they were much harder to convince.

He sighed heavily. The choice was always between good living plus danger or simple living and greater safety. He was too old now, and too slow, to risk the danger. Better to choose a village well away from any place where trading ships might call; but it meant a long and tiring journey.

It was almost dark before he found a suitable landing place, and he was near exhaustion. The cove was large, but the entrance was dangerously narrow. The bottom of the boat scraped ominously on a rock, but the next wave carried him over the obstruction and safely on to the sandy beach. His foot hurt ferociously as he stumbled up the shallow incline dragging the boat behind him to the shelter of the rocks. Fortunately the dark shadows that he had seen proved to be caves, as he had hoped; and he found one that was splendid for his purpose.

He needed to haul the boat onto its side to manoeuvre it through the entrance, but then it was easily drawn up into the depths of the cave. A few loose rocks pulled in front of it and he was satisfied. He sat down gratefully and leant back to eat some of the bread. He was hungry, but ate sparingly. He might need the rest of the bread tomorrow. The light he had seen on the eastward heights could have come from a village. He hoped so, but it might easily have been the torch of a shepherd or even a traveller.

When he had eaten, he explored the injury to his foot. Something had pierced it. He could feel something, but the flesh was too swollen for him to grasp whatever it was and pull it out.

He remembered uneasily the boy's reference to 'poison spine'. He had never heard of such a thing before. He knew of many poisonous creatures that bit or stung or pricked and left their poison in the wound. He also knew that some such injuries were best left alone, spread with coan oil and wrapped with cool leaves. Others needed the poison sac removed, and as soon as possible. He did not know what to do for the best and sleep was essential. So he slept.

The morning brought the warmth of the sun. He woke late, waking only when the light struck his face. He lay and listened. The only sound was the call of the birds and the waves stirring the shingle. No voices. No footsteps. No cries of sailors.

He sat up. His foot was still swollen and in the daylight he could see the angry red flesh around the wound. He crawled outside, unwilling to stand until it was necessary. He heard another sound when he reached the mouth of the cave and it was most welcome – the sound of falling water. A tiny rivulet flowed between the rocks and fell in a thin stream onto the sand. He fetched his cup and drank deeply. That was better.

He held his foot under the cold stream for a long time. It was a good feeling though it did not appear to reduce the swelling by any appreciable amount. He washed the salt out of his hair and beard and considered eating. No, he ought first to take a look around; see if there was a habitation nearby and, if there was, what manner of people lived there.

He cursed several times as he climbed the steep rocks, but it was relatively easy. He could not have managed a hard climb. His foot was too painful.

There was a house, not far from the cliff edge. More of a shack really, rough logs of wood fastened crudely to make a frame and covered with bundled stalks, but there was smoke rising thinly from one corner. As he watched, concealed behind a clump of thorn bushes, a woman emerged with a bucket and fetched water from the nearby stream. If she had ever been pretty, it was long ago. There was no spring in her step, her back was stooped and the hair that escaped from her headscarf was grey. When she turned back with her filled bucket she shouted. Morrell went cold with fear, but she had not seen him. She was calling to someone in the house.

"Gery! Gery, you just get up off that blanket this moment. There'll be no cockles nor crabbies to find if you lie longer and your father'll not be pleased when he gets back for his breakfast."

There was a shouted reply and a boy came out, rubbing his eyes. He made no move to take the heavy bucket though he was a sturdy lad.

"I can't go till you've fetched the water. I need the bucket." His speech was slow.

Morrell drew a satisfied breath. This boy was ideal. Stupid enough to be awed by a man rising from the sea, and just about to go alone to collect shell fish. The woman looked foolish, too. Any spark of curiosity she may once have had had been crushed by the hard life of a shepherd's wife, for such she surely was. He made his way quickly down to 'his' cove, wolfed down the remainder of the bread and made his preparations; one of the hollow straws he had brought and his cloak and boots in an oiled sack.

He was at home in the water. He swam more easily than he walked and soon found his way to the place where the boy was digging in the sand. He stayed hidden behind a rock and waited. Shellfish made a good breakfast. He was in agreement with shepherd on that point and wanted to make sure that the boy had time to collect an adequate supply for everyone. He was hungry, but it would not do for a holy man to show greed on his first miraculous appearance.

When he was sure that the bucket was full and the boy ready to leave, he made his move. With the hollow straw in his mouth he swam under the water towards the shore. His luck was changing! There were some flat rocks close in, just covered by the water. His rising from the sea would be even more wonderful if he could manage to convince the lad that he had walked on the water. The stupid child might think he was Namier himself – if he knew the stories of the Visitations well enough.

There was a slight hitch. The boy was so unobservant that his first careful emergence went unnoticed. He ducked quickly under the water again and the next time gave a great cry as he raised his head. That worked perfectly.

The boy turned and watched with open mouth as he rose to his feet and, rather unsteadily, climbed onto the first rock. After that it was easy. He timed his steps with the waves and was sure that from the shore it seemed as if he was walking on the water.

He greeted the lad with a blessing and his usual words about coming at Namier's bidding to teach the people of this land the error of their ways; neither appeared to be understood. He was obviously a boy of very limited intellect. He was, however, amazed and impressed – and too stupid to be frightened.

Morrell was led in silence to the shack at the top of the cliff. He was introduced, if one could call it that, to the woman he had seen earlier and her husband. He *was* a shepherd. He smelt strongly of sheep, and of the even less fragrant goats. No one meeting him could mistake his occupation.

They were bemused; but they did believe. He was given the best stool at the plank table and breakfast was set before him with cautious deference. The food was satisfactory, but the black and bitter tea was not to his taste.

After the meal they expressed their regret at their inability to provide him with shelter. He must go to the village at Fort Bellue.

He contained his surprise. Bellue was at the eastern end of the coast. Had he come so far? He asked if that was the nearest village and was assured that it was. It was a fair walk but there were a few small houses on the way. Gery would lead him. He was known and would be welcomed.

Gery objected. He did not wish to take the man to Bellue, even if he was a messenger from Namier. The Bellue folk were strong and their leader, Frelius, was frightening.

His mother soothed him. Neighbour Woodman would take the holy man to the boundary of the Fort. Gery need go no further than the Woodman's. They could stay the first night at Neighbour Cobb's house. It would be cramped, for the Cobbs had five children, but she was sure they would be welcomed and made comfortable.

Gery looked almost cheerful and asked if he might stay there on his way back home. The affirmative answer obviously pleased him.

His mother continued. The name 'Frelius', she explained, was a tribal name, taken by every leader of the tribe that lived around Fort Bellue. They were a fighting tribe, the Frelians, but they fought only the pirates and raiders, and that because they were fishermen. They traded peacefully and dealt fairly with all the farmers in the area.

The farmers were nearly all Maleans. They did not fight nor did they wish to do so. They kept houses and stock well hidden from the seaward side and paid their taxes to the Great Lord in Bosron. He controlled the coast all along the great bay, or so it was said. It was a large bay. The far side of these hills was one coast, and even from the highest point you could not see the other coast. He was a powerful lord.

Morrell listened avidly. The more he learnt about this area, the better he could 'prophesy' and the more he would be revered. He prompted her discreetly. It was of no use to ask the shepherd. He gave short and noncommittal answers that were useless to a seeker of information. Eventually he said more than two words. They were addressed to his wife.

"You talk too much."

She was much less communicative after that, talking only of the food and attending to her domestic duties, but Morrell hoped to have further conversation with her, when her husband had left to tend his animals.

He did succeed in having the conversation, but it was not especially useful. She was obviously not as intelligent as he had first thought; certainly brighter than her husband and her son, but she volunteered only general remarks and her answers to his more searching questions were very vague. He gave up after a while and watched as she prepared and packed a substantial amount of bread and meat for their journey. She knew something of healing herbs, too, and bound up his swollen foot with a great many of them and a trace of coan oil. She asked no questions as to how he had hurt it, and he volunteered no information.

Later, as he tramped painfully along, he tried talking to the boy. It was not easy. The youngster could not, or did not, answer all his questions. He knew the names of the plants and the sea birds that they saw, and gave them readily enough; but anything else elicited only a shake of the head. Comments on the nature of the terrain or the beauty of the coastline produced no response at all. Morrell gave up and walked in silence.

He learnt something when they stopped for lunch. The substantial pack was not just for one meal, nor was much of it intended for him. It was for Gery – enough for the whole journey. After careful questioning, Morrell came to the dismal conclusion that neighbours might share their supper and make a place by the fire for a traveller whom they knew, but they would not provide food for the ongoing journey – not unless it was paid for.

Holy men were different. Neighbour Cobb might provide for him for tomorrow, as Ma had done for today.

The holy man was not pleased.

The Cobb's household, however, was much less forbidding than Gery's. Its head was also a shepherd, but he was more contented. His wife was cheerful and the children were lively. The elder girl was plump and pretty.

Morrell understood why Gery was pleased to stay overnight with them. His palette by the fire was comfortable, but he would have been happy enough to share the big bed with the children, as Gery did. The lad might not have a great brain, but his physical attributes were obviously adequate. Morrell shut his ears resolutely to the noises from the other room. He was a holy man, he reminded himself sternly.

He was also ageing, and in dire need of sufficient funds to support him when he chose to retire. He did not wish to join a Community. They were strict – early rising, plain food, no wines or ales and no contact with females of any age.

This time, he promised himself, he would make an Impact; and be appropriately rewarded.

The following day he made plans as he walked. They had set off early and Gery had set a fast pace, but he made no complaint. Mistress Cobb had clearly felt that supper and breakfast fulfilled her charitable obligations. She had resisted all his persuasive talk and had suggested another household where they might seek hospitality around midday.

According to his guide, they needed to walk fast to arrive there by midday and there were no other dwellings nearer. He was hungry and tired when they scaled the final hill and looked down at the house and the fertile valley.

He was impressed by the size of the house. It was large, two storeys high, and boasted glazed windows and patches of flowers on either side of the door. He felt more cheerful at once.

"They will have good food there," he commented, but the boy was not enthusiastic. He had learnt early that the rich did not often share with the poor. He said so in very few words and was proved right.

They were not sent empty away, but the bread that they were given was stale, the cheese end rancid and the meat little more than skin and gristle.

Morrell ate without enjoyment. He was hungry and had no prospects of eating other than what he could beg. He was also rather further from his boat, his belongings and the possibility of exploring elsewhere, than he would have chosen to be. As they continued their journey, he concentrated hard.

The poor food lay heavy in his stomach and he needed to think deeply to distract his mind from the discomfort. He must remember the paths, and the habitations. Whenever he decided to move on, he announced well in advance that Namier had called him to leave, but he never gave the day. He did not always know himself. It depended on opportunity, and sometimes on necessity. He told his followers that Namier would bless those who helped him on his onward journey and his mission, and he encouraged them to leave suitable non-perishable gifts.

When he had pressed them as much as he dared – they rarely gave enough, but a man needed to exercise fine judgement in such matters – he left. He did so at night, unnoticed, and if possible just after a storm or a meteor sighting. If nature did not oblige, he had a few tricks; he could start a mysterious fire, produce an apparition or make an animal behave strangely. A seemingly miraculous departure was as much a part of his plan as a spectacular arrival, but from Bellue it would be hard, with his boat a two-day journey away.

The path turned inland quite suddenly. The cliffs had changed. The rocks were darker and the vegetation more sparse. It clung precariously in the narrow clefts. There was little grass. It grew low, in tiny clumps behind the hardier shrubs that could withstand the salt and the wind.

He heard the crash of waves against the rocks and looked out to sea. The peaks of the long thin island of Shyran were well behind them and only its shallow tail and a few scattered rocks protected the shore of Salima from the force of the ocean. A gust of wind emphasised that they were past the sheltered stretch of coast. Ahead both sea and shore were inhospitable – no place for a lone man in a small rowing boat. He turned thankfully inland.

Ahead he saw a possible shelter/hiding place. The land rose sharply and beyond the rise he could see the tops of trees. He assessed the height of the rise and concluded that the trees were small and stunted, but they *were* trees; and trees usually offered cover. He smiled; to himself as he thought, but a moment later his satisfaction was diminished. The stupid boy had seen both his smile and the direction of his gaze.

Gery nodded. "Aye. That's Neighbour Woodman's place," he said.

It was, supposed Morrell, reasonable that a man named Woodman should live and work near trees, but he did not feel reasonable. He felt annoyed. The last few days had not been at all promising, nor had the last few years been very profitable.

It had been a mistake to leave the west. He ought to have tackled the city of Kaldor when he was young and keen and able to adapt. Then, he acknowledged sadly, he had believed – in both Namier and in himself – and when a man believed, he had more chance of convincing others; but his mentor had been old and had avoided the worldly men of the great city. Such men were traders and merchants, dedicated to the pursuit of money and progress and an easy life. They were little inclined to think about the afterlife, when their spirits would roam free with Namier or be confined to the dark shadows of Hadron. He had feared to go alone, so he had stayed with the older man. It had been a mistake.

The small villages on their route south had been unsophisticated. It was easy to attract followers, but they were poor and could not support spiritual leaders in any more comfort than they lived themselves. It had not satisfied him and he had said so. His mentor had rebuked him. He had been a holy man and had been shocked beyond measure when he had discovered that Morrell had seduced a young girl. They had been obliged to move on.

It had not been the first girl, nor was it the last. They had parted company the following year when Morrell realised that at least two of the young women he had introduced to the 'special rites' of Namier were with child. He had left secretly one night, 'appropriated' a pony and ridden hard to the coast. There he had exchanged the animal for a boat. Whether the owner desired such a trade or what became of his mentor, he neither knew nor cared. His original enthusiasm had long since waned. Now he found exhorting sinners to change their ways or instructing unbelievers in the Visitations of Namier dull work.

His very first lesson in the ways of performing 'miracles' had started the decline. His mentor was sincere in his belief that such small deceptions were justified if they persuaded folk to live a better life, but he remained unconvinced. He doubted, too, that the 'better' life – a life of unselfish devotion and unending work for other's benefit – brought happiness. He did not find great contentment in sharing the fruits of his labours with the sick or the aged. He liked his own comfort too much.

He began to despise the followers and to doubt the truth of the Visitations. If the wonderful happenings in the books were simply tricks that had deceived the people of the time, then its message was also suspect. There was no reward for goodness, nor was there any punishment for faults.

Like many who were idealistic in early youth, when he became disillusioned the change was drastic; he became corrupt. Now he had no belief and no thought beyond his own comfort on Erion.

Neighbour Woodman lived with his elder son. His wife had died some years ago, the younger boy had moved to Fort Bellue to fish or to fight, and his daughter had followed some passing traveller to marriage or perdition, he did not know which. He did not seem to care very much either, but it was obvious that he cared for the trees that grew, more sturdily than Morrell had imagined, on the north side of the peninsula. He told their history as he walked with them to gather some mushrooms for Gery to take home. There would be some too, for Mistress Cobbs.

The trees formed a small wood rather than a forest, but it hid the great house on the north shore. The man who had built the great house had employed the first Woodman to plant and tend saplings. There had been no trees then east of the Ament forest. Now they stretched along the north coast as far as the fort at Bellue. They were self-sown out there and provided wood for fires and for boats. It was all due to the Woodmans.

He did not mention years at all. He counted in generations. His father planted one group, his grandfather planted another, his great-grandfather that one, and his great-grandfather's grandfather planted these fine specimens. A few had fallen or been felled, but many were still in their prime. It was there that the mushrooms grew and were gathered: gathered for Gery and the Cobbs, not for the newcomer, or for the community at Bellue. They, it seemed, could find and gather their own.

Morrell limped wearily back to the house. He would not have graced it with such an accolade himself. It was no more than a cave with an extended entrance built of wood and thatched with a patchwork of dried grasses and leaves, but Woodman had lived there for generations – planted like the trees by the lord in the great house and now as permanent as a feature of the landscape.

They ate before they left. The son appeared and cooked seabird eggs and mushrooms for all, followed by a dark and bitter fruit sweetened with a smear of honey.

It was nourishing, thought Morrell bleakly, if not substantial. No one asked about his foot. It hurt and the long walk had not helped. He hoped that Fort Bellue would take better care of him. If it did not, he would be in serious difficulty.

Fortunately the boy did tell of his arrival, briefly at first but in some detail when he was questioned. He was definite too, as simple folk often are. The visitor had risen from the sea. He was wet. There was no boat and he came to shore as if he walked on the water. The lad knew that such things were not possible, but that was what he had seen. That was what Neighbour Woodman was to tell the Frelius.

Morrell was questioned also. He said, as he said so many times before, that he had come as Namier commanded, not knowing where he would be sent or whom he would meet. The boy, Gery, had seen him, and his mother had suggested that Fort Bellue was the best place for him to go. He always followed such suggestions. He presumed that this was Namier's way of directing him.

He was convincing. He almost believed that it was true. Neighbour Woodman certainly accepted it and in his turn was also convincing when he spoke to the guard at the gates of Bellue. They were admitted and taken to the Frelius.

It was not surprising, thought Morrell, that the boy had not wanted to bring him here. The outer wall of Bellue reached from one shore to the other. It was more than twice the height of a man, and squat towers straddled it at intervals. Between two of these hung a pair of gates. They were made of stout wooden planks studded with metal spikes. The spikes were not long, but they were too sharp for decoration. They were to deter an onslaught from man or beast. It was a forbidding entrance.

The man on the gate was equally forbidding – tall and broad and silent. He stood firm, blocking the small opening, and waited for them to state their business. Woodman was clearly used to this treatment. He indicated Morrell, gave a brief introduction and asked to be taken to the Frelius. The guard inspected the unknown man, concluded that he was not a threat, nodded without comment and allowed them in. The gate fell back into place against its neighbour and the wooden beam that locked them together was dropped back into its iron hook. They were led through the village to the fort, by a different, but equally taciturn, guard.

No one spoke, but eyes followed them. Morrell sensed the watchers and was obliged to concentrate harder than usual on the indifference that a holy man ought to have to such scrutiny. Namier might hold all mankind as equal, but he did not. Idle curiosity caused him no problem, but he felt assessment in at least one pair of eyes. He must be careful.

He did permit himself to look at his surroundings. The village and most of the cultivated fields were in the central and northern area. There were cliffs on the north coast but it was to the south that the land rose steeply. It was green enough but obviously not very fertile. Few cattle grazed, but there were sheep and on the higher slopes a few goats.

"Bellue Heights," Neighbour Woodman informed him. "The fort is not so high, but is at the eastern edge and commands a wide view of the seas."

He was right. The fort itself was an impressive structure, seeming to rise without break from the cliff's edge. It was built from the black rock on which it stood. The walls were high and were punctuated with outcrops of natural rock. There were no openings, no breaks in the surface until the crenulations at the top. The eyes that surveyed the surroundings watched through those gaps or from the tops of the towers. There were three of those; two on the eastward wall to watch the sea, and one to the west that spanned the gateway. There were a few slits in that broad tower, but they did not show weakness. Missiles might be flung from them, but little would penetrate such high and narrow apertures and the view from its height would be wide indeed.

Morrell murmured some comment to his guide and Woodman replied with an accepting shrug. "No one comes unseen. They have false eyes that see almost to my house in the west, to Shyran in the south and to the far shore of the Great Bay and for all I know to the edge of Erion to the east. But," he added shielding his mouth so that the guard would not hear, "they do pay tribute to the Lord in Bosron."

They were kept waiting for some time in the courtyard beyond the gate, until the messenger, sent to inform Frelius of their arrival, returned. He led them into a large room but did not stay to announce or introduce them to its occupants. That task was left to an older man. He was tall, broad and armed with a short sword and a dagger. Both hung from his belt and neither was protected with a sheath. A stump replaced his left leg below the knee but he walked upright nonetheless and without the aid of crutch or stave.

"The woodman from the heights of Sairune brings a stranger to Frelius, seventh of that name," he announced. His voice was deep and not impartial. Deference was plain in his attitude to Frelius and in his acknowledgement of the woodman, but his pronunciation of 'stranger' prickled with caution.

Frelius was not a young man, but he exuded strength. He was short and stocky, with coarse curly hair that still retained traces of its original black. Sturdy legs encased in woollen stockings were plainly visible under his tunic, and its short sleeves showed his thick forearms and broad hands. He did not appear to be armed, but sword or dagger seemed unnecessary. Morrell had seen a man of such a build stop a charging ram and break its neck with his bare hands. Besides, there were others with him; two guards at a discreet distance, a man of his own age at his right hand, thin and bald, but wiry, and a younger man on his left. He had hostile eyes, a narrow face with high cheekbones and a jutting beard.

"Greetings, Woodman," began Frelius. "Who is this you bring to my domain?"

Woodman bowed. "Greetings Frelius, Master of Bellue. This man is named Morrell. Gerharst, son of Bayan the shepherd, brought him. The lad would not come to Bellue. The way is long and he is feared of men he does not know; but he told me how he saw this man rise from the water in the cockle cove and walk to shore on the surface of the waves. He is a man of Namier, knows the Visitations by heart and says he was sent by Namier to these shores.

"If that is so, it is surely to Bellue that he must come. My master is away and only the caretakers remain, and at the House there is only Master Rondil. You know him. He is old and welcomes no one."

"Does anyone welcome a man come to tell them to mend their ways?" observed Frelius dryly, but he turned to address Morrell and he was not unfriendly. "You claim to be sent by Namier. Tell me, how do you know when you have arrived at the right destination?"

Morrell bowed and shook his head sadly. "The ways of Namier are not always plain, Master, nor are his directions. I never *know* that I have arrived. I am guided in dreams or in a trance and I travel so. When I awake, I do as all men do, and seek work. My work is the work of the spirit, but I look as others do, for a place where my skills are needed; and I trust, that when I find such a place, I am doing Namier's will."

Frelius looked at his right hand man. He did not speak. A raised eyebrow asked a question and it was answered with a nod. A similar glance at the younger man was met with a scowl and a comment.

"I do not think we have much need of a 'holy man'," he said, "but we have many children in the school. If he can read, write and count he can teach the children, and perhaps he can teach adults to walk on water."

He smiled at his last words. Morrell found the smile more menacing than his scowl. Nevertheless, he bowed to the young man and was about to answer him when Frelius spoke again.

"We have a church here. The schoolmaster reads from the Visitations on Rest Days, but we have had no preaching and no sacrifice since the Padri died several years ago. As my son Jael has told you, we have a thriving population and but one schoolmaster. If you make yourself useful to him in the school, you may stay. There is a room behind the church."

It was not the deferential welcome that he felt was his due, but it was an offer. Morrell bowed again.

"You can teach, I suppose?" queried Frelius.

"I have taught the stories of the Visitations, the prayers and the hymns of praise for all my adult life, Master. I have also taught reading and calculation from time to time, but I cannot teach anyone to walk on water, for I do not know how it is done. I remember nothing of my journey until I came to shore and saw the boy, Gery. He said that I had risen from the waves and I was certainly wet, so I believed him. Why would he lie? But the manner of my arrival and the place, was Namier's doing, not my own."

"Indeed. Well, I am glad that He does not treat me in such a way." Frelius dismissed the topic and his visitors with a wave of his hand. "Show him the church and introduce him to Master Saldar. He will judge what you are worth to him and pay you accordingly."

Chapter 2

So it was that Morrell found himself in an overcrowded schoolroom with the harassed Master Saldar and more than sixty children aged from five to sixteen. The population was indeed thriving and it was not unintelligent. The walls were covered with the youngsters' work and there were designs for buildings and boats, maps with navigation calculations, charts of the night skies and labelled drawings of the skeletons of animals, all vying for a place among the more usual pictures of the Visitations and samples of writing and simple sums.

He was happy to start with the younger children, teaching them their letters. He would keep his knowledge of mathematics and the physical sciences to himself. He would chant over the sacrifices and he would preach, but there would be no 'signs' from Namier until he had thoroughly assessed the talents and abilities of Fort Bellue. Some folk here would be easily impressed, but others – and he thought again of the dark-eyed hostile Jael – would not.

The classroom was remarkably quiet. Master Saldar kept order with a short stout stick. Minor infringements merited a poke in the ribs, but hands and heads suffered sharp blows for more serious misdemeanours. He managed the wide-ranging abilities of his pupils by utilising some of the older ones to teach small groups of younger children. It was one of these groups that Morrell took over.

The girl in charge smiled at him and showed him what she had been doing with the little ones. She was about twelve, just the age he liked, her slender body showing the promise of the curves that would come with maturity. She was not a beautiful child, but she was clean and her brown hair shone. She was too intelligent, though. The bright eyes reminded him of someone, but he could not place the memory. That little mystery was not solved until Master Saldar spoke to him at the end of the afternoon.

"You will be useful to me," he acknowledged. "The older children, at least those clever enough to help the little ones, do not like to miss their own lessons. Tammina was pleased to have her nature class. Her mother is one of our finest Healers and she hopes to follow in her footsteps. She will have noticed your limp and may well be waiting outside to offer her mother's services. When you have had your foot attended to, I will come and see what, if anything, has been done to your room behind the church."

Tammina was indeed waiting to ask if he needed her mother's help. He accepted and she led him to her house. It was her mother's assessing eyes that he had felt as he had first walked through the village. He was sure of that as soon as he met her.

The house was larger than many in the village. The living area was compact and neat, but there were two workrooms. One, viewed briefly through the open door, contained shelves of books, solid benches and equipment for the preparation of infusions and the extraction of oils. The other, into which he was led and given a seat, was a treatment room. It smelt of herbs and was so clean that Morrell felt ashamed of his own body, unwashed for several days.

Tammina introduced him as a holy man who was to live as the priest and teach in the school, but her mother had no need of the information. She knew already, as did everyone. Gossip, especially about strangers, spread faster than the swoop of the sea eagles when they spied their prey.

Mistress Farsay washed his foot thoroughly before she examined it. She had a gentle touch, but it hurt even so. The flesh was swollen, red and angry. Tammina watched.

"Is it poisoned?" she asked and was silenced with a look.

"It has been pierced and is infected certainly," was the noncommittal reply. "And there is something left in the wound."

"A thorn tip, perhaps," offered Morrell. "I took off my wet shoes to climb the cliff. That was foolish for the way was rough."

"Perhaps," Mistress Farsay agreed absently as she wielded a slender pair of tweezers. A few painful moments later she withdrew the offending object and laid it on a dish. It was short, sharply tapered and surprisingly thick at one end.

Tammina was sent to boil water, but not before he had seen her eyes widen in surprise.

He did not look too closely at the dish. He knew that it did not hold a thorn and, alas, the object seemed translucent unlike any thorn that he knew, but it swiftly joined the soiled bandage and swabs in the waste bin.

When Tammina returned with fresh water her mother had cut the swollen flesh and was allowing it to bleed, "- to clear the infection -" as she put it. The girl waited quietly and fetched whatever jars and bottles her mother requested without further comment, but Morrell was not fooled. He remembered that wretched boy's words as well as he remembered the stones that had been thrown. The foreign body was a 'poison spine' and, though he did not know the species or what damage it might do, it was clear that both mother and daughter had recognised it.

There was no challenge as yet. He must bide his time.

Despite the unpleasant feeling that Mistress Farsay had seen through his deception Morrell had to admit that his foot was a great deal more comfortable after she had washed and dressed it. The short walk to the church was almost pleasant. Several people greeted him politely. It was curiosity, he knew that, but it was promising nonetheless.

The room behind the church was more than promising. It had been swept and dusted and there were fresh herbs hanging from the beams. Master Saldar was waiting for him at a table laid for the evening meal. A small fire burned merrily in the hearth and an appetising aroma came from a pot set over it on a trivet.

Frelius had provided the meal, he was told, and would continue to do so for the rest of the week. After that he must earn his own bread, or starve, as did everyone else in Fort Bellue.

The stew was tasty and there was plenty of it. There was a fruit tart and a piece of cheese to finish and Master Saldar had brought ale. Morrell was content.

The schoolmaster was good company. He asked questions certainly, but they were not challenging ones. He seemed genuinely interested in Morrell's life and travels – his aim being to learn, not to criticise or catch him out. After they had eaten, he gave more details about the school, what was taught and how he wanted Morrell to help. It did not seem difficult and would provide an adequate income.

One thing was strange though, and disappointing. He could not teach songs in school. Boys learnt to sing and they might, if they wished, sing in the church services, but females were not permitted to sing, ever.

The songs of Bellue were fishermen's songs or fighting choruses. Women did not fight nor did they go to sea. Therefore they did not sing. Not even, he was assured, to their babies.

Master Saldar had heard of lullabies, but they were not used in Fort Bellue. Men might sing to their sons when they were awake, of the sea or of battle, but women did not sing. If a child were fractious, they held it close in their shawls and talked to it quietly.

Morrell found this strange, and worse than strange, it was annoying. One of the most enjoyable parts of his work was with choirs, preferably, but not exclusively of children. He had a fine voice and the traditional songs in praise of Namier, or in supplication to him, had splendid tunes. Burning flesh in sacrifice was not nearly as satisfying as singing in unison. A choir with a good range of voices was a great pleasure to lead. He felt vaguely sorry for the babies of Bellue who had no lullabies, but a great deal more sorry for himself with no prospect of women or girls in his choir.

It was, however, a small hardship in comparison to the advantages and comforts of Fort Bellue. It was a prosperous community. The men were fine sailors and fished or manned the fighting ships that kept the pirates from dominating the seas.

Many were craftsmen – masons and builders, carpenters and metalworkers. There were some herdsmen and farmers, but they were not so highly regarded in the community. Tending the land was regarded as women's work.

The women grew vegetables in small plots, and washed the wool and spun and wove the cloth. They gathered wild herbs and fruit; they dried fungi, made pickles and collected honey from the hives. They carried buckets of seawater up the steep cliff paths to replenish the shallow saltpans. They scraped the shining crystals from their sides and used them to preserve the meat. And naturally they kept house for their menfolk.

The women worked hard, but none had authority or power. Morrell had seen the same situation in most of the communities where he had lived, but it was only the instinct to breed that kept the females subservient. It was not their lack of intelligence. Some were clever, much cleverer than many of the men. He was as careful in his approach to such women as he was in his approach to the men who held the power. Mistress Farsay and her daughter were high on his 'treat with caution' list.

In the weeks that followed Morrell learned more about Fort Bellue, its inhabitants and its surroundings. Health and strength were highly valued especially by Jael, the young heir. He had many admirers among the young men, but his bold opinions were not so popular amongst the older folk. They honoured his father and favoured his more tolerant views on physical weakness and his conciliatory approach to outsiders in general and the great Lord in Bosron in particular.

Frelius did not like paying tribute to Lord Parandour, either in money, goods or the young men who were conscripted to fight in his wars, but he did not curse or confront the official collectors. He bargained with them. He kept records of the pirate ships that his people had sunk or chased from the area. He backed them with samples of weapons, clothes, foreign goods and even body parts taken from captured ships, and used these as his bargaining tools.

Morrell admired his thoroughness. He too was a careful planner and usually had a choice of lessons prepared for each

Rest Day. He viewed his congregation before deciding which to use. Mistress Farsay did not appear, nor did her daughter, but Frelius came to his first service and to most thereafter.

Happily Morrell had re-read his 'First Time' sermons, all on various passages from the Visitations that told of Namier's arrivals on Erion. He was able to thank his listeners for their welcome and deliver an eloquent lesson on the visitation to Krundel. He did not dwell on the unpleasant fate of the villages that had turned the stranger away. He enlarged instead upon the blessings and the wonderful flower that had been given to the village that gave him shelter. Nor did he refer to the passage extolling the wise leader of the village. They were educated here and would know it, and it would not do to appear obsequious.

He waited for several weeks before he preached on malefaction.

Chapter 3

Tammina spent most Rest Day mornings with her mother. They went out early and gathered herbs and roots and fungi and fresh greens. Sometimes they took her father's bow and a quiver of arrows and her mother shot a pigeon or an unwary rabbit. Her mother had a good eye and a steady arm. Tammina was not gifted in that way so she kept still and silent whilst her mother hunted, but she did more than her share of collecting food and plants for the medicine store and when they returned home she was keen to help unpack and prepare what they had gathered. She was an adequate cook, but her great interest was in the preparation of unguents and potions.

Mistress Farsay was happy to prepare their meal and allow her daughter to steep and grind and pound and blend the medicinal items. Boiling, in oils or water, and distillation they did together in the afternoon. She trusted Tammina, but felt her too young to manage the equipment alone. Accidents did occur with hot oil and distillations. No one was immune, but two people were less likely to miss a potentially dangerous sign than one working alone.

When young herself she had worked with her own mother, and later her husband had sat by whilst she worked. He had amused himself carving driftwood. For years the figures, animal and human, had stood on ledges and shelves in her treatment room. They had served to distract children from the discomfort of their wounds and ailments, and the pain that sometimes accompanied treatment.

Only one remained on view now, high on a shelf half hidden behind a bound book of recipes. It was a fish, a great leaping seasprite with fins like wings and a slender sinuous tail. Tammina had put it there. It was such a fish, they had said, that had been thrown on to the deck of her father's fishing boat by a huge wave, and in its struggles to regain its freedom it had swept him overboard with one of its great fins. His body was washed up on the rocks a week later.

By then, her mother had packed all the figures into a box and put it behind the piles of wood and kindling in the outer store. His knife was there, too, his old boots and his favourite cup. Tammina knew that they were the things that even her practical realistic mother could not bear to see, but could not give away or consign to the rubbish heap.

The fish was Tammina's. She thought it the most beautiful thing he had made and had been allowed to put it by her bed. Mother had not taken it away and a few months after his death, Tammina had put it where it now stood. She had missed the figures almost as much as she had missed her father himself and now that the hurt had gone and she had almost forgotten his face, it reminded her of his hands. She wondered still, as she had wondered when he gave it to her, how such gnarled and sea-worn hands could create something so silky smooth and beautiful.

Sometimes on Rest Days the crippled child, Margren, would come to visit. It was usually late afternoon, when Margren's father had recovered from the previous night's drinking and could tolerate, perhaps even play with, her three younger brothers. If she had finished her chores, and they were many, her mother allowed her a free hour or two before she was required again to help with cooking or fetching water. Her father did not hold with men or boys helping with household duties and her mother had long since given up trying to persuade him otherwise.

Margren was a few months older than Tammina, but she was smaller in stature and much less confident. Her twisted leg made her slow. She could not run and she could not straighten her left arm. It hung awkwardly by her side, the elbow bent one way, the wrist another. According to many in the village she had been cursed from birth. The birthing woman was now dead and Margren's own mother did not deny it, but Tammina knew that it was not so.

She had asked her mother long ago about Margren's problems and had been answered enigmatically. It was a curse of sorts, she had been told. Margren had been born with straight limbs, but she did not feed easily and cried a great deal. Mistress Farsay had been present at the birth, not as healer, but as a friend. A familiar face was a comfort in a new and frightening situation.

"You were there, too," and Mistress Farsay had smiled. "I had just begun to believe that at last I had conceived. I told your father that evening."

That information had distracted Tammina, as had been intended, but not for very long. She asked no more questions but she thought a great deal.

Margren's father was a harsh man, much given to drinking ale. He would have little patience with a crying child, especially a girl child. Ale was sometimes called a curse by those who imbibed too much of it; and Margren's mother was a timid woman prone to bumping into things and bruising.

Her mother said that there was nothing to be done for Margren, but Tammina tried anyway. She took the herbs that they used to deaden pain and pounded them with fat instead of infusing or distilling them. She rubbed the ointment on the twisted limbs and sometimes into Margren's back. There was no improvement, the limbs did not straighten, but Margren was grateful. She never complained, but Tammina was sure that she suffered pain.

It was Margren who told them of Morell's sermon on malefaction. She was not sure of the exact meaning of the word, but she knew it was not good. Her mother had been very troubled, thinking that the sermon had been directed against her husband. Contact with the evil things of Hadron prevented people attending church on Rest Days, and ale, in the quantities her father drank, could be considered an evil thing, and it certainly prevented him from attending Rest Day services.

Mistress Farsay was reassuring. The Padri was talking in general terms about evildoers. It was true that Margren's father was not a great worshipper of Namier and he did drink too much on Rest Day Eve; also he had a short temper, but such faults did not make him evil. He was a fine fisherman who supported his family and was loyal to his wife. Those were good things. Certainly Erion would be a marvellous place if everyone was faultless, but alas everyone was not – not even the Padri.

Margren wondered at that. Surely Padri was very good. His whole life was devoted to the service of Namier. She accepted, however, that he might have small faults.

Tammina also accepted her mother's words and her warning glance. She did not see why it was such a great secret that the man had had a poison spine in his foot. She knew that they were found only in one or two coves. She had travelled with her mother on one of the healing missions that Frelius allowed on rare occasions, and the journey was so interesting that she had made great efforts to remember everything.

The cove near the Bayan house did not have poison spines, but there the Padri was supposed to have walked on the water; and he could easily have forgotten when he hurt his foot. A man of Namier would not be occupied with mundane things. She imagined that he would be so involved with higher thoughts that he would not notice where or when he suffered an injury; but as her mother normally allowed her great freedom, she respected rather than questioned her mother's wish for her silence.

Weeks later she began to understand and to fear. Margren whispered at school that she was not allowed to visit any more. Her mother thought Mistress Farsay was an evil one, a witch. Several other children began to avoid her company. Her mother's help was not sought so often and another healer who went regularly to the Rest Day services gained patients.

Tammina had never sought popularity; she had scarcely thought about it. People were there. You liked some much more than others and some you simply tolerated. She had always had friends and never any enemies. Now she became less open and more suspicious. She lingered in doorways of shops and in the shadow of trees and listened to the conversations of her elders. Many were interesting and some unnerving.

How could people say that their elderly parent or sick child might have lived if Mistress Farsay had not tended them? Naturally the sick slept more deeply and became less coherent if one gave them a potion to ease their pain, and if death came as they slept was that not a blessing? And how could they even dream that her mother had killed her father by some mystic power over a fish?

The change in Tammina did not go unnoticed. Her mother dismissed the antagonism towards herself as a passing phase that would fade as easily as it had arisen, but the whispers 'like mother, like daughter' worried her; so too did her daughter's secretiveness. She sought, and was granted, an audience with Frelius.

He guessed why she had come. Morrell had been subtle, but Frelius did not like his talk of evil, of witchcraft and association with the Shades of Hadron. There may well be such things and such people – he had an open mind on that point – but not in his territory.

The audience was brief. He was aware of the problem and would deal with it. Her living would not be in jeopardy much longer. He had great respect for her skills though he had not so far had need of them. Her worries about Tammina were waved away. It was her age. Girls became moody and difficult sometimes. They grew out of it and became pleasant and lovely young women. Tammina would be no different. Her happy relations with her mother would then be restored. He smiled and dismissed her with a wave.

Mistress Farsay was not satisfied, but she could ask no more of Frelius. She did try to talk to Tammina, but not with any great success. Perhaps Frelius was right, she thought, and her daughter's behaviour was due entirely to her age. She tried again, a discreet question.

Tammina glared at her. "Do you think I would be so troubled about my first bleed," she answered contemptuously. "I am troubled about the rumours and the side-long glances; and it is for you I am concerned. We should have exposed him when we first met him, before he had time to establish himself. He lied; and you would not have me confront him nor tell of his

38

deception. You did not confront him either and now he is trying to destroy your reputation."

"He will not succeed." Mistress Farsay hoped that she sounded more confident than she felt. "I have spoken to Frelius. He knows the situation. He despises such nonsense and assured me that my reputation will soon be restored."

"Did you tell him about the poison-spine?" demanded Tammina. "No, you did not! I can tell from your face. Now it is too late. Frelius may speak, but he will have little effect. He is a plain man and that Morrell that they call 'Padri' is devious – and he is clever. You should not have accepted his explanation."

"I am a Healer, Tammina," answered her mother gently. "I heal, if I am able. I do not challenge or argue or accuse those who seek my help. Nor do I judge them. Besides it is quite possible that poison-spines are now found in other coves. We travelled only once beyond Bellue and that was several years ago. Trust in Frelius, my dearest girl; he is a fine and fair ruler. Do not worry. We shall be fine."

Her daughter said nothing. She stared at her mother for a moment before she lowered her eyes, shrugged her shoulders and walked away.

What stupid parents she had! Her father had gone out fishing when the wind was fierce and the waves high, and he had been swept overboard; and her mother, who knew so much about plants and the effects of their various parts, was so simple that she thought Frelius a match for the cunning Morrell.

She could not understand why her mother was so blind. Mama was straightforward, that was it; and she was not. She felt guilty about that. At the same time, she felt proud. One day she would be as devious as Morrell. She would scheme and deceive people and use their foolish fears to her own advantage; but now she could not compete with the older man. She had never practised such talents and Morrell, she was sure, had had plenty of practice.

The following Rest Day they climbed the cliff to the south of the Fort in search of a particular flower. Tammina was interested in spite of her fears for the future. Mama had a drawing of the plant she sought. She carried the paper carefully between two pieces of wood, for it was old and fragile and the wind on Bellue Heights was often strong.

They found only a single specimen bearing two flower stems, but Mama did not pluck either of them. It was the seed that was most useful, she explained, and not even the lowest of the seedpods was ripe. They would come again in two weeks, and collect a single pod. Other seed they would scatter. If it proved to be as beneficial as notes on the drawing indicated, she wanted a healthy colony.

They climbed higher, up to the spring. The water was sweetest from the high springs, or so it was said. Perhaps because when one had climbed so high any water tasted sweet, but the view was almost worth the effort. They were high as the fort. Its great black bulk lay to the north, but beyond and to the east and south there was just the sea. Only white wave edges and the sails of ships disturbed the blue-green expanse and to the southwest the low line of Shyran separated sea and sky.

"I love this place." Tammina's voice was heavy with regret. "I do not want to leave."

"Why would you leave?" her mother asked sharply. "No women leave Bellue."

"They think you are a witch. You will be sent away and I with you."

"No." Mama was very firm. "I have spoken to Frelius. He is aware of the rumours. He thinks, as I do, that they will soon fade, but he has promised that there will be no more sermons on evil and association with Shades. He will speak to Morrell."

"And Morrell will obey, but it is too late. The seeds are sown. They must be uprooted. Morrell will not do that and Frelius will not think it necessary." Tammina looked at her mother in despair.

"Is this what has been troubling you?" A gentle hand stretched out to touch the girl's arm.

"Troubling me! Oh Mama, I cannot sleep for worrying about you."

Tammina flung herself into her mother's arms and buried her face in the familiar breast. "You are so good that you do not see the badness and stupidity of people; but I have heard the talk, and there is hatred in it. Oh, it is not everyone, not even most, but it is enough. I am afraid for you."

Mistress Farsay soothed her daughter's fears as best she could. She promised to be careful and do nothing that could be construed as fixing anyone with an evil eye or casting a spell. She even promised to stop feeding the lame cat that prowled about the houses looking for easy pickings. She did not think that anyone seriously believed that the poor creature was a thing from Hadron that carried messages for her or brought her special powers, but Tammina was distressed and she would have promised much more than that to calm her child. She did not, however, feel able to attend the Service. That would be too obvious, and to have any credibility, she would have to attend all, or most, Rest Day Services. Even Tammina thought that too much to ask.

True to his word, Frelius did have a quiet word with Morrell, but it did little to stop the chatter and it pleased Morrell. No more sermons on Hadron's influence were necessary. As Tammina had realised, he had sown the seeds.

He watered them judiciously and in private. He knew the women who harboured resentment, those who had lost a family member treated by Mistress Farsay and those who liked nothing better than to castigate others. It was easy to make seemingly casual remarks to them. Some brought him food and there was opportunity to chat when he thanked them. Some had children at the school and he could stop a parent to comment on the child's progress. Others he simply waylaid after the Service. He was an intelligent man and now he was sure that Mistress Farsay had not spoken to anyone about his injury, he was enjoying his little intrigue.

He was very pleased with his sermon the following week. A woman had died after carelessly throwing oil onto her fire and burning herself badly. He was able to offer sympathy to the family and exonerate the Healers who had tended her from all blame. Death was inevitable and must be accepted. Not, of course, that all deaths were the will of Namier. Some were certainly due to the evil ways of men or women.

He was particularly pleased with the 'or'. In Fort Bellue, death was usually due to accident, sickness or old age, though there had been instances where it was due to a fight between belligerent men. He knew how certain members of his congregation would interpret death due to a *woman's* evil ways.

Frelius was also pleased. He was not a subtle man. He thought that Mistress Farsay had been included in the Padri's praise for Healers just as much as those who attended the unfortunate woman. Jael was less sure, but his doubts were brushed aside. He did not argue. He could think of only one reason why Morrell would wish to harm Mistress Farsay. With the mother out of the way or disgraced, the man would have easier access to the child who was growing nicely.

Jael did not want to discuss that point with his father. It would inevitably lead to suspicions of Jael's own interest in the village children and though he was innocent of any impropriety on that score, he did know one of the young mothers rather well. So he held his tongue.

Unsurprisingly one of Mistress Farsay's patients died before another topic dominated the local gossip. It was a child, no more than a baby, who had suffered from fits almost from birth. His mother grieved, but most of her grieving had been done long before his death. She knew he was not destined to live long, but her husband was distraught. He had witnessed few of the fits and had expected that his child would outgrow them, as so many children did. He railed against fate and Namier, the Shades of Hadron, the Healers who had not healed and any other thing, real or imagined, on which he could vent his anger and despair. His wife's meek praise of the woman who had helped her so much, and often in the middle of the night, was lost in his loud complaint.

Someone mentioned that the fits had not started until Mistress Farsay visited the mother to soothe her afterbirth pains, and everyone knew of babies who had survived such fits and grew to healthy adulthood. It was clearly witchcraft – or plain murder. None who spoke of such made exact differentiation between the two; and reasons for the killing of an innocent babe were plentiful. The grandfather had annoyed the Witch. That was reason enough.

He had indeed spoken sharply to her on several occasions when she was a young girl. So had his wife. Their small plot was not well tended and had many plants that were of interest to an apprentice Healer. She had trespassed more than once to collect samples. It was so much quicker than scouring the wild land and time was important to a young woman who wanted to meet the boats, and one particular fisherman, when the day's catch was landed.

The rumours spread rapidly and grew more vicious. None who talked of witches could remember a witch test being carried out, but they all knew how it was done. Witches could fly. They would fly if thrown from a height. Hadron protected its own. They would not be hurt, but they would fly away.

Tammina saw the group from the schoolroom window – about ten strong and mostly women. She watched without understanding for several minutes. Master Saldar called her to attention. Morrell, after the briefest glance, bent his head assiduously over the work of one of his charges. He heard the sharpness and the surprise in Master Saldar's voice and the slam of the classroom door, and he knew that the girl had gone. She would go to warn her mother, but he did not think that she would be in time.

Nor was she. She raced along narrow ways and scrambled over fences and through the plots. It was shorter than the proper path, but she arrived home only moments before the group. Her skirt was torn and her breath came in ragged gasps, but she screamed loudly.

"Run, Mama! Run to the Fort!"

Mistress Farsay heard and came at once to her door. She gazed in amazement at her daughter and at the gang of people who were marching towards her. She approached them thinking to reason with them and by the time she realised that her daughter was right and that her best chance was to run, it was too late.

Tammina did not attempt to stop them. She had no chance against so many. She continued screaming to attract attention, and paused only long enough to see in which direction those who had seized her mother were heading. She ran to the fort and hammered on its gates, calling out her problem. They were opened almost at once for the guards had seen her running. One knew her well. He had cause to be grateful for her mother's skills.

He wasted no time. He called to his fellow to inform Frelius and ran with Tammina in the direction of the northern cliffs. He saw the mass of people on the cliff top and others scrambling up the slope to join them. Some, like him, were calling to them to stop; others seemed more intent on seeing the spectacle. It was not everyday that one had the opportunity to see a witch flying.

Four of them flung her out over the edge. The wind caught her skirts and they billowed out around her, and for a moment or two it did seem as if she were flying. If she cried out, the sound was lost in the wind or deadened by the screams of triumph from her accusers.

"See! She flies! She is a witch!"

Tammina's agonised "Mama" was lost too; first in the noise and then in the folds of the guard's coat as he caught and held her firm, lest she throw herself off the cliff after her mother.

The unbelievers lay on the ground and peered over the cliff, but they could not see a body. The cliff overhung the shore so that not all was visible, but the believers felt vindicated.

Later, they were even more confident. Frelius sent men down to search the shore below the cliff, but they found nothing more than a shoe. There were neither bloodstains on the rocks, nor torn limbs nor scraps of clothing. There was nothing to prove that Mistress Farsay had fallen and not flown.

Tammina was more persistent than Frelius' men. She searched for days along the northern coast, clinging to the rocks at high water and scouring the caves when the sea was low, but she found nothing. One cave was long and narrow and the sea that filled it whirled and foamed; but she braved its darkness at low tide and found herself on the shore beyond the walls of Bellue.

She wandered along the shore, still searching for traces of her mother's body, but also considering her own position. She had left Bellue; but she knew little of the land beyond and she had no more than the clothes she was wearing. She kept close to the cliff edge so that she was not seen and she waded back through the cave at the next low tide.

She did not immediately return home. She stood for hours watching the currents beneath the overhang as they swirled and sucked. She tossed, first sticks, then larger pieces of firewood into the sea and saw how they were flung against the rocks and pulled under and out to sea. At last one night she dragged a long heavy plank up the hill and pushed it over the edge. Not a fragment remained when she searched next morning. It would be washed up somewhere, sometime, near what remained of her mother's body. Only then did she return to the village.

The first few folk who saw her averted their eyes. None greeted her. They rushed away to spread the news that the Witch's daughter was back. It was Darl, one of her contemporaries, on his way to school who spoke to her.

"I am sorry about your mother," he said simply. "I am not surprised that you hid after that. Frelius wants to see you, though. My father said he is cross that you disappeared."

He thought of adding more, of telling her that there were rumours that her mother had returned to collect her and they had flown over the walls together; and another rumour that she too could fly, and had flown away.

They were ridiculous ideas and once she would have laughed with him at such silliness, but now she did not deny that she had disappeared. She nodded gravely, and he said nothing. She would not laugh again for a long time.

"Thank you. I was looking for Mama's body. I have good reason to search more carefully than the guards. She was my mother. But there was nothing to find. That cliff is a good place to fly a witch. I wonder who knows that."

The boy looked at her nervously. The last words had been spoken calmly but the tone filled him with apprehension. He hardly recognised her voice as that of his school friend. He had expected her to be full of sorrow, weeping perhaps. Instead she sounded menacing and he did not know how to respond.

"I must go," he said hurriedly. "I shall be late for school. I think you should go to the Fort."

Tammina stared after him. She was puzzled. Why had he felt uncomfortable with her? They had frequently worked together in school, always at ease.

She thought back. They had said only a few words to one another. True her thoughts had come unbidden to her lips. She had not intended to pronounce those last sentences. She was pensive as she walked towards the Fort.

Chapter 4

Frelius was angry. His failure to stop the dreadful treatment of the woman was humiliating and the subsequent disappearance of her daughter annoyed him further. He had managed to prevent the fools from burning down her house with all its store of medicaments and hand-written books, but that was little consolation for the loss of the girl. She was a mere schoolchild and she had eluded his guards.

Now she had arrived at his gates. She had not thrown herself over a cliff, but it was possible that she had left Bellue and returned again by some means other than the gate. Now she stood before him with meekly bowed head, but he found her difficult to assess.

He had already asked why she apparently fled from his protection and she had answered with a question.

"Did not my mother have your protection, lord?"

"I had not realised that things had reached such a state," he had said defensively.

"I knew," she stated. "But I did not know when, or how, or where."

He could not object. She was not defiant nor contemptuous, merely regretful.

"Where have you been these last few days?"

"Along the north shore, lord. Looking for my mother."

"There was no need. Did you not know that I had sent men to search and they found nothing? The currents are strong there."

When she did not answer he repeated the question, his voice sharper and more demanding. She spoke then.

"Yes, I knew that men had searched, but she was not their mother, she was mine. I wanted to see for myself."

Again he was angry at her answer, but could not in fairness object to it. She had lost her father several years ago, and now had witnessed her mother thrown from a cliff. He set his teeth and drew a deep breath.

"We must decide what to do with you, now you have no parents," he said eventually. "You are too young to live alone. Your father's sister and her husband will care for you, and later, when you have finished school, Mistress Penge will no doubt accept you as an apprentice Healer. I believe that is what you want?"

She lifted her head and regarded him gravely. "I have now finished with school." Her answer on that point was quite definite. "And I do not think that either lady you have mentioned will welcome those arrangements. Nor do I; but if that is what you have decided, lord, then that is what will happen."

Jael was standing with his father and another older man. He gave a low growl of disapproval.

"What may well happen is that you will be beaten for your insolence!"

Tammina curtsied low with bent head to acknowledge the correction, but when she rose and looked at the man she found that she was not afraid. What could frighten her now? She stood up straighter and spoke clearly.

"My apologies, lord, if I have offended. The Frelius asked me a question, and I have answered it; but I do not argue with his decisions."

He made to speak again, but Frelius said softly, "Do not threaten her. She is a mere child and has some cause for complaint."

He turned to Tammina and addressed her in a louder voice.

"I do not wish to force you to do anything, but your aunt is your only female relative and Mistress Penge is a respected Healer. Where else would you live? What else would you do?"

"I will live alone and I will continue my mother's work. I know what she planned to do and I can study her books and papers if they are still there."

48

"They are still there. Nothing has been damaged. They are yours." Frelius spoke firmly. He had no problem with that, but he shook his head in doubt at the prospect of her living alone. "You are still a child. You need the care and guidance of an older woman."

"I need my mother," thought Tammina and widened her eyes so that tears that threatened to fill them would not spill down her cheeks.

Aloud she said, "My aunt would have me till the land and tend the sheep, fetch the water and help her to cook. I can do that more easily for myself than for her, her husband and her three sons. Also I would prefer to be the first to benefit from my labour, and not the sixth."

Jael coughed and raised a hand to his mouth. This girl was interesting and she certainly had spirit, but his father and his old adviser would not be amused at her boldness so it was wise to conceal his smile. He suggested a compromise. If Master Saldar judged her competent the girl need not attend school, and she could live alone for most of the time, but spend a few days each week with her relatives. If Rest Day were one of them she could attend the Service with her family. That way she would not be over-worked, as she seemed to fear, and all rumours that she also was a witch, would be quashed.

Frelius looked at his son in surprise. His contributions to the management of Bellue were not usually so reasonable. He turned to the girl. She had bent her head again. He would have liked to see her expression, but could not.

"That seems a fair compromise," he said slowly. "Will you accept those conditions?"

Tammina kept her head bowed. She was taken aback by her own fury and did not look up lest her anger show in her face. How dared that arrogant young man make her attend Service? She was sure that he had no great desire to attend himself and did so only at his father's behest. He was envious of her previous freedom. This was his way of curtailing it. She hid her clenched fists in her skirt.

"Yes, I will accept," she said.

Frelius was delighted. A ridiculous confrontation with a child had been avoided and it was Jael who had provided the answer. He dismissed Tammina with a wave of his hand. A guard would escort her to her house and he would have all concerned informed immediately of the decisions about her future. She must present herself at school tomorrow to see Master Saldar, and later visit her aunt to discuss arrangements with her. She need not come to inform him of the outcome. He would send to the adults to find out.

Tammina curtsied. "Thank you lord," she answered as meekly as she was able.

Frelius smiled benignly and did not notice the baleful glance that she cast at Jael as she left. He did though, and this time he did not disguise his smile. It drew a frown from his father.

"A good outcome," he said, but added severely, "Though I do not find it amusing. Not at all amusing."

"No. I do not think the girl found it amusing either. She agreed, but she did not like it," conceded Jael. "The mother was no witch, but the daughter will cast spells of her own in a year or two. I have no doubt about that."

His father scowled. "Well see that *you* are not charmed." His voice was sharp. "She is too young and you are married. Your wife and your other – two or is it three – interests here in the Fort should be enough. I do not want you rutting in the village, too."

"No Father, I would not think of it." The answer came swiftly and with deference. It was no secret among the Fort's society that Jael found his wife dull and amused himself elsewhere, but he had thought that only one affair was commonly known. He must be more careful.

Master Saldar was sorry to lose a bright and interested pupil, but he had no hesitation in declaring her competent. She could read, write and calculate as well as many who had left school. He made use of this small opportunity to plead once again with the Frelius to allow the cleverest children to attend school outside the Fort area. He did not expect a favourable reply so he was not unduly disappointed with the curt refusal. Bellue needed its bright youngsters – to pay for them to be educated elsewhere was madness. They might not return and Bellue stock would be weakened. An intelligent man ought to realise this.

Aneda Valwy was not so sanguine. At first, she had resigned herself without enthusiasm to accepting responsibility for her niece, but on further consideration she realised that having a young and fit girl about the house would be an advantage. She could fetch water and do washing – there was always a great deal of washing with four men in a household and their thick tunics and hose were heavy when wet.

The girl could help with mending, too. She could help gathering and preparing vegetables and carry the heavy load of shopping home. And, thought Aneda happily, there would be no need to return the favours, as she was now obliged to do when she begged assistance from some neighbour for help with the tasks that were becoming too tiring for her to manage alone. She was downright disappointed when she was told of the arrangement that had been agreed with the Frelius, and Tammina turned up on her doorstep.

Coming to sleep on the eve before Rest Day, indeed. The meal was always prepared by then and waiting to be heated when the family returned from Service. Now Tammina would claim a share and have done none of the work. A single day's labour in the middle of the week was poor return for providing two breakfasts and two evening meals and a place to sleep; and all for the daughter of the high-thinking woman whom her brother had married.

No sons she had borne him, only a girl like herself, who thought fine thoughts and spent more time boiling leaves and flowers than cooking proper meals for her man. No surprise that that man had been swept overboard by a fish.

Aneda had always blamed her sister-in-law for her brother's death; not that she had ever considered witchcraft, but a man fed proper food – good stews with plenty of root vegetables to thicken them up – such a man would have swept the fish overboard, not fallen into the sea himself. And such a man her brother had been before that woman captured his fancy. Her cooking had no substance – bread as light as air with little seeds and scarlet fruit in it and stews with scarce a trace of rich fat, and flavoured with mould that grew on rotten trees. 'Fungi' *she* called them, but Aneda knew they were the same as mould. Mind, the new Padri was said to be fond of them, but he was not sturdy like a fisherman. He was thin, as befitted a man of Namier whose mind was full of spiritual things.

Aneda did not try to be tactful. She had never hidden her views from her sister-in-law and saw no reason to hide them from her niece. Tammina stood at the door and listened without comment to her aunt's complaints. When that lady paused for breath, she said quietly that it was not her choice either. She, too, had been obliged to accept the Frelius' ruling. She would come next Rest Day eve.

She walked away with no more farewell than an inclination of her head. She did not wish to offend, but she expected to do so, whatever she did or said. Her aunt was easily offended and hard to please. Mama had tried often and had always failed; and Mama's tolerance and patience were unending. Tammina was not like that. Her aunt annoyed her and though she rarely lost her temper she did not stay a second longer than was necessary in that irritating presence.

She walked towards the road where Mistress Penge lived. Unpleasant tasks were better tackled as soon as possible. They did not become any easier if postponed. Meeting Mistress Penge was never an easy experience. She was always so uncertain and apologetic.

Tammina wondered how and why she had ever become a Healer. She did not seem to have the confidence and authority that a good Healer ought to display. Perhaps some sick people liked to feel that their particular illness was strange and unusual, but Tammina was sure that the majority preferred their suffering to be instantly diagnosed and easily cured.

Mistress Penge fluttered nervously when she saw who was at her door, but she did invite her young visitor into the house and began several expressions of sympathy, none of which she managed to finish. She also talked of apprenticeships; they were so important, knowledge must be passed on, she was honoured, she had such admiration for, and it was the Frelius' will. All her phrases, however, ended with 'but'.

"What troubles you, Mistress?" asked Tammina. The woman's fluster irritated her almost as much as her aunt's blunt hostility had done.

"Well, you are her daughter, and they might think I am a witch, too." Mistress Penge completed a sentence at last.

Tammina closed her eyes. She could not bear to look on the foolish frightened woman any longer.

Mistress Penge regarded the girl with a worried frown. She was pale and swaying slightly on her feet. Her eyes remained shut for a long time, and when at last she opened them and spoke, her voice was strange, high and uncertain.

"There is no danger of that. No danger for you. For some, perhaps; they may not live long."

"You are sure. Sure that I am not in danger, even if I take you as my apprentice?"

Tammina took a deep breath. She was near to fainting. She ought not to have embarked on these unpleasant tasks without food. Now she had given away her fears for herself. She shook her head, not trusting herself to speak.

Mistress Pemge pushed a chair towards her. "Sit down," she said. "You look very pale."

Tammina sat down and thrust her head between her knees. She stayed still and counted slowly to fifty. When she lifted her head she saw that a beaker of water had been placed on a stool by her hand. She drank gratefully. She felt it strange that Mistress Penge did not touch her or even come close, but as she had no wish to become one of the woman's patients, she was not sorry. Best to finish this conversation as soon as possible.

"You will not be accused of witchcraft." Her voice was confident and reassuring. "And I will help you, but will not intrude too much on your time. We will satisfy the Frelius that his will has been done and in two years, when I am sixteen, I will make my own decisions."

The Healer did not seem reassured, but Tammina had done her best. She suggested a day, received a nod in reply and she returned to her own home. There were eggs and cheese still there. The bread might be stale, but she would eat and rest and prepare herself for her new life.

When Tammina had gone, Mistress Penge sat and thought. If the mother had indeed been a witch – and after all no body had been found and many said she had flown – then it was likely the daughter had some strange powers. She did not think the girl was evil, but perhaps she had the Power of Sight.

There had been a woman in Bellue long ago who had that power and she was said to go into trances when she used it, or when it came on her. No one seemed sure if the Power could be called upon, or if was involuntary, but the signs were clear - unseeing eyes, unsteady stance and a high unnatural voice. That was how her grandmother had described the trance, and she had been told by her grandmother who had witnessed it.

The more Mistress Penge thought, the surer she was that she too had witnessed such a trance. Tammina was not much more than a child, but the Power did not come suddenly at a given age. It was latent in a person's head and could be nurtured or quelled according to their upbringing. She was sure her grandmother had told her that. She was also confident that she would not be accused of witchcraft; and it therefore seemed a good moment to have a chat with her fellow healer and great friend. It clarified one's ideas so, talking about them, as if the very act of saying them aloud made them plain.

She was pleased to find her friend at home, but less pleased to see the butcher's wife there. She had come to have a new dressing put on her foot. A cleaver had dropped form the board and cut her badly. It was healing nicely and caused her little pain or inconvenience, but the dressing needed changing frequently to prevent infection from the raw meat and blood-stained straw that surrounded her. That task had been completed and she was sitting comfortably with a steaming beaker in one hand, plainly prepared to make the most of her visit. A plate of spiced bread lay on the table. Naturally Mistress Penge was invited to join them.

She hesitated for no longer than a second. The butcher's wife had contact with many of the villagers and she was not known for her reticence, but news of the Frelius' decision on Tammina's future would soon be common knowledge so it would not matter if the butcher's wife heard it before some of the other gossips. She sat down and accepted a beaker of hot brew and a slice of bread.

It was a long and interesting chat. Mistress Penge enjoyed it enormously. Her colleague was always attentive and encouraging, but the butcher's wife was also a good listener and made several useful and interesting comments. Her knowledge of Tammina's early childhood was very illuminating.

Mistress Penge had never heard the tale of her becoming lost at the tender age of two, and finding her way home again. Nor had she heard before of the fall down the mountain. It was most remiss for any mother to allow a small child to climb so high without careful supervision, but Mistress Farsay had been a great advocate of 'independence' and 'learning through experience'. Of course, one could let a child do that without much concern, if one had the Sight, and had seen that child grown and healthy at some future time. And the Sight was selective. One did not see all the future, so it was quite possible that Mistress Farsay had had that Power, but it had not warned her of the accusations. But then if she was a witch and had flown away, perhaps she had not minded. Her daughter was almost grown and not at all helpless or frightened. And, if she could fly away, she could presumably also fly back from time to time to visit said daughter.

All these suppositions and 'perhapses' had been discussed in detail and at great length. Mistress Penge was glad of that. It had been enjoyable and she was now much clearer in her mind. They had all agreed that the Witch's daughter had the Sight and that Mistress Penge had witnessed her Speak. Happily she herself was in no danger, but others were. She could now wait and watch to see who those unfortunate 'others' might be; and observe, maybe at first hand if they were her patients, what would happen to them.

The butcher's wife also went home contented. Her visits to have her foot re-bandaged were a welcome opportunity to sit down for a while and this time there had been the added pleasure of conversation – good gossipy conversation. It had given her a fund of little snippets to mention casually as she packed up the customers' meat. That kept them in the shop so they would buy something more, or it brought them in again the next day. She was very skilled in her choice of words and in her timing, and frequently, when she wanted to keep her listeners in suspense, used the excuse that her husband disapproved of her chatting too long.

Chapter 5

It was some weeks before Tammina noticed the strange behaviour of the villagers. She had expected all those involved in her mother's death to avoid her or perhaps accuse her, but accusations against her were forestalled by her attendance at church on Rest Days. She sat with her aunt and cousins and she stared uncompromisingly at the Padri throughout the Service, as if she were challenging him to preach about witches again. He did not, and nor did anyone else mention such things in her presence, but several people gave her odd glances and moved away.

She did not mind the older folk turning away, but it troubled her that those who had been school friends did not speak to her and some younger ones, whom she had helped to teach, ran away when they saw her.

She did not confide in her aunt. That lady worked her as hard as she had anticipated on the one weekday that she spent with the family, and fed her meagrely on Rest Day. She slept on straw with a rough blanket. It was uncomfortable, but clean, – even Aneda Valwy baulked at the prospect of her neighbours believing that she had given her niece bug-ridden bedding. Tammina, therefore, had no desire to discuss anything with her aunt.

She wanted to ask Master Saldar, but did not like to visit his house in the evening, and to wait outside the school for him to emerge might precipitate an encounter with Morrell. That she did *not* want. She tried instead to corner some of her young friends. Most of them brushed aside her questions and hurried away. Even Darl was cautious, but she persisted and at last he answered her.

"They are frightened of you," he told her. "They think you have strange powers. They think you can see the future. Some think that because you can see, you can influence it and change things."

He shrugged his shoulders at their lack of logic. "It is rumoured that you have prophesied that some in the village are safe and others will be harmed, so they fear your eyes on them." He shrugged again.

"I do not believe it, but you were always a bit – strange – apart – different." He tried to find an acceptable word but could not. Nor could he offer much comfort. "It will pass. They will forget as soon as the older ones find a new topic of conversation."

"No, I do not think they will forget, though some may talk to me again in time. This is a part of what happened to my mother. Am I to forget that? Am I to allow those who killed her to forget? And those who stood by and watched her killed? As long as I am here, I will remind them of that day; and *I* will never forget."

Darl shivered. She sounded venomous. "It would help if you behaved more normally," he pleaded. "Come back to school and learn with the rest of us. It is not good to hide yourself away with your mother's books."

"Good? Where am I to find good? My mother's books are more useful to me than school; and the experiments that she was doing – I will continue those. They were not evil. They were for the benefit of the sick. I may use them so, or perhaps I may not. I have not yet decided."

Tammina was angry. She was also hurt and confused, but the anger was stronger. She liked Darl and trusted him, but she would not take his advice. He did not know why her mother had been targeted, perhaps he did not even realise that she had been. It was simply his ignorance that made him urge her back to school where she would meet daily with the Padri.

"I have no special power," she told him in a gentler voice. "But if I had, why would anyone fear me? They did not fear my mother though they accused her of having Hadron's powers. And now I am obliged to come to the church. Does that not absolve me?"

"Of witchcraft, yes; but not of other things."

They talked for a long time. Darl tried his utmost to explain the superstitions of the villagers to his friend, but she was too angry and hurt to understand. It was the current that had taken her mother's body. She did not fly. No one could fly. She was dead; and Tammina had not been able to bury her or scatter petals on her grave. What remained of her when the fish had had their fill would be washed up on some shore far away. How could anyone of sense believe that she flew back under cover of darkness to speak to Tammina? Or that she gave or taught her daughter the power to hurt people or to influence events? And what was in Tammina's eyes that made them fearsome? She saw as others saw. No more and no less.

Darl looked hopelessly at her eyes. They were bright, intelligent eyes; grey as the sea on a cloudy day; and calm. He realised with a shock that they were beautiful, not because they were large or of brilliant hue, but because her strength shone out of them; and they were fearsome because they also showed the intensity of her feelings. He felt suddenly embarrassed, seeing her as female and for the first time conscious of his own gender.

"You asked why people avoid you. I have answered as best I can. If you do not believe me, you do not believe. I cannot do more." He walked away.

Tammina stared after him sadly. They had learned to read together, faster than most members of their class. He had been her preferred partner for experiments and discussions and her helpmate in solving those 'testing' problems that Master Saldar had occasionally set in mathematics lessons. She sensed the difference in him, but did not know what had caused it. It left her bereft – almost more so than the death of her mother. Mothers were different. One expected to grow up and away from them, but Darl was one of her own age and, as such, ought always to be there.

She turned for home. There were few people around, but she did encounter an old man. He was too slow to slip between the houses at her approach. He felt her eyes on him and trembled.

Tammina stared harder. He was an old man, prone to the shakes. He looked up for just a second, before shrinking back against a tree covering his face with his hands. She saw the fear in his eyes, but she did not alter her gaze until she had passed him. Perhaps Darl was right.

Old men were fearful, though, and he was a simple soul. She would need to try again, on someone younger, stronger and more intelligent.

Her attempts were not conclusive. Some people shied away, but that could be embarrassment. She did not know precisely what part, if any, each person played in the death of her mother. Some stared back at her boldly, as she herself might well have done had anyone stared so fixedly at her.

Things changed the following week. The old man became ill, as old men do, and he died the day before Rest Day. Tammina did not hear of his death until she arrived at usual at her aunt's home.

"Old Narry died this morning," said her aunt suspiciously. "Did you know?"

"No, I have been in the woods today. He was old and ill."

"You were expecting it, then, were you?"

Tammina set the plates on the table as she usually did and repeated her comment. "He was old and ill."

"Humph!" Aneda snorted. "Well, you mind you keep your eyes off my man and my sons!" she warned. "I nursed you as a babbee, and I'll box both your ears if you give 'that look' to one of mine. I'm not afraid of you."

Tammina kept her gaze low. "Why would you be afraid of me? I could stab you with a kitchen knife, in the night whilst you sleep, but why would I want to do such a thing? You are my kin."

It was the last sentence that calmed her aunt, Tammina knew. They were kin, and kin did not harm one another. She kept her eyes on her plate during the meal and did no more than glance at her uncle and cousins during the evening.

It was Rest Day when she relished her new power. She stared even more fixedly than usual at the Padri. He was not disconcerted, but then he knew that her mother was innocent of witchcraft and guilty only of recognising a poison-spine when she saw one; but she was gratified when later she overhead the comments.

'The Padri will be next,' and 'Did you see how she cast her eyes on the Padri?' and 'He is man of Namier. The evil of Hadron will not touch him'.

She smiled to herself. It no longer worried her that people avoided her. It was amusing. They were all uncertain, a little afraid; even the toughest of the fishermen. It had a disadvantage, though. Her aunt was even harder on her and the weekday work was exhausting. Aneda also began cooking the occasional dish for the Padri and took pleasure in making Tammina help her with the preparation.

Tammina tried to hide her resentment from her aunt, but she was not always successful. Also, she was allowed merely to help with the initial preparation. There was no chance of taking a small revenge by sending undercooked vegetables or burnt meat or over-spiced stews to the Padri. That was the stuff of daydreams.

Weeks later and quite by chance, she did have an opportunity. She had been weeding and cropping all morning in her aunt's vegetable plot and had filled two large baskets with root vegetables and fruit. As she was leaving she noticed some fungi growing by a rotting fence. She picked one and studied it carefully before selecting one or two more of the freshest ones and balancing them carefully on top of the vegetables. She did not want to crush or bruise them. They were similar to a fungus that was widely used in cooking, indeed her first intention had been to collect them for that purpose, but these were not for eating. They were not common. She had rarely seen them growing before; but she was sure that they featured in one of her mother's books on potions.

She could not recall the recipe or its purpose, but the carefully drawn picture, she did remember. It had a bold arrow pointing to the faint dark spots on the creamy skin.

She carried the heavy baskets back to her aunt's house. She walked slowly. Her arms ached after the day's work, and it was hard to keep the baskets steady. She was later than expected and she knew that her aunt wanted the fruit for the evening's dessert.

Tammina intended to conceal the fungi in her pocket when she neared the house, for her aunt might be waiting at the door, but she had no chance to do so. Her cousin Benel had been sent to meet her and he rounded the corner of the track just as she had set down the baskets.

"I've been sent to meet you. Ma's waiting for those," he announced without preamble, and he pointed to the fruit. "And Pa's waiting for his meal, so you had better hurry." He picked up the other basket and was surprised by its weight. "This is heavy! I'll bring this, but you go ahead. I want to see someone."

"Those fungi are for me. Your mother thinks they are mould, so shall I take them?" Tammina smiled as ingratiatingly as she could, but she was waved away and told again to hurry. He walked away with her basket.

She had finished preparing the fruit when he arrived at the house. He dumped the basket on the floor beside her.

"There. Best get on with preparing those for tomorrow," he said.

"My fungi?" Tammina asked anxiously.

He grinned maliciously. "I saw Mistress Kellein as I walked back. She knows Ma does not like them in the house, and asked if she might have one. I gave her all three. Seems she is making a stew for the Padri – again – and he is fond of them. I knew you would be happy to give them to *him*."

Tammina started to protest, but her aunt called her. Her assistance was required immediately. She was annoyed, but it was not worth the argument that would ensue if she objected. Besides it was too late; and if Mistress Kellein used fungi, she ought to know them. Also, it was unlikely that she was intending to take the stew to the Padri tonight.

Tomorrow Tammina would be home and able to look up the book and check why those particular fungi were useful. If they were poisonous, and that she did not think was likely, there would be time to ask whether they had been used, and to warn the Padri if necessary. So Tammina contained her anger, obeyed her aunt's many instructions and eventually sat down to eat her meal. She ate in silence. She had nothing to add to the men's talk of their day's fishing, or to Aneda's gossip.

She almost laughed the next day, when she looked up the fungus in the old book. It was recommended for severe cases of blockage of the bowel, but was to be used judiciously. 'Very palatable' she read, 'and likely to be enjoyed rather than refused by the patient, but one small cap is sufficient for a man, a half for a woman and the merest sliver for a child. Only for otherwise healthy people.' The warning was proclaimed in capital letters and the important words were heavily underscored with what had once been red ink. The colour had faded now to a sad brown, but the urgency remained.

'NOT TO BE GIVEN TO SMALL OR SICKLY CHILDREN, TO THE FRAIL OR THE ELDERLY, OR TO ANYONE WHO SUFFERS FROM PALPITATIONS'.

Tammina shut the book and returned it reverently to its place on the shelf. Her mother had started copying the pages from the oldest of the books, but it was not an easy task. They were so fragile and the ink so faint that it needed good light to copy the drawings, but bright light damaged them further. There were not enough hours when the sun was continuously shielded by thin cloud and could provide the clear diffuse glow that Mama had declared perfect for the task.

One day Tammina had brought the pens and fine paper out of the cupboard and attempted to continue the work, but it was too soon. The vision of her mother's head bent over the desk and her steady hand carefully selecting a pen was still vivid in her mind. Her own hand had shaken with the effort of holding back the tears. In a year or two the grief would dull and she would try again. Now she must content herself by taking great care of the books.

She considered what to do about Mistress Kellein and her stew. The Padri was in her opinion neither frail nor elderly and did not appear to suffer from palpitations. A wound from a poison-spine did sometimes bring on such heart irregularities, but as far as she knew the effects were immediate and not long lasting. Also, Mama had been confident that the spine from Morrell's foot had been from a baby.

"Practising," she had commented, "otherwise the poor man would be suffering more than a sore foot."

Tammina spent some time searching for more information on the combination of effects, but could find none, so she abandoned the Kellein family and the Padri to fortune. If Mistress Kellein had used the fungi, then the fault was hers and all anyone would suffer would be an uncomfortable day or two. That would serve them well: especially the Padri.

Fortune favoured the Kellein family, and capriciously ignored the matriarch's carelessness in using the fungi at all. The largest portion of the stew, and the one with the most generous proportion of fungi, was given to the Padri that morning for his evening meal.

Morrell was grateful, especially when he lifted the pot lid and smelt the contents. He was greatly tempted to abandon his dull lunch and eat the stew instead, but he decided against the idea. Sometimes the women told one another of their plans to cook for him and one would provide an accompaniment for another's main dish. So he waited. Nor was he disappointed. Later in the day some vegetables and a small loaf of fresh bread appeared, and later still a portion of currant pie.

"Nice and sharp after the rich stew," he was told by the donor. The pie was unadorned. She obviously considered that cream was not necessary after 'rich stew'. He disagreed, but it was a minor omission and he looked forward to his evening meal.

As the old book had predicted, the fungi were very enjoyable, as was all the food. Morrell rarely drank alcohol, but he had, several weeks ago, been given a small barrel of the local ale and that evening he treated himself to a large glass – the perfect accompaniment to an excellent meal. He went to bed contented, happy to stay in Fort Bellue for the rest of his life.

The early rising fishermen found him the next morning. He lay with wide-open eyes on the path to the harbour. They were at a loss to know *why* he was there, but there he was, and he was dead. That was obvious.

They called the Healers, but they knew a dead man when they saw one. Nothing could be done.

Inevitably there was a great deal of gossip and, because he was the Padri and the Frelius was involved, there was discussion – entirely different from gossip. Questions were asked, and answers were given, but those in authority reached no firm conclusions. All those who had provided food were adamant, and truthful, in declaring that they had given only portions of what their own families had eaten or drunk. All the Kellein family kept quiet about the rather unusual trips to the latrines. Such things were private matters. They did not even mention it to one another. None ever considered putting it down to Mistress Kellein's cooking.

Nor did she. *She* thought it was the pie, or perhaps the ale. The Padri might not know how to keep ale. But then, there was no certainty that he had drunk ale that evening, not in the opinion of the donor of the barrel; and the woman who gave the pie was adamant that it was a small portion. Her family had eaten all that remained, and none had suffered any harm whatsoever.

The report given to the Frelius blamed no one. There was no reason to suppose that what he had eaten the previous evening had caused him problems, and no one had the least idea why he would be on that path. It was some way from the church and his room. A strange event, perhaps due to a bad dream, but no one could be sure.

The truth was that Morrell had rushed out to the latrines, which were situated discreetly some distance from the church, in the middle of the night, half-asleep. After a prolonged and uncomfortable visit, he had at last managed to stagger out into the fresher air and to start on his way back to his bed. Unfortunately, he had become disorientated and had wandered down the path towards the harbour.

He had suffered pains in his chest from time to time, but nothing that had lasted long or troubled him overmuch. In the darkness and in his uncertainty, the pain became much worse.

A nighthawk had screeched and he had jumped at the sudden harsh sound. He had stumbled, fallen, and had not risen again. The startled expression remained on his face.

The gossips enjoyed the uncertainty. It gave them plenty of opportunity for speculation. Once the contributors to the Padri's meal had been cleared of blame, they discussed the possible causes of his fear and pronounced upon them.

Who or what had frightened him, frightened him enough to drive him out of his bed and down the harbour path? Normal night scares were not considered terrifying enough; but *induced* night scares, *deliberately inflicted* night scares, what of them? And who could perhaps induce such terror? Who was the daughter of the Witch? Who had strange Powers? Who had stared at old Narry just before he died? And who had stared at the Padri every Rest Day for weeks? Perhaps even a man of Namier was not proof against the Shades of Hadron.

Many in the village believed that the Witch's daughter had such powers; and they came to the inevitable conclusion that she had used them. Tammina was regarded as a witch; and, because it was believed that she still had contact with her mother and had powers of her own, she was feared.

Tammina had mixed feelings about the Padri's death. She had not intended him to die. She had not intended to hurt him in any way, but she had not done all that she could to prevent it. All Mama had taught her was gentle and forgiving, and Mama had never judged anyone. Revenge was wrong, she knew that, but she could not help wanting it. Oh Namier! How she had wanted revenge!

Now she was troubled. She had done nothing actively to seek revenge, but she could have done more to prevent the mistake that had caused his death. Torn between guilt and triumph, she shunned all casual contact.

It was not difficult to avoid people. Mistress Penge did not take her on visits nor did she make arrangements for patients to come and see her on the days when her apprentice was there. Tammina's 'training' was limited to collecting raw ingredients and preparing potions and salves under strict supervision. She found it almost as wearisome as the day she spent with her aunt.

Mistress Penge did not divulge her secrets and without experiment or knowledge of the blending and eventual use of the items that she so carefully made, Tammina found the exercise as dull as raking weeds and preparing vegetables.

Rest Days were different now. She was still obliged to attend church. One of the men who had assisted the Padri at the services was now in charge of the weekly sacrifice and prayers, but he did not preach. He read from the Visitations and said a few words on the text he had chosen. The service was shorter but smellier, because he had not perfected the art of burning.

Tammina pleaded nausea and was allowed to sit at the back of the church, near the open door. She was usually alone there for it was always draughty and, when it rained, wet. She did not mind that, though she thought it ridiculous that the door was not shut at the start of the service. A house was not unwelcoming because its door was shut against the weather – why should it be considered that a welcoming church needed an open door? She had voiced that opinion in the past, now she kept silent, and was glad of the fresher air that blew in.

Tammina suspected that the Padri had used a preheated bowl and some oils that burned fiercely and fast, so that the smell of scorched food rose with the hot air to the roof vent, and did not spread throughout the church. He had not shared his knowledge with Master Dregan though, so his acolyte struggled with the firing of the offerings and Tammina was able to sit at the back, away from others, to the satisfaction of all.

She had attempted, after Padri's death, to miss the service altogether, but Jael had noticed immediately and had pointed out her absence to his father. On being requested to seek her out and remind her of their agreement, he had assented dutifully and had concealed his delight. It had not been difficult to accost her when she was alone. Apart from the days she spent with Mistress Penge and with her aunt, she was almost always alone.

"You are growing independent," he had opened. "In fact you are growing up in many ways."

She had flushed at his tone and at his gaze, and for the first time had become conscious of her swelling breasts.

"In what way am I growing independent, lord?" she had asked meekly, and was told that she must still attend the Rest Day service.

"I like to see you there," he had continued smiling. "Indeed, I like to see you anywhere; you are worth the seeing. So few are."

She had coloured in a mixture of anger and embarrassment, but she had retorted sharply.

"Mistress Leanstor being another of the few, I think!"

She had immediately regretted her lack of control. His eyes had narrowed and his smile had disappeared.

"Keep a guard on your tongue, girl. You have need of friends, not more enemies. Talk in the village comes eventually to the fort and to my father's ears. If such talk as *that* comes to the castle, I shall not be pleased and I shall know where to lay the blame."

He had uttered no threat, but it was not necessary. She understood. She had lowered her eyes, but she did not need to see the cruel twist of his mouth, the tone was enough.

"I will attend the service in future," she had responded meekly; and she did so. She also considered her wardrobe more carefully.

That was not a huge task. She had but three dresses and she realised that only the newest was fit to wear. Looking down at her chest, she wondered how she had dared to walk out in either of the other two. She had scarce been aware of the changes in her figure and the way that the front fastenings strained across the new curves. Now she was.

She had no female cousins and no one in the village would buy her old clothes, for no one would care to dress their child in anything that she had owned. There was no money to be obtained from that source to help buy another dress.

She investigated her mother's clothes. They were too large and they were mostly black and of a style more suited to a widow than a girl of her age. Regretfully she concluded that for the next few years they would be useful only as a guide to her cutting and sewing. The skirt of one of her dresses would provide enough material for two bodices and the sleeves could be re-used without much alteration. Dressmaking was not one of her skills and she disliked it, but she managed to fashion a new dress from the two old ones. It was noticeable for its strange colouring rather than its style or fit, but at least her 'bulges', as she referred to her growing bosoms, were decently covered.

Strangely, it was her eldest cousin, Karron, who drew the matter to his mother's attention. He walked into the kitchen one evening when she was helping her aunt with the cooking.

"Evening Cousin Tam," he said and demanded that she turn round to let him look at her. She was about to object, but Aneda was quicker.

"Leave her be! She works little enough for her bread as it is, without you wasting her time!"

Tammina turned and smiled at her cousin. "Why do you want to look at me today?" she asked pleasantly. "You see me every week."

"Linnie said you needed a new dress. Said she will not walk out with me again if you do not get one, for it makes her ashamed." He surveyed her critically. "She is right too," he commented.

"That girl should mind her own affairs not interfere with ours! We have no money for new dresses." His mother was sharp in her complaint.

Tammina said nothing and turned back to her task, but her cousin was not deterred.

"There are few enough girls who will walk out with me, related as we are to one they call 'the Witch's daughter'. That cannot be altered, but her dress can be, and it will be if Linnie wishes it. Tam, you are growing and that dress is too small. Ma will take you to get a new one, if you do not like to go alone."

"I do not mind going alone, but I have very little money left. Mistress Penge does not pay me, though she gives me a meal at mid-day."

Her cousin's opinion of Mistress Penge was so forcibly expressed that it drew a rebuke from his mother. He made no apology for his rudeness or his language; he merely offered to buy a new dress for Tammina.

"Thank you," she answered, genuinely grateful, "but it does not need to be new. If Linnie has one that she has grown out of or no longer uses, I would be grateful for that. I cannot sell my own clothes or my mother's for no one would buy them; and I am not a good seamstress."

"Many girls would like Linnie's unwanted dresses," sniffed Aneda. "She is given far too much. She has new dresses so often that those she sells are almost unworn, but they are too fine for an orphan like you, who has scarce a fen to her name!"

"Linnie spins the finest yarn in Bellue, *and* she weaves it into fine cloth. She is a good seamstress too, so she deserves fine clothes." Karron was quick to defend his girl. He was proud of her skills. "I will speak to her," he added quietly to Tammina.

Chapter 6

Linnie called on Tammina one evening. She was cautious in her approach. She did not want to offend. She knew little of Tammina and, though many girls wore second-hand clothes, not every girl was happy to do so.

She was, however, warmly welcomed and reassured – Healers were not always paid for their time or their potions and Tammina was more used to having second-hand dresses than she was to buying new. Linnie opened the large bag that she had brought and displayed all its contents.

The girls spent a happy hour or two deciding what suited Tammina and what fitted her. Tammina accepted only two dresses, insisting that that was all she needed, but she did also accept several pairs of stockings, two petticoats, a scarf and a warm hooded cloak. In return, she found a jar of soft cream for Linnie, to protect her hands and face. If it proved effective, she said, she would make more. It was one of her mother's recipes and was easy to make though some of the ingredients were difficult to find.

Linnie was pleased with her evening, but she did report to Karron that his cousin had no lock on her door, neither was there a bolt. She did not think that safe. It was bad enough for a young girl to live alone, but to live in a house with only a latch as fastening was inviting trouble.

Karron duly fitted bolts to his cousin's door.

Tammina did not at first think it necessary. She had lived in the house all her life and there had never been a lock or a bolt on the door. In Mama's view, a Healer ought to be easily accessible to people in need. She thanked him for the kind thought, but she did not begin to use the bolts until the following Rest Day.

She had put on the prettiest of the dresses for the Service, and had brushed and dressed her hair as Linnie had suggested. She did so as a gesture of gratitude to that young lady rather than a conscious effort to make herself attractive, but she was attractive and she did attract more than a casual glance from a number of people. She noticed, and was amused.

Only one stare caused her the slightest concern, and that was from Jael. Frelius might not be aware that his son frequented the village at night, but Tammina was. She had no wish to annoy either of them, but nor did she wish to become Jael's latest 'convenient woman'.

It was easy enough to avoid him by day, but she began to bolt her door at night. Linnie, she thought, was wiser than she looked – she would be a valuable friend.

Waste was not encouraged in Bellue, so Tammina looked around the village for a suitable recipient for her own outgrown clothes. She did not have to look far. Margren was older than her, but smaller and not yet coming to maturity.

Slow to learn, perhaps because she was often in pain, and unable to undertake many tasks because of her twisted arm, poor Margren was little valued in her own home.

Her mother seemed ashamed of her and considered her useful only for the most menial of tasks so that her clothes were usually much mended and stained with mud or worse. She helped to wash the salt-encrusted clothes of her father and her brothers, but she rarely had time or energy left to wash her own.

Few in the village washed assiduously and few smelt sweet, but Margren smelt worse than most and was thus avoided by her peers. She was a lonely child and was pathetically grateful for Tammina's offerings. At least on Rest Day she would have a clean dress to wear.

Linnie found Tammina's cream effective and sweeter smelling than others that she had tried, so she came back for more. Soft hands spun finer yarn and finer yarn produced finer cloth, she declared, and certainly her yarn was valued.

Tammina produced more cream and some lotions, and in return was supplied with clothes of a quality she would never have dreamed of buying. Their friendship grew. If Linnie's parents objected, their objections did not deter their daughter, and Aneda's disapproval soon waned.

Karron was determined, and although the girl was spoilt and did not cook or clean with any enthusiasm, there was no doubt that she was skilled. It was not long before she began to choose the wool and goat hair that she spun, and to weave only with her own yarn. Even the ladies in the Fort came to the village to buy Linnie's cloth. It was not quite as soft as the silks and fine fabrics that the merchants brought to Bellue, but it was not at all uncomfortable to wear and did very well for every day gowns. Also, it was more readily available and cheaper.

If Linnie could make money from her cloth and her sewing skills it did not matter so much to Aneda that she was a poor housekeeper. Cooking and cleaning could be bought and Karron would be well cared for.

Margren continued to benefit from the friendship. Tammina was still called 'the Witch's daughter' and was avoided by many, but she became less of an outcast and Margren was able to visit her occasionally. Her mother made sharp comments, but did not forbid her to go or to wear the clothes that she was given. Tammina began once again to try to alleviate the crippled girl's pain. She was not entirely altruistic in her efforts; she needed to practise her healing skills. Mistress Penge was not encouraging and the 'apprenticeship' faded away as soon as Tammina was old enough to determine her own future.

The Frelius did not appear to object. He made no comment or criticism and she assumed that he was content.

He was not. He had noticed, but there was an internal conflict in his court at that time and some village disagreements about grazing rights and land ownership that demanded his immediate attention. By the time he felt able to consider the particular village problem of 'the Witch's daughter', it was too late. She had abandoned her studies and was selling her cosmetics to the ladies of the Fort.

They came highly recommended by the girl who made the cloth. He had no wish to upset this arrangement. If cloth fine enough and creams soft and sweet enough were made in Bellue, then the ladies would spend less on imports and his domain would prosper. He watched, but did not interfere.

Karron also watched over his young cousin, though both his reasons and his anxieties differed from those of his ruler. He watched firstly because Linnie demanded it, and then because he saw the dangers.

Tammina was an attractive young girl, and an orphan. She worked hard and was making a reasonable living for herself, but gathering the plants and fruits that she needed meant wandering alone in the early morning far from the protection of the village. He gave her a round pebble to keep in her pocket, and he showed her how to use it.

"You may encourage whom you choose," he told her, "And if it pleases you, then lie with them. That is your choice. But if you do not want an embrace, this will discourage a persistent man. The boys will probably leave you be, if you are firm enough, but if anyone presses you against your will, a round stone is a handy weapon."

He wound a thick pad of cloth around his head and made her practice. A single blow, but hard; that was the best practice for self-defence. It would not kill, but it must be hard enough to fell her assailant and leave him staggering, or perhaps unconscious, for long enough for her to run away. Only when she had landed several accurate blows of sufficient strength on his head, was he satisfied.

"Best not tell Ma," he added as he left her. "She might be concerned."

Tammina smiled. "Why would I tell your mother?" she said; and Karron wondered if he had been wasting his time.

He had certainly wasted his breath with his warning. She did not volunteer information to anyone. Her slow, knowing smile made him uncomfortable and would deter most men he knew. Still, she was attractive, and when Ma realised that, she would want her safely married to the first young man who showed a serious interest.

None did.

Tammina knew the effect of her smile. She used it often. She would have welcomed the friendship of several young men in the village especially Darl, but she did not want their courtship and was uncertain as to where one ended and the other began. Linnie's answers to her tentative questions were not helpful. Such things were obviously learnt by experiment and experience, but she lacked a family home. She knew that she would never have asked for her mother's advice on courtship, but the presence of a parent in the background provided a certain security, or so she assumed.

Other girls seemed confident; she was not. She felt it safer to remain aloof, so she encouraged no one and made great use of her smile. It kept everyone from coming too close and she did not realise how much mockery it conveyed. She was left alone, as she wanted; but she was also disliked, even by those who bought her products, and that was not her intention.

In time, Linnie and Karron were married with great ceremony. Despite strong objections from her family, Linnie asked Tammina to be one of her attendants. Tammina refused. She appreciated the thought, but she was well aware that even her tolerant cousin did not really want her to play such a prominent role at his wedding.

It was the largest the villagers could remember. Frelius did not grace the proceedings with his presence, but several lesser residents of the Fort attended, dressed in fine silks. Linnie also had a silk gown and looked so lovely that even her mother-in-law praised her beauty and did not declare more than twice that silk was a shocking waste of money.

Tammina dressed carefully for the occasion. She did not wish to shame her family. She knew the ladies from the Fort, because they bought her creams, and although she did not push herself forward she spoke to them politely. It did not endear her to the villagers.

'None of her superior smiles for them,' noted Aneda caustically and many agreed with her. The Witch's daughter had set her sights way above farmers and fishermen; only one from the Fort would do for her.

It was not a happy situation. Tammina was not unduly concerned about the village talk, but she hoped it would not reach the Fort. She did not want her best customers to think that she had designs on their sons, brothers or husbands. They might stop buying.

Fortunately they did not, but it was not because the gossip had failed to reach the Fort. Society there assumed that any attachment between a village girl and one of them would be transient. It would certainly not involve marriage. They thought of themselves as aristocrats, though lords from farther afield may have held less flattering opinions. Frelius was disturbed by the talk; his son was delighted.

Jael was convinced that the few words he had spoken to the girl had charmed her and that she was his whenever he chose to take her. He was in no hurry. She was young and he had mistresses at the Fort in addition to his two current interests in the village. Also, his father was pressing him to show more interest in the running of Bellue and its finances, and to beget another child with his wife.

The girl would keep. A smile and an occasional word would hold her interest, and, if he had the chance to give one unobserved, a telling glance. So Jael bided his time.

Tammia did not realise that Jael's interest in her had grown, but she knew his habits and there were others, villagers, whom she did not trust. So she was careful. She always bolted her door at night, and often during the day when she did not wish to be disturbed. Now that she was earning money she was able to buy some new items for her house – crockery and pans and a large chest with a lock.

She was very particular about the lock. The carpenter carried her purchase home for her and set it against the wall in the main room.

"It is a stout chest and a good lock," he assured her. "It will keep your things safe from thieving fingers."

She had nodded gravely and later she had moved it into the treatment room. She still called it that though none had been treated there since her mother had been killed. Margren always sat on a stool by the hearth when she rubbed salve into her shoulders.

There were several cupboards in the treatment room. They all had stout doors and good locks. Mama had always locked up all but the mildest and most well known of her remedies. It was not the chest that Tammina had wanted, but the hinges and the lock.

She set about removing them from the chest. It did not take long; she was a practical girl and often used her father's tools both for cutting firewood and for small repairs around the house. Now she tackled a more difficult task. She wanted another door, a small one that opened into the lean-to store at the side of the house, but one with a lock and key that could be fastened from either side.

She tackled the lock first and it proved easier than she had expected to adapt. The front of the house was faced with stone, but the main structure was of wood so it was not especially difficult to cut an opening from the treatment room into the store, but fitting it tightly took some time. She attached the hinges and lock on the outside and moved a couple of pegs on the inside. When the blankets that usually hung on them were put back, the door was inconspicuous. Now she could leave her house locked if she chose to do so, and she had an exit if anyone tried to force a way in at night.

As it happened, the first person to bang on her door at night was Karron and she had no hesitation in opening her door to him. He wanted her help for Linnie. She was in labour and he was frightened at her pain.

Tammina was reluctant. Linnie's mother was there with one of the birthing women and a Healer. They were experienced. They knew what to do. She did not.

Karron was insistent. His aunt had made a most effective potion against pain and Tam was the only person who knew what it contained. He begged her to find or make something to ease Linnie's suffering.

"Remedies cannot be made in a moment," she had told him, "but I have something that might help. I will bring it, but I will not give it to Linnie without the agreement of those who are in attendance. I do not know what effect it may have on the child or on the progress of her labour. It may not be good to slow it down."

Those in attendance were not welcoming, but they were anxious. The labour was not going well and Linnie was becoming exhausted. The Healer asked many questions about the ingredients of the potion. Tammina expected that and answered as fully as possible without revealing her mother's recipe. The Healer was sceptical. She used similar things. It would do no harm, but she doubted that it would help.

Linnie screamed suddenly and Karron snatched the bottle from his cousin and started to pour the contents down Linnie's throat.

Tammina stopped him. She was surprised at her own strength and firmness, and at her anger. She scolded him roundly for interfering as she poured a small measure of the liquid into a glass. She asked before she held it to Linnie's lips. It was quite possible that the girl's mother might want to give it.

She did not; and Tammina saw that she was almost as distressed as Karron.

It was some time before Linnie's moans and cries became quieter, but the potion did work and it did not seem to slow the contractions.

The birthing woman took charge. If Karron insisted on staying, she declared, he could do something useful and lift his wife into a sitting position. She cried out as he did so, but he had been shamed by Tammina's angry words and he did not flinch nor did he panic. He was still supporting his wife when his son was born.

Tammina stood back and watched. She was not unmoved by the joy of the birth nor was she uninterested in the care of the baby, but the new mother was her main concern. Linnie lay very still.

Aneda came. She brought gifts and was ready to celebrate the arrival of her first grandchild. She was not pleased when she noticed Tammina.

"What is she doing here?" she demanded, and when told she added tartly, "Well she can go now."

"Mistress Farsay will want to stay until your daughter-in-law comes round." The Healer's voice was soft and calm, but definite.

Tammina was startled by the formal address. She looked up, half expecting to see her mother in the room. No one had ever called her Mistress Farsay before. The title was an acknowledgement of her maturity, and the comment acknowledged her skills. She was grateful.

"Yes, I would like to do that. Thank you, Mistress Dreke," she said; and she stayed.

Karron escorted her home, much to his mother's disgust. *She* had walked alone, she declared indignantly. Why did her niece need a companion?

"I asked her to come," answered Karron mildly, "and so I will walk with her back to her home." And he did so.

She bolted her door when he left, for though it was morning it was still early and she was tired. She did not sleep – she was too excited, her mind too full of the night's events – but she did rest. Later she copied out the recipe for the potion she had used. She was not a Healer, perhaps one day she would be, but now she was not. She could not use the potion, but Mistress Dreke could, and at least something of Mama's work would continue to benefit the people of Bellue.

She underlined carefully the advice on the picking of the plants and the instructions for the preparation. The age and the state of the ingredients were important, but so also was the preparation. She would give it to Mistress Dreke the following day.

She rose early, as planned, before it was light. There were several leaves and berries that she needed that were best picked in the early morning, before the sun had dried the dew. She left, as had become her habit in early morning, by her secret door, for she was not going far and would be home again long before anyone was alert enough to notice her movements.

She was happy. She had witnessed a birth, with all its pain and its joy. Her mind was occupied with the events of the previous day and her perusal of the village streets was not as careful as it normally was. She did not notice the shadow in one of the doorways as she walked past. Nor did she hear Jael's soft leather boots on the damp path. She was startled when he came up and walked beside her.

"Ah!" he greeted her, "the Witch's daughter, now the purveyor of creams and lotions designed to make women feel more beautiful, and certain to make their husband's pockets lighter."

He smiled, intending to make his disparaging remark amusing, but she did not find it so and she was wary of his smile. She greeted him politely and quickened her pace.

He followed. "And where are you going, so early? Or are you returning from somewhere?" There was no mistaking his innuendo.

"I am going to pick leaves and berries, lord. They are best picked early."

She answered as coldly as she dared, but it did not deter him. He moved closer and put an arm around her, under her shawl.

"I can think of much pleasanter things to do," he murmured in her ear.

They were passing one of the trees that surrounded the small square, and he pushed her gently back against the trunk. At first, she was puzzled. She hardly resisted when he pulled at her shawl, took her basket from her arm and tossed them both aside. She was not alarmed, simply surprised. Only when he pressed his body against hers and began to kiss and caress her did she begin to struggle. She did not scream, but she objected loudly and strongly. Jael took no notice.

She remembered Karron's lesson and searched her pocket for the stone. Her hand closed on something, but it was not the stone. She could not reach that. She held a jar of the cream that she used for Margren. She had put it into her pocket when Karron had roused her the previous night, in case the draught had been considered unsuitable. She had forgotten about it.

Now she held it firmly, but she did not strike. Mama's ideas and her example were foremost in her mind. Healers did not hurt – they healed; and they did not judge. So she pushed him away as hard as she was able and told him clearly that she did not want his attention, but she did not strike. Not until he laughed.

"Come, that is enough," he said, and his breath was hot and heavy on her cheek. "You have resisted very properly as a good girl should, but we both know that you want this just as much as I do."

She caught her breath at that, and he laughed and pulled at her skirt. "I will make you cry out in ecstasy, my little witch," he promised, thinking that her indrawn breath signified pleasure.

It did not; she was angry. Her hand had tightened around the jar at his first words and his added remark roused her further. She struck out with all her strength.

It was not, as Karron had taught, a calm blow, carefully judged and well aimed. She swung her arm in wild fury. She missed Jael's temple, but the base of the jar made violent contact with his cheekbone. He staggered and gazed at her in amazement. Then she remembered another lesson from long ago – from older girls giggling in tight groups in the playground – and she kicked him.

She held the tree trunk with one hand to steady herself and she swung her leg back as far as she could. This time she did not miss her target. He doubled over and fell, and she ran.

She did, for some strange reason, pause long enough to scoop up her basket and shawl, but then she ran without a backward glance. She turned off the main street, down one alley and into another, twisting and turning so that Jael would not see where she had gone. She ran past the back of her own house, dropped the basket containing shawl and jar into the open mouth of the outside store, and ran on to the schoolhouse. There she knew a hiding place where he would not find her.

She had not played hiding games for many years, but the bushes still grew thickly in the narrow gap between the wall of Master Saldar's house and the fence of the schoolyard. She threw herself down and crawled underneath the branches. It was not easy. A prickly creeper grew amongst the bushes and her hands and face were scratched long before she reached her haven. The space was much smaller than she remembered – the bushes had grown, and so had she – but it was safe. The branches sprang back to hide her entry point and the dense growth concealed her.

She lay without moving for some time, recovering from the shock. Her own reaction shocked her more than Jael's behaviour. As long as she could remember, she had wanted to be a Healer like her mother. The last few years had changed her expectations of how that might be achieved, but they had not changed her hopes or her intention. Now she had struck someone in anger, and struck again after the first blow. Healers did not do such things. That was why Karron had been so careful to teach her how to defend herself with minimum hurt to an attacker; but she had waited too long and hit out wildly – and then a second time, deliberately. She felt ashamed, and worse, unworthy to follow in her mother's path or apply her teaching.

She had another concern. Jael's touch had appalled her. Everyone considered him a handsome man and so did she. His face and figure were certainly more pleasing to the eye than most men she knew and though she had never responded to his words with anything more than quiet respect, she had been flattered that he thought her good-looking. Yet she had loathed his closeness and she wondered why.

She did not want to be his latest woman, but that was because she disliked his behaviour. She disapproved of promiscuity and adultery and in addition she regarded his actions as a misuse of his position, but she was not a prude. She had not been offended by Karron's assumption that one day there would be someone whose embrace she would welcome; she had thought the same.

Now she was not sure. Jael's hot breath on her cheek and the smell of his maleness had aroused nothing but disgust. Did all men smell the same? Would all be so repellent when they came close?

After a while she sat up cautiously. She could see very little from her hiding place, but she could hear. There was no sound of pursuit and no angry cries. There was birdsong and the occasional rustle of leaves as some small creature searched for food in the soft carpet under the bushes; and a few sounds of people starting their day. She had waited too long. She was concealed now, but sometime she would have crawl out and make her way home. Her hands and face were scratched and bleeding, her dress was torn and she had neither shawl nor basket. She did not want to be seen in such a state. The sky and wind promised rain today, but when and how much she did not know. If the rain were heavy enough, it would clear the streets; so she waited.

She heard the children arriving for school – the chatter of the early risers and the pounding boots of the latecomers. She heard them in the yard at mid-morning and then at mid-day. It was quieter when the afternoon lessons started, but not silent. There were people walking by and she heard snatches of their conversations.

She had resigned herself to waiting until dark when the first drops of rain fell. They were large and she heard them splash on the leaves above her head. She heard running footsteps, shouted farewells and a distant growl of thunder. It began to rain in earnest.

She was grateful for the first few drops that penetrated into her hiding-place. She caught some on her tongue – she was thirsty – and she pulled down a couple of large wet leaves to wipe the blood from her hands and face. She was scratched again as she crawled out, but the rain was so heavy that any fresh blood was washed away. The village was temporarily deserted and the visibility so poor that anyone looking through a window would see little more than a sodden figure making its way to shelter. She reached home without incident.

It was two days before she ventured forth again. This time it was in the middle of the morning and she took a pot of oil, suitable for a baby's skin, to Linnie and she delivered the recipe to Mistress Dreke. She was well received in both houses and heard no news about the son of the Frelius. Neither lady was renowned as a gossip, but both would surely have heard, if it were known that such an important person had been badly hurt.

There was talk when Jael did not appear at the Rest Day service, for though the official reason was that he was suffering from a minor indisposition, there were no statements as to its exact nature. Speculation was rife.

Tammina took no part in it. She began to go about her daily business again, but she took good care not to be alone in the village at any hour of day or night.

It was several weeks before Jael appeared at the church again. He looked at none directly and paid much attention to his expectant wife. This was so unusual that the faint traces of bruising around one eye went unnoticed by all but the most observant. There were various opinions about how it was obtained – a fight, perhaps with a jealous husband, a fall after imbibing too freely, a collision in the dark when creeping to a forbidden bed, even a blow from his long-suffering wife. The village was more aware of Jael's habits than he realised. There was no mention of Tammina, however, and she was grateful for that.

When she next wanted to gather ingredients in the early morning, she decided to leave home in the early evening and spend the night on Bellue Heights. She knew of a tiny cave there. It was scarcely more than a fissure in the rocks and did not offer much comfort, but it did provide shelter from the elements. The night passed without incident.

She was woken at daybreak by the calls of the seabirds. The smaller birds were also singing, but their melody was harder to hear. When she strained to hear their sweeter song, she heard another sound. It was strange and yet familiar, and when she listened more carefully she realised that it was a woman's voice – a woman singing!

She crept out of the cave, but only so that she could hear more clearly; she did not show herself. A woman who broke the rules on singing would not welcome an audience. It was a foolish thing to do. The punishment was harsh.

As she listened, she realised why the poor lady had come at this time to this place. It was not a song of the sea that the woman sang, nor was it a hymn of praise or pleading to Namier. It was a love song, a lament for a love that was unrequited. It was sung to a tune she had never heard before, a simple tune. There were none of the complex rhythms or subtle changes of key that occurred in some of the hymns and made them interesting to hear, but unpopular with all but the finest of the singers and music makers in Bellue. Tammina had never heard a woman sing before so she could not judge the quality of the voice, but it sounded sweet and true and it conveyed a hopeless yearning that brought tears to her eyes.

She waited for some time after the singer had finished before she ventured into the open. She saw no one near the spring or on the high ground so she moved forward and looked down the slope. The woman was making her way down the steep path. She had not gone far, hampered as she was by the heavy bucket and her twisted leg. There was no mistaking the limp. It was Margren.

Tammina stepped back and cursed Namier with an intensity that surprised her. She stood and let the tears run down her cheeks. Was it not enough for a girl to be crippled, unable to run or jump, unable to spin or weave, scarcely able to wash her own body or to comb her own hair? Why should she also be burdened with a talent that was barred; a voice that she could not use unless she struggled up the slopes in the semi-darkness and sang to herself before other villagers came for water?

Some of those others arrived soon after. The water from the high spring was fresh and clean, valued by many above the well water that was more easily available in the village. Tammina brushed aside her tears, gathered the plants that she needed and followed the group of women – it was always the women who fetched water – back to the village. That was safe. She resolved to use the same tactic whenever she needed the leaves, fruit or flowers that were best picked before the sun dried the dew.

A year passed. The messengers came from the great lord in Bosron. They brought back three men, still in their twenties, but with such dreadful wounds that they were less able to work than many three times their age. The messengers demanded five more young men. Frelius argued and bargained, but his success was limited. The wounded were left to the care of their families and three other young men were taken away. One was due to be married. His girl was torn from his arms as they were marched to the gate. She swam out to sea the following week and her body was washed up on the rocks, scarcely recognisable, ten days later.

Tammina did not admire Jael as a person, but she was as indignant as he at the arrogance of the Bosron lord. Frelius ought not to have allowed any young men to be taken away against their will. He had not been resolute enough; and he was ageing. Tammina was sure that he was sick. The 'fading sickness' Mama had called it. It was not the spirit that faded, but the body. Frelius' eyes remained sharp and bright as ever, but his sturdy figure became gradually less substantial and his limbs weakened until he could scarcely walk alone.

He died six months later, and Jael became Frelius, eighth of that name.

Chapter 7

As Frelius, Jael did not come so often to the village. If he still had extramarital interests, he confined them to the Fort, and he did not attend Rest Day service regularly. More often than not, he asked Master Dregan to give a service at the Fort. On those occasions the village service was lead by another acolyte. He was prone to read long extracts from the more obscure parts of the Visitations and to preach on them.

This did not reduce the congregation. Most snoozed contentedly whilst he spoke and only roused themselves when he burnt the sacrifice. That inspired more amusement than prayer and it also provided a topic of conversation for the week ahead. In addition, everyone felt virtuous.

It was true that the more profane laid bets on various aspects of the sacrifice, but they did so in advance and settled their debts well away from the sacred precincts.

Tammina neither slept nor gambled, but she attended, as she had done since her mother died, as a counter to any accusations of witchcraft. Sometimes she dwelt on her latest experiment or a new recipe for a cream or lotion, but sometimes she listened to the reading and to the attempt to explain it. When she returned home she read the passage herself and found her own interpretation. It was a peaceful time.

Jael had ruled as Frelius for almost a year before Parandour, Lord of Bosron, sent his messengers again. They were seen approaching, as visitors always were, by the lookouts on the boundary wall. They came in a carriage marked with an official crest and accompanied by an open cart.

It was a large empty cart. Everyone knew what that meant. Parandour was fighting another battle and needed a great many more strong and fit young men. The fact that the cart was empty meant that those already conscripted in his army were still able to fight, or they were dead. There was little hope of discovering their fate. The messengers would certainly plead ignorance; and perhaps in truth they did not know.

Frelius made no attempt to keep the impending arrival secret. Nor did he interfere when a great many men suddenly decided that it was a good time to fish. All serviceable boats, and some that were far from being in prime condition, set sail to somewhere.

Tammina saw them leave next morning from the heights. She was not sure that it was a good idea, either for the men – for many of the boats were overloaded – or for Frelius and his domain. The fittest men in Bellue were now his soldiers and his guards. He would not wish to lose them. The villagers might be happy enough to see fewer guards, but it did reduce the defences.

In theory, Bellue was vulnerable to invasion on two sides, but the coasts were rocky and there were few places where even a small boat could land safely. That, and the reputation of the soldiers and sailors who guarded the ports and manned the fighting ships, kept the stronghold unmolested.

The following day, at the market, Tammina heard that Karron had gone.

"I encouraged him," Linnie assured her. "There will be another child soon, and I do not want my little ones to be fatherless."

Tammina acknowledged her wisdom and turned to her customers. She and Linnie had adjacent stalls at the market and both were usually busy.

That day Tammina was exceptionally busy. The ladies from the Fort were out in large numbers and were buying more than usual. It was strange – as if they were preparing for a siege. Tammina dismissed the notion. If they were preparing for a siege, there were more important items to hoard than hand and face cream.

She and Linnie had closed their stalls and were packing away their goods when Frelius strode through the village. He was finely dressed, armed and accompanied by a cohort of guards.

The girls stared. Was he going to meet the messengers in such state?

It seemed that he was. He stood with his guards in a semicircle about him and commanded that the great gates be opened.

The messengers were surprised. They were not usually welcomed, nor invited to choose the men they wanted from a uniformed group. They hardly noticed that the cart was kept outside, and that the carriage, once they had alighted, was forced backwards.

The driver was puzzled at the crowd of boys teasing the horses by waving bits of greenery, and he called out a warning. It was then they noticed.

"Those lads may be hurt." The messenger's voice was sharp, but there was little concern in his tone. "They are fools to torment animals like that. You had best call them to order."

Frelius smiled. It was not one of his genuine smiles.

"I will, when I am ready," he answered and watched the heavy creatures back unhappily away from the branches.

Tammina, standing at the back of the worried, but fascinated, crowd, wondered how Frelius knew that horses, and indeed many other animals, disliked the smell of the seawillow.

He must know. The boys were trained and seawillow did not grow near the village. Someone must have gathered it from the cliffs as soon as Parandour's people were sighted. She felt uneasy and began to move away. She would go home.

She was too late. A hand closed around her arm, and when she tried to pull away another large body blocked her way and another hand gripped her shoulder. Frelius' personal guards had a firm hold on her.

"Enough!" Frelius spoke crisply.

The branches were dropped immediately and lads vanished into the crowd. The gatekeepers were ready at their posts. They did not close the doors completely, but the gap they left was narrow, wide enough for a man on foot, but not for a vehicle. The visitors began to realise that this was not a welcoming committee. They were effectively cut off from their transport and their group. They were armed, but they were also surrounded and outnumbered.

Frelius regarded them with amusement. His plan had worked perfectly and he was relishing his position.

"Do not fear. We will not harm you."

He smiled, but they were not reassured. Nor was Tammina. She struggled again, hoping that her captors were distracted by the drama that was taking place in front of them, but they merely tightened their grip without even looking at her.

"You have chosen well," Frelius continued, "as I expected. I know that Lord Parandour is generous enough to return some conscripts, but only when he has sapped their strength and they are of little use to anyone. I wonder that he does not breed his own soldiers. I have heard that he is successful in most of his battles so there must be many strong young men in his armies. Perhaps it is the women in his domain that lack the right qualities. That is speculation; of interest, but of little value, and I have much to do today so we will return to the business in hand."

He became brisk again, and stood taller, proud and defiant.

"Alas, I cannot spare any strong young men; not now and not at any time in the future. Give that message plainly to your lord. I will pay the taxes due on our trade and my ships will keep the Great Bay clear of pirates, but I will send no more men for his army.

"He will not like the message, but I will not send you away empty handed. Here," he gestured to one of his court and was handed a heavy bag, "here are my taxes, as *I* have calculated them; and in addition you may have two of our women. Breed your next generation of soldiers from them!"

Tammina caught her breath in alarm, but frightened as she was, she gave credit to Jael for his plans. They had been well laid and were carried out with precision. Frelius moved forward and swung the bag towards the messengers. They took it, but its weight and thrust caught them off balance. They staggered back and were swiftly pushed through the great gates.

Tammina's captors lifted her easily off her feet and carried her forward. She saw another woman also being carried, but only one man was needed for that task. He carried Margren.

They were both flung through the narrowing opening and Tammina was still lying where she had fallen when she heard the gates crash together and the thud of the bar as it fell back into its hook.

She struggled up and would have run, but Margren was beside her and clung to her skirts wailing.

"Oh Tammina, what are we going to do? What will happen to us?"

"Run!" hissed Tammina fiercely, answering only the first most urgent question, but she knew that was not an option even as she scrambled to her feet.

Margren could run, but not nearly fast enough, and though the most important of Parandour's delegation were still flat on the ground, there were at least half a dozen others. They were not so elegantly dressed, but they were alert and on their feet. One of them overheard her and caught her arm. He twisted it behind her back.

"Bring the other," he said with a nod to one of his companions. "We'll put them in the cart. Keep them safe until The Honoured Ones decide what to do."

His tone did not convey much respect for 'The Honoured Ones', but as they were still struggling to their feet and trying to maintain some semblance of dignity, Tammina doubted that they had heard.

The cart was dirty and even at its best had never been comfortable. The seats were rough sawn wooden planks that no carpenter had touched with his plane. They were sturdy though – sturdy enough to hold iron staples with heavy chains attached to them.

'So this was why the conscripts did not flee back to Bellue,' she thought as the men pushed her onto the seat, looped the chain around her and fastened it with a stout padlock. In so much as she had thought about the conscripts' fate, she had assumed that they were, at least in some respects, happy to go and fight in Lord Parandour's army. Now she knew that they had had little choice.

Margren was weeping, and still asking questions that had no answer.

"Be quiet! I need to think!" Tammina silenced her more harshly than she had intended. She also was frightened. It was only pride that prevented her from weeping, for she had no wish to be used for breeding and had no idea how to avoid that fate.

Ironically, it was Frelius who gave her hope. He had climbed one of the gate towers and now stood on its roof, looking down at those outside.

The Honoured Ones were having an agitated discussion. They were standing now with the open bag beside them. Two large stones lay next to it. Despite her predicament, Tammina smiled at the sight. The bag had been heavy, but not with coin. The calculated tax had not been nearly so generous. She could not see clearly from where she was sitting, but she thought it rather meagre. The Honoured Ones obviously thought so too.

She heard the laughter from the tower and looked up. He was there and now that she had seen him, she would not look away. She stared back at his smiling face. She was not the sole recipient of his mockery. He addressed Lord Parandour's men first.

"You had best leave now. Get on your way before dark. You can do nothing else. Bellue will not fall to a handful of men with swords and knives. It will not fall to an army equipped with a battering ram and a ballista. Tell that to your lord when you present my gifts."

He laughed as he looked down into the cart.

"I see that you have secured the women. Wise of you, though I doubt that the cripple needs chains to keep her from running, and the Witch may summon demons to break them when the moon is high. Still, they are yours now. Do what you please with them."

He stared down at Tammina before he turned away and he smiled in satisfaction. Jael had taken his revenge and he revelled in it.

Tammina did not change her expression nor did she turn away until he had left the roof of the tower. She was sure that he did not believe that she was a witch – sure indeed that he believed in little but the power of might – but he had given her hope. They were surely sophisticated people in Bosron, but it was possible that they might still believe in witchcraft, and in its power. She must work on Margren.

Tammina liked Margren. She was sweet natured and forgiving and totally lacking in aggression. It seemed sometimes that she had been born to oblige and to obey. She also accepted. If Tammina implied, she would not question. If Tammina hinted, she would agree.

There was little to be gained by sharing her intentions with the girl, though. She would worry and make mistakes. So, when Margren asked, in the hearing of the drivers, if the Frelius really believed that Tammina was a witch, she did not shake her head in denial. She smiled slowly instead, and answered clearly,

"I am a witch's daughter. Does not everyone believe that I have – unusual powers?"

She was rewarded. The man at the horse's head turned and stared at her curiously. She held her smile, and his gaze, until he turned away. She closed her eyes as if in slumber, but her mind was active. There was much to think about.

Jael was pleased with himself and his guards. His orders had been carried out and his plan had worked perfectly. He had not only defied Lord Parandour, he had made fools of his representatives. He had also rid his land of that thorn in his flesh, Tammina Farsay. No one would object to that.

It had been a masterstroke, too, to get rid of the crippled girl. She would not be missed, except perhaps by her mother who might cry for a few days, and it had been wise to send two women. He had made the choice, and to single out just one might have given rise to comment; but a cripple and a Witch's daughter – that was a fine insult to the great lord in Bosron. It was good to hear the talk about his defiance, especially among those who frequented the port. He wanted all of the country to know of his stand.

His complacency was short-lived. The rumours started only a few days later and after the next market day even the Fort was full of disturbing talk.

Two boys started the rumours. They had been dared, the very evening of the confrontation, to enter the Witch's house and see what was inside. They walked boldly enough to the door and lifted the latch, but the door would not open. They were surprised and after some discussion decided that there must be another entrance. They walked round the house searching and peered into the store.

It was dark, the only light came through the narrow opening and that was almost blocked by a great stack of wood for burning, but they crept in and made their way cautiously round the obstacle. The first thing they saw was Tammina's store of fruit, carefully laid out on a bed of straw.

She had treated the fruit as her mother had done. Leaves from a certain plant were boiled in ale and the fruit, carefully selected for unbroken skin, was dipped into the strained, cooled liquor. The smell and taste of the coating deterred both insects and vermin, according to her mother, and it seemed to do so, though Tammina had never found either especially strong or unpleasant. Mama had always insisted that the fruit be peeled before they ate it, 'to avoid bad dreams', and she had always done so.

The boys were not so particular, and they were, as boys usually are, hungry. They ate several. It seemed a pity to waste good food. Still eating, they moved on to investigate a few boxes – one containing carved figures, one full of old clothes – before approaching some large jars.

The owl that roosted in the rafters was disturbed by their voices. It moved closer to the wall, not wanting to leave its perch, but the boys came closer and began to laugh. Just as one lad reached out to investigate a jar, the owl launched itself from its perch and flew out over their heads. They heard the flap of great wings and felt the draught. They clutched one another in terror.

That was not all. A great dark shadow emerged from the behind the jars and reached out towards them. Both staggered back, tripping over the clothes that they had dropped carelessly on the ground and not recognising them in the darkness. It seemed that black tendrils were catching at their ankles. They tumbled out into the twilight and ran.

Their hallucinations did not last long. An hour later they were quarrelling bitterly about what they had seen. One was certain that it was a huge crow whose great wings were tipped with fingers, the other that it had been a disembodied cat's head with whiskers like arms. They agreed on one thing; a figure in a billowing cloak had flown across the sky and come to rest on the roof of the house; and they knew that the Witch had come back to protect her own. They did not keep their fears to themselves.

Karron also went to his cousin's house. He went as soon as he returned from his sea trip and heard what had happened. He hoped to rescue some of her belongings from looting or destruction, but he could not open the door. He returned home puzzled and asked Linnie if there was another entrance to Tammina's house. He could not recall one, but he had not often been inside.

Linnie was angry and upset. She was not as familiar as she believed with her friend's home, but she was quite definite in her answer. There was no other door.

If the door in front of the house was bolted, as Karron was sure it was – and he had fixed the bolts – then Namier must have intervened to protect the home of a good woman. *He* had ensured that it would not be easily raided. She did not believe those two young rascals who said that the Witch had returned.

The village was divided. So was the Fort. Some thought it was witchcraft that protected the house from intruders, and some thought it a miracle. Either way, Tammina's house was left alone – and Jael was troubled.

Chapter 8

The journey to Bosron was uncomfortable for Tammina and Margren. It was also longer than strictly necessary. The Honourable Ones were in no hurry to return and vented some of their anger on their prisoners. At the first camp, when they were still fastened with chains, one approached Margren. He was rough and she cried out in protest and in pain. Tammina was scathing in her objections.

Did they not think that the Great Lord Parandour would want his gifts unspoiled? They had no conscripts for him, but Frelius would make sure that all the land knew what he had sent instead. Bellue traded with all the ports on the shores of the Great Bay. It was Bellue ships and Bellue men that kept those seas free from pirates. They were respected, and so too was their news.

It was likely that Lord Parandour would hear, and be expecting two women, but he would expect two virgins, because none in Bellue wanted either of them. It was an insult and he would not be pleased, but nor would he want them to be violated and breeding already. He needed more soldiers, not more messengers.

She spat out the last word with contempt and was slapped hard for her insolence, but the Honourable One moved away to confer with his colleague. He was angry, but he was not stupid. The Witch was right. They could not abandon the women, or even kill them. Parandour would hear sooner or later of Frelius' insulting gift, and their lord's temper was uncertain. However unpleasant the prospect was, it would be wise to bring him his 'conscripts' unspoiled.

There were no further attempts to molest the prisoners, but they were not well treated. Water was given sparingly and food not at all. One of the drivers tossed some crusts of bread into their laps when he could, but it was little enough. This was possibly just as well, because the opportunity to relieve themselves was given only once a day. The time allowed was short and the privacy available almost non-existent. Tammina managed to keep herself clean, but Margren did not. She was pulled back to the cart almost before she had reached the nearest bushes and when she fell she was dragged along the ground. Her hair came loose and the muddied strands fell round her face. She wept, and streaked her cheeks with dirt when she tried to brush the tears away.

Tammina could do nothing to help. She sat silent and thought.

Their first view of Bosron came on the third day. They were moving north through the forest. It had rained earlier in the day and the water dripped from the trees and ran in cold rivulets down their faces and their backs.

They emerged quite suddenly from the dark wetness of the trees onto a stony plain. The clouds had thinned and small patches of pale blue were visible and rays of golden sunlight wavered through the damp air. They were on a high plateau and before them the ground fell steeply to the sea. The northern shore of the Great Bay was lost in mist, its southern shore lay hidden beneath the cliffs, but to the west they could see the city. The walls on the seaward side ended in two towers that guarded the harbour entrance and a castle graced the high ground on the south bank of the river. All were built of lighter stone and in a less brutal style than the fortifications at Bellue, but they were formidable none the less. The quays, the storehouses and the dwellings clustered in their shelter, and the dark shadow of the city spilled across the green plains on either side of the river Bos and reached inland along its banks.

Margren was too cold and wet to admire the view. The city was their destination and though she was miserable now, she feared that worse would come when they arrived.

Tammina stared with interest. She too was afraid. There was little hope of escape, but an opportunity might arise, and if it did then even a small knowledge of the city would be useful.

She noticed a large building opposite the castle. It was built on a great mound and was surrounded by trees. Further upriver another edifice caught her attention. It stood on flat land in the city centre, completely different in style to the house but just as imposing. The first was the seat of government, she thought, the second, a church – but such a big church ought to have a tower and before she could discern one, they had crossed the open ground and were back among the trees on a steeply descending track.

Progress was slow and it was late afternoon when they emerged from the forest. Ahead loomed the wall and above them towered the castle. It was still light enough to see.

The Honoured Ones were annoyed. They had hoped to pass through the gates in darkness, so that the sex, if not the number, of the 'conscripts' would be unnoticed. They were too early for that and were forced to bear the mocking laughter and the taunts of the gatekeepers.

It was a festival day – the Festival of the Sword of Gerharst, the soldier's day – and the men were drunk enough to be bold, but nowhere near drunk enough to mistake two women for the expected cartful of sturdy young men. Tammina and Margren were not handled gently when they were freed from their chains in the castle courtyard.

The castle was functional, or so it seemed from their first sight of passages and stairs. The Fort at Bellue was more richly decorated than this. Soon, however, they came to a wider passage. The flagstones were spread with clean straw that deadened the tramp of feet and the walls were hung with tapestries. The armed guards who preceded them held their weapons close to prevent the clash of metal on metal. They were approaching the great hall and Lord Parandour and most of his court were celebrating the Festival there. Dinner had not yet been served but the entertainment had begun. They waited in an outer room for a suitable break in the proceedings. Lord Parandour enjoyed music and did not like the playing to be interrupted.

The Honoured Ones had already stopped to wash and brush the journey's dust from their clothes, but as they stood and waited they ran nervous hands over their tunics and removed any stray wisps of straw. Tammina smoothed down her dress but she left the strand of hair that had fallen over her eyes. She could see well enough and it made her interest in her surroundings less likely to be noticed. Her eyes moved restlessly, but she turned her head as little as possible and allowed her shoulders to slump dejectedly.

Margren was in a very poor state. She stood, but only because she was held upright by a guard. He held her at arm's length and did not hide his disgust at the sight and smell of her. Her head was drooped to her chest and her arms hung limply by her sides. There was no sign that she heard the music though it was sweet. Tammina was no musician, but she thought the instruments finer than the pipes, tambours and lyres of Bellue.

Someone began to sing. It was a woman's voice, high and clear. Tammina caught her breath and immediately regretted her lack of control. If she was to play the witch, or the seer, she ought not to show surprise. On the journey, she had been unable to assist Margren and any attempt to escape with her would be doomed from the outset, but as she listened to the song she thought again.

If the ability to sing was valued here, she could perhaps help the poor girl, not to escape, but at least from being killed or thrown to the coarsest of the soldiers for their amusement.

Margren lifted her head in surprise when she heard the woman's voice, but it fell again. The sound did not bring hope; merely another reason to despair. Fate had granted her talent, but had brought her too late to a place where it was valued.

The song ended and the applause followed. It was enthusiastic. The singer was clearly appreciated. When the noise abated, the return of the Ambassadors was announced and permission was given for them to enter and bring the men from Bellue with them for inspection.

Tammina smiled inwardly at the title 'Ambassadors'. She preferred the driver's contemptuous 'Honoured Ones'. The guards shared his disrespect. They grinned maliciously as they moved aside to allow the party to enter the great hall.

There was uproar when the two women were thrust forward. Tammina stumbled, but she recovered and stood upright. She pushed the hair back from her face and looked openly around seeking out the great Lord.

Margren staggered, fell and lay beside her in a tumbled heap.

The greetings and explanations were lost in the noise from a crowded hall. Amazement was the first reaction. Lord Parandour's demands had been refused!

A loud voice called for silence and Frelius' message was repeated and, this time, heard. There was some laughter, hurriedly stifled, but full realisation of the situation brought ominous quiet.

The bag containing the tax was held out.

"Count it!"

The order was given by a man of average height and indifferent colouring. He had an air of command, though, and piercing eyes. The jerk of his head and the prompt obedience of one who was plainly a gentleman confirmed Tammina's suspicion. This was the Lord of Bosron.

The silence was so profound that the click of coins was audible throughout the hall. Parandour did not turn to watch the count. He stared at the two women and at his ambassadors, but he was counting too. When the noise ceased he asked,

"Is that all?"

There was a murmured assent. The precise amount was given in a whisper. It was left to Lord Parandour to announce, if he so chose. He did so choose and also stated the amount that had been required. The shortfall was not insignificant.

"Frelius rebels, it seems," he continued, "I doubt that these are the finest in Bellue."

He walked towards the captives as he spoke and wrinkled his nose in disgust as he neared Margren. "A stinking cripple and a supposed witch."

Another man spoke, angry and indignant. "You have been insulted, my lord; you and all your court. This young upstart has defied you and held you up to ridicule. We must make an example of him. Send a force and bring him back in chains. We will hang him from one of the towers so that all shall see that Lord Parandour is not a man to trifle with."

There were shouts of agreement, but Tammina did not think that that agreement was entirely shared by the man who stared at her. She threw back her head and laughed aloud.

"Frelius thinks to mock you, lord. Send a force and you will compound the mockery."

Someone struck her hard. "Do not speak woman, unless speech is required of you."

Tammina staggered under the blow, but she did not turn to see who had given it. She lifted her head and stared again at Parandour.

She knew little of him, but a man who had extended the boundaries of his command as he had done, could not be a fool and had surely experienced the difficulties of mounting a siege. She tried again, very softly.

"And you, lord, do you silence truth with blows?"

She was hit again and this time she fell. She did not attempt to stand, but she did look up, this time at the men behind her, and she laughed.

"Save your strength for pounding at the gates of Fort Bellue. They will not be felled so easily."

"Leave her!"

She was edging away from the anticipated kick, but the command prevented its delivery. She stayed still and waited.

"Stand up, woman, and tell me why Frelius only *thinks* to mock me." His voice was challenging.

She stood up slowly and pulled back her hair before she spoke.

"The Frelius does not know what he has given, lord."

"I can see what he has given! Less than he owes in tax and two useless women instead of the strong men that I need."

"Are women useless, Lord?"

"They have their place, and their uses; but a cripple offered for breeding soldiers is certainly a mockery." He turned away. "Take them away. I must consider how to punish this insult."

"She was not born crippled." Tammina moved after him and spoke boldly.

Lord Parandour glared at her. "The Witch speaks again without invitation, does she?" he said sourly. "You remember her birth, I suppose?"

Tammina smiled her special smile. Her heart beat fast. She had no idea whether these nobles of Bosron believed in witchcraft or magic, but she had no weapons to use other than her supposed power. She must speak with confidence.

"I was there," she said, "and yes, I remember. She was born straight as any I see here. So were her brothers and her parents. If she breeds, there is no reason why her children should be twisted."

"Oh, Tammy! Is that really so?" Margren lifted her head, forgetting her situation in her surprise.

Lord Parandour ignored her. His eyes were on Tammina.

"You are not old enough to remember her birth."

"I am younger than she," Tammina nodded in agreement, "but I was there at her birth and I remember. The Frelius does not know, but I do.

"She is crippled, and now she is soiled and dirty, but if she is given water she will wash, and if she is given food and drink she will be able to stand; and if she lies with a healthy man she will bear a healthy child."

Tammina smiled again. She was pleased. Margren could not have reinforced the message better, had she practiced for a week. She was sitting now with joy and amazement plainly written on her dirty face.

"There is another thing that the Frelius does not know – she can sing."

Again Margren did not disappoint. Her exclamation was audible. "How did you know?"

Parandour studied the girl on the floor before he spoke. She was in a sad state. This scene might have been planned, but Frelius had labelled one woman a witch, and one a cripple – was the cripple so skilled that she could pretend to the shock and the fear that showed in her face? He did not think so. The shock perhaps, but the fear was surely instinctive. Women in Bellue did not sing.

"I have heard that women in Bellue do not sing."

"It is forbidden," – Tammina stared back at him boldly – "but nevertheless she can sing."

"Well, it is a simple thing to test. We shall see. Master Hallarden!" He beckoned to one of the musicians who came forward.

He was a young man, fair-skinned and brown-haired, and he held a stringed instrument of a type unknown in Bellue.

"Try her," commanded Lord Parandour.

The young man crouched by Margren and plucked a string.

"Can you sing that?" he asked her gently.

A strange sound emerged from Margren's throat and there was some laughter, but the musician nodded gravely and stood up.

"She will do better standing, lord," he said, "and her throat is dry. May I give her water?"

The brief nod of assent brought a serving-woman with a glass of water. Master Hallarden stooped and helped Margren to stand. If he felt disgust, he hid it well. Only pity showed in his face. He offered her the water and held it to her lips when she feared to handle the glass. She had only a crudely made wooden cup at home. She drank greedily and Tammina envied her.

This time the musician sang a note for her and when she repeated it, he sang another, and another. Her confidence grew with each note, the uncertain waver disappeared and her voice though soft was clear and true. He plucked a note and when she sang it, he tried others, higher and higher still. Margren did her best, but she had sung softly in Bellue and she had never attempted to sing such high notes.

Tammina tried to seem disinterested. She kept her head high and her eyes on the middle distance, but she listened. She thought that Margren's voice was beautiful, but she was ignorant in such matters. She did not look directly at Master Hallarden, but she thought him encouraging, even pleased.

She was sure of it when Margren failed on one note, for he did not repeat it. He smiled and turned to Lord Parandour.

"She is untrained, lord; but she can sing."

Lord Parandour was unimpressed by the young man's enthusiasm.

"I can hear that for myself," he answered, and to Margren, "You know a song? 'The Ballad of Bara' perhaps, or 'Sighs of the Sea Maiden'?"

Margren shook her head and trembled at his words. "No, lord," she answered. "I know no songs."

"She has a song."

Tammina focused on the middle distance. It was becoming surprisingly easy. She was thirsty and so tired that keeping her eyes open at all was an effort.

"One of her own – of a fisherman and love given, but not returned."

Margren's frightened gasp was ignored. She was abruptly ordered to "Sing that", but the lord's next words were, by his standards, gentle and reassuring.

"You have no need to fear. There is no punishment for singing in Bosron."

So Margren sang her song.

From highest spring, I early fetch the water,
As rising sun turns sky and sea to gold.
Above my head sea birds are harshly calling,
On shore below, the fishermen's rites unfold.
And maybe, there is one with golden hair.

I watch them dance and know that they do sing,
Yet cannot tell if he I love is there,
But at song's end, when high their caps they fling,
The sun will light upon his golden hair.
And I will see the boy with golden hair.

All day, for fish, he'll brave the waves at sea,
And I on land will pray the wind is fair,
For though I know he never thinks of me,
I cannot help but love his golden hair.
Oh how I love that boy with golden hair.

All day I tend the flocks and weed the land,
And wash the wool for fairer hands to spin,
And pray that evening tasks will let me stand
Where I can rest and watch the boats come in,
And see again the boy with golden hair.

He'll mark me not, but none can chide my dreaming,
For none do know, my dreams I do not share.
When catch is beached and birds above are screaming,
He'll doff his cap to free his golden hair.
How bless'd the breeze that stirs that golden hair.

Work done, I seek the pathway from the sea,
And sweet I dream, he sees me waiting there.
He waves a hand, and he does smile at me,
And evening sun will shine on golden hair.
Oh favoured ray, that kisses golden hair.

But sweeter yet, he stops, he stays to greet me.
I stretch my hand and he will speak me fair.
Oh, sweetest dream, I touch the boy I love,
And twine my fingers in his golden hair.
And maybe steal a strand of golden hair.
I long to own a strand of golden hair.

She began uncertainly, but at the end of the first verse
Master Hallarden played the notes of the last line and
accompanied her when she started to sing again.

Her eyes widened in surprise and delight. She pushed the
tangled strands of hair away from her face and stood straighter.

Someone was playing her song and she was singing it. Her
voice swelled. She did not need to sing softly. Here she could
lift her voice and it was not swept away by the wind or drowned
in the cry of the birds. It filled the hall and the Bosron court
listened to the unwashed cripple in her soiled clothes and they
heard the anguish and the longing of a woman who had no
expectation of life beyond pain and drudgery.

There was silence when she finished, and then applause. Lord Parandour did not applaud and after a few moments he held up a hand and the clapping ceased.

"You can sing," he stated and demanded where she had sung before.

Margren shook her head. "I have never sung like that before, lord; only in secret, far from anyone who might hear, and softly because I was afraid."

"Your friend," he jerked his head towards Tammina, "she has heard you."

She shook her head again. "Oh no, lord. Tammina sees. She sees things that others do not. That is why they are afraid of her and call her a witch. I am not afraid of her because she has always been kind to me."

He considered them both before he said impatiently, "Whatever talents you have, Frelius has still mocked me."

"Four thousand soldiers and seven ships to besiege Bellue." Tammina spoke regretfully as if even that number would not have an impact.

"The Fort at Bellue has never been taken, lord," someone murmured, and Tammina spoke again, softly. Those standing further away heard no more than the hiss of the sibilants, as hard to grasp as a snake.

"Reverse his jest, lord. Send thanks for the seer and the songbird, and save your ships for the sea, and your soldiers for skirmish on the northern reaches."

"What do you know of the northern reaches?"

"They are not peaceful, lord." Tammina's reply was unchallenging, a statement of fact. "They are recently conquered, are they not?"

"Aye."

He glared at her, but he asked, "She will have good sons?"

Tammina shrugged her shoulders. "I see the future in a mist as others see it. I cannot draw the clouds aside at will. She was born straight, and a soldier who has lost a limb does not breed children with the same lack. A child may be well or ill as Namier decrees."

He considered, but not for long. He turned and scanned the faces of the assembled company until he found the one he wanted.

"Verryon."

The man who came forward was or had been a soldier. That was evident in his stance. He was no longer young, nearing forty perhaps, but he was tall and straight with regular features and clear eyes. He was not lavishly dressed, but his tunic was of good cloth, his boots were polished and his beard neatly trimmed. He bowed to his lord without undue deference.

"Take her, Verryon. Her voice will please you, and perhaps her loins, when she is clean. You do not have as far as some to escort a filthy bundle, and you have slept alone for too long."

There was some laughter at that, but it was quiet. It covered Verryon's hesitation. He stood silent and twisted the ring on his finger several times before he answered.

"As you wish, lord."

Tammina raised her head and looked into his eyes.

'A lonely man, still grieving?' she wondered.

Aloud she said, "A bloom is lost forever if it is pulled too soon, but a tender hand may grow a different flower in the same ground."

Margren was hardly flower-like in her soiled gown; perhaps she had chosen the wrong words. It was too late to change now. She could do no more.

Verryon acknowledged her speech with a nod and turned to Margren.

"Come," he said and walked towards the door. Margren limped after him, and all eyes followed them as they left the room.

"Now," Lord Parandour regarded Tammina. "What do we do with this one?"

"She needs water, lord."

It was the musician who spoke and to Tammina's surprise the lord made no objection and a glass of water was put into her hand. She drank slowly, but it was hard not to tip the sweet wetness into her mouth all at once.

"Will you lose your powers if you lie with a man?" asked Lord Parandour when she had finished drinking.

"I do not think so, lord, but I do not know." That was truthful enough.

He studied her more closely and flicked an assessing glance at the Honoured Ones.

"Has no man lain with you? You were not molested on your journey here?"

"No, and no, lord."

"And the other?" he demanded, suddenly realising that 'the other' might not have been so disgusting when the party first left Bellue.

Tammina did not feel that she owed anything to those who had brought her here.

"There was an attempt, lord, but they are not quite fools. They listened when I told them that Frelius would publish the details of his defiance over all the Great Bay. Wiser to deliver his gifts unspoiled, for if you choose to mock Frelius by breeding as he suggested, it would be soldiers that you wanted, not more – messengers."

He laughed at the contempt in her voice, but he was still angry.

"No, I want no more messengers, but I want soldiers now, not fifteen years hence!"

He walked away giving orders as he went. They were not harsh. He was not sure what to do with her yet, but at least she was not to be thrown from the castle walls immediately.

Master Hallarden smiled encouragingly as she was led away and she saw in his eyes an admiration that she did not seek nor want. She followed the guards as meekly as Margren had followed the soldier.

Chapter 9

Margren lay back in the large bath and wondered at her situation. She was in a large well-furnished room, a fire was burning cheerfully in the grate and a woman and a girl were waiting on her. The water was blissfully warm and it was scented. She had eaten tender meat and creamy cheese, and a pastry so light that she thought it might have flown away had she breathed too hard upon it.

She was a little anxious that her clothes had been whisked away, but the older woman had assured her that such fine cloth would not be discarded. They had not thought that a distant place like Fort Bellue would have such stuff, but Mistress need not concern herself. It would be carefully washed and dried. In the meantime other garments would be provided.

Her hair was washed and her hands. The twisted arm was lifted and the bent fingers gently straightened. The nails were scrubbed and the sores exclaimed over.

"I did not have chance to wash," explained Margren. She did not wish them to think that she was dirty from choice.

They did not. They bathed the sores, patted them dry and spread cream on them. When they helped her from the bath, she was swathed in a warm soft towel. She breathed deeply.

It smelt of coolgrass; there was no lingering trace of sheep or of fish. It was a nightgown that was pulled gently over her head – a reminder of why she was here – but it was so soft that it caressed her skin and the wrap that followed it was, she was sure, made of silk.

"This is too fine for me," she said, fingering the soft folds.

She was contradicted. The Commander's sister, who had looked in whilst they were bathing her, had chosen it specially. She was married to a Lord and would be very happy if Mistress could please and comfort her brother. So would they and all others in his service.

He was a good man; he was kind, even-tempered and just. He had grieved so when his wife died and had not shown the least interest in any woman since. It was not if he were old, he was not yet forty and a fine figure of a man.

Margren had no difficulty interpreting the admiration in their last words, but the meaning of the subtle note in their references to his wife, eluded her. Tammina would have known immediately that they did not consider said wife entirely worthy of such devotion.

When her hair was dry and dressed to their satisfaction, they dabbed a sweet-smelling liquid on her neck and breasts and helped her to her feet.

"There, you are ready now," the woman declared and the girl stepped away and pulled a long curtain to one side.

Margren stared. There were three women on the far side of the curtain. One was dressed in a silk wrap. It was scarlet, but the sheen took the harshness from the bright colour. It glowed softly and set off the dark tresses of hair that swept the woman's cheeks. They curved under her ears, before they were drawn back and left loose to join the shining mass that fell softly down her back. Large brown eyes stared back at her.

She stretched out a hand to touch the shiny surface. "Is that – me?" she asked in wonderment.

They had had a mirror at home, a small square of polished metal, strictly for her mother's use. She had never pined over that. The reflections that she had sometimes spied in still pools or on the greasy surface of the tub where she washed the fleeces, had never inspired a desire to see herself more clearly. Now she looked at the vision in the mirror and stood a little straighter.

"Oh, yes." The woman was full of encouragement. "That lifts your lovely bosoms. You will surely please him. Is it hard for you to stand like that? Do you need a stick?" She was clearly anxious that Commander Verryon be pleased.

Margren smiled. The Commander must be a good master.

"No, I do not need a stick," she answered, "and I hope he will be pleased; but I do not know how to please a man. What should I do?"

A bell sounded from the next room.

"He is ready for you. Just do what he asks. That will please him."

The women led her to a door. They opened it and pushed her gently through. They had done their best. This soft-spoken girl so full of gratitude for every little service would be a much more acceptable mistress than the ambitious widow who was pursuing the Commander with great determination; and had been almost since the day of his wife's burial.

It was true that said widow had not so far made any impression, but many a man had given way to persistence, especially when he had no inclination to seek a woman for himself. Socially the widow was acceptable, but no one in the castle thought that she would make their master content and several felt that she would also cause considerable disruption in their own lives.

It was obvious from the silk wrap supplied by his sister, who was visiting, that she had similar fears. It was fine cloth and not much worn.

Margren moved no further into the room than was necessary for the door to be shut behind her.

She was frightened. She had no notion of where Tammina was or whether she would ever see her again. She wanted to please the man to whom she had been given, but she did not know how to do so, and the kindly women whom she hoped would help had said nothing useful. Margren was well aware that every man, even those with no claim to authority over her, expected her to do as they asked.

He was standing by the fire looking at the portrait above the mantelshelf. It was not large, but it was the only picture and it dominated the room. Even the curtained bed seemed insignificant compared to the large blue eyes that stared out from the canvas.

Margren waited in silence. Her surprise at her own appearance was forgotten. The woman in the portrait was beautiful. If she had been his wife, he would not want Margren.

It was some time before he turned and saw her; and even then he was silent, staring at her as if he had no idea who she was or why she was there.

"Forgive me," he said at last. "I have not been in this room for some time. I had forgotten this picture. I have others."

"Is it your wife, lord? She is very beautiful."

"She was my wife and she was beautiful, but she died, and the child with her, some four years ago."

His answer did not encourage comment and Margren made none. After a while he spoke again, less coldly.

"You have washed, I see, and have clean clothes. Have you also been given food and drink?"

"Oh yes, lord. I have had a hot drink and meat and cheese."

"I am not a Lord. I am a soldier. This castle does not belong to me, I merely have rooms here whilst I am in command."

There was a pause.

"They are fine rooms, lo – sir." Margren felt that she ought to say something and she certainly thought the rooms fine. She had never been inside such a large building before. In fact she not entered many buildings other than her own home – the church and the village hall, and one or two houses in Bellue. That was all.

Verryon cast a brief glance around. The curtains that hid the stone walls were plain and barely adequate for the purpose. The furniture was serviceable and the fire surround was unadorned; the few parallel lines gouged from its surfaces could not be called carving.

Etheldra had not considered any rooms in the castle 'fine'. She had been used to large comfortable houses filled with upholstered furniture, wooden panelling, embroidered hangings, wide staircases and large windows.

She was the daughter of a lord; an old family whose estate had been one of Parandour's early conquests. He had loved her from the moment he saw her. He had been no more than a captain then, and was not of ancient lineage. He had thought her unobtainable, but Parandour had intervened.

Verryon had his lady, her father was permitted to remain in his house and to keep a good part of his land and Parandour could delay the payments due to his skilful captain until revenues from the conquered lands began to fill his coffers.

It was a poor bargain for Verryon, though he was content with it. Such a delicately bred girl could not be expected to follow the army on its marches, so she had continued to live with her family and he had visited her whenever Parandour's wars had allowed it. Each time he returned, he had hoped to find a child and each time he had been disappointed.

Promotion had come and eventually a posting that did not involve living in a tent. Proudly he had brought her to Bosron and shown her round the castle. She had been excited and happy on the journey, but her expectation was of a fashionable house in the city and a husband who visited only on evenings when he was free. Shared quarters that were neither spacious nor well furnished, in a castle across the river from the main town, did not meet with her approval. She had said little, but he knew her thoughts. Alas, the higher ranks in the army were for the nobler members of society. This was the best he could do.

The closer contact had brought the pregnancy that he so desired and it had also brought her death. He had been faithful whilst she lived, and he remained so after she died.

Now Parandour had given him another woman. As like as not, she was the daughter of a fisherman, an ignorant girl in addition to being a crippled one. His lord was mocking him, venting his anger at the defiance of Frelius.

He thought of the Fort at Bellue. It was not an easy place to besiege let alone to conquer. The other girl was right; better to bear the defiance and keep the manpower to quell any who tried to copy it. She too might be the daughter of a fisherman and ill-educated, but she was clever. 'Reverse the jest' she had advised.

He broke his reverie and looked at Margren.

"Come, we will test that voice of yours," he said and moved to a corner of the room.

Margren was glad to obey. She had not dared to move and standing still for any length of time made her legs ache.

He was sorting through some sheets of paper that he had taken from a shelf. He selected one and held it out.

"Can you read?"

She looked at the page. It was a sheet of music.

"I can say the words, sir, but not sing from that."

"I will give you the notes," he said and began to sing.

They sang together for some time. He gave only a cursory explanation of the music and was surprised when she sang from the score a note that was beyond his range. She was not stupid.

He gathered the music sheets and returned them to their place.

"Were you raped on your way here?" he asked abruptly.

Margren was startled. She had been watching regretfully as the music was put away out of her sight.

"No, it was not -. He only -." She gathered herself together and stared down at her hands. "Someone tried. He was rough and hurt me and I cried out. Tammina stopped him and no one tried again."

He questioned her gently and discovered that her attacker had been stopped by an excellent argument before much harm had been done. He was also assured that though she had cried out, it was only because it was unexpected and the man was rough. She did not think she would cry out in different circumstances. She was not sure how to please a man; she had never wanted to before because she did not wish to bring a child like herself into the world, but Tammina had said that she was born straight. That changed everything.

"You believe this Tammina, even though she is labelled 'Witch'?"

"Oh, yes. She is not a witch. Witches are evil and I cannot think her evil. She has always been kind to me. She knows a great deal about plants and how to use them but I am sure she uses them only for good."

A trace of uncertainty crept into her voice, and a tiny frown creased her forehead, but she straightened her shoulders and continued stoutly, "I do not believe that she killed the Padri, for all that she glared at him at Rest Day Services. I think he slipped in the dark and banged his head on a stone. It is perfectly possible to be hurt without having a mark."

She had her qualities, this fisherman's child, he thought; but it was Etheldra that he wanted and she was gone.

"You sing well," he began, "and that pleases me and you are not ill-looking, but I would be of no use to you. I have no desire; I am too old; and besides your heart is given to a young man with golden hair."

He smiled gently. He did not want to hurt her.

Margren was used to rejection. She smiled too, but she shook her head. "I do not think you old, sir. Many men in Bellue wait until they are established in their work before they marry. And my song was just a song, a girl's dream. Many girls in Bellue village dream of Jan, for he is handsome and has beautiful hair, but he did not notice me. Oh, he never pushed me to one side or cursed me. If I was in his path, he simply walked around me, as he would walk around a boulder that was in his way."

"The lack is not in you, it is in me." He sought for her name and realised that he did not know it. "I do not remember your name. What are you called?"

Margren was thinking of Bellue, trying to distance herself from this gentle man who had treated her so well, but did not want her.

"I am called many things, snail-tail and sea-crab and twisty-vine, but my given name is Margren."

He had never heard the epithets before but there was no doubt as to their meaning.

"Margren," he repeated slowly. "I do not know that name. Is it a common one in Bellue? Does it have a meaning?"

"It is not common. It was my great-grandmother's name. She was from Shyran. In the old Shyran language it means," – she looked at him and smiled slightly before turning away and finishing her sentence – "'The Wanted One'."

He was silenced. He stared at her, but she did not look up. A strand of hair had escaped its fastening and hung down the side of her face. She lifted her hand, but the bent fingers could not put it back in place. He moved forward.

"Allow me," and he tried to help. He was not overly successful. The tress did not stay as he intended. He tried again. It was strong hair and the ladies had brushed it well. They had not attempted to curl it. The dark locks were straight and shiny and they smelt sweet. A different scent, he noted, from the one that Etheldra had used. This girl was different in so many ways.

She was sturdy despite her twisted limbs, the sun had darkened her face and hands, her eyes were soft and brown and her breasts were round and full. She reminded him of the women who had followed the camps when he had gone to war. Some were wives, some were not, but they all bore whatever hardship they encountered and rarely complained. He had never desired any of them, nor did he desire this woman, but her singing had pleased him.

'Reverse the jest.' It could apply to him just as well as to Parandour, and he too had been mocked and did not like it.

He was not used to being mocked, not as this girl was. He was not used to being angry, either, but anger shook him now, and sympathy. She needed care, not rough words. He looked down at the dark head and made his decision.

"You know that I still mourn my wife. You know that I am many years older than you are, and may have difficulty in satisfying you. You know that I am a soldier and do not own this castle. I have a house in a village by the shore, but it is not large. Knowing all these things, Margren, will you marry me?"

She whirled round so fast that she almost overbalanced. "Marry you!"

He steadied her, but kept a careful distance.

"I do not like to share women," he said carefully. "Nor do I want a woman who shares herself with other men."

"No, what man does?" She dismissed his words with a shake of her head. "But the Lord Parandour, did he intend that? Will he allow it?"

He answered lightly. "No, I do not think he intended it, but he is aware of my views on women; and as to his allowing it, I must admit that as I am a grown man, I had not thought of asking his permission."

"Oh, but if he did not like it, he would be angry. I have heard he cuts off people's heads or hangs them from towers. You must not risk that – not for me."

Her anxiety was for him, fears for herself took second place.

"He can exact harsh punishment for some offences, certainly," he agreed, "but I am a citizen and even Lord Parandour cannot act outside his law. He ordered me to take you and see if you pleased me. You have done so and he can hardly object to the consequences."

"You are sure?"

"I am sure."

"Then yes, sir, I will marry you."

The words were simple, but no one had taught Margren the correct way to accept a proposal of marriage. She did not look modestly down nor did she speak calmly. Her tone was unashamedly enthusiastic and she flung both arms round his neck and kissed his jaw because she could not reach his cheek.

He did not object. He wondered about repeating the things she ought to consider before accepting him, but as he looked down at her full breasts and felt her closeness, he felt that one item on the list was becoming irrelevant, and he did not.

"Then I will send for a Padri. I think that we shall both be happier if we marry first and take our pleasures later."

He adjusted her wrap and retied the sash. "And we will find a gown for you. You look delightful in this, but it is not suitable for a wedding."

Chapter 10

Tammina counted meticulously as she strode back and forth across her cell. Fifty times was the minimum she had set herself – fifty times skipping, fifty times marching, fifty times at the stride. She had started the second day when her request for exercise time in the open air had been refused. She was accustomed to walking and climbing, every day and in all weathers. The journey had left her stiff and sluggish though the lack of exercise had been the least of her concerns at the time.

Now she was more comfortable. The cell was dry, the bedding clean, the food adequate and she had been allowed pen, paper and ink. That was a luxury she had not expected.

She wrote a great deal – all that she could remember of her training. She wrote in a simple code, in neat lettering and as small as she could manage in the dim light. Rarely had she, or her mother, prepared a cream or a potion without first checking the written recipe; and with the recipe there were the notes on its use – when, how much, how often, for how long, and most importantly the warnings. Even the mildest and most often prescribed mixtures had their dangers – and those dangers were easily forgotten.

Less easily forgotten were her mother's adages. They came unbidden into her head the first night of her incarceration. Many had been prefaced by 'as my mother said' or 'it is family knowledge that'. She had recited them. Somehow it had given her a tiny sense of security, a tenuous link to a life that was familiar. One of the first had been 'Knowledge is power' and another 'Active muscles, active mind; lazy body, lazy brain'. So she exercised and had asked for writing materials.

Paper was precious so she marked the days on the wall. Others had done the same thing, but she found a clear space. In her pocket she still carried a round stone and she also had two small pots of face cream. She had expected to be searched before she was locked in, but the guards were male and their orders had been plain. The punishment for molesting her had been vigorously expressed. No one came closer to her than was necessary. The stone made no mark on the wall, but it pounded the leaves that she found in her bedding and the juice made a greenish paste when mixed with a little of the cream.

She used her finger to make the marks. They would fade sooner than scratches, but they would last a while. None of the sets of scratches recorded more than a few weeks. She did not dwell on that, as she did not know whether it boded well or badly. In the event it was sixteen days before the routine of imprisonment was interrupted.

She had eaten her midday meal and the dish had been removed as usual, but she had scarcely settled back to her writing when the door was unlocked again. There were four guards, instead of the usual two and she did not recognise any of them.

"You are to come with us," announced one.

"May I know why?" she asked mildly.

"No."

"Very well." She rose and walked away from them. "I will bring the brush that I have been given. Perhaps we will pass a mirror on our way and I will have an opportunity to see that my hair is tidy. It is as well to be neat, whatever one's destination."

Her remark did not produce a noticeable reaction, but that might be because they were used to leading prisoners to their deaths. She collected the brush and followed the guards.

She did not recognise any of the passages through which she was led, but she had been very tired when she was taken to her cell and the passages in the prison area were stark and unmemorable.

They passed through a door and emerged into a pleasanter area. The guards' boots still sounded on the stone flags but the sound was deadened a little by the wall hangings. Another passage and the hangings became more ornate. There were more of them and they were thicker. The rhythm of her escort's steps did not change but it seemed to Tammina that its members placed their feet more carefully.

They halted in front of a door. A man was standing there, waiting. Tammina recognised him immediately, it was Verryon; but it took her a moment to recognise the woman who was approaching. It was not just the fitted riding dress, the shining hair or the neat headdress that was tied over it; it was the stance. Never had Tammina seen Margren carry herself so well. She limped still, as she always would, and her arm hung awkwardly, but her back was straighter and her head unbowed. And she spoke first.

"It has begun to rain so we came back early. Have you finished your discussion or are you still waiting for Lord Parandour?"

She addressed Verryon, and he was not pleased to see her. A frown creased his forehead and he held up his hand to halt her steps. He was too late.

"Tammina!" she exclaimed. "What is happening?" and she hastened forward.

"Lord Parandour has sent for -," he paused, not knowing how to describe her, "for 'the Witch'. That is how he expressed it. I do not know why he wants her. If I did, you may be sure that I would tell you; but as yet I do not."

Margren reached the group and held out her hand to Tammina. Verryon took it, and kissed it.

"I have done all that I can to ensure her comfort and her safety. I am not in charge of prisoners. I would not keep news from you, however bad it might be, but I had hoped to spare you anxiety."

"You look well, Margren." Tammina regarded her calmly. "I am glad," and she turned to Verryon. "If I am to see Lord Parandour, may I first have chance to tidy myself. A mirror, perhaps?"

"I can fetch one." Margren was almost pitiful in her desire to help, but she was thwarted.

"No." The word was uncompromising. "I will deal with her request. You are wet; go now and change."

Margren gave Tammina an apologetic glance and limped away. She was used to obeying. Verryon was equally used to giving orders and to being obeyed. He did not pause.

"Come," he said to Tammina, and, "You wait here," to her escort. She followed and they waited, but she thought them anxious.

She was taken to a side room furnished with chairs. He gestured to a small mirror hung above a table and watched as she brushed her hair and re-braided it. She had no clips or pins – they had been lost on the journey – but she had a short length of ribbon that she had removed from her dress. She preferred plain gowns, but this had been one of Linnie's, and her dresses were often adorned with lace edgings and bows. It had been useful. She tied the end of the braid firmly and let it hang over her shoulder. That was neater than a long tail swinging at her back.

He led her back. He did not speak and nor did she. Her escort was waiting and she returned to her place in the centre of the group. Verryon opened the door and announced that the Witch had been fetched. Were they ready to question her?

The answer was not audible, but it was obviously in the affirmative for Verryon opened the door wider and Tammina was marched in.

The escort came to a halt in front of a small dais. Lord Parandour sat on the central chair. He wore a dark red tunic, a short fur-trimmed cloak and a heavy gold chain bearing an ornate pendant. A narrow gold coronet circled his head. He was flanked by four men. They were also formally garbed, but their cloaks were not so lavishly trimmed and their chains of office were considerably lighter. This was an official meeting.

Tammina wondered if a judgement was to be given – a death sentence, perhaps, or a witch trial that would have the same outcome. She was afraid. She bowed her head as she curtseyed, and when she rose she lifted it only a little, so that she focused on the officials' feet and not their faces.

"So, Witch, you have not flown away?" Lord Parandour uncrossed his ankles and planted his feet squarely on the floor. "Why I wonder? Do you not have the power?"

"Why would I fly, lord? I certainly prefer freedom to imprisonment, but I was not ill-treated. Power ought not to be used wantonly; as you will know, lord, because you are powerful." She looked up as she answered, but she did not stare boldly and lowered her eyes the moment that she stopped speaking.

He was unsure of her, she had seen that, but she did not know why. It was as well to keep her eyes hidden so that she could conceal her surprise if he voiced reasons for his caution.

"The green marks you make with your finger, does that not use power?"

Her gesture of assent was not so much agreement as a desire to hide her smile. "It is a small skill," she said, "and as such needs little power."

"And what do you write, that none can read?"

She looked up at that and spoke plainly. "I write what I can remember of my family's recipes for salves and potions. It is in code, for Healers in Bellue do not divulge the details of their methods. They pass them on only to their apprentices. My forebears have studied such things for generations and have recorded their findings, but I was obliged to leave all behind. I do not want to forget."

"Healing is it?" He exclaimed and gave a short rather unpleasant laugh. "We have heard that death, rather than health, followed *your* attention."

Tammina smiled openly at that. Frelius had spread news of his defiance, and with it had come tales of the 'Witch' that he had sent in lieu of strong young men.

"You hear the gossip of the gullible, lord. I heard it too; but there are laws in Bellue and killing contravenes them. Had there been evidence that I was responsible for anyone's death, I would have been tried, and punished if found guilty. An old man died in his sleep as old men do, and a newcomer out one night missed his way and was doubtless alarmed by a noise that was strange to him. I could kill, for many healing plants can be poisonous. It depends on how one uses them. I have used such plants, but I have never killed."

Lord Parandour accepted her answer, but a frown creased his brow and his next words were thoughtful and questioning.

"It seems though that you have strange powers. It is reported that your house in Bellue is protected by such power. No one can enter, for the only door is bolted on the inside; and no one dares to break in, for dark shapes protect it throughout the night."

"Ah!" Tammina gave a long sigh as she remembered. On market days the streets were busy. She always left by her front door and she carried her goods to her stall in a handcart. That last morning in Bellue she had done just that, but she had returned in a rush. She had been curious to hear what Frelius had to say to the visitors and had intended simply to push the handcart into the outer store and leave it there, but the crowd had been anxious. She had picked up the sense of unease and so had opened her secret door, returned her stock to its usual place and bolted the front door. Only then had she left and joined the crowd at the gate.

Thus her door was bolted and her cart and stock box was in the store. No one would even notice that the stock had gone unless they opened the box, for she had closed the lid after lifting out the bags. She had sold so much that the bags were light and she had been very quick.

"Yes, the door is bolted. I have other ways of entering or leaving, but I know nothing of dark shapes. Perhaps those who thought my mother a witch and threw her from the cliff top, might mistake a nighthawk for a Shade from Hadron sent to guard her home."

"I doubt that Bellue folk mistake a bird for an evil Shade."

It was the man at Lord Parandour's right hand who spoke and his voice was urgent. "The tales have come from several sources, lord. The mother was a witch and they did well to fling her from Bellue Heights; and we would do well to toss her daughter from one of the towers. It is dangerous even to talk with witches."

Tammina raised her head. Even now her anger flared when her mother was maligned.

"My mother was a Healer, not a witch; and it was not from Bellue Heights that she was thrown. It was from the Great Overhang, to the north, west of the harbour wall. Even from its very edge the shore beneath is hidden to the eye, but it can be heard. The sea crashes against the rocks and fills the caves. None swim nor take their boats there for the undertow is fierce. I threw branches and logs over that edge and after I found no trace of them; neither twig nor splinter was on the rocks and nothing floated on the waves."

She was robust in her speech, but her eyes filled with tears at the memory of those dreadful days following her mother's death. She opened her eyes wide and the tears did not spill over, but she did not think that her emotion was unnoticed.

Lord Parandour regarded her steadily, but a young man, standing to one side, moved forward.

"These things should be checked, sir. Commander Verryon's wife may know from which cliff the woman was thrown, and if she does not know of the currents, we can summon sailors. Some of them will know that coast."

There was some dissent, but Parandour overruled it.

"The Frelius," he observed, "is troubled and I want, if possible, to trouble him further without the expense of a long siege."

He bade someone summon the cripple. He had used her – her singing was a delight to his court and she had made one of his army commanders happier than he had been for years – and now he wanted to use the witch.

He had not yet decided precisely how to use her, but he was a subtle man.

Verryon returned with Margren. He had been gently insistent on his going to fetch her, to spare her unnecessary alarm. He called for a chair and stood behind her when she was seated.

Tammina smiled once and turned her head away. Margren would tell whatever she knew in her own way. And Margren did.

She had been in school. She had not seen them throw Mistress Farsay from the cliff, but they had been running north.

The Heights were to the south and though that hill was the highest point in Bellue, it did not have the highest cliffs. She did not know the north coast. There were ways down to the sea, but few went there for there was no reason. She had never climbed down. The ways were difficult and she did not tackle difficult climbs.

Mistress Farsay had been a Healer, well respected until the Padri had come. He had never *said* that she was a witch, but his preaching had somehow implied it and she, Margren, had been forbidden to visit the one house where she was welcome. Evil people are not kind, she had pronounced firmly, and Mistress Farsay was kind.

Parandour commented that evil folk could be kind if it suited their purposes and was answered with wide-eyed wonderment.

"But I am crippled, lord. I was despised. *I* had no influence. What possible motive could anyone have for being to kind to *me*? Other than that they are good people."

She turned her head slightly and looked at the hand that was resting on the back of her chair.

Tammina had kept her eyes on the edge of the dais, but she raised them when Lord Parandour gave a short laugh. It was a gentle laugh and when he spoke he sounded almost genial. She was grateful, for Margren's sake.

"Well, you may complain to me if at any time you are treated *unkindly*, and I trust that, as I will be tired this evening, you will be kind in your turn and sing for me after dinner."

There was a pause in the formal proceedings at that point, for sailors to be found. Tammina was allowed to sit and was given food and water. No one spoke to her, but she had good opportunity to watch and to listen to some of the conversations. The man who had recommended tossing her from a tower had his supporters. Witches were feared.

She was sure that Lord Parandour wanted to use that fear, and her, for his own purposes though she had no idea how. She did know that it was a narrow and dangerous path for her; too much emphasis on witch power and she would die as her mother had died, too little and she would lose her mystery and be of no value to him. She must keep alert.

She looked for the young man who had addressed Lord Parandour as 'sir' and she studied him covertly.

He was tall and slender with fair skin and light brown hair that almost reached his shoulders. His blue eyes were bright and intelligent, but they did not pierce. He was not at all like Lord Parandour, yet he had not called him 'lord'. As she watched, he brushed back a lock of hair with delicate fingers. She looked away in case he felt her eyes on him, but she had seen his ear.

She allowed her gaze to drift over the assembled heads, and ears. Most wore their hair short, as did their lord. His ears were in plain sight; they were almost triangular, flat-topped and with large deep lobes. She had hardly noticed before because his eyes were so compelling, but they were not elegant ears. She would not have described them as ugly, but the younger man obviously considered them unattractive enough to conceal them with his hair. He was speaking with more confidence than most young men would display in such company, so he was surely a son, or perhaps a nephew. She could hear only a word or two of his conversation. It concerned Healers. She ate and drank and she listened as she waited.

It was not long before the formal proceedings began again. The seamen came and confirmed that the currents along the northern coast were treacherous, the cliffs overhung the sea and no one went ashore there. Further west the shore was accessible, but that was beyond the outer wall of Bellue.

The Healers came next. There were three, the most senior being a man. He did not speak at first.

Tammina was shown leaves, berries and roots, sometimes singly, sometimes two or three similar ones. There were some that she did not recognise, but most she could identify and say how and for what they were used. She gave no details of preparation, and the Healers gave no reaction to her answers.

When they had produced all their samples, the man took over. He questioned more closely and for a long time. Several times she shook her head and answered that she could not remember. She had not finished her training as a Healer and she needed her books for reference. That was no more than the truth. She was tired when he finished and glad to be escorted back to her cell.

She had her evening meal and was given more water when they took away the platter. That was usual. She did not expect to be disturbed again.

The first night she had sat up and tried to stay alert, but no one had bothered her either that night or any other since. She took off her shoes and stockings and her dress. She sacrificed some of her drinking water to wash her face and scrub at a stain on her dress. It, like all her clothes, was in dire need of a proper wash, but there was not enough water, nor was there soap or any means of drying wet clothes.

The sound of the key startled her. She had no time to pull on her clothes; she pulled the blanket from the bed and wrapped it hurriedly around her.

There was a discreet tap before the door opened, but she did not call out. If they had come to rape her, they would not be hindered by her state of undress; and if they had come to kill, it hardly mattered.

It was Verryon whom she saw first, but he stood back, murmured something inaudible to his companion and allowed that gentleman to enter before him. It was Lord Parandour.

She bowed – easier than a curtsey when one was clutching a blanket – and regarded them warily.

Verryon spoke first. He apologised for the lateness of the hour and the lack of warning of their visit. Then he offered her a bag.

"Margren was concerned that you were wearing the same dress. Fresh clothes have been sent, but perhaps they have not been delivered to you."

She shook her head in answer – they had not, took the bag and thanked him. Lord Parandour scrutinised the cell before taking the only chair.

"You will have to stand," he said to Verryon and turned to her. "You may sit on the bed," he told her.

"I have come because I want to speak with you, privately and without the knowledge of my advisors or any of my court.

If at any time you speak of this visit, I will deny it. So will the Commander. Do you understand?"

Tammina nodded. She understood perfectly.

She wanted this discussion; she had worked for it, but now was not a good time. It was late and she was tired. She sat down and gathered her wits. She had, she told herself, been at a great disadvantage when she had first met this lord, and that encounter had gone well enough. There was no reason why this one should be different.

In fact it was easier than she had feared. Lord Parandour did not believe in magic powers, but he was less sceptical of the ability to see the future. Many successful rulers had employed seers. Tammina suspected that some had also believed in wizardry and witchcraft, but her only comment was a warning.

The gift of Sight – if it was indeed a gift – was unpredictable and its revelations were frequently difficult to interpret.

He nodded briefly. Such a gift could be used though, especially in conjunction with a reputation. She, Tammina Farsay, had such a reputation. She was feared.

The bolted door of her house was easily explained – there must be another, secret, entrance to her house, just as there were secret entrances to this castle – but the dark shadows guarding her house, they were generated by fear; and fear was a powerful tool. A ruler needed to be feared.

Tammina did not agree, but she said nothing. She had never been a ruler, nor had she any desire to rule. All that she had ever wanted to be was a Healer, and now that she felt unworthy of such work, she wanted only to learn more about plants and how to use them. She doubted that any lord would value her for that.

"You are also clever."

It was a statement, not a paean of praise.

"The Healers were impressed with your knowledge and with your reticence. They expected someone from Bellue to know little and tell all. You did not. They respected that, and so do I."

Lord Parandour stared at her in silence for a moment before he continued. "There are, however, two things that I want to know, before I make a decision. One: why did the Padri preach against your mother? My Songbird is sure that he did. And two: why did Frelius, eighth of that name, want to be rid of you?"

Tammina drew a deep breath and began with the second question. She told him that as a child, she had stupidly let Jael know that she was aware of the nights that he spent in the village, and with whom he spent them. When she was older he had made advances towards her, and she had repelled them.

He nodded, but he was not satisfied. "Gossip tells me that this Frelius is a vigorous young man. I doubt that his 'advances' were limited to mere words or offerings of flowers. How did you manage to repel them?"

Tammina coloured at the memory. It still troubled her.

"I could not simply push him away," she said at last. "I was not strong enough, but I had a small jar of cream in my pocket. I hit him with that. It was not enough. He still held me, though he was off-balance. So I kicked him. He fell and I was able to run away."

Her voice was not quite steady. She was ashamed of her actions that day – her anger, the wild blow and that kick – but Lord Parandour laughed.

"Yes, that would have wounded his pride. If he fell you must have kicked hard and found your target. You have strength, then, as well as subtlety."

He did not prompt her to answer his first question; he simply sat back and waited for her to continue; and after a pause to order her thoughts, she did.

"When he came to Bellue, the Padri had an injured foot. My mother treated it. He said that it was a thorn in his foot, but it was not. He had stood on a poison spine. Fortunately for him it was not mature and its poison was weak. Mother was able to remove the spine. We both recognised it, but I was not able to conceal my surprise. Poison spines lie in shallow water, half covered in sand, and they are not found in the cove where the Padri had supposedly risen from the sea and walked on the water to the land. They are found further to the west, and they are not common.

"I know this. I travelled with my mother on two of her visits outside Bellue. Frelius, the seventh of that name, sent her occasionally at his expense. He was a considerate man and he regarded all the population of the peninsula as far west as Fabbae as his people. At times they brought goods to Bellue, but I do not know whether they paid tax or acknowledged his rule.

"My mother cut the poison flesh from the Padri's foot and dressed it. She would never have spoken to anyone about his injury or its cause. She was a Healer. She did not criticise her patients, nor did she question them unless she needed answers in order to determine the best treatment. And she never gossiped."

Tammina twisted her hands together in her lap as she remembered. She still burned with anger, both against her mother who had been so good that she had not seen the danger, and against the man whom she considered evil. She kept her turbulent thoughts to herself and said only,

"He did not know this. He did not know my mother, but he knew that he had lied, and that we knew it."

Lord Parandour watched her as she answered. They were truthful answers, he was sure, though not necessarily complete.

He was glad that he had sought this interview. She would not have been so direct had his advisors been present. No wonder that Frelius had wanted to be rid of her. That young man had his skills. He had planned his defiant stand very well, but he did not know how to manage this woman, or how to use her.

Tammina felt his eyes on her and looked up. Perhaps she had sounded too venomous.

"It may be that he wanted only to discredit us; I do not know."

"It is useless to speculate on the motives of someone who is dead. You have answered me fairly, I think."

He stood up. "And you were right. Frelius does not realise what he has given, but I, I am learning. Tell me, Mistress Farsay, what do you want in your life?"

She was so surprised by the question that the only answer that came into her mind was the truth.

"I have hurt in anger, so I cannot be a Healer, but there is much to learn about plants and their uses. That is what I want to do."

"And if I allow you to do that, will you work for me?"

Tammina did not answer at once. The question was large and though an unqualified 'yes' might win immediate freedom, it might bind her to things she did not wish to do.

"I will work for you, lord, if that work is for good. I do not wish to harm anyone."

"Nor do I, but sometimes it is inevitable," he commented dryly and started towards the door.

Verryon moved to open it and Lord Parandour frowned at him.

"There was something else," he said. "Ah, yes. After your mother died, you disappeared. It was thought that you left Bellue. Was that so?"

Tammina had relaxed.

Just as he intended, she thought, before he asked the crucial question. She felt suddenly cold and pulled the blanket closer. That piece of information was so old that it could hardly have been part of the latest talk among travellers. It had come from Margren. She glanced up at Verryon, but his face told her nothing. She resorted to the middle distance and the third person.

"A weeping child seeking its mother's body remembers little but its grief."

"A way out of Bellue would not be forgotten." His voice was harsh. "And there are ways of improving people's memories."

She lifted her head and stared at him.

"I do not doubt it, Lord," she said, "but how do the torturers tell whether their victims lie or tell such truth as they know? Is it when they give the desired answer? A tunnel under the walls, for example; or a tree that stretches over them; or a time when the tide allows smooth passage round the wall and safe landing on the shore? In ten years, tunnels may be blocked, trees may fall and tides will change. And memories blur. That is the nature of things."

He was not pleased. "And I am assured that it is the nature of man to scream out all he knows, if the right pressure is applied."

Tammina turned away. She knew about pain. Sometimes it was necessary to inflict pain in order to heal. She quoted a family saying; she did not know whose.

"So quick and easy to hurt, so hard and long to heal."

There was an angry exclamation, but the sharp steps that followed it went out of her cell rather than towards her, and it was Verryon who spoke.

"Forgive her," he said quietly. "She thought to enhance your reputation, not to put you in danger."

"She was not bullied then?"

"No. I will not allow that. I have served Parandour for many years and count him a friend, but I have married Margren and I will protect her with my life."

He smiled slightly when Tammina looked up in surprise.

"No, I was not pleased when she was given. He intended to mock me, as he had been mocked; but I too can 'reverse a jest'. I did so, and I do not think that I will regret it."

He left before she could answer. The door closed and she heard the key turn in the lock. She was alone again, and more weary than she had been before, but it was a long time before she was able to sleep.

Chapter 11

Usually Tammina woke early and dressed before the guards brought her breakfast, but she slept late the following morning, rousing only when the plate rattled on the table as one of them set it down.

"You are leaving this morning," said the other and flung a small sack into the cell. "If you have any belongings, put them in that."

The food was adequate but rarely appetising and the words did nothing to increase her desire to eat. The egg was hard cooked and cold – an insult to the bird that had laid it – and the bread was stale. She broke it into small pieces and dropped it into her water. In time it would soften and be easier to eat

She dressed before she ate, rejoicing in the clean clothes that Margren had sent. The fabric was soft and cool against her skin. She folded her own garments neatly and packed them in the bag. She retrieved her stone and the jar of cream from their hiding places and buried them in the bag of clothes. She put that at the bottom of the sack and laid her papers, pens and hairbrush on top. She had nothing else.

The escort numbered four. It was not the same four who had escorted her on the previous occasion, but they had the same air of apprehension. Presumably they feared being blamed if she disappeared into thin air whilst she was in their charge, but not if she had disappeared from her cell. To her, the difficulties seemed equally insurmountable, and had she been less apprehensive, she would have found it amusing.

They marched her along the same passages as before, but this time they came to a halt sooner and in front of a smaller door. One of them tapped on it discreetly.

A woman opened the door, looked at them in surprise and stated with more than a touch of asperity that they were too early. Commander Verryon was not there. He was not expecting them for another hour and had gone out. The door began to close.

The leader voiced a vigorous objection and the door was left ajar.

"I will ask," conceded the woman reluctantly, and obviously did so, for there was a murmur of voices.

The door was opened again, the woman announced that their charge could be admitted and an authoritative voice declared, "The guard may go, or wait outside, as they choose."

It was clear to Tammina that her guards were not happy, but she wanted to know her fate so she did not hesitate. She moved into the room and the door was closed behind her.

Margren welcomed her warmly. "Oh Tammina, come in and sit down. Lakis – er – that is the Commander, has gone to check on the transport, but he will not be as much as an hour. We are still at breakfast," she added, somewhat unnecessarily, as she was seated at a table bearing a variety of dishes. An older woman, elegantly dressed, sat beside her.

She was the imperative one. She did not smile in welcome, but she indicated a seat at the table, and it was she who nodded when the serving woman asked if another cup was needed.

Over her second, much nicer, breakfast Tammina learnt that the lady was sister to Lakis Verryon. She had prolonged her twice-yearly visit to Bosron to help his new wife adjust to life in the castle, but she was returning to her country home that day. Her husband was Lord Cumbler and they had two children, but he was devoted to his land and did not care for the city, so she usually visited Bosron alone. She always stayed with her brother because her sister had a large family and a small house.

A gentle comment from Margren gave the impression that the sister's children were young and lively and her house untidy, whereas, Tammina was certain, Lord Cumbler's place in the country was a haven of peace and tranquillity; any disruption caused by the younger members of the family being contained in distant rooms by well-trained servants.

In spite of her conclusion, she felt that Lady Cumbler was genuinely fond of her brother and though she obviously did not approve of the precipitate manner of his marriage, she did accept his bride. It was clear, too, that Margren was grateful to her and thought her kind; but then Margren considered that anyone who acknowledged her existence, without scolding, tormenting or demanding work, was kind.

Tammina reserved her judgement. She also refrained from asking the one question to which she most desired an answer, and she was savouring her second cup of black tea before that question was answered.

Margren mentioned that her husband liked to visit his sister's family for he was fond of children, and would probably call in on them after he had delivered Tammina to the Sick House.

"The Sick House?" Tammina set down her cup and looked at Margren. "I am not sick. Why would I be taken there?"

Margren stared at her in surprise. "Do you not know where you are going? Or why?"

"No. I was told to gather my belongings, such as they are, but that was all." Tammina indicated the bag that she had put down beside her chair.

"You must understand," put in Lady Cumbler firmly, "that we do not know for certain what is to happen. My brother is -," she paused and considered.

It was a long pause. Margren did not presume to interrupt and Tammina regarded the lady quietly. She did not seem unsympathetic and her hesitation was surely significant.

Mama had always waited when her patients hesitated. Tammina had teased sometimes when a consultation took a long time. Now she remembered her mother's advice. 'The usual symptoms are easily told. The important ones are often harder to express. People need time. If you rush them, they lose courage. Wait and the crucial information will be given.'

So Tammina waited. Lady Cumbler drew a deep breath and began.

"My brother has served Lord Parandour for more than twenty years and has known him for longer. He can claim friendship, but he does not have a place on the Council. He is not -." The lips tightened. This was the difficult part. "That is, *our family* is not, of sufficient standing."

Having admitted her less than aristocratic origins, Lady Cumbler continued more easily.

"Thus my brother does not know exactly what has been decided, only what he has been told. He has said that you are to be taken to the Sick House. It is not simply a place where the sick are cared for, it also has rooms where the Healers work together and try new treatments. We assume that that is where you will go to work, but we have no details. It is probable that the Commander is equally ignorant of what will be expected of you."

Margren smiled. "You will like that, Tammina," she said enthusiastically. "You have always liked pounding leaves and seeds and boiling them into potions."

Tammina smiled gently at her friend and agreed. Margren's description of her experiments was as simplistic as her understanding of the words 'what will be expected of you'. Lord Parandour would want something from her in return – and it could be something that she was unable or unwilling to give.

Margren surprised both her companions with her next words – the one by her perspicacity and the other by her knowledge of the latest court gossip.

"Lord Parandour also wants to use your powers," she said comfortably, "to predict things. That is what I have heard; for it is rumoured that he plans another attack on the north and might take his son to fight. Perhaps he thinks that you can use witchcraft to help him to win, because I cannot see how knowing the outcome will help if it cannot be changed. But then I am not clever."

Margren gave a deprecatory shrug and applied herself to the last morsels of her breakfast. There was no time for comment on her thoughts, for at that moment the door opened and Verryon appeared.

"See, she is still here. You may rest easy," he said to the men waiting in the passage. "In fact, you may go. I will take responsibility for her now." He walked into the room and shut the door firmly behind him.

"They profess not to believe in witches, but they are not quite sure of you, Mistress Farsay. They are afraid that you may have disappeared into thin air or flown through a window whilst out of their sight."

"I do not think that witches can disappear," said Margren practically. "Otherwise why would any wait to be imprisoned and killed? Lakis, you are cold," she added, watching him rub his hands. "There is hot tea, for some was made fresh for Tammina."

"Good. It is certainly cold outside. The wind is in the north. I have ordered hot stones for your feet, Jenna, but you will need them reheated at every stop."

He nursed his warm cup in his hands as he informed his sister of the arrangements for her journey. Tammina listened with interest.

Lady Cumbler had her own carriage and outriders, but she was travelling in a convoy with another family and a group of merchants. The country as a whole might owe allegiance to Lord Parandour, but the forests to the north of Bosron were home to numerous bands of marauders and travelling alone was inadvisable. Beyond Mees hamlet the party would split and go its separate ways, as the roads were more open and safer, but some of the merchants were going on to Winniss hamlet. They would accompany her to her home, and on their return to Bosron would report to him and deliver any letters that she or her husband chose to send.

Margren waited impatiently for him to finish. She was anxious to know if he was intending to visit his sister in the city, and if so, could she accompany him.

The answer to her first query was 'I may do,' and to her second a definite no. He was on official business, escorting a prisoner. The fact that she knew that prisoner did not alter the situation. Besides, the transport provided was not suitable for her. It would be cold and uncomfortable.

Margren immediately offered to lend Tammina a warm cloak, but that too was denied her. The purchase of plain clothing from prison funds was not at all the same as the loan of one of her own garments.

Margren's normal compliant expression showed signs of wavering.

Tammina hastily gave her an assurance that she had no need of a cloak. It was hardly a long distance to the city. She would be warm enough.

Lady Cumbler had also noticed. She began her farewells and the Commander had no need to repeat his forbidding words. Margren bade her sister-in-law goodbye and stayed meekly behind when they left.

There were no guards to escort them and Tammina was free to move as she chose, but there was little point in trying to escape. She did not know the castle and she was certain that there was little chance of her finding an unguarded exit.

Verryon confirmed her thoughts.

"You are still a prisoner, Mistress Farsay, so although I have no hold on you, do not attempt to run. You would soon be caught. The punishment is the axing of a foot, but I would also break your fingers. I do not care to be humiliated."

"Nor do I, sir," answered Tammina softly. "The time for escape was outside the gates of Bellue, but Margren cannot run."

She stared ahead and did not meet his angry glance, but she knew that he understood. He conversed with his sister until they reached the doors of the Keep.

He left them in the dubious shelter of the archway beneath the tower that guarded the drawbridge. The bridge was down, the gates were open and the wind drove cold through the narrow space.

Tammina stood close to the wall. The light wrap that had been round her shoulders that day in Bellue, had been lost somewhere along the way. She thought wistfully of the cloak that Margren had offered. It reminded her of a barely heard comment and she turned to Lady Cumbler.

"My thanks to you, my lady," she began, "for your kindness in lending your own clothes to Margren."

The sharp look that she received in answer told her that she had heard aright. Lady Cumbler gathered her cloak around her more closely.

"Yes, I found something for her." She stopped abruptly, but there was no convenient distraction and after a while she continued.

"I was very angry when he gave her to my brother. It was an insult; or so he intended. Everyone knows that Lakis has never looked at another woman since he first married. I therefore went to supervise her cleaning – to see what she was like."

There was another pause. Tammina had no reason to comment. The 'he' was not difficult to identify and the lady's opinion of him was evident from her disparaging tone.

"And I saw," the lady continued in a much softer voice, "and found her so very different from Etheldra; physically, but in her character too. I thought it would bring him back to life if he lay with her. I did not want the women to put her in one of Etheldra's garments; that would have hurt him, so I chose something of my own for her to wear. I did not expect him to marry her!"

Tammina permitted herself a slight smile. "No, I had not expected that either, but I have heard it said that he is pleased."

"Oh! She pleases him and he is happy now, but -." Lady Cumbler sighed.

There was no one in all Bosron in whom she could confide her doubts. This 'Witch' was not a suitable person for that role either, but she was somehow sympathetic.

"But she is much younger than he is, and she is growing more confident and prettier by the day. The man who teaches her to sing is young and well favoured. So also is the one who takes her riding. I do not want him hurt again."

Tammina did not consider how Etheldra had hurt her husband. That was not her concern. She considered Margren.

There were women in Bellue village who were free with their favours and unfaithful to their husbands, but they were few. Margren's mother was not one of them. Her family was respectable apart from her father's overindulgence in ale. Tammina could not imagine that Margren would be unfaithful; not in Bellue – but she was in Bosron now, and her present position was possibly more like that of the ladies in Fort society.

Tammina knew little of that, but she did know that Jael had had his interests there, as he had had in the village. And Margren would change; people did.

She stared ahead, at the stonework of the opposite wall.

"I do not think that she will hurt him or be unfaithful. She cares for him now, and though situations change and people with them, I believe that she will always be grateful and that her love for him will grow in the future." She turned then and said with an open face, "But I do not know."

Wheels sounded on the cobbles of the courtyard. Lady Cumbler's carriage had arrived with Verryon walking alongside. A cart followed behind, so similar to that in which they had travelled from Bellue that Tammina could not control her shudder.

She stood silent as brother and sister made their farewells, and was a little taken aback when the sister turned to her and held out her hand.

"It has been an interesting encounter," said the lady. "I hope that things go well with you."

Tammina took the outstretched hand and curtseyed. "I too," she said and drew back.

Verryon had almost closed the carriage door before she stepped forward again on impulse and made a final plea.

"Oh, my lady, support her. Please support her, for I may not see her again."

There was no reply. The door closed, the carriage moved on through the archway and across the bridge; and the cart drew alongside.

She was glad that Margren was not with them. The cart was indistinguishable from the one that had borne them from Bellue. Even the stains on the seats seemed familiar. She climbed in and sat as impassively as she was able, whilst the chains were fastened around her.

Verryon sat opposite and two guards joined him. One held three whips. It did not fill her with confidence.

They set off slowly. Tammina was not sure why – the horse seemed willing enough. She tried not to think of the uncertainties and to concentrate on the wider surroundings.

There were few buildings near the castle, so she studied the vegetation. It was not greatly different from that which covered the rocky outcrops of Bellue. Here though, all trees had been cut down. There was no cover for an attacking force. The road wound its way down to the river and gave wide views of the cliffs to the east, the forests to the north and west, and the city nestling between them, clinging to the waterside. From time to time she caught sight of Lady Cumbler's carriage below them. When it reached the flatter land near the river, it moved faster, and faster still when it gained the straight stretch that led to the bridge.

There was a muttered query from the driver.

"Yes, fast as you please. They are well ahead now," said Verryon in answer and they too quickened their pace. The horse seemed glad enough, but Tammina was not. The cart bounced on the uneven surface and sometimes landed too close to the edge of the track for her comfort. Fastened as she was to the cart, she would not be flung clear if it tipped over and fell down the steep slope. No one else showed any concern, however, and she supposed that they must have great trust in the driver, or be inured to the danger.

It was fortunate that there were few people on the road and they did not encounter another vehicle until the sharpest bends had been safely negotiated. They passed it without problem and carried on to the bridge.

There were buildings close to the bridge and clustering alongside the river, and there were people; some on foot, some pushing handcarts. They moved swiftly out of the way as was clearly expected of them, but several also raised their right hands to their left shoulders in a gesture that reminded her of death.

In Bellue it was made by the mourners at a burial. All stood by the grave, right hands on left shoulder, palms facing outward, whilst the men sang the Farewell to Erion. It symbolised Namier using the crescent moon to drive the Evil

One from the land, and was meant to ward off the Shades of Hadron and allow the spirits of the newly dead to rise unhindered to the Skies.

She wondered again if she was to be killed.

Verryon also noticed the gestures and he stood and spoke to the driver. Tammina heard only a few unconnected words, 'trouble', 'whip' and 'horn'. The last puzzled her, but immediately Verryon took just such an instrument from a box beneath his seat and gave it to one of the guards.

"We need a clear way, so sound it loudly. The market place will be crowded and I do not want to have to stop for some careless fool."

The guard nodded. He took the horn and one of the whips and stood facing outwards. His fellow took up a similar position on the other side of the cart and Verryon, taking the third whip, stood at the rear.

They were across the bridge and into the city before Tammina heard the first cry of 'Witch' and saw the first pointing finger. That was a man. The first threat came from a woman. She ran towards the cart waving her fists and shouting, "We want no witches!"

No one followed her, and the guard on that side flicked his whip. The woman fell back and did not shout again. She had not been struck though she must have heard the vicious hiss of the leather strip close to her face.

The driver was not so tolerant, though just as accurate. The young man in the market place who tried to rush for the horse's harness, cried out as the whip cut across his cheeks. The horn sounded its warning loud and clear and the whips cracked continuously. A few missiles were thrown, and some hit the cart, but none stopped its progress. They were through the market place swiftly and continued down the less populated streets at the same speed and with the same noises. They passed a long building that boasted several signs proclaiming that it was The Sick House, but they did not stop in front of it.

They turned instead at the corner and again at the next, and slowed slightly as they approached a pair of large gates.

Uniformed men were already dragging them open, and they were shut again as soon as the cart had passed through.

They were in a courtyard at the rear of the Sick House.

The back of that building was not nearly so pleasant as the front. The windows were scarcely more than slits. They were unglazed and they were barred. The yard was enclosed, bounded by a high wall broken only by the gates through which they had come. It seemed to Tammina that she had exchanged one prison for another, and she was right.

The front portion of the Sick House did cater for the old and ill and the wounded, but it also had a Trial Area where the Healers and the Cutters made their remedies and tested new ones. It was ruled by a woman whose title was Lead Healer, though she had such a cold and unsympathetic air that Tammina doubted that any would willingly seek her help.

Healers from Bosron and its environs organised the work, but men and women from recently conquered lands were the labourers and they were not free. Their skills and knowledge were valued – Lord Parandour used what he conquered – and they were well fed, but they were prisoners. And Tammina joined them.

She was taken first to the workroom. It was a much larger version of her room in Bellue, full of pestles and mortars, bottles and jars, vats of oils and bubbling stills. There were also several slabs where remains were being dissected and examined. Most were animals, but some looked human. Four sullen women pounded vegetation, an older man tended the stills and another, much younger, stood at one of the slabs on which lay the remains of a rabbit. Two bored-looking guards stood at the door.

No one spoke, though six pairs of eyes assessed her. Undoubtedly the most intelligent were the dark eyes of the man who, with knife in hand, was examining the rabbit.

She did not like his scrutiny. It was irrational, she knew, but he was too much like Jael. He was darker in complexion, but his face was narrow and his features sharp. Even his neat beard was trimmed in a similar fashion.

She ignored all the eyes and studied the workbenches with genuine interest. The Lead Healer entered.

The atmosphere changed. The guards stood straighter and the workers bent their heads to their tasks. They were not at ease.

Tammina, too, felt the same antipathy towards the woman that she had felt when Verryon had introduced them in the courtyard. He had been unfailingly courteous in face of brusque words that bordered on rudeness. His reference to 'Mistress Farsay' had been countered with 'the Witch', and his brief explanation of the position of Lead Healer had been interrupted with a curt, 'She will find out', and an order to an underling to take her to the workroom.

Now the Lead Healer walked in and announced without ceremony, "We have an addition to our team – the Witch from Bellue. You ought not to have heard of her, but there is so much loose talk in this place that I do not doubt that you have. It is most probable that you also know that she is rumoured to have green liquid in her veins. We will find out."

She swept the room with a calculating glance. "You," she said, pointing to the narrow-faced man who had a small knife in one hand, "cut her."

There was no way out other than passing the guards, and one of them moved to Tammina's side and grasped her arm.

The man did not move, but nor did he lay down the knife.

"Is she ill?" he asked softly. "Does she have some growth that must be cut out?"

"Cut her arm," came the harsh reply. "Let us see what it is that flows in her veins."

"She may be a witch, I do not know, but first she is a woman, and she will have blood in her veins. I have met and treated Frelians from Bellue. They are no different from my own people."

His attitude and his tone were respectful, but the other guard strode swiftly towards him and struck him with a mailed fist. There was a collective sound, like a sigh, but no one seemed surprised.

"Cut her!" The order was repeated.

This time his answer, though still respectful, was a firm statement and not a question.

"I cut those who have need of surgery, and only those."

The guard struck him again and he staggered, dropped the knife and raised a hand to his bleeding cheek.

Tammina was appalled, but she was also angry, and she behaved just as impulsively as she had when Jael had tried to force himself on her. She jerked an elbow back into the ribs of the one held her, pulled free from his grip and pushed unceremoniously past the Lead Healer. She placed herself between the man and the guard who had struck him.

"That is enough," she declared as if she were the superior. "We will allay this foolish superstition. I will cut myself."

She picked up the knife that had been dropped and regarded it, and the remains of the rabbit, with distaste.

"Not with this, though. Is there a clean knife?"

Nothing was offered and nothing was said, so she asked another question. "Where then is the clean water?"

Someone waved a hand towards an open trough and she took a step towards it. There was a dark slime around its edge.

"No. The clean water," she repeated, "the water that you use for making potions and salves."

"That is it." The guard was indignant, as if she had accused him personally of being dirty. "That is clean. Fresh water is added every day from the river."

"Then you waste your labour," declared Tammina staring round in amazement.

The workers bent their heads, but not before she had seen the smiles. They knew, but they were not interested in this work – it was for their conquerors not for their own people.

The Lead Healer sensed that she was being mocked. She had not wanted the witch in her establishment. Witches were trouble whatever skills they had. There were too many rumours about them, too many fears; and she was determined to know the truth of at least one of them.

"Stop this," she said angrily to the room in general, and to the guards, "You are both armed. Cut her! Run her through if you must, but I will see what she has in her veins."

They hesitated. The Witch had a knife in her hand and running her through could prove fatal – to her first and to them later. If Lord Parandour had wanted rid of her, he would not have sent her here.

"Fire will clean the knife," said one of the women softly. "My husband used fire to clean his knives."

"Your husband was a butcher!" The Lead Healer was contemptuous.

"Aye, he was. And my daughters were virgins before the Bos came."

Tammina had regained her control. "There is no need for violence, one against another," she said calmly. "I will clean the knife in the fire."

Her hand was not quite steady, but she held the knife in the flames of the nearest fire. Someone handed her a cloth. It was not over clean, but it was of some sturdy material that deflected the heat. There was silence as the blade warmed and glowed red, then orange. Tammina drew it slowly from the flame and waited for it to cool.

"A burn will not bleed," she noted, and held the knife out so that everyone could see the glow die away.

When it came to cutting herself, she was not so confident, but the man moved closer.

"I will cut," he said and took the knife. She held out her arm and he made a neat incision so swiftly that it did not hurt.

"See," he said, and she could almost feel his anger, "she has red blood."

The Lead Healer watched the scarlet trail as it ran down her arm and dripped onto the floor.

"Put her to work," she said and walked away.

Chapter 12

Tammina worked for the remainder of the day alongside the butcher's wife. Her companion said little, but she did prise from her that her husband had indeed killed and cut up farm animals, but he had also practised as a Cutter. He had been killed trying to protect his daughters from victorious soldiers bent on the rewards of winning a battle.

The other workers had been very surprised at her advice on the use of fire to cleanse. She did not usually offer information. She had been there when her husband was killed. Tammina assumed that he been run through with a sword and that the poor woman did not wish to see another killed in the same manner. She was duly grateful.

The prisoners had little interest in the experiments they were conducting, but their attitude changed when they helped at the open clinics that were held twice weekly. There the poor of the city could have their injuries and ailments treated without payment.

Tammina was glad to see it, not only for the patients' sake – some were near starvation – but also for the sake of the prisoners. There was neither joy nor satisfaction in pointless work; and they had surely chosen their calling because they wanted to heal the sick.

At the first clinic, she sat and observed. She was to learn, she was told, what was available and where it was to be found. At the second clinic she was given a table. She objected at once. She knew something of remedies and how to prepare them, but she was not a Healer. Her objections were overruled.

The first comment, from the Lead Healer was delivered with a shrug. "It is the lower orders who come. No one will complain if they die."

The second, from Tomar Shean, the Cutter, was only marginally more encouraging.

"She is right. No one will complain, and if they do no one will listen; but you have knowledge. Use it. And various remedies are available to dispense; use them. Some do have a beneficial effect."

So she sat and listened as she had watched her mother listen. The selection of remedies available was limited, but she did her best and hoped that what she offered would indeed have some beneficial effect.

The queue of patients was orderly. They were directed to one table or another by a large man who carried a heavy wooden stick. He must have made an initial diagnosis for some were sent directly to Tomar, and some, with long term problems, were allowed to wait for a particular person to become available. Everyone else was sent to the next available Healer.

She had treated several people before she noticed the unease in the waiting line. She tried to ignore it, and to convince herself that any new face would cause the same apprehension, but she thought it more likely that she had been recognised.

"Witch!"

The word was whispered along the line and the patient's faces became more agitated as they neared the front of the queue.

Tammina applied lotion to a rash, bandaged the arm and handed over the bottle with strict instructions as to how to apply it. She finished with a warning, "Keep it covered and try not to scratch. It is not infected now, but could easily become so," and she turned to greet her next patient.

It was a man, broad and strong, but with a badly inflamed eye. He was definite in his objection. He was not going to allow a witch to tend him. There was a stir of interest as he defied the man with the stick. A fight was always good entertainment if one was not directly involved, and one in the Sick House of all places, had the makings of a good story that could last for weeks. The newcomer who interrupted, therefore, was not particularly welcome, though he was regarded with curiosity.

He had polished boots and wore a fine cloak over his tunic and his stockings were without holes or darns. He walked in boldly and spoke with confidence to the director of the queue. He wanted most particularly to consult the lady for he had cut his hand and it was bleeding profusely. He displayed the dark-stained bandage, slipped a coin discreetly into the director's hand and smiled in apology at the man with the inflamed eye.

The apology was gratefully accepted and inflamed eye sat down. If those with fine clothes and coin to spare wanted to consult a witch, he would not stop them.

Master Hallarden sat down in front of Tammina and greeted her with his most charming smile.

"I have cut my hand," he said.

Tammina was not impressed, nor was she attracted. She recognised that he was good-looking, but she suspected that he was accustomed to using his undoubted charm to get his own way. He had, though, been kind to Margren. She was not too severe when she spoke.

"This treatment session is for the poor. I surmise, from the quality of your clothes, and your position when I first saw you that you can afford to pay for a Healer to cure your ills."

"Ah! Yes, I can; but I *have* cut my hand and Mistress Verryon *has* extolled your skills as a Healer. Besides, she is anxious for news of you, and I wish to see you again. This way, I can do both."

He gazed at her with large eyes and she immediately recalled a classmate in Bellue. He was a handsome boy with blue eyes and had used just such tactics with great effect to lessen his due punishments; but, as her mother had declared when she had complained of this injustice, anyone who expected life to be fair was bound to be disappointed.

It took her longer to identify Mistress Verryon as Margren.

"Do you give Mistress Verryon her singing lessons?" she asked as she unwound the bandage. He nodded, and she understood Lady Cumbler's concern.

There was a cut on his hand. It was not long nor was it deep – a minor injury. Tammina studied the stains on the bandage.

"It does not look very serious now," he admitted, "but there was a lot of blood."

"The bandage is certainly heavily stained," agreed Tammina, "but not much of that stain is your blood. What is it?"

"We-ell," he began, and reminded her even more of a small boy caught out in a lie.

She waited. He started another explanation, but foundered after the first few words. She continued to look interested – and implacable.

"It is blood," he assured her at last. "At least, I think it is. They would not let me into the storerooms where the raw meat is kept, but I persuaded one of the kitchen maids to dip the bandage into some blood for me."

"I see." There was no suggestion of amusement in the stern comment. "A foolish thing to do. Blood from meat can cause infection in contact with a fresh wound, even such a small one." She waved dismissively at his hand. "You should also have been more specific, or chosen a kitchen maid with more sense. There *was* blood in the liquid that caused this stain, but there are herbs too; thyme and" – she picked a dark sliver from an edge of the bandage and laid it down for his inspection – "rosemary. She dipped it into a marinade."

She went to fetch a salve, and he sat in anxious silence and stared at his hand. His voice and a few singing lessons would not keep him. He could not afford to lose the ability to play. He sighed. This woman was not even pleased to see him, and he was more used to avoiding women than seeking their company.

He said nothing as she washed the cut on his hand. She was careful, but then she was clever. The shrewd glance that she gave him when she commented on his probable need for flexibility in his fingers, removed any doubts he may have had on that point.

She told him sternly that if the cut became sore or inflamed he must seek help immediately and she gave him a value for her services – in Bellue terms, for she had no other. He should put a suitable sum in the collecting box.

"Will you not at least give me a message for Mistress Verryon?" he asked as she finished. "She does want news of you and does not like to ask it of her husband."

"You may tell her I am well. I am a prisoner still, but the food is better here." She paused and added suddenly. "And she? She seemed happy when I saw her; but I spoke briefly with Lady Cumbler and she had some concern."

He understood at once, and answered gravely, "I teach her singing, Mistress. No more than that. Lady Cumbler has no cause for concern." He smiled. "Indeed she will have cause to rejoice with her brother if the rumours I have heard are correct. It is reported that Mistress Verryon will soon increase her husband's joy."

Tammina's pleasure at this news was short-lived. The smile she had given on hearing it had been noted by her colleagues, and later, in the workroom, she was teased unmercifully about her handsome admirer. She protested in vain that she had no interest in him. He had brought good news of her friend from Bellue and that had caused her to smile. They did not believe her, and in desperation she declared angrily that even if he was attracted to her, she was not attracted to him. He was handsome enough, she could see that, but she had no interest in men.

That silenced them, but it was an uneasy silence and she did not know why. Did they fear her anger? Did they give credence to the 'Witch' label?

The Lead Healer certainly did. She attended the next clinic and those who chose not to seek help from Tammina were allowed to wait for the next available Healer. She had few patients.

At the end of the clinic she was told curtly, "You are no use here. I shall report to Lord Parandour. He will decide what to do."

She must have done so quickly, for it was only days later that Tammina was order to gather her few belongings. She was leaving the Sick House. She saw the other prisoners as she was led away, but only Tomar acknowledged her.

Her status had risen, she noted. She was told where she was going, and although it was an open cart that took her there, she was not chained to her seat.

There were still three men with whips and they were needed. Her actual departure from the Sick House was more sedate than her arrival, but they attracted unwelcome attention very quickly. They drove fast to the quayside and there they lost all but the most persistent of the witch hunters. Uniformed officials barred the way and only a dozen or so managed to evade them. Their passage disturbed the usual bustle of the docks, but the traders either did not recognise her or were too busy with their business to do more than stare.

They reached the quay's end and turned up into the city with great noise and cracking of whips but no serious danger. They were soon in a more prosperous area where the streets were quieter and they arrived at their destination without further incident.

Lord Parandour's Official Residence was the large building that she had noticed from the other side of the river. It was protected with high walls and entered through splendid ironwork gates.

Arrows might be fired through such gates, and missiles thrown, but they would not reach even a quarter the distance to the main building and either of the lodges beside the wide drive could, and probably did, accommodate a small army.

She looked with interest at the grounds. There were trees in Bellue, and small wooded areas, but this woodland boasted trees as tall and fine as those in the Forest of Ament, and as varied. She had not been able to appreciate the Forest, but here, briefly, she could marvel at the size of the trees, and she gazed curiously at those that were new to her.

They reached the formal gardens and there was more to admire – beds of flowers and coloured foliage, stone-edged ponds with water lilies, clipped hedges, bushes neatly trimmed into fancy shapes and paths winding this way and that between them. People walked the paths or rested on the stone benches. They were finely dressed and colourful as birds in the mating season. This was Lord Parandour's court and some of its members were enjoying the sunshine.

The cart attracted a few curious glances, but not many. No one of importance arrived in a cart.

They drove to the servants' entrance at the side of the house. The steps were narrow and steep and there was but a single door, but it was not the kitchen entrance. Tammina was met and greeted with courtesy.

Lord Parandour was not ready to see her yet so she was taken to a bedroom. It was small, but neatly furnished with a chest and a tall cupboard for hanging longer garments. Two blankets lay on the bed and a sheet of unbleached linen covered the straw mattress.

This was not a prisoner's room – and she was not a prisoner. Her guide had hardly finished speaking before someone tapped on the open door. She did not recognise him until he spoke. He was one of the musicians, the pipe player, who had been entertaining when they had first entered the castle.

"Master Hallarden has been watching for your arrival for the past hour and now he has been obliged to work for a change. I am charged with welcoming you and introducing you to the household on his behalf."

He smiled pleasantly and the guide surrendered her willingly to his care.

"I am afraid that here you cannot lock your door as I believe you are accustomed to do, but your belongings will be respected and there is a bolt for when you are within."

His eyes held laughter, but not the admiration that she had seen in other eyes. She felt able to respond lightly.

"I will not miss a locked door. I have few possessions and in recent days, though my door was locked, it was not I who held the key."

He laughed and commented that he was glad she had not lost her sense of humour.

Tammina felt inordinately pleased and wondered why, but as she followed him down the stairs to the hall again, she realised that it was years since she had made a pleasantry. Her cousins had joked amongst themselves but not with her, and her only female friends were Margren and Linnie.

Margren was too worn with work and pain to be amusing and her conversations with Linnie had been mainly about clothes, business and her child. The first two Linnie took very seriously and though they had often laughed together at the child's antics, his play did not give rise to witticisms. Darl had been the one with whom she had sparred in that way, and she had scarcely spoken to him since her mother had been killed. She had grown used to being alone, and had not been conscious of her loneliness. Now her heart lifted as she walked into a room filled with the sound of people.

"This is the servant's hall," said the pipe player. "Musicians have more free time than most – we are required to practice – but all who serve in Lord Parandour's household can be found here at some time or another."

He led her up to one group. Only one, a girl younger than herself, seemed familiar. At least, the small stringed instrument that she held had caught Tammina's attention that first day in the castle. Then it had been laid across her left arm, now it was held casually in one hand.

"This is Mistress Tammina Farsay, the Witch of Bellue," he announced formally.

She did not like the introduction, but he raised her hand to his lips and continued before she could object.

"Her powers are proven. Hal is totally under her spell," and he introduced his friends.

He gave names and occupations. Four were musicians; the other girl, Annia, was a lady's maid and was, as he put it, '- the reason why Hal trusted me to take care of you.'

"I am not in need of care." Tammina's comment was tart for she did not like being considered helpless, but she softened it with a smile as she asked for his name, – "for you have not mentioned it and no one has introduced us. My powers do not run to divining names."

"I am called Pip," he answered, "because I play the pipes."

"And he likes it, because he considers his given name very old-fashioned and cumbersome," added Annia. "It is

Oberisaval – from the First Book of the Visitations. At least, I am told so. The first book is so dreadfully dull – mere lists of the many descendents of the men that Namier blessed – that I own that I have never read further than page six."

Tammina smiled in sympathy. As far as she could recall, the early pages of her grandfather's Book of Visitations had never been read. Her mother liked 'a good exciting story' and picked them unerringly from the thumbed edges of the sheets. They were, she recalled, all stories of a god unaccountably ignorant of the dangers in the world he had himself created, being rescued by the good sense and courage of mere men.

Perhaps fortunately, she did not have time to speak. A bell rang loudly. It was a summons and all occupants of the room turned to hear who had been called.

"The Witch from Bellue," announced the ringer, "you are wanted."

All eyes fell on Tammina and she had no option but to go.

She had expected that the house of the Great Lord in Bosron would be more splendidly furnished than his castle, but it was still difficult not to stop and gaze in awe at the high painted ceilings, the carved wood pillars, the gilded niches with their statues or vases and the woven hangings that everywhere decorated the walls.

"You are to sit there." The messenger who had collected her indicated a particular chair. "You are to wait and watch. Three men will appear through that door."

Another wave of his hand showed the particular door, but it was scarcely necessary as no one seated in the chair could fail to see it.

"You are to study them."

Tammina sat down. "In what way am I to study them?" she asked.

He shrugged and dropped his formal manner.

"I don't know. You are the one with magic powers – you are supposed to know. I am just repeating what I was told."

He walked away, but he did throw a few words of advice over his shoulder in a more friendly tone.

"Best show willing. Remember as much as you can about each one of them. He likes willing; and he doesn't like -".

The last word or words were cut off by the closing door, but they were not important. There were several alternatives. She would have liked to know who had sent for her. She assumed that it was Lord Parandour, but no one had confirmed that assumption. She was the witch; she was supposed to know. She clasped her hands in her lap and waited.

The men came through the door one by one and she had ample time to study them. By their bearing, they were all soldiers. The first barely glanced at her. He was the eldest, in his forties at least. The second was much younger and he was curious. He greeted her and she returned his greeting.

"Bellue?" he asked. "The one they call Witch?"

"You, too, are from Bellue," she said, and it was not a question. The trace of accent was still present. She studied him as she had been bidden. He had done well. His clothes were good and there was gold on his fingers.

"You are the one they call Witch?" he asked again, and he smiled when she nodded.

"Ah! So that is what he is about!" The comment was not addressed to her. It was simply a thought, voiced aloud.

The third was a grim man, lacking an arm. He stared at her, and he stopped to consider, but he did not speak. She stared back at him. She would not be intimidated, though he was obviously wealthy and unused to such a bold gaze from a woman so plainly dressed.

He glanced towards the closed door and waited, but she did not rise to open it and after a moment he opened it himself. He swung it wide, and quite deliberately left it so.

His steps still sounded in the passage when a fourth man appeared. She recognised him, or thought she did. Plants were so much easier to recognise than faces, but she thought him one who had been sitting with Lord Parandour the last time she had been brought before him. She could not remember his name. Perhaps she had never been told.

"Mistress Farsay," he said. "Come."

It was polite, but it was a command. Tammina rose and followed him.

It was quite a long walk. There was no dais in this room, as there had been in the castle, but it was none the less intimidating for that. It was more hall than chamber, so long and high that it seemed narrow, but it was not; and its occupants were seated at the further end. She recognised them all, though none now were wearing chains of office. She was left standing before them when the man who had fetched her took his seat.

"So, Witch," said Lord Parandour. "We will make use of your powers." He leaned back in his chair and smiled unpleasantly. "Which of those three who just left us made your skin prickle?"

Tammina hesitated and someone spoke. It was the lord who had recommended that she be thrown from one of the towers, but as she had no wish to answer the question she was grateful for his interruption.

"My lord, I object. This is not proper. I understood that you wanted her to use her powers of prediction, not to comment on our High Command."

"A prediction might be useful, Caterend; but I have other questions for her."

It was a bland reply and Lord Parandour allowed his lord some time to consider it. He did not, however, allow him time to speak again.

"We have finished our main deliberations, though, so if you do not wish to sit in the company of the Witch, you have my permission to leave. I understand that you feel strongly about the Powers of Evil, though the woman has red blood in her veins, not green slime. Your own daughter has proved that."

The casual remark had two consequences. Tammina stared hard at the floor, hoping that her surprise was not too obvious and Lord Caterend sat stiffly, clenching his teeth. It was several seconds before he rose and took his leave, agreeing that he did not care to sit in company with a witch.

No one spoke as he walked down the hall. His steps were clearly audible, so too was the click of the door as he closed it behind him. The silence continued.

"Bralmoor, go." The order was given very softly. "Make certain that he has left."

One man rose quietly, another said, "Surely, lord, you do not suspect him of listening at doors?"

"It does no harm to be sure," was the soft answer.

Lord Bralmoor returned with less care than he had gone. His chair clattered as he resumed his seat. "He has gone. Poor man; he may be a fool, but he did not deserve such a daughter."

"Who does deserve a daughter with no interest in men?" Lord Parandour shrugged off Caterend's problems and addressed Tammina. "What was your opinion of her?" he asked with every appearance of interest in her reply.

His first words had shocked her. She had used the phrase 'no interest in men' about herself, but from the expressions on the faces before her, those words had a specific meaning. She was not certain what it was, but it explained the reaction that her own words had produced.

"His daughter is the Lead Healer at the Sick House?" she queried seeking time. She saw no point in lying but she needed to phrase her opinion carefully.

There was a nod in reply, and she continued.

"I thought her abrasive, but I never saw her with a patient. She may have been more sympathetic towards the sick. Her orders were obeyed and the place ran smoothly enough."

"But?"

Tammina was annoyed with herself. She ought to have finished her sentence firmly. This lord picked up on every nuance.

"But she does not lead the team. Most days are spent in wasted effort, and she seems unaware of it. Your prisoners are willing to serve the poor who come for treatment, but they see no reason to serve her – their supposed leader; or you – their conqueror."

He was disturbed she knew, but only the trace of a frown ruffled his bland expression.

"They are trying new methods, new leaves and roots. Why is that labour a waste?"

She smiled slowly, mocking him. It was dangerous; she was still his prisoner but she would not betray her fellows.

"You need a Healer to tell you that, lord. I am a witch. I gather ingredients for my spells at special times of the month and I whisper wicked words as I pick them."

"You do nothing of the sort, woman!" he snorted. "But if you will not tell me what is wrong at the Sick House, I will discover that another way. Meantime will you give your opinion of those three fellows who passed by you?"

"Fellows, were they? I thought them soldiers, all used to command. Two who were born to it, one having risen through the ranks. He is probably most able."

She spoke casually, but she watched everyone closely, especially Parandour's son, who stood behind him. He was the youngest, the least experienced and he gave away the most.

"That may be so. And when do you think the most propitious time to launch an attack in the north?"

"Another attack? To consolidate your rule or to extend it?"

"Does that matter? Either way I want to win."

She smiled again, slowly as she had done before, but this time it was not dangerous. Now she knew what he was about.

"If you attack tomorrow, you will win," she said.

"Tomorrow!! The woman is deranged! We cannot attack tomorrow." It was the young man who exclaimed so indignantly, but there were nods of agreement from some of the older men.

"Ah!" Tammina smiled. "There are other considerations, then?"

It was only half question and she did not wait for an answer. "The attacking force must be in position, for example, and the weather must be favourable – the wind at your backs. Also there is the terrain to consider, the numbers of the opposing force, the availability of food and," – she paused and very deliberately walked round in a small circle in the opposite direction to the travel of the sun – "and you must wait, until the rumours have reached the north. The enemy must know that Lord Parandour has sought the advice of the Evil One via his Witch."

Her speech was met with amazement from the young man, uncertain frowns from the elders and a great belly laugh from Lord Parandour himself.

"By Namier's Powers, if she knew battles as she knows people, I would take her advice on throwing the first spear! Roddori, take heed. Do not dismiss all women as foolish creatures. Many are shrewd, and some are clever. Here we have one who is both."

"Did she not change her mind when I said that tomorrow was impossible? What is clever about that?" The young man was indignant.

"She has no opinion on the most propitious time to attack, but she knows that tomorrow is impossible. She knows, too, that I will make my own decisions on who will lead my army and when I will attack. She teases. She bade me use her powers and enjoy the talents of the songbird, as the neatest way to pour scorn on that impudent leader of the Frelians. I have done so; and now she tells me in her own manner that she knows how I plan to use her."

He stood up and stretched himself.

"In four days it will be full moon. I will have her dance on Low Lea where she can be seen from the Common Land. That will confirm her reputation and keep the talk lively. It will reach the north within two months. We will make our preparations and leave in six or seven weeks from now." He turned to his son and clapped him vigorously on one shoulder. "There will be time enough for you to marry Drusil and start a child before we set out."

"I do not dance," declared Tammina, "not at full moon nor at any other time."

Lord Parandour stopped smiling.

Learn," he commanded. "You have survived so far by your wits, but you have now fulfilled one of my purposes. I can use you further, but I do not need you. How long would you last if I put you out of my gates?"

Chapter 13

At midnight when the moon was full, Tammina dressed in a black dress and cloak and danced round a small fire on Low Lea. Her arms and legs were coated with a white pigment so that they shone in the moonlight as she leapt about with her skirt lifted high. She was glad that none of the books on witches had talked of naked dancing.

She had searched the library and had studied their rites with the thoroughness that she usually reserved for plants.

After the interview with Lord Parandour she had hinted to Pip and Annia of her desire to escape, but neither had been the least encouraging. She would be caught, she was told, and they described, in more detail than she wished to hear, what she might suffer when she was brought back. On one hand, the lord was fair. Prisoners could and did earn their freedom. They knew of several in the household and in the town who had done so; but they knew of none who had successfully escaped.

Tammina was not convinced. A successful escape would be kept quiet, not announced, but she soon realised that it would be difficult. She had freedom to wander in the servant's part of the house and grounds, and she saw the security. Her desire to escape did not diminish, but her hopes receded.

She was, however, treated well. She was not despatched to the kitchen, to scour the platters and pots; she was given work in the library. She did not consider it easy, scrambling up the ladders to dust shelves, polish doors and keep the fire at the correct level, but she had learned long ago how to manage a fire to produce a steady even heat. Too low a flame, too hot a blaze or too much smoke was bad for books, just as it was detrimental to the proper preparation of potions and salves.

Her first request for permission to read the books was refused, but must have been reported to higher authority, for the following day permission was granted. She was directed particularly to those on witchcraft, and her hours on duty were slightly reduced. Lord Parandour had his own methods of reinforcing his commands.

She had been taken to Low Lea by one of Lord Parandour's personal guards and she knew that someone was watching from the shadow of the trees, and waiting to escort her back to the house. She had protested – she was not afraid of the darkness – but she was overruled. Whether anyone watched from beyond the high thorn hedge that bordered the meadow, she could not tell.

She danced until the fire was low, no more than embers, their glow almost lost in the brightness of the moon. She swept them away with a bundle of twigs, down and across for the dagger of Gerharst. That would banish any evil power that fire at full moon might possess. A few orange sparks marked her sweepings, but they quickly died away and left only the grey ash.

She was not an ardent believer in Namier or the powers of Darkness, but she did not like her actions. The dance had symbolised the triumph of Evil over Good and that was a bad message to endorse.

She walked slowly up the slope to the trees, scattering the twigs as she went.

"Excellently done." The voice was soft, but that did not diminish the approval. "Tales of my Witch will spread all over my domain."

"Is that a good thing, lord?" she queried as the three of them made their way along the shadowy path back to the house.

"Namier's Power! You have a sharper brain than most of my so-called advisors! No, it is not entirely good. Some will think I am moved towards Evil, but they are more likely to be the ignorant and that usually means the poor. They are too busy surviving to make trouble. The powerful will bide their time, and if I do nothing that seems evil to them, they will not disturb the peace either. If any make plans to do so, I shall hear of it."

They were nearing the more open ground that surrounded the house. Tammina stopped suddenly. A shadow wavered at the edge of the trees.

"There is someone there," she breathed.

"I hope so," came the laconic answer. "I have no intention of escorting you to the rear of my house. Ferren will go with you and Drask with me. Tomorrow you will be free from your duties in the library, though you may continue to consult what books and papers you wish. You will have a workroom to make your magic. To many, a Healer is not far removed from a witch. Both are known to pick leaves and roots and mix their spells."

The shadow darkened into another guard and Lord Parandour moved away without bidding her goodnight. Ferren led her back to the house by a circuitous route, avoiding the open moonlit paths as far as was possible.

"There is little danger, but I have no wish to arouse the antipathy of Master Hallarden," he explained with a smile, as they skirted the walls of the house and arrived at the side door.

The workroom was no more than a hut in the grounds, but it was close to a spring and equipped with all she needed to mix creams, lotions and remedies; and also to experiment. It pleased her and she was grateful, but she did note that it was overlooked by both a windmill and a church tower. He left nothing to chance.

For the next few weeks, she spent most of her time in the workroom or searching the grounds for plants that she knew. The library had many books about plants and trees, but few mentioned their uses other than as flavourings, and the whole household was busy with preparations for the wedding. She had no part to play in that so she kept her distance.

Several times she forgot to go and eat and Hal came to fetch her or brought some bread and meat from the table. Early on, he brought a request from Margren for some of the cream that Tammina used to make. The Healer who came to the castle was very good, but nothing she had provided was quite as effective. Tammina was willing to oblige, but she was cautious. The Commander ought to know.

He came one day, appearing unannounced at the door of her hut, and he left with a jar of cream. Margren trusted her, he said, and so did he. She had protected Margren to the best of her ability. He was sure that she would continue to do so, though he hoped that the need would not arise again.

A kitchen drudge came next, with a badly cut finger. There was a Healer who cared for the live-in servants, but cleaners came daily and were not provided for. They earned very little. Tammina protested that she was not a Healer, but the woman shrugged her shoulders. What was good enough for Mistress Verryon was more than good enough for her.

So they came with their cuts, their coughs, their rashes and their intractable problems. She told them all the same thing – she was not a Healer – but she did her best to help. Even a mother, pleading for something for her child's cough, went away with an infusion. Tammina worried about that, but Hal just smiled.

"They are poor. They work every hour of every day. They do not even have the time to wait in the Sick House. They may believe that you are a Witch, or think you an angel from Namier. They do not care what you are, if you can help them. And you do, and for nothing."

The wedding was celebrated in great style. The two young people appeared suitably delighted with one another and it was generally predicted that there would a child within the year. It was a confident and jovial procession that set out for the northern reaches some six weeks later.

Tammina travelled with the group attached to Lord Parandour. It included several advisors and their personal servants. There were no musicians among them, though Master Hallarden had pleaded for a place. His opinion of the army musicians was not flattering. His lord had laughed at it, but he had not relented. He intended, he declared, to secure his northern boundary and if that separated lovers or interrupted courtship it was unfortunate. The various parties must bear it. Some might well find it a relief.

Master Hallarden did not find his last comment as amusing as some of the listeners. He feared that in Tammina's case it was true.

It was. She did not dislike him; she enjoyed his company. He was intelligent and interesting, he was amusing and he was kind. He made no assumptions and did not press her in any way; but others made assumptions and she did not know how to counter them.

In Bellue terms he was 'a fine fish to pull in', but she did not want to 'pull him in' and her lack of either triumph or desire troubled her. She was happy to shelve the problem even if it meant travelling dressed in dramatic black robes as 'The Witch'.

The mode of transport caused a minor upset. Lord Parandour had intended her to ride on a black horse and was most put out when she said that she could not ride. He should have realised that, she told him. There were no horses in Bellue. Even the Frelius found them more trouble than they were worth. In Bellue, everyone walked or was carried in a litter. Handcarts or donkeys with panniers were used for heavy loads. Horses ate too much and did not like the terrain.

So instead, she rode in a small open carriage. It was painted the colour of sand, decorated with a fanciful design of black moons and swirls of dark grey smoke and had a hood that could be raised to protect her from the weather should that be necessary. She had no duties and was provided with two guards who stayed beside her during the day and slept outside her tent at night.

The journey was interesting. Lord Parandour did not want his soldiers exhausted from the march and it did no harm to display his strength throughout his lands, so the pace was moderate. They marched through the towns during the daytime and camped in the fields for the night. There was time each evening to explore the countryside before the light faded.

Tammina was not the only one to use the evening so. Enterprising soldiers hunted game and camp followers searched for greens to flavour the stews that complemented the basic rations. One evening she met one carrying a basket of fungi and she looked at them with interest.

"I can spare one or two," offered the woman extending her basket for inspection, and she named her price.

Tammina picked one out and studied it. The light was not good, but she thought that there were faint dark spots on the creamy skin.

"Thank you but no," she said and pointed out the spots. "Look in better light and if they have spots on the skin, do not use them."

The woman was not impressed. She had bought many a 'curdy' in the market. She knew a good one when she saw it and did not like being told otherwise by someone who spoke with a strange accent. She peered suspiciously at Tammina.

"Where do you come from?" she asked, and answered her own question when she saw the guard hovering. "Bellue! That's it I warrant! The one they call Witch! Well, I need no advice from you."

She sniffed, gathered her skirts and walked away.

Tammina stared after her.

"What can I do?" she asked.

The guard shrugged. "She picked them," he said, and added when he saw her anxious expression, "Are they poisonous?"

"Not exactly, but oh! They are not good."

He sighed and called out a name. A man detached himself from his two companions and came towards them.

"Yes?" he said.

"That one, with the basket," began the guard gesturing towards the departing woman, "she has picked some curdies, but the Witch thinks that they are not good. One had spots on."

He was interested immediately. "Spots? On the skin?"

"Very faint, they were. Dirt marks or blemishes more like. Probably they will peel away."

"If they are spotcaps the marks will certainly peel away, but that will not change the fungus underneath." He chuckled and turned to Tammina with interest. "You are familiar with spotcaps? They are not particularly common here. Do they grow in Bellue?"

"I do not know what they are called. I have seen them only once before in all my life, but they are pictured clearly in one of my books and it tells of their effects. Please follow that woman and tell her not to use the ones with spots. She did not heed me, and she has a full basket. They may *all* have spots."

"You have books with such information?" he asked with even greater interest.

"I did have in Bellue," she answered impatiently. "Now go and warn her. You can find me at any time, but she will disappear into the camp if you stand here any longer."

"She and her friends will be obvious enough tomorrow," he commented and did not move.

"It is not *funny*." She was vehement. "In certain people those fungi can cause death!"

He moved then and called to his companions, telling them that there was some question about the fungi that a camp follower had picked, possibly spotcaps. They came closer.

Tammina recognised one man. It was the Cutter, Tomar Shean. The woman she could not place, until she spoke.

"You thought they were spotcaps?" she asked staring at Tammina.

Tammina nodded. It was one of the Healers who had questioned her at the castle.

"She will know," she said crisply, "so we had best get down there and warn everyone. If one has found some, others may have, too, and if they are cooked and eaten we will spend the best part of the night dispensing remedies. Come."

She caught the sleeve of one companion and hurried away pulling him along beside her. Tomar stayed.

"Spotcaps?" he queried. "I know the name, but cannot recall their effect."

"They are used, in *very* small quantity, to open the bowels," answered Tammina primly.

"Ah! Yes!" He stared after the two departing figures and audibly wished for their success. An army crowded into tents and with poor facilities for hygiene did not need a mass attack of flux.

"Are you now free?" asked Tammina.

The answer was given slowly, and after some consideration.

"I have been re-assigned – to the army and without pay. Army deserters are commonly despatched without trial."

He smiled at her and added, "So, therefore, no; I am not free; but how many are?" and he walked away.

The army marched north and west away from the fertile lands near the coast. At Winniss Hamlet, where they crossed the River Lairn, the weather was clear and crisp and the white-tipped peak of Valke shone on the far horizon. Tammina gazed at the mountains with interest. She had learnt of them in school, of their size and of the snow that capped the highest peaks. She had thought that she could imagine something higher than she had known in Bellue, but seeing them in reality was entirely different.

She had time to gaze on Valke, for they headed west along the north bank of the river. She enjoyed the view, but did not discover the reason until they halted.

North lay the first tributary of the great river Felt and that was best crossed on the higher ground to the west or at Pittern to the east. The eastern lands between the Felt and the north shore of Bosron Bay were already under Lord Parandour's control; recently conquered it was true, but peaceful, managed by his commanders and paying due tribute. Tomar was from that area.

"There are some who consider him a fair ruler," he commented sourly, "and he keeps out the raiders from the north shore, but we were well enough before, and many were killed or maimed – to extend his domain."

He walked away and someone else explained that Parandour's aim on this expedition was to secure the northwest area at least up to the Aishe River, the most northerly tributary of the Felt. North of that was salt scrub or forest and the folk who lived there were wild. They did not work, their land was poor and they were forever raiding the more fertile and prosperous areas to the south.

"Is not the Aishe a barrier?" asked Tammina, and was disappointed at the weary laugh and the shaken head.

She learnt more of the geography of the area. She already knew of the great swamp of Warne, but she had not realised that the Aishe had its swampland too. It was not as large or so all pervading – more a series of small streams that split, rejoined and split again before coming together into a single channel.

That was a barrier, but the tiny streams, though they made the intervening ground too moist for crops or cattle, were easily crossed; and from there the invading hordes could ravage the land, kill and rape and steal; and that was what they did.

The local lord and many of his people did not want Parandour, but there were those who would welcome his strength, and would willingly pay his taxes if he kept out the raiders.

Tammina was intrigued by the discussion. She could see advantages to the local lords in cooperating with Parandour, even paying his taxes. She had loved Bellue, but she had not liked its restrictions and she realised that the vigour of the community would decline if its people remained for long in such strict isolation. She was glad that not all of Parandour's aims were unworthy, for in order to survive, she was obliged to work for him. She wondered what he intended to do about the lack of defence at Aishe swamp.

She had no opportunity to ask, even had she dared to do so, for she had little sight of him for the next few days. He did not need her for the few small skirmishes that occurred and nor did any other. There were casualties, but she was not called upon. The Healers and the Cutters dealt easily enough with the wounded, and the dead were buried. Graveyards were used for the purpose, if there were any nearby, and plots by the roadside if there were not.

She felt idle and did not like it. She was used to work. She tried her guards severely by her wanderings and her questions.

One village, close to the source of the Aishe, was skirted by the main body of men. It was deserted. Its inhabitants had experienced the incursions of the northerners, and an army approaching from the south was equally feared. They had abandoned their homes, taken their livestock and what goods they could carry and had fled. The forested hills offered some measure of safety.

Tammina, curious as to how the people lived, explored the village. She was investigating a vat of dark berries when she heard the scream.

Her guard wanted her to leave at once. A scream meant danger, and that was best avoided.

She pushed him aside. "A scream means that someone is in pain and needs help," she said, and ran towards the sound, still carrying her basket. The noise came from a row of buildings, but she did not know which one. She called out, but there was no reply.

The guard followed anxiously as she ran along the row, trying the doors. The third one opened. It gave onto a small dark room, simply furnished, and apparently unoccupied, but there was a curtain at the further side. Tammina entered. Her sharp ears caught the faint sounds from beyond the curtain and she pulled it aside.

A woman lay on a bed, with a man kneeling beside her. Four children, all girls, cowered against the wall.

"Do not hurt my children," begged the man. "Take what you will, but do not harm us. My wife is in labour, but the child does not come. We could not leave her; she is dying."

Tammina stared at them. The eldest child was about twelve, younger than she had been when her mother was killed. The others were younger still. They were frightened, but they did not understand.

"We need help." Tammina turned to her guard and realised that he would not leave her. He was a soldier and he would not go against his orders whatever the circumstances.

"Do you know the names of any of the Healers?" she asked, but he shook his head. They were the Healers. Names were not important.

She turned back to the eldest girl.

"I cannot help your mother alone," she said. "Go outside and shout. Shout for Tomar Shean. Do you hear? Shout 'Tomar Shean' as loudly as you can. When he comes, bring him here."

The girl hesitated, waiting for her father, so Tammina pressed him too; promising that Tomar Shean would come, would help; and what other hope was there?

He was crying, but he went and she heard his despairing shout.

Alone, she delved into her basket. It contained only what she had gathered that morning. She had no salves, no potions, nothing more than a few raw leaves, but one type, she thought, had narcotic properties.

She commanded one of the children to light the fire, but there was not time to wait for boiling water. She tore the leaves, crushed them between her palms and rubbed the juices into the woman's swollen belly. She crushed more and covered her patient's mouth and nose with her warm hands.

"Lord Parandour is seeking you." The guard was brusque, but he added more gently, "Tomar Shean is coming."

"Good," she said. "Parandour must wait."

When Tomar arrived, he repeated the guard's words. She was wanted.

"We do not have time." She was urgent. "The child is not well placed for birth and I cannot feel it move. It may be dead already and she is near to dying. Can you cut it out? I have heard that babes can be cut from their mothers."

Tomar was horrified. "I have *heard*, but I have never done such a thing, nor have I seen it done."

"But you know the organs, you will recognise the womb. You know what to cut and what to leave? She will die if nothing is done." Half was question, and half was plain statement.

"Now is a good time to try," she said softly, all encouragement. "You have your knife?"

"Yes." He was reluctant, but he could see for himself that the poor woman was exhausted. He opened his satchel. It held all his tools. He wore it all day and it lay beside his bed at night.

"He needs good light," she said to her guard, and though he repeated Parandour's name he did so without expectation. He found a lamp and lit it. It gave light, but it smoked.

"Poor people, poor oil," thought Tammina as she shooed the family away. She bade the guard block the door and warned him not to watch unless he had a strong stomach. He hesitated, but gladly turned away at the murmur of reassurance from the man holding the knife.

"Now," commanded Tammina, and Tomar took a deep breath.

How had he been drawn into this situation? Was she indeed a witch? But the thoughts were fleeting; he needed to concentrate.

He was aware of her throughout the operation – her soft words of encouragement and her unobtrusive efforts to keep the patient still, – but they did not speak, not until the child was visible and she offered to take it.

It was still, lifeless he thought, and was sure that she felt so too, but she tried. As he finished his work, as best he could remember from dismembering animals, she was cleaning the small face, massaging the tiny chest and slapping gently. There was no response.

He heard her indrawn breath and the sharp crack of flesh on flesh, as she struck harder, and harder still.

The first sound was small, but it was followed by a vigorous cry of protest that so startled him that he almost dropped his knife.

"He was slow to start, but he has a fine pair of lungs," he said.

She looked at him in wonderment, and then at the child, and they both smiled. She flung back her head and cried out in triumph,

"It is a boy!"

They were still smiling when they heard the commanding voice outside. The woman was lying quiet, exhausted and in pain, and her husband sat beside her, still bemused. He had offered all that was in his meagre store of coin and they had taken nothing.

The eldest girl was seated by the fire nursing her brother. She was used to nursing babes, and Tammina was not.

"Where is she?" demanded Lord Parandour, flinging open the door. He ignored the other occupants and glared at his Witch.

"How dare you bid me wait? Do you not realise that I could have you killed this very moment!"

Tammina curtsied low.

"Indeed, Lord, you can kill me whenever you wish, and in whatever manner you desire," she answered meekly, "but you will not – not yet," and she looked up at him and smiled slowly, "for I have not yet served my purpose."

"By Namier's moon, woman, you try me!"

"I did not choose to try you, Lord, but Master Shean needed help," she said, dutiful again, "and neither birth nor death take heed of wishes, even those of a great Lord."

He looked about him then, saw the family and ordered her to come. She was no longer needed.

She agreed at once, but she remarked to no one in particular that in her area it was the custom for the first visitor following a birth to bring a gift, but that was in Bellue, and might not be so here.

Parandour turned in the doorway. It *was* the custom here, and he was sure that she knew it.

"There are coins on the table there," he said. "Is that not the first gift?"

She shook her head and came closer. "That belongs to the father. He offered it to us. All he had, he said, and I believe him. Master Shean is very skilled, but he is yours, as I am, and would not take payment."

"I thought that Master Shean, as you call him, was a Cutter, not a birthing woman."

"The child was in the wrong position. He had to be cut from his mother and that takes great skill. She will not have another child, but she is alive."

That startled him. He strode over to the bed and pulled aside the covering.

"Namier's moon," he muttered and dropped the sheet.

Tammina pulled it straight and tucked it around the woman, who was still barely conscious.

"She must still be in pain, Lord, and I have no preparations with me. A Healer? With some soothing draught?"

"Aye." He was still shocked. "Send for a Healer," he said to his attendant, "and a gift -".

The man bowed and held out a handful of coins, the entire contents of his purse.

Parandour nodded. It was enough. He smiled, and gave a dry assurance that the money would be reimbursed.

As Tammina followed him, she felt a tug at her skirt. The eldest girl had caught the hem as she passed and was kissing it. She felt an urge to protest at the humble gesture, but she said nothing, for Master Shean had shaken his head.

The thanks were due to him, she thought sadly. He carried his knives wherever he went. He was a Cutter. She carried no salves or potions. She was not a Healer. She gathered plants and was called Witch, but even that unflattering title was undeserved. All was pretence.

She walked in silence, as did Parandour. She thought him angry, but in fact he was deep in thought. He was severe, though, when he finally spoke.

"You are to dance again; on a mound by a walled estate. I want you seen; and by as many of my enemies as possible. Perhaps tomorrow night will suit. It is not a witch's moon, but I cannot wait for that. Stay where you can be found; and make sure that your dance strikes fear into all who see it."

Chapter 14

Tammina did not like to be restricted, but she obeyed. She did not wish to strike fear into anyone either, but she thought deeply about her dance.

She must please Parandour. She had tested his patience and he had borne it, and given a generous sum to the poor family; at least his attendant had, but she felt sure Parandour would keep his promise and the man would be repaid.

Despite her thoughts, she had no specific idea about her dance when they made camp the following day. It was midday. In the distance, a high wall was visible, and a small rounded hill. Was that the mound?

It was, and she was given leave to go and study it during the afternoon. She was warned not to go alone. Both her guards were to accompany her, for they were not in friendly lands and were within sight of the River Aishe – and the enemy beyond.

There were trees and shrubs on the lower slopes, but the crown of the hill was almost bare of vegetation. The view was splendid, but the grass was thin and sparse and there were outcrops of gravel and some rocks. They were low and some were smooth, but it was not the best surface for barefoot dancing. It would be dark, too. Even if the clouds cleared the moon was slender now and its light would be faint.

She walked carefully around, studying the ground. She would need fire, and she returned to the wooded area to collect dry leaves and tinder.

She saw the man before her guards did, but he did not alarm her. He was old, with thin hair and a straggled beard. One eye was plainly useless and she suspected that he had little sight in the other, for he was seated on the ground, his back against a tree trunk, and was staring at the unexceptional undergrowth that grew in his line of sight.

She called softly and he turned his head. He was not deaf.

"Rose?" He frowned, and called again, more urgently. "Rose! Where are you?"

"I am not Rose," answered Tammina, "and I am not alone, but we will not harm you."

He was not reassured. Awkwardly, and with difficulty, he pulled himself upright and called again. This time there was a response.

A woman's voice, weary and cross, told all that she was coming, she was coming, and a moment later she appeared, still talking. "I was searching for the black lovas that you wanted, but I found only the small red ones."

The cause of her weariness was evident. She carried two baskets, both loaded with various fruits, and on her back was another filled with wood for the fire. She stopped short when she saw Tammina and her guards.

"If you gathered those, you wasted your time," complained the old man forgetting that there were others near. "Red ones are useless. They have juice not oil, and it stings on my sores."

"I am not familiar with lovas, but I found some black fruit further down the hill." Tammina reached into her own basket and carefully picked out a thorny twig with leaves and fruit attached. She held it up.

The woman nodded without moving, but the man came closer and squinted at her.

"You're not from hereabouts if you don't know lovas," he said. "With the Lord's army from Bosron are you?"

"Yes, we have come with him, but we will not harm any who do not threaten us, nor will we steal from you. I do not think Lord Parandour will either. He comes to secure his lands – and his people – from the raiders who cross the river Aishe."

The woman gave a bitter laugh. "The raiders have always come. He will need to leave his army here to stop them and the army will eat as much as the raiders take."

"The raiders have not always come, Rose." The man sounded angry. "I have told you before! They did not come before the rock fell. But you do not believe me, do you? You think I am a fool, but I know. My grandfather told me, and he remembered those days when the river flowed fast!"

Rose picked up her baskets and pulled at his sleeve. "Come, we should go."

"Do you not want some of the black lovas that I have picked?" asked Tammina.

"Yes, I do," and "How much?" they spoke together.

"No money." Tammina answered the woman, "but I would like some of the red lovas and some information." She turned to the man. "Will you tell me some of your memories?"

He remarked sourly that no one listened to him, but he sat down again.

The guards grumbled, but were better pleased when Tammina suggested that they sit further off. They need not listen to the old man's ramblings. They could see her plainly and so might play at cards or dice.

Rose took some of the black lovas.

"You drive a poor bargain," she said, as she tipped all her red ones into Tammina's basket. "He can tell you nothing of value, he has trouble remembering his own name, and red lovas give oil so thin that is almost useless. Burns too fast for lamps and gives a bitter taste to anything cooked in it."

She gave a scornful laugh, and sat down as far from them as the guards, but in the opposite direction. She began to crush the black fruit to collect the oil.

Tammina also sat, but she listened as her mother had taught her; neither questioning nor interrupting, but encouraging the flow of conversation and, when opportunity arose, directing it towards the topics of greatest interest.

She was pleased with her success. Mama would have been proud of her skill in obtaining various pieces of information, but she would not have approved of the use to which they might be put.

The old man would have talked for hours, but Rose would not wait. She returned to his side when she had obtained sufficient oil and she applied it, without much sympathy, to the open sores on his arms and legs. She then hauled him to his feet and dragged him away.

Tammina felt sorry for him, but she also felt sorry for Rose. Caring for the sick was never easy, and when they were old and there was little hope of recovery it was depressing as well as difficult.

When they had gone, she resumed her inspection of the area. She would need a fire in order to be seen. The grey clouds showed little sign of lifting and at this time in its cycle the moon would not give much light even if the sky were clear. She collected dry leaves and twigs and some larger pieces of wood and piled them carefully on the crown of the hill. She marked a circle around it with stones and walked round it and out from it, counting her steps.

"Seven directions," muttered one guard to the other as they watched her, but then she confounded them by trying two more. Nine did not have the unique properties that the number seven possessed.

She did not mind if the guards saw that part of her preparation, but she did make a second pile of dead wood under the trees and out of their sight. She was not yet sure what use she would make of it, but she had ideas and it was not easy to gather tinder in the darkness.

When they returned to the camp she sought Lord Parandour. He was in conference, but his son was not.

Roddori was striding unhappily about the camp. He had wanted to join this expedition, though it had meant leaving his new wife, but he had not expected to be shut out of a conference.

He scowled when Tammina approached him and made her request. Nor could he keep the surprise from his voice when he answered.

"You dance tonight, do you? Well, if you must, you must; but you can practice in the camp. There is no need for a private room. We are scarcely surrounded by elegant buildings, are we?"

"No, Lord, we are not. Here the elegant buildings are enclosed behind high walls. The lord who lives there protects his own from the raiders, but leaves his people to defend themselves. He has no love for your father. I am to frighten him as well as others when I dance tonight. That is why I cannot practise in the open camp. There would be no mystery."

Roddori considered. The reply had been calmly delivered, the argument plainly stated. There were no hidden meanings and certainly no obsequious words or gestures. Perhaps it was the omission of the latter that gave her that air of difference. She had made no effort to persuade, and yet she had done so.

"Very well. Come with me. I will find you somewhere private."

She followed in silence. There were other things that she needed, and the list needed thought, for she was not sure what would be useful. If she requested something superfluous it would not matter, but she did not want to omit anything essential.

"I will need a fire, and some pots," she began when Roddori stopped outside a large building. It was the village chapel and meeting place and had been commandeered by the army. "I will also need water, herbs and salt" -

"You are intending to cook?" he asked and raised his eyebrows in disbelief.

"I am intending to make spells, and that is much the same as cooking. The results are different, and cooks do not chant as they prepare a meal, but the processes are similar.

"Clothes from the dead I shall need, to conjure up their spirits to take revenge. Hair or bones would be better, but I doubt that those will be available."

She gave a resigned sigh and added with feigned annoyance, "- and I must also do without the heart of a deer killed at full moon. A rabbit leg must suffice, or a rat's hind foot; and perhaps -", she listed several things she considered of possible use, interspersed with other, stranger items that she recalled from the books on witchcraft that she had consulted.

Roddori was uneasy, but he bade her guards bring what they could find from her list and promised to stay with her whilst they were gone. He would answer to his father, he told them, if by chance she vanished in a puff of smoke.

They left and he pushed open the door. A few officers were sitting playing dice. They grumbled when he ordered them out, but they obeyed. Parandour might have faith in his Witch, but they preferred axes and swords.

Tammina walked to a long table and swept it carefully with a leaf before setting out the contents of her basket. She felt sorry for Roddori, given a wife, torn from her side after a few weeks and turned out from one of the conferences as if he were a child.

"Your father is not sure of my powers," she remarked, concentrating on arranging leaves, "but he wants others to believe in them. You do not, so, whilst he talks of how he will use me, he has sent you away. Do not blame him. You are young and forthright and might disturb his plans."

She wanted to squeeze the red berries and test the properties of oil, but that must be done in private. She used them instead as the centre of a flower.

Roddori watched in silence as she drew the sacred symbols of Namier on the table with the various items from her basket.

Perhaps she was right. His father was certainly using her, thought highly of her intelligence and half-believed that she had unnatural powers. He did not believe that anyone possessed mystical powers – there were tricks and illusions, and they could be used for good or for ill.

Despite that belief, he was unhappy when she circled the table in the wrong direction, bowed to each symbol, and changed them. The depictions of the horned head and the poison root were crude, but the five-pronged fork was clear, and the tip of each prong was flecked with red berries.

"Blood?" he queried, trying to seem amused.

"What you will?" she answered. "Hadron has no need of symbols. They are for men whose lives are uncertain – and brief."

He was relieved that he had no need to comment for the guards returned. They had found most of what she asked for, they assured her, casting wary glances at the table; and they were clearly happy when Roddori declared that they might keep guard outside the door and leave the witch to her own devices.

Tammina was also glad, though she did not make it quite so obvious. She wanted to experiment and the results would be more effective if that were done in private.

The oil from the red fruit did indeed catch fire easily and burn fast, but it was not spectacular. It burned with soft blue flame that was scarcely visible.

She tried soaking strips of cloth in the oil. Some took fire almost as easily as the oil itself, but burnt less quickly and, if sprinkled with a little salt, gave a bright yellow flame. A small amount of black smoke was given off. That was undesirable, but only a small disadvantage.

Some types of cloth burned better than others and she discovered that small pieces of the braid produced flashes of red flame.

She made her plans, not for the movements of the dance – in the darkness they would hardly be noticed – but for the fires. The fires would be seen and she wanted them noticed.

It was late and she was tired when she was finally satisfied and she packed her basket ready for the night's work.

There were few people who did not see at least some of her dance that night.

Those who had chosen to stay within their shelters or to turn away their faces were soon persuaded to come and look.

The central fire on the mound burned merrily and lit up the dark shadow that twisted and turned around it, white limbs shining in the glow from the flames. Every so often the flames turned red and a streak of bright yellow fire leapt from a white hand. Sometimes the flame started a new fire where it fell; sometimes it did not. When it did, the dark shadow with its white limbs danced round the new fire, and that too flamed red for a brief moment. Six fires were started before the shadow disappeared.

The seventh fire began slowly from a tiny spark rather than a ribbon of flame, but soon it burnt brightly, red and yellow, and the figure appeared again, dancing, first around the newest fire, then around and between the others. In and out it went until the fires faded into embers.

Tammina was annoyed that she had only managed to light only six of the nine piles she had set around the central fire. Six was hardly a magic number, divisible as it was by two and by three. She had hoped to light seven.

Now she was obliged to change her plan; dropping down to the ground, covering her white-painted arms and legs, and crawling to one of the unlit piles of leaves and twigs with a glowing stick. She burnt her hand hiding its light from the watchers.

The oil-soaked rag she had laid at the heart of the pile caught slowly – it had grown cold and damp in the night air – but it caught. When the flame was stronger, she sprinkled salt and tiny pieces of the braid onto the fire. Only then did she leap up and uncover her pale limbs.

She danced around the fires until their light faded.

When she was confident that she could no longer be seen, even by the night guards who awaited her more than halfway up the slope, she dropped to hands and knees again and scattered the debris over a wide area. She left the ashes of the central fire to smoulder. There was nothing there to give a curious seeker any clue about her methods.

She was exhausted when she picked up her basket, now containing no more than a few empty pots, and went to meet her guards.

They were silent, and that pleased her. She was further pleased when they reached the outskirts of the camp. It, too, was silent and the few who had not retreated into their tents stepped back when they passed. More than one made the sign of the crescent moon. She had succeeded!

Her elation was short-lived. Roddori was waiting at the entrance to her tent. She thought him uneasy and that was satisfying, but his message was not. His father wanted to see her.

She wanted to sleep. She had not the least desire to see Lord Parandour, but she did not dare refuse.

She was unsurprised to find him alone. He would not have sent his son to fetch her to a formal meeting. Roddori sat down beside his father, but she was not invited to sit.

She was sure that Parandour was pleased with her efforts and his first words confirmed it.

"Well done," he said and smiled, "A very effective display. Even some of my senior commanders were impressed."

"You bade me strike fear into the hearts of those who saw me, Lord, and I did my best, but it is the enemy that must tremble, not your own soldiers. They should be told that the spirits I called up were not evil. They were those of their dead comrades. They will not harm their friends, but will seek revenge on the enemy for their own suffering and death. Your son and my guards know what garments I used – the garments of those killed on our way here."

He frowned. He asked for advice and on occasions followed it, but he did not care to have it given so freely.

"I saw no spirits dancing, but I saw flames come from your hands and start fires. How did you do that?"

"Great energy is needed to make spirits manifest, Lord, and it would be wasted tonight for we have not yet engaged the enemy."

Tammina did not expect that such a limited answer, gleaned from one of the books that she had studied, would satisfy him, but she stood quietly and added nothing further.

"How did you start the fires?" he asked again.

She prevaricated. She had no intention of telling him her secrets. She told him that she had carried a hot ember from her campfire, as everyone did when they moved to a new site.

"That was to start the central fire, woman. I want to know of the yellow flames that flew from your hands and the small fires that burned bright yellow and red!"

"Why do you wish to know, Lord?" she queried gently. "I was flung out of Bellue and labelled Witch. So I am known, and as such I am of use to you. You know that I am of no value without mystery.

You are a wise man; angry and insulted as you were by Frelius' action, you did not react impulsively. You used your judgement. Had you not, I would have been tossed from the castle tower and your ships and army would still be surrounding Fort Bellue."

She paused, looked up at him and added so softly that he had to lean towards her to hear, "And all your conquests in the north in danger of being lost."

He straightened again and thrust one fist into his other hand in frustration. It was hours past midnight. She had worked without food for most of the previous day, she had climbed the hill and had danced for hours; she was tired – Namier's Moon the woman must be exhausted – and still she avoided his questions with her clever answers.

"I do not need to give you my reasons." He scowled at her. "I wish to know. Tell me."

Tammina was suddenly tired of word games. She shrugged her shoulders.

"Spells or tricks, they are my secrets. I will tell you nothing. Find out for yourself – you have the means. I am going to bed."

She walked towards the door.

Roddori followed and stood in her way.

"You cannot leave without permission!" he exclaimed, appalled.

"Yes, I can – and he will not punish me. Not yet."

She smiled at him, but he was tall and lifting her head made her dizzy. She focused on his chest. That too was difficult. It was far too easy, she thought, to seem in a trance and talk nonsense when one was tired and had eaten little.

"Learn wisdom," she said, and her voice sounded far away. "You will inherit most of the land east of the mountains. It will be called Eastland. Practice justice, and your people will prosper. The north will come in time to Eastland's ruler."

"Let her go," said Parandour. "Call someone to carry her to her tent."

"I will take her, sir," and Roddori reached towards her.

"No. No man must touch me!" Tammina spoke sharply and drew back against the wall. She was startled at her own reaction, and it took a great effort to collect herself.

"Some water please; and I will be able to walk without help."

Parandour himself brought the glass and offered it to her. The water was cool and sweet; she had not realised how thirsty she was.

She accepted an escort to her tent, but she had no need of their support.

"Why did you not punish her, sir?" Roddori was puzzled at his father's attitude.

"Would you have whipped her?" asked Parandour, and laughed at his son's hesitation.

"Nor would any other," he continued, "not willingly. And they would wonder why. What reason could I give? She has done exactly what I asked of her. Only in private did she refuse to do my bidding, and she knows that I cannot make that public. I spoke to her in private because to admit that I question her powers would undermine all my plans for this campaign."

He shook his head in frustration and strode about the room before he spoke again.

"*I* am more in *her* control than she is in mine! Wisdom – she bade you learn wisdom. Good advice, Roddori, but do not learn it from my actions today. I ought to have known that her tongue would well be guarded, however tired she was.

"Women have more resilience than men. Learn that. A prisoner in a strange land, unfed and unwashed; and yet she kept her head and told me that Frelius did not know what he had given.

"She was right! She is a finer fighter than many I have conscripted – and she has won hearts. Many think her a witch and will not go near her, but others have sought her help and are grateful for it."

He paced in silence, up and down the hall, and Roddori did not disturb his thoughts. He had many of his own.

It was several minutes before his father came to a halt beside him. He clapped him on the shoulder.

"Come, my son," he said, with more affection than he normally displayed, "Come to bed. It is late; and tomorrow, though the journey is short, we have a battle to plan. And I must make peace with my Witch. I do not want her to disappear into the northlands. She is valuable."

"She puzzles me," said Roddori. "I do not believe in witchcraft, but I do not understand her."

His father smiled. "Nor do I," he answered, "but she is clever and she is valuable. She was given as an insult, but if I use her skills wisely all the land will laugh at the Frelius of Fort Bellue for throwing out such a treasure."

Roddori smiled in return.

Tomorrow would be his first experience of planning for battle and likely the following day he would be fighting one. A tough fight it would be too, for the enemy would regard his death as a triumph; but he would live, and his father would win the day.

The Witch had said that he would inherit his father's lands. He could not do that if he were dead.

He had grave doubts about witchcraft and magic, but prophecy was not evil. Namier had had his prophets. Her words gave him confidence.

Chapter 15

Tammina did not have a restful night. The day's events filled her mind and she could not settle.

She was worried also that she had been too bold. When Lord Parandour had won his battle, and had no further use for her, he could order her killed. Such an action would not be just, not in her eyes, but false charges were easily brought against a person without family, influence or friends.

Half asleep, she toyed with the idea of escape, perhaps during the fighting, when all minds were on their own survival. She might be safe from pursuit if she went north – but there was Margren.

That thought brought her to wakefulness. She concentrated on relaxing one limb at a time and she fell asleep, but in a dream she heard Margren screaming and she woke again. She was glad that the hours devoted to rest were long.

They were close to their final destination, so camp was struck earlier than usual. It was never a quiet procedure and excitement and apprehension gave a sharper edge to the shouted orders, and the answering voices were shriller.

She rose before she was called and was ready to leave before her breakfast was brought. She always ate alone – no one wanted a witch's company at mealtime. It was obvious later that it was not wanted on the march either.

Her place was to the fore of the army, not far behind Lord Parandour's impressive entourage. She did not travel with the straggling followers. Even so, the troops kept their distance, and rode or marched as far from her cart as discipline would allow.

The village was supposedly in Parandour's realm, but some of those who watched them leave showed their resentment and there were mutterings of 'evil' and 'witch'.

She had grown accustomed to scanning the crowds so she saw the man raise his arm and jerked back her head. The stone flew past her, but it was so close that she heard the swish of air, and it struck one of her outriders. It clanged against the shield that hung at his side. The noise caused a ripple of alarm through the soldiers and it reached Parandour.

He was not pleased.

"Hold that man, and hang him! I will have no opposition."

Tammina watched as the man was captured and dragged towards the tree that had been indicated. A woman followed, carrying a child and pulling ineffectually at the soldiers' arms. Both were wailing.

Tammina stepped out of her cart and walked towards Parandour.

"You are come to watch, and drag his spirit down to Hadron?" he asked dryly.

She had not approached for that, but before she could deny it, the woman ran forward.

She did not dare to spit upon the Witch, but she made the sign of the crescent moon, almost dropping her child in the process.

"You are evil!" she shouted. "My man is a good man, and cast his stone against you to show it."

"I am from Bellue and am called Witch," answered Tammina mildly. "But I am Parandour's Witch and will bring no harm to his people. The spirits I called forth last night, when I danced, are the spirits of his soldiers. They will fight his enemies, but they will not harm his friends. Your man had no cause to hurt me."

She turned to Lord Parandour.

"I do not know if the man is good or bad, Lord, but he has a straight aim. When you are in need of troops, it would be a waste to hang a man with a good aim."

"He missed," retorted Parandour, and sighed inwardly as he saw her slow smile begin. She was about to say something enigmatic, and, whilst he was using her to put fear into the mass of the population and did not much care how she went about it, *he* liked to understand.

"Did he?" she said. "The stone did, but a single stone is easily deflected. Enemies are best before, and friends behind."

Parandour scowled. He understood her perfectly. He liked the implication that her dark powers had saved her from being struck, but he did not care to be told that hanging a man would make enemies.

He felt that prompt punishment showed strength, but the wretched woman did have a point.

She was speaking again, addressing the wife in a normal voice.

"He is not armed today, but he is an archer is he not? And keeps your pot well filled?"

"Aye." She was bewildered and wary. "But only with little things, the vermin. He does not take the lord's deer or his birds."

Looking at the man's face, Parandour thought it likely that he had, on occasions, taken both. The punishment for that was also hanging, but one could not hang a man twice.

He called one of his archers.

"Try him. Give him a bow and a target," and he added dryly, "A tree. We ought not to take one of Lord Nestor's birds."

The man was not confident. The weapon he was offered was larger than his own bow and the arrows were smooth and straight with metal tips, very different from the sharpened willow twigs that he made himself.

He hefted it to test the weight, plucked at the string and raised it several times to sight before he took an arrow. That too he weighed and measured. If he missed, he would be hung; if he hit the target there was a slim possibility that he might not. He took great care.

There was a whimper from the woman and a sigh of disappointment from the small crowd of villagers when the arrow did no more than shave a sliver of bark from the young tree.

"Close," commented the archer, who was a man of few words. "A moving target will be a better test."

A moving target was duly provided. It was not large, a strip of hide tied to an arrow, and was fired by the one sent to retrieve the first missive.

Tammina watched with sinking heart. She was ignorant of the skills of archery, but it seemed a small target. She clenched her teeth, determined to show no emotion at the outcome.

The villagers were not so cautious. They cheered when they saw the two arrows meet and tumble together from the sky.

"A fine shot. I can use a man with such skill," and the archer bowed to his lord.

"Very well. Conscript him."

Parandour spoke as if it were a concession; but it was not. He had been impressed with the man's skill. The first target had been little more than a sapling and at a good distance; the second had made him believe that the archer had wanted to see the man hang.

He wondered at the thought – the archer he would ask later in the day, but he would not ask his Witch. She was his creature, his prisoner; but increasingly she made him feel uneasy. She held herself aloof and had an air of being different from the rest of humankind – just what he wanted. He had planned to use her to instil fear into his enemies, both within his borders and beyond them, but he had intended to control her; and now, too often, it seemed that she had her own plans.

The woman was wailing again, though not so loudly as her child.

"Does she *want* her man hanged?" he demanded impatiently.

"No, Lord, she does not; but neither does she want to be left without support. The child has croup. The Healers can help, but it will cost. Give her money and both will cease wailing."

It was Tammina who replied, in a voice devoid of emotion or interest, and having answered, she turned and began to walk back to her cart.

He was not pleased, nor had he any idea what sum would be deemed sufficient for a peasant woman in this area, but he commanded that she be given a week's pay for an archer.

Judging by her face as the coins were counted into her hand, it was too much; and her man looked anxious.

"See that you take the child to the Healers," said Parandour.

"It is only a girl." She seemed contemptuous. "Girls cry."

"My Witch is 'only a girl'," he noted, "but she sees. Take your daughter to the Healers, care for her well and await your man's return.

"I care little for you or your child, but the Witch is strange. She may care, and she *will* know. She does not need to be close to a victim to cause pain, and she can sap a man's vigour from a hundred leagues away."

The man looked better pleased and the woman rather less so.

"You had best earn your wage," Parandour warned him curtly, and turned away to order the army onward again. He heard the earnest assurance that was given, but he did not comment. It was no more than he expected.

Lord Parandour had brought his son on this campaign to give him practical experience and he ensured that Roddori was kept busy. It was, therefore, some time before the young man had opportunity to question his father.

He rode up beside him, and the Commander who had been making desultory conversation with his lord, tactfully dropped back.

"You do not really believe that the Witch can affect people from great distances, do you Sir?" he asked quietly.

"I sincerely hope that others do," replied his father grimly. "I have based this expedition on the belief that tales of her powers will keep half of the opposing forces at home."

He looked at his son's doubtful face and smiled.

"Understand, my son that you and I do not have to believe. Many do believe, and others are uncertain, but will show caution. So a simple sentence has ensured that our new recruit is happy. His woman has money, but she will spend it on the child and no man will dare to lie with her whilst he is away. He can put his mind to honing his skills and using them in my service – and he is highly skilled."

Roddori agreed. He had spent time training with one of the archery cohorts and knew how few were able to hit such a target.

"But do you believe her a witch, Sir?" he finished.

"Witches are Hadron's creatures. They must surely be evil. Is she evil? She has a strange manner, and she is clever. She uses her knowledge, and all that she sees and hears."

"She dances and she makes the symbols of Hadron."

"You sound uncertain. Think! Many prostrate themselves before the altars of Namier and make his signs with flamboyant gestures, but do little good. She has danced at my bidding and may have made the signs of Hadron, but do you know of any whom she has harmed?"

Roddori shook his head, and before he had a chance to speak again, his father gave a curt nod signifying that the conversation was over, and reined in to allow his Commander to draw level.

They discussed various aspects of the terrain ahead and the best deployment of their troops for the battle that they anticipated. The uncertainties of weather, of the numbers against them and of the possible tactics of the enemy were all considered. Roddori put the Witch to the back of his mind. She seemed simple in comparison.

He knew that the fiercest opposition would be from Lord Telmarr, but he learnt why Lord Nestor was not expected to stop their progress. He grew vines and made wine and was interested in little else. He collected rent and taxes from his tenants, but took no other interest in them.

His fine house was built on a southern facing slope in the foothills of the Kevaine Mountains and was well protected by its two walls. The inner one was little more than a garden wall, but the longer outer wall was formidable.

It was a fortified wall, high and wide with towers at frequent intervals. It enclosed the low hills near the house and a wide area of fertile plain to the east. Armed men patrolled by day and by night and loosed their arrows at any who came within range of the bows. They defended against all comers, but rarely emerged to fight.

It was, however, deemed prudent to leave a small force behind to guard against the possibility of an attack from the rear.

Roddori was shocked. Surely even a man who taxed his people but did not defend them, would not attack from the rear. It was not honourable.

Parandour regarded his idealistic son with a wry smile.

"No, it is not honourable," he conceded, "but it can be very effective. Nestor will not be deterred by considerations of honour, but he is lazy and may be deterred by the effort needed. He does not like to be disturbed; so, we will not disturb him. A few men, discreetly placed, and with only hand arms will not worry him. Besides, we need every ram and ballista that we have to threaten Telmarr's castle."

He was right, and every man and woman knew it the moment they caught sight of the massive pile.

To Tammina's eyes it was not as forbidding as Bellue, for that was black. This castle was built of golden stone, though like Bellue its walls seemed to grow from the cliff on which it stood. Two slender towers guarded the entrance, but they seemed more for ornamentation than for defence. The entrance could only be reached by crossing a narrow bridge that spanned a deep ravine, and the bridge itself was defended by another castle, albeit a much smaller one.

It deserved its reputation as impregnable. Tammina could not see it falling under attack. A long siege might bring surrender if the people within were starving, but walls that stood on such high cliffs were safe from battering rams and surely beyond the range of a ballista. She hoped that Lord Parandour did not expect her to bring them down by witchcraft.

Besieging the castle was not the first task. Lord Telmarr also defended his lands. Long before they reached the castle, they encountered an armed force, well positioned on high ground. Though fewer in numbers and less well equipped than they were, it was still an obstacle.

Roddori almost laughed, but his father did not.

"Men fighting for their own, fight fiercely," he warned. "Besides, I want Telmarr as an ally, not an enemy. I do not want to lay waste his land or destroy his castle. I want them as part of my own domain, his fighting men on my side, his castle part of my defences against the wild north. I want his friendship and cooperation.

"To get it, however, we must fight. They will fight to kill, but we must fight to take prisoners. Enough prisoners and we can bargain."

So they prepared for the battle.

Tammina was not involved in the preparations and no restrictions were placed upon her so she explored.

She also cultivated the acquaintance of Master Vearle, the chief engineer. The mechanical devices were not of great use in hand to hand fighting. Swinging beams and falling boulders did not distinguish between friend and foe. Therefore his skills were not much in demand and he too had time to wander.

He did not seek the company of the Witch, indeed he would have chosen to avoid it, but she was persistent; and he discovered that she was both sensible and intelligent when she was not being 'odd', as he termed it.

Together they walked along the bank of the River Aishe.

The headwaters tumbled down from the mountains, crashing through the rocks in white flurries of foam, but further east the land fell in a gentler slope and it was possible to walk beside the flow.

They admired the fine defensive wall that some predecessor of Telmarr had built on the further side of the river. Wisely sited, it ran between the Aishe and a tributary, crossing the main stream and ending with a round tower at the confluence.

There the river widened, but its bed was shallow and strewn with boulders and a little way downstream it split into small streams that criss-crossed a wide area.

'Swamp,' he called it, but though the land was well watered, it was not swamp. Men could cross with no more inconvenience than wet legs. There was no danger of being sucked under.

He searched around the final tower, voicing his thoughts. There must have been a further stretch of wall. There was no sense in building to this point and stopping.

She bowed to his superior knowledge about defences and said nothing, but she looked at the trees. On the higher ground they were large, some two or three hundred years old, but further down the slope the growth was younger.

The old man had been right. Here a cliff, eroded by continuous flow, or undermined by a sudden flood, had fallen into the river and changed its course.

"I must follow the southern-most stream," she declared.

Master Vearle did not think that advisable. He warned her of the dangers of going beyond the protection of the wall, but he could not persuade her to change her mind.

"I must go," she repeated. "There is no one in sight to the north and there is something I must see."

Her guards had agreed with the warning. They did not want to walk in that open exposed plain, but they did not try to stop her. They shrugged their shoulders in resignation.

"If she must go, she will go," they told the engineer, "and we must go with her, because those are our orders. You need not come."

"What must she see?" he asked, as Tammina set off in her chosen direction.

"Who knows," said one, and the other gave a longer answer before he too walked after her.

"She sees things that others do not see; secret things, sometimes into the future. So it is said; and Lord Parandour believes it."

"I know her reputation. She is called Witch, not Seer. What is she?"

The engineer was obliged to follow to hear the answer. It was not worth hearing, for the guard did not know and did not speculate, but he continued to follow, even when Tammina tucked up her skirts, removed her shoes and began to cross the streams and the muddy ground between them, making for an outcrop of rock.

She was leaning against it when he caught up with her, staring back across the flat ground to the round tower. She was pleased that he was there, but she said nothing; she did not even acknowledge him.

This, she was sure, was where the south bank of the Aishe had been many years ago. She shut her eyes and tried to picture the landscape as it once had been.

The old man had described many things in great detail, including the fall of the rock, but he had not seen them with his own eyes. They were his grandfather's grandfather's memories and had doubtless lost accuracy in the telling and in the passage of time, but then, the raiders had not crossed the river.

"Peace," she said, her eyes still shut. "Naught to hear but sheep calling lambs, and birds in trees above the river."

She opened her eyes and discovered that one of the guards was offering her a cup of water. She accepted it gratefully.

"You are dreaming, Mistress," said the engineer. "There are no trees in this place and no sheep either."

"Not now," she answered, "but some day. This is the place I saw, but there was just one river. Could the waters flow in a single stream?"

She poked at the bank on which they stood as if to direct the trickle of water on one side into the larger stream on the other.

"Not here. Perhaps further upstream."

It was a casual answer, followed by silence.

Tammina did not think it necessary to say more, but she looked upstream again. The tower was easy to see and she did not doubt the intelligence of her companion.

"Did you see the past, or the future?" he asked.

She answered slowly. "I do not see the past. If I see, it is the future, but it could be that once, years ago, there was but one river, and no swamp."

Suddenly brisk, she added, "We have been here long enough. Now we must return."

He watched as she moved away and he trailed behind as he had done on the forward journey. He had the oddest sense of being manipulated. He did not like it, but he could not turn his thoughts from the possibilities – a wide river was a useful boundary; more easily defended than flat land, however many tiny streams meandered through it.

When they reached the tower, he asked if she could see the future of that area. She shook her head.

"My talents are whimsical and drift away; yours are sober and stable. You would do better to rely upon your own vision." She smiled and walked away.

Her role in the fight against Lord Telmarr did not involve dancing. Her position was on the top of a mobile tower. From there she was to throw small objects into the opposing forces.

Fifty small clay pots with lids had been made and it had been suggested that they contain hornets. The pots would break on impact, or when stepped on, and the hornets would be angry when released and cause considerable concern amongst the enemy.

Lord Parandour had smiled when he told her that. As no doubt she had noticed, he added, there were many hornets in the nearby woods, feeding on the blossoms of a particular tree, but alas no one had offered any suggestions as to how she was to entice the insects into the pots.

She might do what she wished, but it was expected that the missiles would instil fear; so that his men would note where they landed and concentrate their efforts there.

Tammina was not pleased. She had no fear of heights when her feet were firmly placed on solid ground, but a platform on the top of a slender and hastily constructed wooden tower fastened to a cart, did not inspire her with confidence. Nor did she wish to have such a good view of men fighting and killing one another. Lord Parandour's forces were instructed to take prisoners, but a soldier could not be expected to exercise restraint when faced with an opponent who desired to kill him.

She put her doubts aside and thought about what to put in the pots. She attempted to attract hornets by placing blossoms in them, but it was not successful. In order to concentrate the scent she tried distilling the flowers. As was so often the case, ale produced a stronger smelling distillate than water, but the process was unpleasant. Several times she became so dizzy that she was obliged to walk away to recover.

She did not abandon the experiment. The distillate did attract a few hornets and she trapped them, but the effect of the vapour was more interesting. It did not appear to cause permanent harm and missiles that produced temporary incapacity were far more magical – and fearful – than those that merely released stinging insects.

She was called Witch, but it was Namier whom she thanked for her discovery. She grieved that she had no time to draw the tree and record the effect of the blossoms. Such things were for the benefit of all mankind, but at this moment she must use her knowledge in Parandour's cause and hope that his rule would improve the lives of the people whom he conquered.

She insisted on a rope and pulley to lift her carefully packed basket of pots to the top of the tower. The edifice was difficult enough to climb without being encumbered by a collection of pots containing angry insects and a substance that caused faintness.

She also fashioned some breeches for herself. They were inelegant, but preserved her modesty as she mounted the tower. The wide black skirt decorated with symbols of Hadron was neatly folded and placed on top of her basket.

Her efforts were more successful than she expected. She had not anticipated being able to do more than scatter her missiles at random.

As a child, she had always failed miserably at games involving throwing stones at targets. She must, she thought, have improved with age, for several pots landed close to the standards that she had been told were important. They broke easily, often on impact with a shield or helmet, and they caused consternation.

Unsteady soldiers were disarmed and killed or captured before they regained their senses. The prisoner pens began to fill. The opposing force quickly realised that objects flung from the tower were unhealthy and they moved away out of range.

Lord Parandour ordered cart and tower to be driven nearer. Tammina clung tighter to the flimsy rail around the platform and called out as she flung her pots. What she called was not clear, but those who heard believed that she was cursing the enemy. They charged forward ahead of the tower, weakened foes were easier prey.

Despite her pots and her curses, the fighting was fierce and victory was not achieved until Lord Telmarr was taken prisoner. A few fought on to the death, but most surrendered or took flight.

Lord Parandour was delighted, but he did not waste time congratulating his Witch. He left the skirmishes to the direction of his High Commander and went to parley with his prisoner.

Tammina was left to watch the final stages of the battle. It was not pleasant and it came close. One soldier, determined to make his mark, attacked the tower. He was quickly overpowered, but not before he had charged the cart and caused the tower to sway alarmingly.

She searched for Lord Parandour and could not see him. Lacking instructions and having thrown all her missiles, she decided to quit her post.

The descent was worse than the climb. The ladder had been hurriedly made and the rungs were not of similar size. She was obliged to look down several times to see where to put her feet. The ground seemed far away and it was hard not to consider the irony of the situation.

If she fell, she knew that she could not fly.

Chapter 16

She walked away from the fighting, but she did not escape its consequences.

Tomar Shean called her to help tend the injured. She was tired and dispirited. She had hoped to prevent bloodshed, but she had been a part of it. She answered sharply, declaring that she was not a Healer; but a Witch.

He neither smiled nor frowned, but said simply, "Come then and work spells, for there are many in great pain. Can you ignore their cries?"

She could not, and she remembered how he had come when he was needed.

"I must change my clothes and fetch another basket," she said. "I will come back."

She did so and was glad, for there were many in need of help. When at last she returned to her tent and crawled in, she fell asleep without removing even her boots. She slept deeply and did not dream, and in the morning her conscience was quiet – and before long she was busy again.

Lord Parandour did not send for her, but Master Vearle came to her tent before she had finished breakfast. He wanted to talk about the river.

He had considered her vision, spoken to his lord and walked with him to the round tower. His ideas had been approved, but no work had been started.

Much to his disgust, Lord Parandour had insisted that the Witch be consulted. Also, she must cast a spell on the completed structure, for it was her vision; but she would need time.

It appeared that witchcraft needed planning, and she was not cooperative if she was not given plenty of notice. It was therefore preferable that she be informed from the start and updated at every stage of the project.

The engineer had been further annoyed when told that he must not bother her until after the battle with Telmarr, but he did not dare to disobey. He had sought her as soon as the hostilities were over, but he had not found her and had been obliged to wait until the following morning.

He took care to hide his impatience as he gave the reason for his call, but when she agreed to accompany him only after she had done her washing, his patience was at an end.

"Women!" he exclaimed as she disappeared with various garments over her arm. "Witch, Seer or charlatan, she is just as aggravating as any other of her sex!"

The guard who had remained behind, grinned.

"Be grateful," he said and indicated his fellow guard. "He joined the army to escape from troublesome females, and is now ordered to follow one from morning to night!"

Master Vearle did not want details, but they were given regardless. He learnt that she was not like other women; she made few demands, but she did wander. She gathered plants and knew how to use them. The Healers respected her knowledge and accepted her help. She had tended the wounded until late and had now gone to wash her bloodstained clothes.

"It is strange." The guard became unusually philosophical. "None will touch the Witch; not when she is dressed in black and sitting in her carriage. They are afraid, and she does not welcome contact; but if you are hurt, and she touches you – that is different. A few days ago I fell and cut my hand on a broken branch. She washed and bound it for me. She bade me see a Healer, but it did not trouble me and I did not see a need. I remember her touch, though; gentle as a summer breeze."

The engineer was happy that she was considered undemanding and was also cheered to hear that she had worked most of the previous day and had had little sleep. He expected that his discussion with her would be a simple matter. He would tell her what he planned to do and she, being tired, would ask no questions.

It was not as easy as he had hoped. He began, in simple terms, to describe what he intended to do and was interrupted – very determinedly interrupted.

"Lord Parandour wishes me to curse the new flow, I understand, so that the northerners, who are considered primitive, will be afraid to cross?"

"Yes, when all is completed," he answered comfortably.

"No, no. That will not do. They will be watching. Blocking one path and forcing water to take another is not magic, and though a wider stream will certainly be harder to cross, they will not fear it. To be effective my curse must be dramatic."

She told him what she wanted.

The upper stream must be temporarily blocked, a ditch dug along the line of its path and a wall built on the south side. That work need not be concealed. Work on the damning of the other streams must be done as secretly as possible. The new channels must be dug, but not connected, and blocks built, but not set in place until the last moment. She would stand on the wall – a low wall would be quite adequate – and call the waters. Only at her call would they remove the block on the higher stream and allow the water to flow back into the deepened ditch. One by one, as she chanted her curse, they would open the new channels and dam the streams. The Aishe and its tributary would be one river again.

That, she declared, would be suitably dramatic.

He regarded her with dismay, unhappily aware that his men had drawn closer and were listening avidly.

She had not yet finished. She frowned.

"We must think how to keep the work hidden, and it must be done quickly. Full moon is the best time for curses and the next one is in about three weeks. Can it be done in that time?"

There was silence. Master Vearle had bitten back his first unflattering and impolite retort and was searching for more suitable words when someone laughed.

"You are the Witch," he said. "We are mere men. We must cut wood and stone with tools. We cannot build a wall with a wave of our hands!"

"Nor can I!" she said and gestured as if to prove it. "Do you think witchcraft requires no effort, no planning, no work? Have you not read how the Lord of Darkness laboured before he made his attack on Erion? He did not produce the scaly giants, the six-legged fire-breathers and the insatiable beasts in a fleeting moment. He bred them and he planned the destruction that they would bring – the giants to destroy the buildings, the fire-breathers to burn and the beasts to eat every green blade that sprung and every animal that stirred. And he released them in the holiest of places.

"He took time, gave thought and spent energy. Had he not, his terror would not have been so effective."

"Perhaps we should call on Namier," the engineer put in softly.

She rounded on him.

"I do not doubt that he also planned. To pull the moon from the sky would cause great disturbance among the stars, and to slice it into a thousand and one weapons would surely need energy. Much better to make a great sickle from silver-gold and have a thousand of the faithful make copies. It is written that Namier waited for the crescent moon and persuaded a cloud to hide it before he launched his attack. Only then did he show his weapon and lead forth his followers to drive the evil beings from the land."

He was impressed. He was a practical man and she had given a practical explanation; a heretical one, by many standards, but he liked it.

"The Flower of Krundel?" he asked.

"Namier gave a flower, a single plant, to the people of Krundel. It thrived in the sour soil certainly, and that he must have planned, but it did not miraculously make the whole area fertile in a single night. The people tended the plant, collected its seeds, planted them and cared for the seedlings; and when the leaves faded they dug them into the ground. They worked, and it was hard laborious work, but gradually the area became fertile again."

She did not stare at him as she spoke. Her eyes were often on the ground, searching. Eventually she selected a long thin pebble and crouched down beside one of the small streams.

With the pebble, she made a shallow channel and let the water flow into it and run into the grass. She marked another channel leading back to the parent stream, but she connected it to neither, and she stood the pebble upright at the edge of the tiny new stream just beyond the second channel. She moved aside to let all who wished see what she had done.

Satisfied that she had their attention, she stooped again and dug further, joining the two channels and, at the same time, tumbling the pebble across the flow. The tiny splash that it made as it hit the water was audible.

The men had watched without speaking and now they sighed softly as the second channel filled and a flick of her finger allowed the water to flow back into the main stream.

"That is very small scale," said someone, voicing doubt, but not derision.

She stood up. "Very small," she agreed. "We need to experiment on a larger scale," and she walked towards the cart that contained their tools.

The men looked towards their chief. He sighed again as he stared after her, and recalled Lord Parandour's expression when he had spoken of his Witch. It had puzzled him at the time; now it did not. Tired and short of sleep she might be, but she knew her own mind. She was alert, and would, he felt, be adamant.

"It seems we must experiment," he began, "but we can start by blocking the upper stream and digging a trench. I have been promised soldiers, to keep watch whilst we are working. Perhaps I can enlist some labour also. Three weeks is not long."

"No," agreed his right-hand man, "but it is not a dam that we are building. It does not have to *contain* the water. We need a blockage to redirect it. That is less stringent. If there are some leaks, they can be dealt with later – when she has worked her spell."

He laughed. "I liked her interpretation of the Visitations."

"So did I, but do not speak of it to others. Her words could be considered heresy, and you know how heretics are dealt with

– and how evidence is obtained for their trial. Keep a guard on your tongues. I will warn her to be more careful with hers. It maybe, that in Bellue, Holy Ones are not so powerful."

He did so, and she listened to his warning. She thanked him politely and, having overheard some of his men discussing how best to divert water at a moment's notice, turned the conversation to the next most urgent item, the matter of concealment. He followed her lead with resignation.

It was a week before Tammina encountered Lord Parandour again; a busy week for all save the fighting men, who did naught unless their commanders called them for drill or target practice.

Tammina felt obliged to continue caring for those she had treated immediately after the battle, for she had used her own preparations and, where they seemed successful, did not like to change. Unfortunately she had brought only a minimum and was near to running out.

In the early morning, therefore, she went searching for ingredients to make up more supplies. Her search was long for it was not easy to find what she needed in terrain that she did not know. Later she ground and mashed, diffused and distilled, mixed and potted and labelled.

After lunch, she went to the tower to observe, encourage and, where possible, assist the engineers; and after she visited her patients. She knew that in her own interest they ought not to be her priority, but they were. Only when she had checked their progress did she apply herself to planning her next appearance as a witch.

She was worried about that. So far her appearances as Witch had been very satisfactory – dramatic and seemingly magical – but though she had ideas for her curse of the waters, her experiments so far had been unsuccessful.

She could simply dance; but that seemed almost insulting to the team of engineers. She wanted to produce at least one spectacular occurrence and no obvious failures. Such events had been unnoticed when she was dancing alone on a hill on a dark night, but it would not be so when she was in clear view under a full moon.

Lord Parandour did not appreciate her tireless work. She was never accessible when he wanted to speak to her. He was obliged to seek her at the tower in the afternoon.

She came obediently when he beckoned, but he regarded her sourly as she approached. The battle had been won more easily than he had anticipated, but the negotiations had been difficult and protracted.

Despite his being a prisoner, Lord Telmarr had given little ground. He had sent despatches to the Commander of his castle at every stage of the proceedings and the replies had been as obdurate and uncompromising as the structure itself.

Agreement had finally been reached and the contract signed the previous day. It was barely acceptable – one to be mentioned with discretion rather than paraded as a triumph – and thus he was not in good spirits.

"You are elusive, Madam Witch," he greeted her. "I have sought you on several occasions, and again this morning."

"I am not available in the mornings, Lord," she answered, much to the amusement of Master Vearle who had expected her to apologise, "but I am not elusive. I come here each afternoon."

"So I am told. I have also heard something of your plans – or shall we call them instructions – for the changes to the river flow. I want to know more. What else do you plan?" It was more a demand than a question.

Tammina studied him before she answered, and she smiled slowly.

"I will not tell of my plans or methods any more than you will tell of your negotiations with Lord Telmarr. Are they now concluded?"

He assented curtly, for that much was common knowledge.

She smiled again. "But not entirely to your satisfaction."

He glared at her, but he needed to voice his frustration, and to whom better than to this woman who seemed to know everything anyway.

"No, I wanted more; but the Commander safe in the castle was not as flexible as Telmarr and strengthened his resolve. Strange, for when we eventually met him, he did not appear such a resolute man."

"He, then, was not the negotiator, though he may have been in Command of the forces. The one with the strength, and the ability to toughen her husband, was Lady Telmarr."

Tammina spoke confidently, but her statement was surmise.

Her searches had brought her into contact with several of Telmarr's people. She knew that he was well respected, as was his wife, and that they had three young sons. A woman bargaining for her children's inheritance would, she reasoned, prove tougher than the hired help, however loyal.

"Women do not negotiate!" The words burst from Lord Parandour's lips, and as soon as they did so, he realised the foolishness of the comment.

Tammina curtseyed and bent her head to hide her amusement.

"Naturally not," she agreed sweetly, "but we are keeping the men from their work. What was it, Lord, that you wished to discuss with me?"

Master Vearle took advantage of the pause that followed. He requested, and obtained, permission to leave his lord's presence and he turned swiftly away.

He was grinning broadly as he approached his men.

"We can continue," he announced cheerfully, and added more quietly, "We will not be troubled much longer by Him. He is sparring with his Witch and I'd lay a week's wage that she will be the victor."

No one took up the wager. It would be hard to prove the outcome, and they did not doubt that their chief was right. Lord Parandour's expression, as he paced up and down with the woman, was not that of a contented man. She appeared serene, but they had learnt that that did not indicate weakness. She was calm and pleasant at her most implacable.

They were not sorry to see their lord at a loss; it was comforting, for they too were wary of her. She did not look like a witch, despite the black clothes, but she had an air about her. It kept them at a distance and none dared to remark on her physical attributes. They scarcely dared to look on them.

Tammina did not speak to the men or to their chief that day. She was tired after her talk with Lord Parandour. It had not been easy to appear confident about her appearance at next full moon, and it had been all too easy to keep silent about the plans that were in such disarray.

She felt depressed and worried as she made her way back to her tent. She hoped that her visit to the injured would cheer her, but it did not. Some were recovering, some she was sure would not, but one young man had succumbed to an infection.

He had remained cheerful through the pain and shock of an amputation and had calmly discussed the prospects and difficulties of a life with only one leg. Now he lay dying, burning with fever; and she could do no more than damp his face with water as she sat beside him to wait and watch.

Before she returned to her tent, she unwound the blood stained bandages. No one would miss them now he was dead, and she might have a use for them.

She had composed a chant for her curse of the river. She recalled the verses as she walked.

Come, waters, come; called you are by Bellue's Witch.
Flood, water, flood; scour and stretch this puny ditch.
Flow, river, flow, spread your waters deep and wide,
Oh! Aishe flow true, and north and south again divide.

Come, waters, come; for Bellue's Witch doth call.
Come forth, in toss and tumble, froth and fall.
Flood, river, flood; make new and deeper way.
Dark Shades of Hadron, hold it in your sway.

A full round moon it is, that walks the sky this night
And Hadron's fire it is, that gives the water light.
The Aishe grows strong, flows full and fast towards the sea,
And all who cross, by Hadron's power accursed will be!

Not all would hear the words, even though she planned to repeat them several times. A visual effect was needed – a dark stain on the water for verse two and a flash of fire for verse three. So far none of her ideas had pleased her, but it was possible that blood would show dark in water in the moonlight.

She tried it that evening, but a length of stained bandage turned the water scarlet and it remained so no matter how she cast the light from her lamp upon it. When the colour was visible, it was red; and red would not do. Blood was not strange or mysterious, and it was all too easily obtained. A red river would not be feared.

Tired and disheartened, she lay down to sleep, but her dreams were not sweet.

Chapter 17

She made two discoveries the next day and was so excited about the possibilities that she did not even attempt to sleep until it was almost dawn.

The first was made as she searched for a particular plant and happened on some children playing by a pond. They were firing small objects into the air by blowing through hollow stems. She did not speak to them, for they ran away when they noticed her, but she picked a few of the stems out of curiosity. She was always interested in vegetation that was new to her.

Much later in the day, when she was testing mixtures of oils for flammability, she tried the samples on small pieces cut from the uniforms that were left from her previous dance. The tough woollen cloth repelled water and she hoped that it would float for long enough to light the oil.

The samples did not sink immediately, even when she stirred the water in the bowl, but she did discover one combination of oils that drew the dye out of the cloth.

She soaked a fresh piece in the mixture and squeezed out the coloured oil. That spread beautifully on the surface of the water, dark as any Shade of Hadron.

She laughed in delight and made a light-hearted attempt to shape the stain into a five-pronged fork. She was not successful and her finger became stained. The means to make the waters dark would need care.

She also needed containers for the colouring. That occupied her mind as she cleared her worktable and carried the bowl of liquid to the waste pit.

The duty guard was seated outside her tent, sufficiently awake to smile at her. Spell-mixes or whatever else was in her bowls, he was never asked to empty them. He did not accompany her, but he watched as she moved unobtrusively through the camp, avoiding late carousers, tent lines and other hazards with apparent ease. Nor did she jump at the distant howl of a wolf or the sudden, much nearer, screech of an owl as it flew overhead. She was used to night.

She returned as quietly as she had left, but he noticed that her step was lighter than it had been of late and she was smiling to herself in the darkness.

It was the flicker of a tallow candle that had made her smile; that and the memory of the hollow stems.

They would be her containers! With their ends plugged with tallow, they could be hidden amongst the growth at the side of the wall. She must make sure that all was not cleared away.

There was still much to try and to prepare, but she did nothing more that night. She bade a fair night to her guard and went to bed. She slept well and did not dream.

Master Vearle did not share her guards' opinion of the Witch. He dreaded her daily visits. It was true that she was generous in her praise for work done – provided it met with her approval – and that she was unfailingly polite. She never mocked, issued orders or raised her voice, but she did insist.

The ditch must be dug along a precise curving line and not too deep. The wall must follow it exactly, but a space must be left between the two and the vegetation in that space must not be cut down.

"That is what I saw," she told them sweetly, "and so that is how it must be."

She was willing to help with the labour, and could wield a spade and an axe to good effect though her efforts with a hammer and chisel were less impressive. He dissuaded her from too much involvement, however, for his team did not like to work beside her.

He half considered that it was because she shamed them by working without pause, but when he spoke to her, he gave them the benefit of his doubt and explained that men did not care to see women doing such heavy work.

"Their wives, I am sure," she answered with wide unbelieving eyes, "take great care that they are not seen tending their plots, or carrying water from the well, or heavy bags from the market, or logs for the fire, or baskets of washing to pound over stones in the river."

He smiled.

"Perhaps they do. I have never met their wives, so I do not know, but they do not like to see you labouring, and neither do I."

The last words were not entirely true. He had enjoyed watching her – strong, supple and more graceful than the men – swing an axe in a steady rhythm; but he did not want to lead an uneasy team.

There was danger, too. The men from the north were gathering, as expected. Groups of them stood in the trees and laughed at the narrow ditch and the low wall.

Most kept out of range of the detachment of soldiers, but one foolhardy soul ran forward and leapt first the ditch and then the wall in mockery. He was swiftly despatched and his body tossed derisively back to his starting point; but the danger was there. No one wanted to face Lord Parandour if his Witch was killed.

She accepted that her help was not welcome, but she did not cease to check on their progress, not did she allow them to alter her plan.

The soldiers would have preferred a straighter wall, it was easier to patrol, but they accepted. Their lord had based his campaign on his Witch, she had certainly assisted in the last victory and even he, according to rumour, approached her with caution; so they were unsurprised that the engineers conformed to her wishes.

The work progressed as Tammina desired and her work also progressed, though at great cost to her sleep.

There were hollow stems to be gathered and dried; tallow stoppers and coloured oils to be made; braid to be sewn in small strips to the cotton cloth, wicks to be twisted and threaded through the hollow stems, thick woollen pockets to be made and sewn to her Witch's dress to carry the pots that would hold the hot embers; and all to be done in secret.

She was weary by the time she had completed those tasks and had still to secret the prepared stems in the rushes by the wall.

She had walked by the wall many times, counting her steps. She knew it well, but did not plan to walk backwards. The top was uneven. She must place her feet carefully to avoid a fall. She would turn to call forth the waters.

They would come. She knew that. The engineers had done their part and she must do hers.

Her determination on that score worried her. Pride alone was not a worthy reason. She argued with herself.

She owed some degree of duty to Lord Parandour, for he had treated her fairly. Also there was a chance that if the raids ceased, the people would be grateful and willing to own him as their lord. Perhaps if she could persuade him to devote the same energy to managing his lands as he had to conquering them, all would prosper; and there would be peace.

There were too many uncertainties. It was hard to find a worthy reason for expending so much effort on 'witchcraft'.

She was fortunate that two days before full moon, the wind changed and brought cloud. The day was sunless and the night was dark.

Lamps and fires lit the camp in the early evening, but few were still alight at midnight. She stole through the shadows carrying her pack of stems and wearing a hood to shield her face so that if she were seen, she would not be recognised.

It was not easy to set the stems in the darkness. She knew that they blended with the reeds well enough to go unnoticed wherever they were, but she needed to find them easily so they must be placed with precision. She felt her way carefully.

She was glad to push the final stem into the soft ground for the clouds were thinning. Fortunately, she was but a few steps from the rock at the wall's end. It would not do to be seen.

Before the clouds parted and the bright moonlight bathed the land, she leapt back into a clump of bushes. Spiny things they were, with few leaves to offer shade, but they were dark against the pale surface of the rock. She crept deeper into the mass, uncomfortably reminded of her hiding place when she had fled from Jael. That at least she had known, and those bushes had been dense.

These shrubs did not offer good cover. She could see the moon, and the area of clear sky around it. She crawled towards a deeper shade, hoping to find a leafier shrub, but there was no change in the vegetation. The shadow was a cleft in the rock.

She squeezed into the narrow space and found herself in a sizable cave. She sniffed cautiously – the cave was a fine hiding place and might already be in use – but there was no animal scent, and when she explored the ground with her hands she found only rocks and damp soil. No bones, no remains, no droppings. She was safe.

She waited for the clouds to obscure the moon again before she crawled out and made her way back to the camp. There was little of the night left, but she was pleased. She did not think that the cleft was visible from the open ground, but she would check tomorrow. If it proved as hard to see as she suspected, then she had found a hiding place.

Her existing plans might not be as successful as she hoped, but when she reached the end of the wall and the last words of her curse, she could disappear! That would be a fitting finale.

It did, however, require more work. She thought ruefully of her words to Master Vearle. At the time she had been speaking part in jest, but the effort needed for this spell seemed to become ever greater.

The following afternoon she cut branches from the woods. She chose a particular tree that had large pendulous leaves. She had heard it called 'the Whispering Tree' because of the noise made by the wind in its branches. That made it eminently suitable both as a 'magic' tree and as a screen, for the trembling leaves would disguise movement.

She set the branches out at intervals along the southern side of the wall, keeping the largest ones for its end, where she most needed cover. The ground was damp and would keep the leaves fresh for a time.

She worked in daylight and the workers were naturally curious. She told them that the branches were for protection – which was true. They were cut from magic trees and would absorb her spell and protect the border.

Whether they believed or not, was not important. They would talk; and some would believe. Also, the walk by the wall enabled her to check on her stems and she was also able to snip a little of the spiny bush to make her 'disappearance' more comfortable.

She was pleased by her final inspection of the practical work and thanked the chief engineer and his team for their efforts.

He smiled at her. She was not at all frightening, he thought. She was not friendly, but she was gentle and courteous. Her patients, he had heard, did not recognise her as the Witch. When she tended them, she dressed as a Healer, behaved as a Healer and was accepted as a Healer.

At full moon, when she was expected to cast her spell, she would no doubt dress as a Witch. That decorated skirt would swirl dramatically as she walked – if she choose to walk. Perhaps she would ride – or fly. He stopped speculating; he had more important things to think about.

Nevertheless, at rise of full moon he was watching for her with as much interest as everyone else; and she did not disappoint.

She arrived in her carriage. The moonlight emphasised its decoration and the black horse that pulled it had silver moons in its mane. A five-pronged fork rose from each shaft and spearheads dangled from the reins.

Similar shapes shone silver in Tammina's long loose hair and decorated the tall pointed hat that she had fixed firmly to her head with tapes. She carried a stout black stick and, with the white cord fastened to its end, she traced circles in the air.

She planned to make the same movement every time she called the waters to come, for she would be plain to see, but her voice might not carry to those who were to damn the streams.

Her descent from the carriage was dignified, but her heavy gown and stick made the climb onto the wall something of a scramble. She was on her knees when she glared at the gathering northerners.

"I come with Hadron's power, to make this wall his own!" she shouted, and she waved her stick.

It gave her chance to move her skirts and rise to her feet. When she was upright she flung both arms to the skies and announced in ringing tones,

"I am the Witch of Bellue and I am come to change a river's course! Come, waters, come!"

She circled her stick around her head and waited.

There was a long silence. It was broken by a single laugh, but before others joined in the mockery, there was another sound. The great plank of wood that had blocked the upper stream did not move silently. The sucking gurgling complaint it made as it was pulled back drowned the grunts of those who pulled and the crudely whispered taunts of those who encouraged them.

Their cries of triumph as it finally moved were lost too, for as the water began to flow in the ditch, the watchers let out their drawn breath in a huge collective sigh and Tammina gave a shrill scream of exultation.

She turned then and began her walk along the wall, counting her steps. After four steps she halted and crouched down, beckoning the water with a crooked finger. She spoke the first lines of her curse slowly and persuasively as she sought one of the pots hidden in her skirt. The stem was easier to find and the wick was dry and caught fire at once.

She stood erect, nudging the pot and its embers into the ditch as she did so. She intended to intone the fire verse as she waved the burning stem, but she had no time. It burnt more vigorously than she had anticipated and she was obliged to fling it away. Droplets of oil, blue-flamed with the occasional spark of red, arced across the ditch. The remains of the stem glowed orange as it fell.

She moved on.

Come, waters, come; called you are by Bellue's Witch.
Flood, water, flood; scour and stretch this puny ditch.

Flow, river, flow, spread your waters deep and wide,
Oh! Aishe flow true again, and north and south divide.

Come, waters, come; for Bellue's Witch doth call.
Come forth, in toss and tumble, froth and fall.
Flood, river, flood; make new and deeper way.
Dark Shades of Hadron, hold it in your sway.

A full round moon it is, that walks the sky this night
And Hadron's fire it is, that gives the water light.
The Aishe grows strong, flows full and fast towards the
sea,
And all who cross will, by Hadron's power, accursed be!

Later, as she rested with her back against the wall of the cave, she considered all that she had read about witches. There had been much about the manner of dress, the most propitious time for the casting of spells and the gathering of ingredients, and the steps of several dances, but she could recall nothing about public curses.

Were witches supposed to show emotion; or ought they to appear calm, indifferent even?

She was annoyed with her preoccupation. Whatever the answer to the question, she could do nothing to change things now.

There was no doubt that she had shown emotion; both when the dark-stained oil had lain on the water and twisted into strange black shapes, and when her last tube of fire had neither exploded nor been extinguished by the water. It had floated and the flames had flickered on the surface.

'And Hadron's fire it is, that gives the water light,' she had shouted exultantly, her joy compounded by her timing.

The cloud that she was watching drifted across the moon before the flames died away. In near darkness she had intoned the final line, tossed her hat high into the air and had leapt down from the wall.

She had found the cave without problem and crawled in, pulling a loose branch across the small gap.

She was glad that she had taken that precaution, for a search started as soon as the moonlight revealed her lonely hat and no other trace of her. They came with torches and sticks to beat the undergrowth, but they did not crawl into the bushes.

She heard some snatches of conversation. More than one frustrated man declared the uselessness of searching for a witch. That stick had probably been a broomstick and she had flown away.

After a while the sounds ceased and the cave became very dark. She was cold, despite the breeches that she was wearing under her skirt, but she drifted into sleep.

A voice close at hand disturbed her. Alert at once, she listened intently. Someone was calling her, but softly formally.

"Mistress Farsay, can you hear me? Mistress Farsay? I have brought water and some bread."

She recognised the voice. It was Tomar. She did not fear him, but she did not answer. He was so like Jael.

"Your guards are still patrolling the wall. Unwillingly I fear." His voice remained soft, but she heard the amusement in it. "I will leave the bread by the sorrel clump, for even a witch must eat," he added.

She was angry at his presumption, but she was also thirsty and had not thought to leave water in her cave. She had also omitted to plan for her re-appearance; a serious oversight. She must not now be seen crawling out of the bushes.

She made a careful survey from behind the branch in the entrance before she even ventured to put out her head. The guards were near the round tower and a figure, Tomar she presumed, was walking briskly in the direction of the camp.

She waited until the figure was out of sight and the guards had completed their eastward patrol and were trudging away from her. Only then did she make her way to the clump of sorrel. It was at the edge of the bushes furthest from the wall

She wondered how Master Shean had known that she had marked it, but she wasted no time in speculation. She gulped down the water, pushed the container into the soft soil, seized the bread and crept round the rock.

She had never explored its eastern side. She had not considered it important. Now it was in deep shade. She cursed her lack of foresight as she crawled along, feeling her way. It was hard on her hands despite the grass, but preferable to a noisy or injurious fall.

As far as she could tell, only a few sheep occupied the land beyond the outcrop, but she sheltered in a clump of trees before she ate the bread. She rested with her back against a tree trunk and waited for dawn. This side the rock was not sheer. Perhaps it was climbable and she could re-appear on the summit. She was used to climbing.

She thought of Bellue and its rocks, its cliffs and the sound of the sea, its hillsides where she had played, and her parents. Silently she sat and cried.

Chapter 18

Tammina awoke when the birds began to sing to the new dawn. The sky was still grey, but there was light enough to see.

She was thirsty, but bodily needs must wait. There was no time to follow the tempting sound of water. She must seek a path up the incline.

She did not find a path, but there was a way up. Even from the ground, it did not look easy, but might be possible. She tied her wide skirt around her neck and made her attempt.

It was harder than she had anticipated. At one point she continued upwards only because she did not dare to make her way back down. These rocks were not like the firm black rocks of Bellue. They were pale and they crumbled. Ledges that seemed solid broke away and bushes that appeared deep-rooted rocked alarmingly at the smallest tug. At one point a large rock tumbled down when she tested it. She clung to her handholds in terror until the sounds of its fall ceased. Only then did she try, even more cautiously, to find another foothold.

She was greatly relieved to reach firm ground at the top of the cliff.

She stared down. The rock fall had obliterated all traces of her ascent and there was no obvious route downwards. She put on her skirt and searched quickly for a suitable place to stage her re-appearance – as a silhouette against the rising sun.

She had no need for haste. She was obliged to move several times before she was noticed, and it was not by either of her guards. Master Vearle had risen early to inspect his team's work and, finding no serious flaws, had looked up at the golden sky.

Lord Parandour was angry. He had been angry when he lay down and though he had slept, he woke early and his anger was unabated.

It had been a successful night. The Witch had put on a fine performance and his engineers had changed the course of the Aishe.

He had watched with his son and the high-ranking Army Chiefs from the top of the round tower. Lord Telmarr had offered and it had seemed churlish to refuse, but it was impossible to accept the vantage point without accepting the company of the Lord, who, though recently bested in battle, acted as host – for such he was.

In addition to that aggravation, the man had also asked questions, and despite his skilfully evasive answers, Lord Parandour had felt exposed and humiliated.

Telmarr, he was sure, realised that his Witch, though supposedly in thrall, did as she pleased and did not tell her lord either what she intended to do, or how she intended to do it.

The questions had ceased long before she had reached the end of the wall, but then the wretched woman had disappeared and Telmarr had commented blandly that she had perhaps flown north.

The remark did not improve his temper.

He had ordered a search that lasted hours and produced nothing. In a fury, he had ordered her guards to patrol the wall until she was found. Only then had he retired to his bed.

Now he knew that she had been discovered perched on a cliff in need of assistance, and was annoyed that he had deemed it beneath his dignity to go and watch the rescue, for it was taking an inordinate amount of time. He was curious as to why, and feared that no one whom he would care to ask would be able to satisfy his curiosity.

He was wrong. People of all ranks went to watch. One was his son, and it was he who came rushing in to announce the successful descent of the Witch. He was accompanied by several of the High Command and also, to his father's disgust, by Lord Telmarr.

Lord Parandour heard, in more detail than was strictly necessary, how four climbers had attempted to scale the cliff and the fifth only managed to reach the top because he was aided by a rope. The Witch had drawn it up by a cord attached to an arrow fired by one of the best archers.

Roddori paused for breath.

"They lowered her in a harness," he began, and continued with a trace of disappointment, "but she was wearing breeches beneath her skirt so there was no improper exposure."

Lord Parandour interrupted before his son commented further. He had long realised that his Witch's legs would be worth the viewing if anyone was ever given the opportunity, but he did not want that opinion voiced.

"Where is she now?" he demanded.

No one answered, for no one knew. Roddori broke the strained silence, offering the possibility that she was having breakfast, for someone had provided food.

"Breakfast is, naturally, important," commented Lord Parandour heavily, and another, more profound, silence followed.

There was an audible sigh of relief when a servant entered and announced that the Witch had come as summoned.

Tammina knew that she had kept her lord waiting, but she had not anticipated so many others. Determined not to be overwhelmed by their presence, she lifted her chin a fraction higher as she walked in and she did not wait to be called closer. She came close enough to touch her lord before she curtseyed and greeted him.

"You sent for me, Lord?"

"Hours ago. Where have you been?"

"I ate, Lord, for food was provided and I did not wish to offend, and I bathed and changed my clothes, for I was not in a fit state to come before you."

Lord Parandour glared at her. "And last night? Where were you then?"

Tammina feigned surprise. "Why Lord, it was full moon. I was laying a curse on the waters of the Aishe and on all who attempted to cross them."

She realised that her answer, though meekly delivered, was too bold.

"It did not go as well as I had hoped," she added hurriedly, "so I disappeared after the final words, for that strengthens the curse. Alas, I had not planned that adequately either, and was obliged to reappear in a most inconvenient place. I am truly sorry for that."

"There is no need to be sorry," put in Roddori impulsively. "Last night's effects were spectacular and your reappearance on top of that high rock has everyone thinking that you flew there!"

"Did you fly?" asked his father gravely.

Tammina shook her head. "No, Lord," she answered. "I have never attempted flight. It requires a great deal of energy and is difficult to control."

She was pleased that he was no longer angry and, though it made her feel guilty, she rather enjoyed playing this game with him.

"And invisibility?" he queried with studious interest.

"That, too, requires energy, but not as much and it is easier to control. A sudden loss of power is not dangerous unless one has been so careless as to drift into the middle of a solid object."

Lord Parandour noted several bemused expressions on the faces of his companions. Lord Telmarr's puzzlement gave him particular satisfaction.

"And were you careless, drifting upwards as you did?" he asked, sure that she would meet the challenge. She did, and he nodded gravely as she answered.

She had indeed been careless, for she was not experienced in invisibility. Drifting was a known hazard caused by loss of concentration. She had foolishly allowed herself to think of the river in its new bed, and had immediately been able to see it from above. It was, she owned, a splendid sight; but it had cost.

She did not know how to unite her mind with her invisible body and had been obliged to draw her body up to her mind. Frightened by the experience, she had reappeared on the nearest ground – the rock from which she could not descend without help.

She apologised for the trouble she had caused, but she was sure that her disappearance would have strengthened the curse.

"I am sure you are right, but I own that I considered your curse strong enough." Lord Parandour inclined his head in appreciation. "I ordered a search in case you had flown north. Had you done so, I would have followed. I am not done with you yet."

He paused, and added more gently, "Did you sleep last night?"

Tammina admitted that she had slept but little and was immediately dismissed with an order to rest.

She walked slowly back to her tent. The exchange had filled her with delight, but she was ashamed of her elation and the words 'I have not done with you yet' added to her concern.

Tomar was standing in her path. She did not want to speak to him though she owed him thanks. It had been easy to thank Master Vearle for his consideration and for the fine breakfast that he had provided. All was done openly.

Master Shean, however, had made his gift in secret, and the coarse bread was the food of the forced labour and been saved from his own meagre rations.

Now he made it easy for her. He did not greet her, nor wait for her to greet him. He asked simply, "Did he praise you?"

"Yes," she said, and after a tiny pause, "Thank you."

He understood, but made no sign for her guards were near.

"Good, for you deserve praise. It was an impressive display. You have earned your place in Eastland's history."

She laughed without pleasure.

"History does not tell of the lowly; it writes of rulers, of battles, won or lost, and of policies, wise or foolish. It will not mention the foot soldiers or the engineers; and if I am mentioned it will be as Parandour's tool, the Witch of Bellue. None will remember my given name, or my parentage."

He bowed, and spoke softly, a whisper that she could barely hear.

"I will remember; Tammina Farsay," and he walked away.

Camp was struck two days later and the journey back to Bosron began. They were to return by a different route, following the Aishe to the ford, the River Felt to the port at its mouth and the coast roads to Bosron.

A long journey, and not only a journey; it was to be a grand parade, spread over many days, to celebrate – and display – the might of the Great Lord.

Tammina was to be a significant part of it. Her carriage was cleaned and its paintwork renewed, the horses were groomed and the harness polished, silver shapes fashioned by the smiths were hung from the shafts and Tammina had several new gowns, all black, but with varied decoration. She did not ask which of the seamstresses had been ordered or persuaded to embroider the symbols of Hadron on her skirts, but she did hear that the Holy Ones had been visited more often of late.

The injured and their carers were to follow the same route and Tammina requested that she be allowed to visit Master Shean's patients each evening when they made camp.

Her request was refused. It would not be possible. The injured were at the tail of the procession and travelled more slowly, and she was to accompany Lord Parandour on his official visits, of which there were a great many.

Her concern at the heartlessness of her apparent desertion was also dismissed. The patients knew that their Healers would change. All who had joined the army as it passed were free to return to their homes, or to stay and take their chance in Bosron. So too were those prisoners who had earned their freedom.

She had almost earned her freedom, but as she must pass through Bosron to reach her previous home, there was little point in discussing the matter.

"Do you want to return to Bellue?" asked Lord Parandour.

Tammina was startled by the question. She had thought of her homeland, and had yearned for it, but she had never considered returning. She did not answer.

He laughed at her hesitation.

"There is no lover there then; but you have possessions. Books. Old books. Would you return for those?"

"Yes." She answered immediately, though she did not know how she could return, "but I would not be allowed through the gate."

"You had a way out, and in again, once," he mused, "And books are valuable. They contain knowledge and I find knowledge useful. You have skills that will allow you to make your way in any town, but the books would help."

"I was a girl when I found a way out, Lord," she protested. "I was a child. Now I am a woman. Besides it is likely that my house has been broken into and my belongings scattered or burnt."

"When we reach the port of Felten we will pick up the latest news from all Eastland, including Bellue, and now you are famed for your powers, the state of your home there will probably be known.

"If your house has been destroyed, the books are lost; but if not -." He smiled. "Think on it."

She thought; a great deal. There was plenty of time for thought and very little for any activity that she considered worthwhile.

In the countryside, she sat in her carriage with no opportunity to investigate the interesting things that she saw, and in the towns and villages the people stared and made signs to ward off evil.

The officials whom she met when she accompanied Lord Parandour to audiences and receptions were too sophisticated to show their feelings. All were courteous, but none stayed long in her company. Even her guards were unfamiliar. Her current protectors were from the cohort that rode with Lord Parandour and his attendants, and they changed every day.

It was at Lairmouth that she finally determined to return to Bellue. The tents were erected on a cliff above the village. Bosron Bay stretched out below them to the south and east. There were rocks, neither as high nor as black as those of Bellue and there was golden sand on parts of the shore, but the sea was wide and the waves were audible.

The first evening she lay and listened, and in the morning she rose early to watch the sun rise over the sea.

It was clear of the horizon when she heard the guard's harsh challenge. It startled her, but there was no mob rushing to throw her over the cliff. There was a lone woman, a woman she remembered from the Sick House in Bosron and more recently tending those injured in the battle.

She was surprised. She had thought the hospital carts were far behind.

She ignored the guard, called a greeting and added a query.

"We have caught up. Several Commanders of the less prestigious units took the inland route from Felten. We joined them. It is shorter and passes close to the hometowns of some of the conscripts. Many have left already; I am one of the last. I go today, but first I must deliver a message from Master Shean."

The guard backed away. There was no threat to his charge and he had no desire to hear women discuss messages from men.

"Where is it?" asked Tammina, expecting a written page.

"He asked me to convey his thanks. That is all."

"His thanks?" She did not understand. He had aided her, not she him. "For what?"

"He did not say, but I presume for your help. I thank you too, for that. Had you not assisted him and tended his patients we would all have had to work harder."

She stared at Tammina and shook her head in puzzlement. "You are called Witch and you make fire and cast spells – but you are a Healer too. I do not understand how you can be both, but those you tended were grateful."

"I am not a Healer." Tammina's voice was bleak.

She felt bereft. Her former guards were not from the elite units. They had gone. Tomar Shean had gone, and all others with whom she had worked.

"I cannot be a Healer," she said bitterly. "I am not worthy."

"Worthy? What has worthiness to do with curing disease and relieving pain?"

Tammina turned and stared across the sea. She quoted her mother's long list of the attributes that a Healer needed. It began with calm and ended with tolerance and understanding.

"I do not possess those qualities," she said. "I did not have the patience to finish my apprenticeship. And I hit someone."

"Not many possess all those qualities," answered the woman with a shrug, "and most of us have been tempted to hit a patient at some time or other."

"Indeed," she said without believing.

Thinking that she had sounded curt, she added a hope for an easy journey and a pleasant homecoming.

"Do you have a spell for good things, or do you only curse?" asked the woman. "It is near three years since I was taken. My parents may have died, my youngest child will not know me and my man may have another wife."

She shrugged. She knew that there were no spells to help her. "But I will go, if only to find out."

Tammina watched as the woman walked away. Was returning simple for anyone?

In Bellue, she had no parents, no man and no children, but her family books were there, and she would go back to find them.

Chapter 19

Having decided to return to Bellue, Tammina began to consider how best she might gain entrance. There were several options.

She could simply arrive at the gates and try to persuade those on duty to admit her, or she could approach by sea. A trade boat would take her to the port or a small boat could land on one of the south coast beaches.

She knew little about the port or how it was controlled for she had had no reason to go there. She did know that the north coast was treacherous and that the dock area was the only place where ships came close, and she was sure that it would be guarded. Visitors might be welcomed, but she doubted that they would be free to wander where they chose.

The problem with both the conventional approaches was that they did not engender fear. She needed to be feared, especially by Jael. Otherwise she would be in his power; to imprison, kill, or hold for ransom.

She considered the south coast. There were safe landing places and paths up the steep cliffs in several places, but it was a busy coast.

The fishermen sailed from there at first light and returned at sunset; herders came at all hours to check their flocks on the cliff top and women and children fetched water from Bellue Heights. In daylight a strange boat would be very fortunate not to be seen and probably reported, and in darkness the passage through the rocks would be difficult to find. They were unmarked; known by local men but a danger, sometimes a fatal one, to strangers.

She decided that only a secret entry would give her any chance of a safe exit; and having decided, she did her utmost to dismiss the matter from her mind. She remembered nothing of the rocks or the cliffs that she had walked, only her desolation and the unrelenting sound of the sea. She could do nothing until she was there.

From Lairmouth they turned inland for the mouth of the river was wide and the nearest bridge was some way upstream. A watch tower on the southern bank was the only defence on this stretch of coast. The vagaries of the shore were sufficient to protect the habitable land from invaders. The seabed changed with each tide and there were patches of sinking sand that swallowed men and boats in minutes rather than hours, though from the water they appeared to be ideal landing places.

Fish were plentiful though, and the local fishermen made a good living. They noted the winds and tides and planned their sailings with care.

Inevitably there were casualties. If they were drowned, rather than buried in the sinking sand, the bodies were washed up on a large sandbank to the south. All the debris in Bosron Bay was said to come ashore there eventually.

Some of the debris was valuable so the bank was a great hunting ground for the local folk. They took what they could use or sell, and left the rest to the sea and sand.

Human remains were treated with respect. They were taken carefully ashore and buried with due ceremony in an area set aside for the purpose. It was close to the village burial ground, but not part of it.

Tammina learned of this in Lairmouth. The Lord there made much of his defences in the hope of reducing the tribute that was demanded of him, and he stressed the goodness of his people in their care for the bodies of strangers.

Lord Parandour pointed out that the defences had cost him little. They were built by nature. All he had done was to choose his inheritance wisely.

The remark was made in a serious tone and confounded not only the Lord of Lairmouth, but also several of Parandour's aides.

Tammina's expression remained impassive, even when improvements to the somewhat inadequate castle were being negotiated, but she did allow herself a nod of approval when her Lord proposed a reduction in tax for the land set aside for the burial of strangers.

Lord Parandour accepted the low bow and words of gratitude from the Lord before mentioning that the reduction ought, in fairness, to be passed on to the community that dealt so respectfully with the remains. He would tell them himself. It was but a short detour and it was fitting that he and his entourage should pay their respects to the unnamed dead.

The detour was along a track too narrow for carriages and not suited for large numbers of people. Lord Parandour picked his companions and they rode on horseback. Any others who wished to visit the burial ground were obliged to make their own way.

He did offer a narrow cart to Tammina, but she declined. Her reasons for wanting to visit were best kept secret and it was foolish to fuel speculation by accepting special treatment. She would walk.

The guard on duty was not pleased, but did not dare to take advantage of her offer to go alone.

Why, he complained later, did a Witch want to visit a burial ground? She did not desecrate anything. She was respectful, keeping a discreet distance from the ceremony that was taking place, though she had watched it. She had wandered around graves that were years old, reading the details that were carved on the markers. Crescent moons, they were – crudely carved, but recognisable.

She had spoken to an old man who was clearing the weeds. He apparently believed it a worthwhile task, for he had known of folk coming to search for someone as much as ten years after they had been lost at sea. They needed to know as much as possible about the bodies. Sex, approximate height and colour of hair could usually be determined and occasionally distinguishing marks. Some bodies were still part clothed and some had rings or other jewellery. The style and colour of clothing was always noted if it could be determined.

"Old fool had no need to tell us that," commented the guard sourly. "Bits of cloth and trimmings were hanging from many a crescent, with chains and rings sewn to them."

"Things worth money?" queried one of his hearers, and was shouted down. No one stole from the dead.

"Did the grave-tender know who she is?" asked another.

"Perhaps. I told him she was the Witch as we were leaving, but he did not seem surprised, or worried. He shook his head and said, 'Not here, she isn't. This is a good place.' And he was right. It was."

Tammina also thought it a good place. She had found what she was sure was her mother's grave. The date, the height, the hair colour were given and some additional information – broken bones including damage to the skull.

She found that strangely soothing. Mama had been killed or knocked unconscious on the rocks. Fear she must have suffered, but little pain. Death had come quickly.

There was a piece of cloth and a ring fastened to the crescent moon, but Tammina had not touched it. There was nothing distinctive about Mama's dress or her ring, and she had not wanted to display particular interest. She had looked carefully at the details on a dozen graves. Most were men and the few women or children she had marked with a quiet murmur of regret. No watchers would have thought that one was more significant than another.

She had long ago determined not to dwell on her mother's lack of burial, but it had mattered and she had almost feared to visit the burial ground. Now she was glad. She had seen a ceremony taking place there and she knew that the dead were treated with respect and buried with due rites. She was comforted.

The journey continued, but more slowly. Lord Parandour had been ruler of these lands for several years now. He wore his finest clothes and rode slowly so that his people could see his grandeur. He was welcomed. His latest victory was acclaimed and the local dignitaries were keen to entertain him. He was also petitioned.

Several days were spent in considering cases, offering opinions, making rulings and giving judgement.

Tammina was not involved in such things, but she was expected to dress in her witch's clothes. Tales of her part in the victory had travelled before them, losing little and gaining much on the way. The folk who gathered to watch their lord stayed to watch the remainder of the procession, in particular the Witch.

She was not cheered. They were quiet as she passed and many made the sign of the crescent moon, but there were no shouted threats and no missiles thrown at her carriage.

In one town, she was taken completely by surprise. She was handed a petition.

It was ill-written and on the poorest of paper. There were few signatures, but many had made their mark and the request was clear: they wanted her to stop the tide.

It was a ridiculous request, but Tammina did not find it amusing. She determined to investigate. The poor folk must be desperate to ask anything of a Witch, and they promised payment; not in advance, for they had little, but if the tide stopped salting the water they would be richer.

The village was north of the town on low-lying ground that had at one time been watered by a stream, but years ago there had been a great flood. Town and village had suffered and the flow of the river had changed. Now their stream was no more than a salty creek and they had no fresh water.

"But if the sea is still we can dig out the channel to the river and fresh water will flow again."

It was the village leader who spoke, but all the watchers, men and women, nodded enthusiastically. One of the women came forward and offered her a shawl.

"We have sheep. They need fresh water, but their meat is good and their wool is prized. It makes fine cloth, but we need water to wash the fleeces. When we have money to buy dyes, we can give you black cloth."

Tammina took the creamy brown-flecked shawl. The lace edge was delicately worked and the fabric reminded her of the fine cloth that Linnie made. She almost trembled at the memory.

"Many of the women spin and weave and work fine lace, but Greda is the best," said the leader, pride and anxiety in his voice.

"I cannot halt the tide. It needs great power to turn such a vast spread of water and I have not such power, but there may be other ways to solve the problem. Show me where the water used to come."

There was no transport, they told her, and the ground was wet; but she hitched up her skirts, took off her shoes and declared herself ready to walk.

It was a long walk. After the flood the townspeople had rebuilt and extended their wharves and now the defences against the river reached beyond the walls, to the edge of the bank on which the town was built. Further on, the river formed a small lake. Only at its head was the water certain to be fresh, and Tammina could see the start of the long pipe that supplied the town and a few village women returning with buckets.

She closed her eyes, but shutting out the sight did nothing to help.

Later she stood with Master Vearle and viewed the area from the top of one of the town's towers. He confirmed her dismal thoughts. The water must be piped – or the tide stopped.

"It is possible to put up a barrier against the tide," he said, and paused.

"But the water must go somewhere, and here it would come up the river and overrun the new channel." She finished the sentence for him.

He smiled. She was an intelligent woman, and a lovely one. The cream of the shawl round her shoulders suited her better than black, but he did not tell her that.

Instead he offered a suggestion.

"The Great Lord might be persuaded to put money into an aqueduct. The pipe is vulnerable to attack, and there is little use building a protective wall if the only water supply is a single pipe, plain to see on the outside."

She did not go first to Lord Parandour; she went to the Public Building in the town and asked to see the Town Master. Naturally he was not available, but she shamelessly used her reputation to terrify some underling into informing him that she was waiting.

He came.

The reception that evening was short, tense, and to some, surprising. Lord Parandour brought a guest whom no one knew, and the leader of the village appeared, looking rather ill at ease. Even more surprisingly, he spoke to the Witch.

Not long after he had arrived, he retired with the Town Master, Lord Parandour and various officials to a conference room. The Witch remained, sitting alone, sampling the delicacies that were on offer and surveying the room with her penetrating eyes. Her presence dampened the spirits of even the most convivial of the guests and spoiled their appetites.

Tammina watched them leave. Some bowed to her but most slipped away as unobtrusively as they were able. None spoke. When all were gone, she sat and waited. The servants, having nothing to do, stood in a silent group in the farthest corner.

Eventually someone appeared and bade them clear the tables. Less confidently he approached Tammina. He had no wish to give an order to the Witch, even if it did originate from the Great Lord of Bosron. He re-worded the message carefully. The Great Lord had been brusque.

The Witch did not seem surprised by the summons; she merely asked if Lord Parandour had returned to the camp, and when told that he had, she gave a general thanks to all who had served her, and left.

She went immediately to the camp. The great canvas structure that housed the Lord and his entourage was still so brightly lit that her guard extinguished the torch that had guided them through the town.

The Witch may have noticed, but she said nothing. She left him at the entrance and went boldly in to meet her Lord.

He was with Master Vearle and Roddori. All three were leaning over a table studying the papers that were spread on it. He straightened when she was announced and she curtsied, but she did not wait meekly by the entrance. She walked towards the table.

"You are bold, woman! Wait until you are bidden to approach!"

Tammina stopped. "I understood that you had summoned me, Lord," she said reasonably. "So I have come."

"I did indeed summon you, but that does not excuse you. Now you may come close, and see what you have done!" He indicated the table with a sweeping gesture. "I keep you to curse my enemies, not my supporters. Nor do I wish you to meddle in affairs of state. You accepted a petition, involved my engineer and had the effrontery to take your findings to the Town Master! And you terrified him!"

"I did not curse him, Lord. If he was frightened, perhaps he misunderstood the explanation of my powers, and I approached him because I thought the matter could be settled easily, without troubling you."

"You were wrong! It has troubled me greatly."

He glared at her. It had been a long day. "And that, after hours of dealing with the petty squabbles of the townspeople."

"They are not petty to the people involved," she said. She did not sound sympathetic, nor was she.

"Besides," she continued, in a tone of genuine interest, "why did you conquer them if you find their problems tedious?"

Roddori looked anxious. He had often wondered at his parent's desire for more land, but he had never dared to ask the question. For a moment he thought his father would strike her, but the raised arm fell slowly back to Lord Parandour's side.

"There are times when I ask myself that question," he replied. "I had not expected to pronounce on a quarrel between two sisters over the inheritance of a particularly ugly bowl."

"Its beauty is not the issue," she answered. "It has significance in the family."

He looked at her sharply. Her expression was calm, and he recalled that any family items of significance to her were in

Bellue. She owned nothing here. Even the clothes she wore belonged to him.

He turned to the table and again indicated the papers.

"This," he said, "is a solution, but it will cost me a great deal of money."

She came forward and saw the drawing – a fine stone aqueduct.

"How many great battles have you won, Lord?" she asked.

"Great battles?" He counted. "Seven. Yes, seven that would count as Great."

"And there is but one Victory Arch in Bosron. It commemorates the first. Here you have six arches. This was meant!" she declared triumphantly. "Each can be a memorial to one of the other battles. Carve the place and the names of the dead on its stones and you will have six Victory Arches in one construction! And it will be of use!"

Lord Parandour bent his head and beat his temples with his fists.

"Namier's Moon, woman, but you have an answer for everything!"

Roddori and Master Vearle exchanged glances and Tammina bent over the drawings and studied them.

"I am your Witch, Lord," she replied casually, her attention on the drawing. "Is that not what you expect?"

Chapter 20

Bosron greeted Lord Parandour's return with acclaim. The crowds were still a little cautious of his Witch and she did remind them that his victory was not entirely due to the courage and strength of his army or to his own abilities as a leader. Never the less the bells were rung and the streets were decked with his standard.

There were more formal celebrations, also, to which Tammina was invited. She had little choice about attending; Lord Parandour sent new clothes for her, with instructions as to when she was to wear them.

She obeyed with little enthusiasm, but was pleasantly surprised to find that some of the receptions were interesting, if not entirely enjoyable.

She did enjoy seeing Margren; a splendidly dressed and heavily pregnant Margren on the arm of her proud husband. Neither of them had any fear of her. They greeted her easily and made pleasant conversation with no intrusive questions.

"I will leave you to talk together." Verryon bowed to her. "Margren has a request for you."

Margren stared after him affectionately.

"He will go and talk to all those he must speak to, whom I do not like. Then he will come and collect me. He is so kind. I sometimes think I am in a dream."

"Does the baby not kick and awaken you?" asked Tammina with a smile.

"Yes, he – it, I ought not to assume it is a boy – kicks hard and reminds me that my time is soon. Will you come, Tammy? I would so like you to be there."

"If I am able; and at present there seems no reason why not."

"And will you bring some of the potion that you gave to Linnie? I have broad hips and I am not afraid of the pain, but Lakis is very anxious. He will stay within hearing, and I do not want him to hear if I scream. Can you remember the recipe?"

Tammina nodded. She remembered it very clearly, and her fear when she had given it to her dearest friend. Now Margren wanted it, and for what, in Tammina's view, was insufficient reason.

"Oh! And some more of my cream, please," Margren added hastily, seeing Verryon coming towards them. "He thinks that that is all that I want to ask."

Tammina was willing to sit with Margren through her labour, but she had no idea what Lord Parandour planned for her, nor did she have opportunity to ask until the following week, when he sent for her.

She was summoned to a full council meeting and it was Bralmoor who called her in.

He commended her formally for her part in the recent campaign and expressed a hope that the next full moon she would dance as witches did, and all Bosron would see the fire flow from her fingers.

"It is not obligatory for witches to dance at full moon," answered Tammina carefully. "The rites of Hadron are best performed in secret, but I will dance if that is required of me."

Trusting that none of the officials present had any deep knowledge of witchcraft, she invented a reason for not producing fire.

Fire, she declared, was used mainly to increase the potency of a curse and it required considerable power. Her power had been depleted on the campaign. She needed time to recover before attempting anything that needed fire, but could curse enemies near at hand very effectively without such an aid.

She caught Lord Parandour's eye and continued with a gentle query.

"Does Lord Parandour have many enemies in Bosron?"

Several voices hastily assured her that he had none, which was unlikely to be true, but his rapid scan of the assembled company convinced him that none were present. Only two faces showed any discomfort and he knew that both those gentlemen had been expecting a longer campaign and were now hastily paying back the monies that they had unofficially removed from his coffers.

He rewarded his Witch for her assistance.

"We will not, then, insist that you dance. Pay your homage to Hadron in your own way in private, but I am still interested in your family books. Have you thought of returning to Bellue to collect them?"

"Yes, Lord. I have thought and I will go; but Mistress Verryon has asked that I be with her when her time comes. If you permit, I will do so. After, I will go to Bellue, but I cannot enter through the gate. I must enter by other means and, once in, I will be without your protection. It may be difficult to leave again."

"We would not pay ransom for you!" Bralmoor spoke and the rest of the Council nodded vigorously.

"She knows that," commented Lord Parandour, but he did not voice his further thoughts.

She would not ask it. She would survive by her wits, or not at all, this girl for whom he cared as he would have cared for a daughter. He did not want to lose her, but she must go back. She had been forced from Bellue before, but when she walked out again – and he hoped very much that she would – it would be her own choice.

He turned to her. "You may attend Mistress Verryon, and, when you are ready, I will provide an escort for the journey to Bellue."

He smiled at her. "And a companion? Master Hallarden perhaps? He has paid you several visits, I believe."

Tammina drew a deep breath. Lord Parandour was not quite up to date with the court gossip.

On her return to Bosron, Master Hallarden's welcome and his frequent visits had cheered her, but their last encounter had not been enjoyable. His assumption that she had accepted him as a suitor had annoyed her, and her refusal to satisfy his curiosity had infuriated him. He had declared that she was an obstinate woman, totally lacking in sympathy or understanding and he wanted no more to do with her; and he had stamped off, in what she viewed as a childish tantrum, but had no doubt that he considered a dignified retreat.

"He has visited me, Lord," she replied, "but I do not think that he will continue to do so. He asked a great many questions and was angry when I did not answer them. Witches' ways are secret. There are books *about* witches and their rites in your library, but there are none that were written *by* witches.

"I will be grateful for your help, lord, but I do not need a companion on the journey to Bellue."

Lord Parandour did not answer that. He dismissed her without comment, but he was disappointed. He had hoped that a handsome young suitor would ensure her return and the musician had seemed keen, but he wasted no sympathy on the man. There was time to consider others.

There was time, but there were no obvious alternatives. Master Hallarden had ample consolation, but the Witch had few callers other than her patients.

She worked alone and visited the castle often. She made up several flasks of the preparation that had helped Linnie and her stocks of cream grew larger. So too did the records of her experiments. She was always honest about the potions that she offered, but those who sought her help were desperate and most were willing to try anything to relieve their various woes.

Margren grew larger, Commander Verryon became more anxious and Lady Cumbler came to visit.

Margren welcomed her. She wanted Tammina at her side during her labour, and hoped that her sister-in-law would sit with and support her brother at that time.

Lady Cumbler did not approve and Margren's gentle reminder that Tammina had been her friend since childhood had no effect on her opinion. The Witch was not a proper person to attend a confinement.

Lady Cumbler tackled her brother, but found that not only had he no objection to the Witch's presence, he welcomed it. Margren's twisted leg might cause problems in labour and the Witch would bring preparations that could ease the pain.

He called her Witch, because everyone called her that, but he had encountered so-called witches before. Most had been old, crotchety and ill natured. The younger ones had belonged to covens, groups of women who met and amused themselves with 'rites' much as their men folk amused themselves with throwing dice and drinking ale. He doubted that any had had contact with the Shades of Hadron.

The Witch of Bellue was different. She was intelligent. Had she not been so quick-witted, both she and Margren would have met an untimely and unpleasant end and he would be living in a tent again, laying siege to Bellue.

"You spoke with her once, I recall. Did you not find her sympathetic?" he asked.

"She had a way, I will allow that," admitted his sister reluctantly, "but since that meeting she has changed. I saw her in her black carriage, dressed in a gown covered with symbols of Hadron; and I have heard much about the strange things that she has done. How can you allow your wife to use anything that she has made?"

She enlarged on the subject for some time, but Verryon was not persuaded by her arguments. He was gentle, but adamant. If Margren wanted her, she would be there.

Lady Cumbler visited her sister. That lady was not nearly as polite as her brother had been.

She laughed.

"You are worried that association with the Witch, however distant, will lower your social standing," she declared candidly. "But you will not ban her from Margren's side. That cream she makes for Margren is very good. I do not know if Lakis has used any of her creams or lotions, but I have. And I would wager that half the castle has. There are so many little things that are not serious enough to warrant a visit to a Healer. And she listens. Margren gave me a jar of her cream one time when I had a rash, just like the ones that poor little Lily has, and that worked. And the following week she came round to see Lily. The cream was too strong for a child, she said, and – -".

It was at least a half hour before Lady Cumbler was able to interrupt her sister and take her leave. She had learned much about the various minor ailments of her nieces and nephews and had reluctantly accepted that she could do nothing to prevent the Witch being present at the birth of her brother's child.

Later, she admitted, but only to herself, that the woman had conducted herself in an exemplary manner. She had soothed and comforted her friend and allowed others to take their proper role.

The senior birthing woman had made the joyous announcement – a son, and he was perfect. The Witch had seen the child, as she had done, but she had not spoken. She had spoken only when Margren insisted that Lakis be brought to see his son, rather than the babe taken to his father.

"It is the tradition in Bellue that the mother shows her child to its father," she had explained. "Please allow her that, she is far from home. Lady Cumbler, will you tell your brother and bring him. He will be anxious still."

He was. He had not heard his wife cry out and feared that she was dead. He did not need leading to her; he rushed ahead faster than Lady Cumbler considered appropriate. She followed at a more dignified pace.

He was holding his son, when she arrived, his eyes full of love and joy.

The Witch was by the door, her basket on her arm, her face reflecting the happiness of the scene she viewed. She stood aside, to allow Lady Cumbler to pass and slipped away without another word.

Chapter 21

Margren's son was a month old when Tammina sought an audience with Lord Parandour. He received her after a meeting of the Council. Not all approved of his use of a Witch, but it was easier to include all, than to pick and choose and consider the implications of his choice.

She was called in, greeted briefly and asked to state the reason for her request.

"I am ready to leave for Bellue whenever you wish, Lord," she replied, "but my choice would be to appear in the village exactly one year after I was forced to leave. I will need, however, to arrive in the area a few days before that time, in order to plan my entry."

Lord Parandour nodded. He approved of her choice of date.

"Sendier owns a small estate on the Bay coast of the peninsula. He is rarely there, but I expect that the house is staffed. Perhaps he will permit you to stay there. It will offer greater comfort than a tent."

He turned to one of the Council members.

"You know him. Is it likely that he will allow the Witch to stay?"

The answer was murmured discreetly, but certain words were audible.

Sendier, it seemed, was a member of the Brotherhood of the Flower. Tammina had never heard of it, but she saw Lord Parandour frown and assumed that it was one of the stricter sects within the church.

It did not appear to ban its members from gambling, however, or from accepting bribes, for she caught the words 'bad luck', 'persuaded' and 'small sum', and Lord Parandour's frown disappeared.

"I will discuss the matter with him," he pronounced confidently, "and make enquiries as to the time that the journey will take. When I have answers, we will talk again. If that is all, you may leave."

It was not, but Tammina left. She did not want to raise the topic of a 'companion', but she did wish to know if it was still considered necessary; and if it were, she hoped that Lord Parandour was aware of the situation regarding Master Hallarden.

That gentleman was far too good-natured to remain angry for long. He had long since apologised and they were no longer at odds, but he had ceased to visit her. Several attractive young ladies were currently seeking his company and he appeared to be enjoying his return to the role of the pursued. He would certainly not wish to be her designated companion on the journey to Bellue.

Lord Parandour was well aware of that and it grieved him. Master Hallarden was not nearly as intelligent as his Witch, but many women were cleverer than their husbands and he had hoped that she would melt a little in the sun of his admiration.

She had more than fulfilled his expectations in her role as witch, and he appreciated that it had necessitated a degree of withdrawal from society, but she was too much alone.

The Songbird had told him that she had been so since her mother died, but that was not a comfort. It merely emphasised the abnormality of her life.

She would need all her wits, all her mystery, when she returned to Bellue, but that, in Lord Parandour's view, was all the more reason for her needing some distraction on the journey. A difficult task needed thought, but it did not do to dwell on it to the exclusion of all else. She needed a friend.

Unfortunately, he discovered that none whom he considered suitable were interested in taking on the role. Bellue was not a popular destination and the Witch was an object of curiosity rather than a sought after companion.

Lord Parandour turned his mind to other matters.

One of these, though not the most urgent, was the progress of plans for the aqueduct. His architect had been most enthusiastic about it, but he was in the happy position of having no less than six triumphal arches to design. Each must blend with its neighbour, but each must have its own character and distinctive decoration.

It was a great challenge, and must be a splendid structure, for people would travel leagues to see it, either to honour their dead or to satisfy their curiosity.

He was confident about its splendour, but he had never designed an aqueduct before. He, therefore, consulted frequently with the engineer.

Thus Lord Parandour renewed his contact with Master Vearle. He thought at once of his Witch, and of how he might bring up her name.

In the event, he had no need. The architect did so. When the business was done, he praised her effusively for the idea. It was strange, he declared, that one dedicated to Hadron should see a vision that was surely from Namier.

"She sees into the future," commented the engineer with a shrug. "Who knows if that belongs to Skies or Shades?"

He turned to Lord Parandour with a wry smile. "Has she had further Sights, lord, of such a dramatic nature?"

"No-o-o." The negative was drawn out as Lord Parandour considered. The man meant 'expensive', he was sure, but had been tactful in the presence of the architect.

"But then," he continued, "She is much occupied at present, with her plans to return to Bellue."

"Return!" The architect was surprised. "I had heard that she was thrown out because she was feared. Will she be allowed back in?"

"She will not knock at the gate; she will arrive in her own way, by her own powers."

Lord Parandour watched Master Vearle as he spoke and he answered the man's question before it was asked.

"She has books there, old books, written by her forebears. She wants them. And I too, I am interested in the contents. Bellue is isolated, but it is not backward. It is more enlightened and its people more educated than many large towns. Even the cripple went to school."

"Books are heavy," noted Master Vearle. "How will she bring them out?"

"I do not know. The Frelius is still young and he is foolish. She is younger, but she is much wiser; also cleverer and shrewder. I believe that she will find a way out. I would discourage her if I thought otherwise. As it is, I am providing transport and an escort for her. And, if I can find the right person, I shall also provide her with a companion."

"I see," said Master Vearle, and nodded. He saw, and understood, perfectly.

Sendier's predecessors had been traders; honest and hardworking, but also shrewd and successful. One had founded the Brotherhood of the Flower. Another had built the house on the Bay and had lived there and loved it.

Its current owner had inherited the possessions, but few of the family qualities. He did not work, cared nothing for the sea or the land and belonged to the Brotherhood only because all his family were members and the annual subscription was not large.

He did not know that the Great Lord was aware of his existence and was considerably surprised to be summoned by him.

When he realised the reason for the summons, some inherited instinct returned. He bargained. He obtained both money and a meeting with the Witch. The former was more than enough to keep his creditors at bay, but the latter, that he had hoped would enhance his social standing, was frankly disappointing.

One could not dine out on a meeting with a young woman, softly spoken, polite and neatly dressed in unspectacular grey. The meagre consolation was that she would certainly not frighten the servants.

She did, however, thwart his hope of having the channel to the jetty dredged out at someone else's expense. She agreed sweetly that Lord Parandour was full of consideration for her comfort and that the sea crossing would be shorter, but she preferred to travel on land. There was so much more to see.

It was a truthful comment. She had enjoyed seeing the countryside whilst travelling with the army, but the restrictions and her duties as Witch had reduced her pleasure.

There were no such problems on the way to Bellue and even the weather obliged. Light clouds softened the heat of the sun, the breezes were gentle and the air was clear. Coast and hills, flowers and trees, huts and castles, all were visible and Tammina rejoiced in the sights.

Lord Parandour had been generous. The carriage was well upholstered, the provisions were plentiful, one of her escorts was an excellent cook and all were polite; and, although she would have chosen to travel alone, she found Master Vearle easy company.

His only questions concerned fruit and flowers, about which he knew very little, but he knew a great deal about the road they travelled and the difficulties encountered in its construction. She found the subject interesting and his delivery amusing as well as informative.

Memories of certain aspects of her journey in the opposite direction did occur, but she did not dwell on them. She and Margren had survived.

Too soon for her liking they arrived at Sentier's house and her last evening free of thoughts and plans for her return to Bellue.

The following day she began her initial exploration and made the acquaintance of the Woodmans. All efforts to turn the conversation to the coastline, alas, failed dismally. Father and son were willing to talk to anyone, for any length of time, about trees and wood, but they knew nothing about the sea.

Its salt spray killed certain species, but others could withstand it and the change in the leaf colour was plain from the high ground to the south. From there the reach of the spray was plain to view.

Unfortunately, Tammina had no desire to climb to the high ground. The far-seeing eyes in Bellue might catch sight of her and a woman in that area would be worthy of note. She would have to view the change in the trees from below.

She spent most of the day under the trees.

Just as she remembered, they reached as far as the great wall, but she had not realised how narrow the woodland became as it approached Bellue, or how steeply the rocks tumbled to the sea.

Years ago she had made her way out of Bellue, but even if the narrow cave still existed she could only return through it from the sea edge. There were places where climbing down was possible, but she needed to find the right place for there was no easy way along the shore. Rocks and currents were treacherous for walkers, swimmers and boats. That was one reason why Bellue was near impregnable.

She was tired and dispirited when she returned to the house and Master Vearle found her poor company at dinner that evening.

He was not surprised that she went early to bed, but he was surprised that she did not set out again immediately after breakfast. Instead, she made preparations and left at mid-morning.

She must go alone, she told him, and she would not return again until she had been to Bellue and collected her belongings. She said nothing of failure, either failure to enter or failure to emerge. She spoke as if her home village was as open and free as any other.

He knew that it was not, but he could not help. He wished her well, promised to meet her on her return and watched her go with a heavy heart.

Tammina walked inland almost as far as the Woodman's house. She was not entirely sure of Lord Parandour's reasons for suggesting her return. Was he really interested in her family books? Or did he want to discover her way into Bellue?

Jael had been treacherous, but his father had been a fair ruler as far as she knew, and she had no intention of betraying her childhood home. She made certain that she was not being followed before turning towards the north coast.

She followed the cliff edge, climbing down to the sea wherever she was able, walking as far as possible in both directions and climbing up again. That way she was sure that she would not miss her target.

Progress was slow. She moved carefully. She did not want to be seen from land or sea. She was the Witch of Bellue and had a reputation to maintain. This piece of 'magic' must, she felt, appear at least as dramatic and spectacular as the others.

The success of the operation demanded it; and so too did her pride. She felt a twinge of guilt about the fault, but dismissed it firmly. This was no time for guilt. She had not sought her title; it had been given and she had used it to survive. That was all.

She did not find the cave that day. She stopped searching when the light began to fade and found a comfortable spot to sit and eat, but she sought shelter for the night. There were no caves of any size so she settled for a hollow tree. She pushed her baggage inside and crawled in after it, pulling stout sticks across the entrance. It was cramped and uncomfortable, but it was best to be safe.

The wood was not large enough to be home to bears or wild boar, but there were smaller animals that foraged in the dark and were best avoided. Some could inflict nasty bites or scratches and others were simply curious and might destroy or carry off her belongings. She could not afford to lose a single item that she carried.

The wind rose during the night. It blew from the east bringing flurries of rain; not pleasant, but it had advantages. Her movements would cause far less disturbance than the wind and there would be few ships on the heaving mass of grey water that was Bosron Bay.

It was easier to stay concealed, but conditions were not pleasant. By midday she was wet, cold and tired. She had dry shoes, but they were stowed in a bag of oiled cloth with a set of dry clothes. They were for Bellue.

She trudged along the cliff top seeking the next treacherous way down. She had found few, and none had been easy. In many places the cliffs overhung the shore just as they did on the north shore of Bellue, where her mother had met her death. The sea scoured the lower rocks and carried the fragments away, as it carried all the debris, to deposit on the sandbank where her mother's body had been found. One piece of land was eroded and another was built by the powerful tide.

Somewhere, she hoped to find a place where the overhang had collapsed; and almost within sight of Bellue's far-seeing eyes, she did. The broken rocks lay in untidy heaps below the cliff, part covered with seaweed. She could see them and the sea that broke so noisily over them.

Tammina needed food before she attempted to go further. She listened to the waves as she ate. She had often listened with pleasure to the sound of the sea, but now it was not soothing. It was as ominous as thunder.

She approached the descent of the cliff in the same way as she approached all tasks; with care and precision. She studied the rocks from above and watched and listened to the waves. Counting them helped to predict the coming of the highest and most dangerous ones. She shut her eyes and counted by sound alone. She would not be watching the sea as she climbed.

She would not be seen. Ships in the Bay were keeping well away from the rocky shore and the leaves of a tree would hide her from eastern eyes. Half of its weathered roots were exposed to the salt spray, but, perhaps because of that, its canopy was low and wide and provided good cover.

When she had planned her route, she took off her skirt and tied it with her various packages firmly to her back. Her breeches had been hastily made and were somewhat the worse for wear, but they did allow greater freedom. She took a deep breath and began her descent.

It proved less difficult than she had feared and she reached sea level without mishap. Only then did she turn to look eastward along the shore.

And there was her passage!

It showed only as a dark uneven shadow in a massive rock, but she knew that the shadow marked a cave, for at its base the water tumbled and foamed as entering waves met and fought with those that were retreating.

Her heart leapt. She rejoiced for only a moment before scolding herself for the burst of excitement.

There was a cleft in the rock, certainly, but it might not be the one she sought. She could not even see the top of the rock from where she sat. She must be calm and concentrate on the next stage.

She had need of calm, for when she edged her way to a better view and saw the high wall standing proud on the cliff top, she knew that she had found her entrance, but she could not approach it yet.

The incoming tide had reached the base of the cliffs at several points and was rising still. She had thought to wait inside the passage and choose her time of arrival in Bellue, but that was not possible. She must wait here for low tide and hope that the moon would light her way over the uneven ground.

She climbed beyond the reach of the sea and waited. One thing was certain – she had not betrayed Bellue. No army could march this way and take the fortress by surprise. The sea had already obliterated the softer shoreline that she had walked as a child. Soon this cliff would fall to its onslaught and soil and stone would tumble down.

She visualised it so clearly that she almost believed that she had seen into the future and did indeed have the 'gift' of Sight.

The night was kind to her. The moon was not bright, but it lit her way, and only a few waves lapped softly into the passage. The water was ankle deep in places, but there was no danger of its flow causing her to lose her footing.

The rocks were not kind. She was no longer a child and was obliged to stoop to avoid hitting her head and to walk sideways to squeeze her woman's body through the narrow places. There was no light and after the first knock, she made her way more slowly, feeling every surface before each step. The moon was at its height when she emerged. She was wet, cold and hungry, but she was in Bellue.

She disturbed a few sea birds as she climbed the cliff, but the sheep scarcely raised their heads as she slipped past to reach the village.

The first building startled her. It was a new house, built on the edge of the village, but further in all was familiar. Most Bellue folk worked hard in the day and slept soundly at night, so the streets were quiet and still and most of the houses in darkness.

Without a sound, she stole through the shadows to her own house.

Even in the faint light of the moon she could see that the store was not quite as she had left it, but she found her key without difficulty and entered her own home.

She lit a small fire and changed into dry clothes. She found a jar of preserved fruit, and, having eaten all its contents, she lay down to sleep.

Chapter 22

Tammina slept serenely until the first rays of the sun crept through the gaps in the wooden walls. She stared around her when she woke. It was familiar – and strange.

She had grown used to her room in the Residence. The bed there was wide and soft, the walls were covered with hangings and light came through a glazed window. Sadly she realised that even if she wiped away the dust and polished the brass decoration above the hearth, this room would not content her. She had grown away from Bellue.

She hurried to the treatment room and the books, fearing that they too would seem poor, unworthy of the risk she had taken to retrieve them.

They did not. Her heart swelled with pride in her ancestors as she took one from the shelf and turned its pages. The drawings were as fine as she remembered them, the details as clearly recorded. Old and frail as some of them were, they would be valued in Bosron.

She unbolted her front door and walked to the store. She laughed when she saw the disturbance. Animals would not have taken a fruit from the centre of the neat rows, nor would they have scattered clothes on the floor.

"Always peel the fruit. If you eat the peel, it will give you bad dreams."

She repeated aloud the warning that her mother had given when she was small, though she knew now that the bad dreams did not come in sleep.

Her voice disturbed the owls perched in the rafters and she looked up. Two owls stared down at her, but she saw no trace of the cat that had sometimes slept behind the jars of oil. It had left for a more reliable source of food.

She delved into the box searching for the carved animals. They were rougher than she remembered, but she chose three and put them in the cart.

She had pulled it outside before she came to a decision.

"You must find a new home," she said to the owls. "When I leave Bellue this time I will take what I most want and I will leave nothing behind."

She added the two jars of oil to her cart and trundled it round to her front door.

Strangely, it was one of the boys who had dared to enter the Witch's house a year ago, who noticed first the cart and then the open door. He was standing, staring with open mouth, when Tammina emerged carrying some clothes. She disliked waste and Linnie's dresses were as good as any that she could afford in Bosron.

She called 'Good morning' when she saw the lad and smiled when he raced away without answering.

He completely forgot that he was supposed to be making the boat ready for the day's fishing. Spreading the devastating news was more important.

The Witch was back!

She continued calmly packing her cart whilst the people gathered in cautious groups at the ends of the street. No one came near. There was time to arrange a section of her 'magic' inside as she carried the books one by one and laid them carefully on top of the clothes. The oiled bag she had put in first, fearing that it might survive the fire she planned and prompt the more intelligent inhabitants to consider its purpose.

Linnie was first to come close, followed by Karron with a babe in his arms and his small son sitting on his shoulders. They had wondered at the strange stories, but they did not fear her.

"Tammy." Linnie was warm in her greeting. "You are back. When did you come? *How* did you come? You look well."

"You too; and your children." Tammina smiled in her turn. "A girl or another boy?"

"A girl. We have called her Callia."

"A beautiful name," said Tammina.

It was her mother's name and she recognised the compliment. They could not call their child Tammina. That name would not be used in Bellue for many years.

"How did you get in?" Karron repeated his wife's question.

"I arrived last night, but I did not come through the gate. I have my own way. You have heard, perhaps, of my part in Lord Parandour's latest victory."

"We have heard many rumours. The Frelius utters threats against what he calls 'idle talk', but travellers bring their tales and they cannot be silenced. Some are very strange. We do not know what to believe. We have heard that the Witch of Bellue can make herself invisible, kill with a glance, stop the tide and send scarlet flames from her fingers."

"Not all is true. I have not killed anyone."

Karron stared at her, not liking her answer. She was his little cousin; she had saved Linnie and his son; she could not be a witch.

"I came to protect your house," he said moving towards the open door, "but I could not open the door."

Tammina stood in his way. "Do not go in. Only I can enter safely."

"Is it cursed?" he asked, and Linnie repeated stoutly that it was Namier who had protected the house.

"Cursed or protected, I do not know," said Tammina.

These two were the only people in all Bellue that she counted as friends. She did not want to deceive them, but she did not dare to deny her reputed powers. If she were to leave Bellue with her books, she needed to instil fear. There might be opportunity for her to slip out when, or if, the gates were opened for Parandour's tax collectors, but not with the handcart – and she had come for its contents.

A commotion in the crowd at one end of the street caught their attention and ended the conversation. There was a scuffle and raised voices.

"I *will* speak with her," they heard, and a woman broke free of restraining hands and rushed towards them.

She was not used to running and as soon as she realised that no one had followed her, she slowed to a walk and stopped before she reached them.

One eye was swollen, but she could see well enough to recognise people. She announced Tammina's full name with satisfaction and added, hesitantly and as a question, her daughter's name.

"Margren is -," Tammina hesitated before she decided how to give her news, "-as you named her."

Margen's mother showed her delight, but Karron and Linnie were puzzled.

Tammina raised her voice as she continued, "Have you not heard that the Great Lord calls Margren his Songbird? Women are encouraged to sing in Bosron and she has a fine voice. She is wed to the Commander of Bosron castle and has borne him a son. A strong, straight son."

"There were rumours, but you – you know this?" Her anxiety was pitiful.

"I know it. I was there at his birth." The answer was soft. "Her husband is a soldier, but he is gentle. He cares for Margren and he delights in his first child."

The woman stared at Tammina, amazed and uncertain. She had not expected her daughter to survive more than a day after she was tossed out of Bellue. For all that she had felt ashamed of her crippled child, she had borne her and loved her; and she had mourned as for one dead, and had not dared to believe the rumours of marriage and birth. Now she gazed at Tammina and believed; and she knew whom to thank for the happy outcome.

"May Namier bless you, Tammina Farsay, for that news," she said and walked away.

"Are you not staying?" asked Linnie, eyeing the contents of the cart with sadness.

"Not if I am allowed to leave," answered Tammina, "but I must pass through the gate. I have come for my books, but they are heavy. I cannot go back the way I came.

"You ought not to stand and talk with me," she continued. "By now the Fort will know that I am here. These," she spread an arm to indicate the wondering crowds, "may not betray you, but it is best if the guards do not see you talking to me.

"I would kiss your children, but I dare not. It would mark them," she said, the sorrow plain in her voice. "Go now, but do not think ill of me."

Karron and Linnie watched as she walked into her house. He made a move to follow, but his wife laid a hand on his arm and shook her head.

He stopped on the threshold and called out, "How can I think ill of you, cousin Tam? Without you I would have neither wife nor children."

Tammina heard and her eyes prickled with tears. They spilled over and ran down her cheeks when she heard Linnie voice the formal words of farewell.

"May Namier's sun rise on your joy and his crescent moon shield you from harm."

There was no further sound, and the door remained shut.

Tammina set the rest of the books on the table and added what remained of her store of creams to the pile. She stoked the fire, laid a trail of dry kindling and spread oil around the floor. The tears were brushed away – witches did not weep – and she picked up the second jar.

This oil did not catch nearly as easily as that from the red lovas had done, but it did burn. She remembered the hollow stem and how it had burst into flame, and she poured small quantities of oil into jars, sealing their lids with tallow and placing them at random around the floor.

She was profligate, using every jar she could find. Economy was not important. She wanted everything, including the house itself, to be destroyed.

A peep through her secret door showed her that the ember she had laid in the store was still smouldering and was satisfied. Tiny curls of smoke were rising from it and the owls were restless. Soon they would fly.

Dry-eyed and with unstained cheeks, she continued loading her cart. All must be stowed safely before the guards came from the Fort.

It was. She had shut her door and was tucking a blanket around her belongings when the crowd parted to make a way.

It was not only guards who marched through the gap. The Frelius himself was there, in his robes of state and accompanied by several of his senior advisors.

Tammina was not surprised at his coming, but she had not expected such formality. She did not waste time gazing, though. She tied the blanket down with a rope and fastened it securely before she stood erect.

She gave a curtsey. It was the custom when Frelius passed by, but he did not pass. He stopped and commanded her to rise.

"You!" he exclaimed, when she did so and he could see her face. "They were right. It is you, not some fool who broke into your house."

Jael was frightened. He knew her door had been bolted. He had sent a trusted servant to test it when he first heard the tales, and he knew there was no other access. One night, years ago, he had spent a futile hour seeking for one.

"Indeed it is I, lord; and no one has broken into my house."

She lifted the latch and opened the door a little way to demonstrate.

"How did you come?" he demanded; and one of his advisors murmured unhappily, "And why did she come?"

"Do not fear," – Tammina's reassuring tone was near to patronising – "I came by my own power. No army will follow me. As to why I have come; it is to collect some of my belongings. I have now gathered all I want and will return to Bosron as soon as I may."

She indicated the laden cart.

"Unfortunately they are too heavy to take back the way I came. I must leave by the gate."

"Perhaps I will not let you leave. If the Great Lord in Bosron wants you, he will pay for you." Frelius turned to his advisors and laughed. "We shall take *his* coin, rather than he take ours."

"He wants me," Tammina spoke calmly, but her heart was beating fast, "but he will not pay ransom and he will show his displeasure if I am held against my will."

He smiled nastily at her and laughed again. "I doubt that he was pleased with the tax and tribute that I sent him last year, but he did not send an army to claim what he considered his."

"He does not need to send an army, lord. He used my powers to increase his own influence, and now he rules from the mountains to the Bay of Bosron. Every port on the Bay is his – and pays the taxes that he sets. He could raise the tax on Bellue goods, and increase the mooring fees of every trading ship that calls in Bellue port.

"If he did so, how long before Bellue has only coarse bread, fish and its own meat to eat," she smiled as nastily as he had smiled and flicked a mocking finger at his chest, "and no new silk for your fine shirts?"

Frelius cast an anxious glance towards one of his advisors.

"Most of our trade is within the Bay," the man answered, "Our deep water fish is valued, but would not sell if it were highly taxed. There may be other markets at greater distance, but fish does not stay fresh for long without ice. And we have no ice in Bellue."

"I know that, you fool! But how would anyone distinguish between ships that trade with Bellue and ships that do not? Tell me that!"

The words and the rude delivery shocked Tammina, but the man merely bowed and neither he nor any other attempted to answer the second question.

"And you?" Frelius revelled in the silence and addressed Tammina triumphantly. "Can you tell me?"

"The Great Lord has his ways, and perhaps I know them; but why would I tell? I am *his* Witch now – you gave me – and he is powerful.

"He subdued the fierce fighters of the north, defeated the Lord Telmarr, took him and half his people prisoner and lost fewer than a hundred of his own men in the battle. And he turned the River Aishe so that its flow marks the boundary of his lands and cannot be crossed."

"By all accounts that I have heard, you did that! And you are here – my prisoner!"

One of the owls, worried by the rising smoke, swooped out of the store and flew, hooting noisily, over their heads to a nearby tree. Tammina stared at it for a while before she said softly,

"And what of my mother, lord?"

A confused silence followed her words.

"Let her go, Frelius. I do not like these tales of witchcraft and magic. Let her take her cart. She has bothered no one and taken nothing that is not hers."

It was an elderly man who spoke, but others nodded and murmured agreement. A young man with ink-stained fingers was more forthright.

"She should go at once. Whilst we are standing here no work is being done and no boats are out. What she takes is not important; none could use her things before, for none could enter her house. Perhaps the curse will be lifted if she has all she wants."

He turned towards her and asked if she had indeed taken all that she wanted.

An accountant, she thought, and answered accordingly.

"All I want is in my cart. There is no curse on the house, but it is guarded and will remain so for some time, even after I have left Bellue. Do not let anyone enter until the guardian has flown. You will know when that happens and after you may take possession of whatever is left."

"Address me, woman, not my lackeys," ordered Frelius. "*I* decide what to do, not they."

His contemptuous tone irked them, she noted, and he scratched his crotch for the third time.

She smiled inwardly at that. A year ago she knew nothing of men's complaints, but working in an army hospital had widened her experience. None had consulted her, but she had listened and learnt.

"Forgive me, lord," she apologised and curtsied deeply. "I addressed the one who asked the question, but I know that you, as the Frelius, make the decisions – and take responsibility for the consequences."

She heard rather than saw the reactions to her words for she had kept her head lowered. Nor did she raise it when she spoke again.

"What is your decision, lord?"

There was silence. Frelius had not made a decision. He had not believed the tale of her return, but here she was; as sharp-witted, insolent and knowing as ever she had been, and, most annoyingly, still as desirable.

Unfortunately, whether he left her in the village or imprisoned her in the Fort, he could not be sure of satisfying his desire, or of curbing her tongue. He had made a good decision a year ago. It was best to be rid of her.

"Go! Now and quickly; and do not return," and he bade two of his escort to accompany her and make certain that she left without delay.

Tammina was more than willing to obey, but as the men moved towards her, one taking the handle of her cart, she was obliged to move backwards, closer to Frelius. She could not resist advising him, but she did so discreetly, her voice barely audible.

"Comfrey leaves will soothe the itch, lord, but rest for the organ is essential."

She slipped swiftly into her place between her escorts and did not look back.

She said nothing to either man. She saw at once that no advice on handling a cart was needed. The leader guided it skilfully over uneven ground and up and down the slopes, and the other was behind her.

She half expected a call from Frelius and was relieved when none came. She ought not to have spoken; he had a quick temper.

Frelius was angry, but he was also frightened. The woman knew too much – she always had – and he did not know how she acquired her knowledge. He was berating himself for his fear and was about to change his orders and have her whipped, when the second owl flew out.

262

The poor creature was distressed. It did not want to leave a perch that had been its home since it hatched. It flew to the nearest tree and glared balefully at all it could see.

"You did well, lord, to be rid of her without offending. It is said that witches always take revenge, and she is surely possessed of strange powers. How else did she gain entrance to Bellue?"

Frelius acknowledged the praise of his senior advisor and he appreciated it. His praise was given as rarely as his advice was heeded.

As they returned to the Fort, the accountant took advantage of his ruler's unusually compliant frame of mind, and suggested that they take from the treasury the full amount of tax, but give some, in the presence of Lord Parandour's officers, to those wounded in his wars; in proportion to their injuries.

He was delighted when the suggestion was accepted. Frelius did not like to part with his money, even to clothe his wife and children.

Thus it was that Tammina reached the great gates of Bellue in safety. They were opened at the request of her escort.

"It is perhaps not fitting to offer Namier's blessing to a Witch," said one softly, "but any who can discomfort the Frelius as you did, has my good wishes."

"Aye," agreed the other quietly. "He is not like his father."

"No. His father was a respected ruler; he is not. He is unworthy to lead the Frelian people. We are a fine strong race."

She took the handle of her cart and thought, as she pulled it through the open gates, 'I am one of them, but there is nothing left in Bellue for me.'

She walked out with her head held high, but she felt as lonely and bereft as she had done when her mother died, and she listened with dread for the thud of the gates as they closed.

She did not turn at the dull sound, nor did she slacken her pace, though she bent her head for the ground became uneven and the cart more difficult to pull.

When she looked up again, her heart lifted. Lord Parandour's standard was visible ahead, fluttering over a coach and a group of riders. One had spurred his horse and was galloping towards her.

It was Master Vearle, and she was no longer alone.

Chapter 23

Master Vearle had not slept well for the last two nights.

When Tammina did not return for the evening meal, he had been anxious and, despite the housekeeper's assurance that she had taken food for two days and was obviously a capable and independent young woman, he had watched and waited until the early hours of the morning before settling to sleep.

The following evening the housekeeper had been concerned, and he had reassured her. Mistress Farsay had business in Bellue. She would spend the night there.

He had sounded confident, but he was not. He had awakened very early and discovered why all the rooms had balconies though they faced northeast, but he had not appreciated the magnificent sunrise. This, he knew, was the day she wanted to 'reappear' in Bellue. The way in, he suspected, would be difficult enough and, once in, even greater dangers awaited her.

He had breakfasted briefly and early and had ridden out to meet the other group from Bosron. He would return for the carriage if it were needed. He sincerely hoped that it would be.

The group was easily found, but difficult to persuade to hurry. The Honoured Ones had scarcely begun their breakfast and were in no mood to rush. Bellue could wait. It did not move and no one of any significance lived there.

He reminded them that the Witch had returned and that they had been ordered to offer her all courtesy on the journey back to Bosron. She would not be pleased if she was kept waiting and she had Lord Parandour's ear.

He felt guilty implying that the Witch was demanding and complained if she was not given due deference, but it did provide the necessary encouragement. They did not know her as he did, and they knew many people who did complain to the Great Lord about the smallest slight to their dignity.

Breaking camp was slower than he desired, but once the party was moving they travelled at a satisfying pace.

The black towers of the fort came into view sooner than he expected, but he felt no elation. They were still some distance away and even from afar they were a formidable sight. So too was the great wall that stretched across the peninsula from shore to shore.

He scanned its length, appreciating the skills of those who had built it, but fearing for the woman whose company he had so enjoyed. How had she entered unnoticed? A tunnel? He did not trust tunnels unless he had designed and built them himself.

Despite all his anxiety, he was taken aback at his reaction when he saw the small figure outside the great gate. What woman would approach Bellue gates without escort? What woman would leave alone? It was her! It must be! He spurred his horse to a gallop.

His heart had steadied by the time he reached her and, though he flung himself from his mount to stand beside her, he did not fling his arms around her. He restrained himself and merely smiled and held out a hand.

"I am so pleased to see you again," he said.

"And I to see you," she responded warmly. "It was good of you to come to meet me."

Her last words were lost in noise. Her fire had grown hot and had reached the oil jars. One exploded, then another and another. The leaping flames that caused her erstwhile neighbours to leave their houses were not visible from where they stood, but the smoke cloud showed dark against the sky.

His horse took exception to the noise and the smell of smoke and Master Vearle was obliged to calm the frightened creature and to lead it away from the gates.

Tammina was pulling her cart towards him, when he looked up again, and the Honoured Ones were approaching on foot. Coachman and grooms had refused to bring the horses nearer.

"There was no need to rush. We are never welcome, but I doubt that the gates will be opened for us yet," said one. "Something is happening."

"You, Mistress, are the Witch. Do you know what it is?" asked the other, addressing Tammina with exaggerated respect.

"I know the cause," she answered, showing nothing of her concern. She had intended to burn her own house and that seemed successful, but she did not wish to damage or destroy others.

"Now that I have repossessed the most precious of my belongings, the guardian of my house has quit its post; and in a dramatic and destructive manner. I feared that some such thing might happen and I trust that no one disregarded my warning to keep at a distance."

They watched as the plume of smoke rose and spread, blackening the sky.

"If you were anxious about folks' safety, why did you not order the 'guardian' to depart quietly?"

Tammina regarded the questioner dispassionately as she answered.

"Witches call on Hadron and summon his Shades, but neither he nor his Shades are biddable. They are unpredictable; as are Namier's responses to the prayers and the pleas of the pious."

Master Vearle appreciated the reply even if the Honoured Ones were shocked at the comparison. He regretted their questions, though. She had been grateful for his presence and her gratitude had disappeared, as had the pleasant and attractive companion with whom he had shared the outward journey.

She was the Witch again.

She also assumed an authority that he thought new. She commandeered the cart to transport her own much smaller cart and its contents, she sent a groom to fetch her escort from Sendier's house and she declared her intention of making a detour rather than returning directly to Bosron. There was a particular cove that she wished to visit. They would not wait for the tax collectors.

They started their journey before Bellue's gate was opened, but the guards on the wall had acknowledged the visitors and though the smoke still rose, it was no longer black.

She sat protectively beside her belongings in the cart and he rode alongside. They did not speak. The smile that had so delighted him was gone and when the escort appeared she declined to ride in the more comfortable carriage. For him it was a dismal journey.

They made camp within hailing distance of a sheep farm and Tammina left him in charge of her precious cargo whilst she went to speak to the inhabitants of the house. She had recovered her money from its hiding place and relished the idea of buying food again.

The area seemed familiar, but the countryside was similar to that of Bellue, and shepherd's houses were simple in structure, not easily distinguished, one from another.

She found the resident, Mistress Cobbs, more than happy to provide food in exchange for coin and equally happy to converse at length with a stranger.

She remembered the Holy Man. He had come with Gery, whom her eldest daughter had married. Her other girls were wed too, and had left, – four girls she had had before her son was born – but Jona, her youngest, surprise child, would be more than willing to guide them to Gery's place. She was fond of her sister and their three children, and she was lonely, but that would soon change. The child would be born soon.

Perhaps there would be two, she added, and gazed with pride on the girl sitting in a rocking chair preparing vegetables. She had grinned cheerfully and commented that it sometimes felt like six.

Tammina was full of concern.

"I have a cream that may ease your backache," she offered, for undoubtedly that was a problem.

Questions had followed, on price and on her experience as a healer. She cited her mother, and her place of birth. That could not be disguised but it elicited a cry of delight from Mistress Cobbs.

"Now I know who you are! I could not place you before, but now I remember. You came here years ago with your mother when my man was unwell."

She continued for some time – a combination of memories, gossip and praise. Her daughter-in- law listened indulgently. She was well used to such outpourings.

When she had opportunity, she spoke; assuming that their visitor was the one known as the Witch of Bellue and further stating that she cared not whether a remedy for backache came from Namier or Hadron. If it worked, she would be happy to use it.

"It does not come from Hadron," Tammina had declared. "It is made from fruits and leaves that grow on Erion. And it is not magic, but it may help."

Thus Tammina returned to the camp with a large joint of mutton, some fresh vegetables and a guide for the next day's journey.

The food was welcomed though it caused some surprise. They had plenty of provisions.

"Lord Parandour is generous," she answered, "but he does not know of this visit. It is my choice, and as I have money I will pay for what I can."

Jona came only to collect the promised cream. She was curious about the company, but had no chance to investigate. Tammina knew exactly where she had packed her jars. She found the one she wanted without delay, placed it in Jona's hand and sent her home.

Neither mother nor sister-in-law was disappointed at her sparse report. The latter seized the jar with hopeful thanks and the former commented that the lady – for Witch or no, she was a lady – had promised that she would see Jona safe to her sister's house, so there was no call to look at any man in that forward way that she had used the last time they went to the market at Highton.

Suitably chastened, on the following morning Jona sat meekly in the cart beside Tammina and directed the small procession along the most suitable routes. The man who rode alongside when the track allowed, took no notice of her. He directed all his attention to her companion, and she, in Jona's view, gave an excellent demonstration of how *not* to encourage a potential suitor.

She was pleased to see her sister's house and pointed it out.

"It is a new house, further inland," she explained, seeing Tamina's puzzlement at its position. "Nell and Gery built it. His parents' house was too small for them when the children came; and Nell insisted. Because," she added with childish candour, "Gery's parents are the most miserable creatures alive."

Tammina and Master Vearle discovered the truth of this statement later. Having partaken of the refreshment offered – bitter tea and a chunk of fresh baked bread – they walked along the rough path towards the coast carrying a still-warm loaf for Gery's parents.

No one else accompanied them, for the path was, as their guide had told them, not suited to carriages or carts. It was easy to follow, but it was narrow where it wound round jutting cliffs and it crossed a stream via a natural bridge of two large rocks that did not quite meet.

One more turn and the path straightened. It ran smoothly down a gentle slope to a shack near the cliff edge. Even from a distance it looked a miserable dwelling.

They were watched as they approached, but they were not welcomed, though Tammina held out the bread with a pleasant smile and announced that it was from Nell.

The man gave them a cursory glance and turned away without speaking. The woman took the loaf and sniffed it suspiciously.

"Sent with strangers, is it? Lazy as ever, that Nell. Does naught but breed."

She banged the loaf down on a wooden platter and addressed the man, "Mind, Gery is no better. All this time to dig a few cockles. Bread'll be hard by the time they're cooked."

"Aye. Always was a lazy ---- ." The man used a coarse and unflattering word to describe his son.

"We seek the cove where many years ago the Holy Man rose from the sea and walked on the water," said Tammina.

The man ignored her and the woman shrugged.

"Is that why you have come? 'Tis still there, just as it was."

Her voice was sour, the toss of her head contemptuous. "Naught changed for the better for all I did for him."

Tammina's polite response was ignored and she turned away. Master Vearle bowed before he followed and did not wait for the courtesy to be acknowledged.

He intended to lead the way down any steep parts of the path, but could not. The way was clear and Tammina started the descent without hesitation. He watched, concluded that she was well used to climbing, and followed her down.

A sturdy young man was coming towards them with a bucket in his hand. He greeted them cheerfully, but showed no curiosity as to who they were or why they had come.

Tammina told him of her desire to see the place where the Holy Man had risen from the sea.

"You are Gery?" she asked and when he nodded she continued. "We have met your family and brought bread to your parents. Will you show me where he rose and walked on the water?"

He recounted his memories enthusiastically, but with admirable brevity. His mother awaited the shellfish he had collected. He turned to go, but stopped.

"I have more in another bucket there, on a rope," – he waved an arm eastwards to where the rocks dropped sheer to sea – "for my wife, Nell. I shall pull it up on my way home, so that they know nothing of it. Do not mention it. It would upset them."

"We would not consider doing so," answered Tammina formally, and Master Vearle grinned.

"We will avoid them, if we can."

"Aye, they are best avoided. I'll get no thanks for these," – he waved the bucket – "but I'll be well thanked for those." He grinned widely and jerked his head towards the further cliff.

"I got my Nell by taking the Holy Man to Bellue. I'll bless him and Namier forever for that!"

As they watched him climb, Tammina imagined the children's welcoming cries and Nell's warm kiss. Master Vearle interpreted the grin differently. The bread had been expected and he recalled several secluded spots between the houses that Nature had clearly planned for joyous tumbles on the turf.

His thoughts were interrupted by Tammina's musing.

"It will not be here," she decided as she walked along the sand. "Too near the house. Here perhaps?"

He followed her into a small cave. She was searching for something. She clambered up the rocks and felt along high ledges. He offered to help, but she could not tell him what she sought. She would know, she said, when she found it, and she added in a tone more chilling than any he had ever heard her use,

"And I *will* find it."

She found the boat after a while but she continued to search every cleft and cranny in the cave for the valuables that she was sure he had possessed. She found nothing, and puzzled, she began to move the sand that had accumulated around the boat over the years.

Master Vearle helped and together they managed to release it and expose the woollen blanket that it had concealed. She gave an excited exclamation, but when she unfolded the blanket she stared in disbelief at its contents.

"He had nothing!" she said. "He was a fraud, but he was clever, shrewd and sly; and yet he had no treasure! All he owned in Bellue was a silver chain and a stone set in a gold pin, and here – only this."

"Perhaps he buried something," suggested Master Vearle, puzzled by her search for a dead man's money.

"No." She shook her head decisively. "No, he had nothing to bury. Who, if they had gold or precious stones, would wrap these in a blanket and hide them?"

She indicated the wooden cup and a metal bowl corroded by the salt air, but she spread out the coat with its crude embroidery.

"Whoever did this considered him a holy man," she said regretfully. "Poor fool."

"He was certainly deceitful," conceded Master Vearle, "but he may have thought that acceptable if it led folk to worship Namier."

"He killed my mother," she answered and immediately qualified the statement. "Oh, not with his own hands. He was subtle. Perhaps he intended only to discredit her, but he did not stop the crowd that flung her over the cliff. And *I* took him to her." Her voice was bitter.

He remained silent and she realised that he knew nothing of her life in Bellue. She told him a little – of Morrell's coming, of the poison spine, of what the creatures were and where they were found, of his lie and her surprise, of his preaching and its consequence.

"I thought him evil, rich and powerful, but he was not. I did not come for his money, but to find out why he had behaved as he did. And it was because he was afraid; afraid that his lie would become known and he would have to leave Bellue."

She was shaking with emotion and he put a steadying arm around her until the trembling stopped. When she looked up he kissed her gently on her forehead. She made no move, so he kissed her again, still gently, but on her lips.

Tammina was curious. Jael was the only other man who had kissed her. He had been rough. She had felt his teeth and he had bruised her head against the tree bark. This soft, questioning caress was entirely different.

Master Vearle, encouraged by her stillness, drew her closer.

Tammina felt that she ought to respond. He was not ill-looking, he was intelligent, courteous and kind; and she liked him. She tried. She moved her lips against his and lifted a hand to his shoulder. He caressed her and his kiss became more demanding.

Suddenly she pulled away, distressed.

"No. No, I cannot. It is not right!"

"I have no ties, Mistress," he said. "I am free to marry you if you will; and just now I ask no more than a kiss."

"I know that," she answered, and she spoke truly, for she knew her Lord. He would not have provided a man with commitments, as her companion.

"You are a good man. I wanted to travel alone, but I have enjoyed your company. I value your friendship. I *like* you! But," – she turned away and stared helplessly at the dark rocks – "but I cannot kiss you. I do not know why I feel as I do. I do not seem to care for men."

"You prefer a woman's touch?"

He ran his hand from her breast to her hip, his touch as light and soft as his voice.

"No. No." She faced him, frowning, as she spoke.

He smiled sadly at the puzzlement in her denial.

"No. I did not think so. You are all woman; and somewhere there is a man for you." He lifted her hand and brushed her fingers with his lips.

"Alas, I am not he," he added and walked out of the cave.

Tammina watched him go, unable to speak. Her mind and her emotions were in turmoil and it was some minutes before she could think sensibly.

There was no point in following him. If he were still there, he would wait and if he had gone, he had gone.

She turned to the pathetic collection that she had discovered. There was nothing worth taking. She had expected wealth, and would have used it to help the poor. She had never considered that Morrell himself might have been poor.

She wrapped everything in the blanket again and returned it to its hiding place. Some day it might be uncovered again, but not by Gery. His illusion must not be shattered. The cave was not washed by regular tides. There were no shellfish, so he would not come.

When she emerged from the cave, Master Vearle was watching the sea, standing so close to it that he risked salt-splashed boots. She walked towards him, but did not venture quite so near the waves. She listened to them before she spoke. It was calm and the water fell softly on the sand.

"The sea is always worth the watching. It is never still, yet each movement is different. Here in the shelter of Shyran it looks tame, but it is the same vast sea that pounds the rocks at Bellue and on stormy days can spatter the guards on the towers with spray. How puny we are in comparison."

"Are you ready to go?" he asked after a while; and she took even longer to answer.

She was not ready to go. There were many things that she wanted to say, but she did not know how to express them in words. She tried to use the sea, sending it her sorrow, her admiration and her confusion. It had been created before man and knew how to communicate without words. The waves, that she hoped had absorbed her thoughts, would return, and he was watching them.

"Yes," she said at last. "I am ready."

Chapter 24

The journey back to Bosron was uneventful. As instructed, they stopped first at the castle, and a messenger was sent to inform Lord Parandour of their arrival.

They were made welcome. The Commander himself came to meet them at the gate and Margren was overjoyed to see her friend. She was disappointed that they stayed for such a short time, but, as her husband pointed out, they had called only to ascertain the situation in the town.

She and Mistress Farsay had had time to talk; exchange news and see Braied. It was surely good that she could return to the Official Residence without danger.

Tammina agreed. The news she chose to share was soon told and although she was pleased to see Margren and her thriving child, she found small babies uninteresting unless they were sick. Also, aware that she would never return to Bellue, she wanted to discover what awaited her in Bosron; and for that she needed to speak to the Great Lord.

Her haste was unnecessary. Her room was ready, her hut in the grounds remained as she had left it, but she did not see Lord Parandour for two days. In the meantime, he had sent various people to look at the books she recovered from Bellue.

When she was summoned to his presence, she was surprised to see two of those people seated at the table; and she was amused at their place, though she hid both feelings. Despite the supposed informal nature of this meeting, they were seated furthest from Lord Parandour and the officials present were ranged at precise distances according to their importance.

She was given a single word of welcome and was invited to sit, at the lower end of the table, opposite to Lord Parandour.

"So," he began, "I know that you have brought what you valued from Bellue – and I have heard that you have destroyed all else that was yours. By fire. You are renowned for fire."

He raised an eyebrow in query, but Tammina ignored it. She did not speak until one of the less patient officials asked a direct question; and she answered as the Witch – obscurely.

"If all that was mine is destroyed, then I am glad. The Witch has left Bellue and it is fitting that no trace of her remains there. The guard on my house has left its post, now that I have taken what I wanted"

She thought of the owls, the cat and the fruit, still whole but sadly dry, no longer nutritious. They had been her guardians, and they were gone.

"I trust that it destroyed only my belongings and did not exact vengeance when it left. The Shades of Hadron are prone to anger and sometimes destroy without discrimination."

"According to the more reliable reports, no one was hurt and the fire was contained."

Lord Parandour spoke disinterestedly, but Tammina was sure that he appreciated her answer.

"It was also said that you spoke to the Frelius. Did you suggest to him that he pay only a portion of his dues to me, and give the remainder to those now in Bellue, who were injured in my service?"

This was so unexpected that she could not conceal her surprise.

"Did he do that? How very clever! It was not my suggestion and I do not know the amounts involved, but in principle I think it fair."

There were several objections to her comment, but Lord Parandour said nothing. Tammina kept her eyes on him as she continued.

"If a man should lose a limb in the service of his lord and can no longer earn his bread, is it just that he be left to starve? And if his family feed him, is it not just that the lord reduce their taxes in consideration? And is Lord Parandour not just?"

No one denied that. No one dared.

"I did speak with the Frelius," she continued. "He threatened to hold me and charge for my release. I told him that, though you might be angry if he held me, you would not pay for my release; and also that even a fine fortress such as Bellue must trade. Now, all the ports of the Bay are in Lord Parandour's control. A special charge on Bellue goods and ships that called in Bellue port could deal a telling blow."

A loud voice interrupted. "That would be difficult to enforce, and could make enemies of friends."

Tammina bowed her head to the speaker. "Indeed so, but the thought was disturbing, especially when I noted that Bellue has no silk, no flax for fine linen and no grapes for wine."

There was laughter at that and she waited until it ceased.

"The Frelius is not a subtle man, but he has a new and young accountant. Giving part of the taxes to the injured was possibly his idea."

A voice commented with sly triumph, "You seem to think it a good idea. Would you be happy if our Great Lord took some of the books that you have brought from Bellue? Would you consider that 'just'?"

"Why, yes," said Tammina. "Lord Parandour provided me with a carriage, an escort and food and shelter for my journey. He is entitled to recompense.

"I do not know what the books are worth in terms of money. Some of the oldest are very fragile. To me, they are valuable for the knowledge they contain. I do not want it to be lost."

The Healer was marginally quicker than the librarian. She most certainly did not want the knowledge to be lost, and he was aware of their worth as objects. Both appeared so anxious that Tammina realised what she possessed.

"You have prepared these remedies and used them," insisted the Healer. "They are yours."

Tammina shook her head.

"I helped my mother to prepare some when I was a child, but I have used very few. I am not a Healer. I am a Witch."

"And you have done well for me in that capacity." Lord Parandour intervened firmly. "I want more, for I want all to know that you are still in my service; but in future, though you will live as before in the Residence, you will be paid a small salary. Master Forlain will care for your books. They will be kept in the library, but will remain yours. You may decide who consults them and the faded pages will be copied at your wish.

"Will that arrangement satisfy you?"

"It will." Tammina bowed her head in acceptance and added, "I have always been treated with justice, Lord."

He noticed the slight emphasis on the pronoun and sighed inwardly. He ought not to have mentioned his unwilling gift to Bellue's injured, but he had been sure that the idea had been hers. Now she would want all those injured in his wars to be compensated, regardless of the difficulties.

Others noticed her omission of any thanks. They had expected her to be overwhelmed by his generosity, but she seemed scarcely grateful. None had time to comment however, for their Lord declared the meeting closed. He beckoned to her as he left and they spoke together, briefly but softly, before both departed.

He had allowed her to rest after the campaign, but now he wanted a witch's dance at next full moon – a spectacular display that would be reported throughout his domain.

She agreed to dance, but reminded him that spectacular displays required power. It would be hard to produce fire so soon after her visit to Bellue.

"But," she added sweetly, "I will do my best. Many tasks are difficult, but nothing would be achieved if no one attempted to tackle them."

He watched her dance, from the vantage point he had used before and he was pleased. The symbols of Hadron that she traced in the air with a flaming torch were not wondrous, but the flickers of red fire that lit the edge of her whirling skirt and ringed her head from time to time most certainly were.

"She does well," he said to his companion, "Always she does well, but how, I do not know. She will not say."

"Why should she? She is your Witch and of no use to you without mystery. She is clever and she is courageous, but that fire is no illusion summoned from the Shades. It is real and she is in danger."

"You disapprove?"

"You know that I do, lord. You waste her greatest talent. She is a Healer. She has knowledge and though she has compassion in abundance it does not prevent her from inflicting the hurt that is sometimes necessary in order to heal."

Lord Parandour sighed. She was a splendid Witch and she intrigued him. She was not afraid of his anger or his annoyance. She prickled him and a ruler needed that. He did not want her to change.

"She does not think of herself as a Healer," he noted, and sighed. "Come, she has finished dancing. She will make her fire safe before she leaves the hill, and she too will be safe. I have men on watch. She will not want to meet me, though I have no doubt that she knows that I am here."

Tomar Shean looked back before he followed, but the fire was dying and he saw nothing of Tammina, not even a shadow against the glow. He stumbled on the rough ground and envied his lord's apparent ability to see in the dark.

"The way is easier here. We can walk abreast and you can tell me what made you leave your village and return to Bosron. Were you not welcomed?"

Tomar smiled into the darkness. His family was strong and loving.

"My parents welcomed me. They believed me dead. My younger brother had taken my place and the girl who had caught my attention was promised to another. It was best to leave – and you had promised me work if I returned. I am a good butcher."

"There are butchers enough in Bosron, but I have never known a child cut from its mother's womb – and both survive. I have enquired, and they both still live. That is the skill that I want."

"I am pleased to know that they live. I had no means of finding whether our efforts had been successful. But in truth, lord, though I had heard tell of such a cut, I had not done it before. Nor would I have done it without her. She – she insisted, so I tried."

He was sure that the Great Lord turned and gave him a sympathetic smile, but whenever he tried to recall the moment all he remembered was the darkness and the voice agreeing drily that she had a way with her.

"But now you have done it once, you could do it again?"

"I would not like to. It is not as simple as cutting a bone. I cut many bones of dead animals before I cut a living being. But a woman in labour – how can one practice such a cut?"

"On rabbits!" Lord Parandour laughed. "They are plentiful. Half of Bosron lives on those poached from my country park. Enlist the Witch's aid to trap them. And you will teach others?"

Tomar, interpreting the remark correctly as more demand than question, answered diffidently that he would do his best to oblige, but the outcome of any operation was uncertain.

"I am aware of that. My first attempt at centralising medical knowledge and investigation was not successful. Was it the Leader, do you think, or the fact that you were prisoners?"

"Both. A more sympathetic person might have managed to inspire us with enthusiasm for what we were doing, but we had been torn from our homes and some of us had seen family members hurt or killed. We had no love for Bosron, its people or its lord."

There was a long silence. Tomar wondered if he had offended, but when Lord Parandour spoke again, he talked only of the school he wanted to found; its position, its leaders, its aims and its requirements.

It was not a one-sided conversation. Tomar was invited to give his views and he was willing enough. He also recounted the tale of his first meeting with the Witch and was assured that the Lead Healer would be fully occupied with administration of the Sick House and would not be involved in any way with the new venture.

"To head this School of Medicine I have chosen a Cutter and a Healer who are known and respected. They will take the salary I offer, but they will do little or nothing to attract or encourage students. They are old and set in their ways. I need young enthusiastic people to set up the school; a Cutter, for example, as talented as you are. Would you accept a post as Deputy, knowing that you would do all the work?"

Tomar was too startled to answer at once, but Lord Parandour asked again, this time asking for acceptance only in principle, with details to be discussed later. Tomar was happy to work to the best of his abilities in any capacity and he said so.

Later, still somewhat bemused, he found himself in a room in the Residence with all he needed for the night provided.

His bed was comfortable but he did not fall easily into sleep. He was tired – he had travelled with merchants and earned his bread by helping with their horses – but he was excited.

When he had been given his freedom, he had been told of the School of Medicine that Lord Parandour hoped to establish and had been encouraged to join it, but he had expected to be welcomed as a pupil – and to pay for the privilege. He had not considered the possibility of taking a leading role in its establishment.

He was also worried. The bag that contained all he owned, including his precious knives, remained in the Guard House and despite the surprising fact that Lord Parandour had remembered him, he doubted that he had impressed the individual guards, and he feared for his knives.

He dreamed of them when he finally slept; of the Witch using her magic to find them and her fire to clean them. She held them out to him, but disappeared whenever he came close enough to take them. It was not a restful night.

Breakfast did not provide relief. The food was plentiful and good, but the room was crowded and the main topic of conversation was the Witch's dance.

Everyone had watched from some vantage point or other and had opinions to voice on both the dance and the dancer. He learnt that she had returned to Bellue to rescue her books of magic and that she had caused a great fire there bringing destruction and death to the place of her birth.

That troubled him, but he said nothing and soon other tales of her wickedness were related. There were the curdies that made people sick. She had put a spell on them, because no one offered her any. She had cursed a wounded soldier, too. He had offended her and he died, though he had been recovering from his wounds.

He was tempted to correct them, but he did not wish to draw attention to himself and it was possible that Lord Parandour wanted such rumours to thrive.

A young woman stood up.

"She may be a witch, and she does have a distant manner, but I doubt that she is wicked." She wagged a finger at one of the others. "You are simply jealous because Master Hallarden still pines for her. Now I must go, and so should you. We will be late."

The last remark caused immediate consternation. All had work to do and all had talked too long. The room emptied quickly, but Tomar sat over his last drink. He had no idea what to do with his day.

A serving woman came to clear the board and he stood up, apologising for delaying her in her work. She smiled and bade him sit down again.

"All are late today, for most watched the Witch dance last night and we were serving ale until long after her fire had died. Though why they watched when they think her evil, I do not know." She shook her head in wonderment as she gathered the platters into a pile.

She realised, as she moved away, that she had spoken more critically than was wise and she turned back anxiously.

"Everyone watches," she said. "It is natural to want to know what is going on and she is strange, but I do not think her evil."

"Nor do I," said Tomar with a smile, and he too, began to collect platters.

"I am new here," he explained, "and do not know yet what to do or where to go."

He was welcome in the kitchen for his height and strength. The cooks were male, but they had tossed their aprons on the floor and left. Those who tidied, cleaned and scoured were female; young and old.

He listened to their chatter as he fetched and carried and stacked clean platters on the high shelves that were difficult for them to reach.

They talked of the Witch and her dance, but they were puzzled rather than censorious. It was not right to praise Hadron or call on the power of Shades, but the Witch made salves and potions that were good. And she did not charge.

A child's cough, a cut hand and a mother's sore legs had been healed. The old lady was now able to walk to Rest Day service. That was good.

The Witch, they concluded, was strange and mysterious, but not evil.

They were not all Bosronians. Several had come as refugees, fleeing from the fighting between their lords. Some were grateful to Lord Parandour. He had defeated the lords, taken over their soldiers and brought peace.

They were taxed, and no one ever enjoyed paying taxes, but it was better than having one's men taken to fight at planting time, or one's livestock killed and eaten by invading hordes.

Tomar slipped away before the inevitable grumbles began. As he made his way back to his room he was stopped and asked his name. The questioner was clearly pleased to hear it, for it was Tomar Shean that he sought. His presence was required at once.

Perhaps fortunately, it was not the Great Lord who awaited him, but three persons of much lower standing. One was reading, the others talking quietly. The details of his appointment were about to be discussed.

It was a satisfactory discussion as far as Tomar was concerned. The salary was more than adequate; the Healer hoped that he could recruit the Witch whose family books were of great interest, and the senior Cutter admitted that he was a figurehead, needed only to make the project acceptable to certain Lords.

Reunited with his belongings at the gate, given a guide to show him suitable lodgings in the town and an advance on his salary to enable him to pay for them, Tomar was more than content.

Chapter 25

In her dance, Tammina had used all the red lova oil that she had brought back to Bosron. She had also burnt her legs. The burns were a minor irritation compared to her dismay at finding that red and black lovas grew only in the northern regions.

Only one book mentioned them. It declared the red fruit useless and the black scarce. Both were inferior to the brown variety that was cultivated in the south. It had no thorns and gave oil that was useful for both cooking and burning. Thorned varieties were destroyed because their proximity to the brown lova weakened the stock and reduced yields.

Now she needed a substitute to make the fire that seemed expected when she danced, and she had scarcely begun to discover the oil's properties. In combination with other oils, it had extracted dye from cloth and the colour from leaves and petals. She had hoped that it would also draw the active ingredients from plants and allow her to make stronger medicines more easily.

She scolded herself for her desire to experiment. She was a Witch, and could not be a Healer. She had struck in anger and she owned a gown decorated with the symbols of Hadron. Her mother would be ashamed of her.

Despite this, she still went out at sunrise to gather leaves and fruits and made potions and healing creams as well as the face and hand creams that one day she hoped to sell.

Usually she saw only an occasional herdsman or folk gathering wood for the fire, but one morning someone startled her. She saw him as a silhouette staring into the sun with one slender hand raised to shield his eyes from the rays.

Jael!

She stepped swiftly behind the nearest tree, her heart beating uncomfortably fast. After the first shock, she realised that it could not be Jael. If ever he left Bellue it would not be to visit Bosron.

She stooped and added a few seed heads to her basket. She knew of no use for them, but the action calmed her. She was alone in an isolated place and the man had neither sack for gathering nor stick for herding animals. She had need of caution, but there was nothing to be gained by trying to hide. He must know that someone was there. Her sudden movement had not been silent.

He turned and bowed.

"Mistress Farsay," he said formally, "It is my pleasure to meet you again."

Tammina drew a deep breath. She had no fear of Tomar Shean, but she had not expected to see him here and her heart was beating fast again.

"Master Shean." She greeted him in her turn. "I thought you had returned to your home. I had not expected to see you again, certainly not in the hills around Bosron."

"I am glad that Irena managed to deliver my farewell. I did return home, and little there had changed. I had changed, though and could not settle, so I came to Bosron and am working here."

He said nothing of his work and she did not ask.

"Someone gave me your message, but I did not know her name."

She remembered the woman clearly and described her. It was Irena.

"Have you seen her since? She too was returning to her home, but she had been away a long time and was unsure of her welcome."

Tammina had forgotten her own unguarded words at that meeting, and she smiled when she learned that Master Shean had indeed visited the Healer's town and had found her happily reunited with her family.

Later she remembered, but she did not spend time regretting. It was surprising enough that Master Shean had sent a message of farewell to her. When he met his colleague again, they would not have wasted time discussing the Witch of Bellue.

She did not see him again for some weeks, but she saw Margren and her child. The boy had a cough and though Margren considered it one of those small illnesses that often troubled children, it did keep him awake and it worried her husband. Tammina would surely have something that would soothe the irritation.

Tammina looked at her friend despairingly.

"Margren, I am pleased to see you and to see Braied, but I am not a Healer. Commander Verryon will surely not want his son treated by a Witch."

"Tammy, do you think I would ever do anything without consulting Lakis? He knows that I trust you; and he also trusts you."

Margren saw that her friend still doubted. It puzzled her. She had grown confident and Tammy, who had always been quick and clever and sure, seemed uncertain.

"He knows, as I know, that you are not wicked. Oh, you have strange powers and you dance at full moon in strange clothes and you make coloured fire. You trace the symbols of Hadron, too, but what of that? They are simply shapes. Shapes cannot be wicked. They have no hearts, and evil is in the heart, not the appearance."

She stretched a hand out and touched Tammina's hand.

"There is no evil in your heart. I have known you all my life and to me you have always been kind. But for you I might well be dead. You are good; and you *are* a Healer."

Tammina turned away. She was more affected by Margren's words than she wished to show.

"I cannot be a Healer," she said sadly. "I struck someone."

"Why?" exclaimed Margren, unable to imagine her friend raising a hand against anyone.

Tammina could not bring herself to explain. "He --he--," she began, and finished, "I struck him twice."

Her shame and regret were evident, and Margren found a reason and laughed.

"You struck a man! And because he was too bold?"

She did not need a spoken answer; she knew that she was right.

"Oh, Tammy, that is not bad. I doubt that there is a woman in all Eastland who has not struck a man for that! Even I have done so. A lad came up behind me once, and put his hands on my breasts. I was washing fleeces and I remember hitting him with a particularly dirty piece of wet wool."

She laughed again at the memory and added, "I might have encouraged him had I known I could bear a straight child."

"Oh! Margren! I ought to have told you, but -," Tammina stopped. She had thought that a mother would have reassured her daughter on that point, but she could not say so.

"I am glad that you did not, for then I might still have been in Bellue. I did not come here willingly, but in Bellue I dared not sing, and here, I am taught and I am praised for my singing, and I -."

She stopped for Braied whimpered and began to cough. His nurse held him out to Tammina.

"Listen," she begged. "It is not a bad cough, it does not shake him, but it troubles him and sometimes he cannot feed."

Tammina listened and asked what remedies had been given. The answer did not please her. Honey would soothe, but was best mixed with a little oil and herbs.

She turned to her shelves and searched for the jar that she wanted.

Margren watched as some of the liquid was decanted into a bottle and her child was given a small dose from a shiny spoon. She smiled as she listened to the instructions – how much to give and when, and always with a clean spoon – and watched as a label was written out and attached firmly to the bottle's neck.

She opened a purse, took out several coins and laid them on the table. Tammina objected, but Margren shook her head.

"My husband wishes to pay you as he pays others who give him service, and that is a fair price. It is a little more than my mother gave to yours when she treated one of my brothers for a cough, but we are in Bosron now and it is more expensive than Bellue."

Margren signalled the nurse to leave and prepared to follow. She smiled warmly at her friend.

"You sound so like her, I could be a child again. I do not doubt that Braied's cough will be cured, just as Jonal's was."

Tammina did not answer. Margren had laughed at her worries. Men tried their luck, and girls agreed or struck them. It was not important. She stared at the closed door, deep in thought.

She met Tomar again the following week. This time he was close to the walls of the Residence because he did not wish to alarm her again.

It was the third morning he had risen before sunrise in the hope of meeting her. He knew little about plants though those in this area were becoming familiar. He picked a large pale green leaf with dark veins and studied it. Some small creature had nibbled several holes in it.

"Master Shean, good morning to you." Tammina greeted him without surprise, but her eyebrows lifted when she saw the leaf in his hand.

"Is that the best you can find? It is sadly damaged."

"Mistress Farsay" He bowed in greeting. "How fortunate I am to meet you, for I was curious about this leaf and you know so much about plants. This would be very attractive if it were perfect. Does it have a medicinal use?"

"Not one that I recall, but it does not grow wild in Bellue. The wealthy grow it in pots for decoration. Here it does grow wild, but is still valued for use in nosegays. I am told that young men seek a small plant and protect it. The mature leaves are then worthy to offer to a girl."

"So, only a perfect leaf is a token of true devotion, and this is of no use whatsoever," and Tomar tossed the leaf aside.

"No, it is not; but a perfect leaf does not necessarily show devotion. A girl may choose to believe so, but a leaf cannot say if the man was thinking of her when he found his plant, or if she is the only recipient of its mature leaves. Men are often faithless and deceitful."

Her voice sounded sour, even in her own ears, and Tomar looked at her in surprise.

"Women also," she corrected herself quickly. "Deceit is common to both."

"Indeed it is," he answered quietly, "but so too is truth and loyalty. There are many happy marriages."

She did not reply at once, and when she did it was with a simple affirmative, but she smiled to herself and Tomar was glad.

He had seen her smile; in triumph when the newborn child had cried, and with compassion when she tended the injured; but she had never smiled at him and he longed for the day when she smiled simply because he was there.

They walked on in silence. Her thoughts were on Linnie and Margren, whose husbands loved them and were loved in return, but her eyes were searching and some berries caught her eye.

"Oh, these are now ripe!" she exclaimed and put down her basket. She pulled the branch with a hooked stick until the dark cluster was within her reach.

"The thorns are sharp. Take care," she warned when he reached for another bunch, "but the berries are useful."

"For jellies?" he asked.

"Yes, they can be used so, but I steep them in oil and use the liquor. A few drops added to a mixture can aid recovery."

He added another cluster to her basket and questioned as to who bought her medicines.

"No one buys. I am a Witch, not a Healer, but some who are poor and desperate ask me for advice. I cannot refuse to help if I am able."

He did not pursue the subject; he could see that it troubled her. Instead he carried her basket and stopped with her to listen to the song of a bird, greeting the morning with particular joy.

Tomar waited several days before seeing Tammina again, and this time he asked if he might accompany her on other occasions, in order to learn more about plants and their uses.

She was doubtful, but he assured her that he was also learning from Healers in the Sick House and studying various recommended books. He was also furthering his skills as a Cutter by treating patients and by dissecting animals, and he lived simply.

He did not mention that he lived meagrely in order to accumulate enough to purchase a house, and a gold ring.

Tammina had rarely felt lonely on her morning forays, but she found herself looking forward to his company. That made her wary. She had not intended to encourage Master Vearle, but she must have been careless, and said or done something that had been misinterpreted. She must not make that mistake again.

Accordingly, she formed a plan; a pleasant greeting, but not a broad smile; instruction and information as the opportunity arose, but no amusing anecdotes or reminiscences; questions such as her mother had asked on their walks, but no laughter or teasing if the answer was incorrect; and *no* halts for birdsong. Inexperienced as she was in such matters, she felt sure that standing beside a man in the early morning and listening to the birds, was liable to be misinterpreted – by him or by others.

Tomar was not unduly disappointed by her strict adherence to her plan. He rejoiced in her knowledge and her ability to teach. He learnt much, and he stood alone to listen to the birds. That gave him time to digest what he had learnt before hearing more, and his mentor had chance to search without offering explanation.

Once she mentioned her mother and he asked about her death. Tammina answered calmly. The anger had gone.

"She taught you well, and you have taught yourself more. She would be proud."

He smiled thinking that the remark would please her, but it did not.

"I do not think so," she responded dully. "She would be disappointed. I have done shameful things."

"So, no doubt, had she in her youth. She would have understood."

"No!" she exclaimed vehemently, "Mama never did anything shameful! She was – "

She stopped abruptly, realising that it was foolish to claim that Mama had been perfect. No one was perfect.

"You were young when she died," he said gently. "Too young to criticise a parent."

She thought more deeply about the mother whom she had loved so much, acknowledged that she had just begun to criticise and walked ahead, ending the conversation.

Some days later he mentioned a woman who came to the Sick House. She had five children, a husband who was a sailor, and an open sore on her leg. No remedy they had tried had helped. The only alternative was to amputate the leg.

She reacted as he had expected. Amputation was surely a last resort. She had nothing to hand that could be tried, but perhaps there was something in her books. She was certain that her mother had treated difficult sores, but it had not been often and she could not remember exactly what was needed. They abandoned their walk and repaired to the library to consult her books.

She located the recipe she wanted with commendable rapidity, but it did not please her. She had some of the ingredients to hand and could find others, but the most important one she did not have. Nor did she know where to find it.

The young man who was carefully copying one of the more fragile drawings, was flattered to be consulted, but was of little help. He *thought* that the plant she wanted grew along the banks of one of the tributaries of the River Bos, but it flowered early in the year and the seed would now be scattered. Full seed heads would be small and hard to find.

Tammina thanked him and praised his drawing profusely. It was a drawing that she loved and of a flower that she knew well, and in truth, she thought it a fine copy.

As they walked away, she promised to try to find the seeds, but even if she did, they would not be at their best and the lotion would take some time to prepare.

Tomar accepted that. It was always so.

"But it need not be!" she exclaimed suddenly. "In Bellue all the Healers kept their recipes and their sources secret, but if one could make a living without the secrecy, the plants could be cultivated and harvested at the best time and made available to all for a small cost.

"I suppose," she continued thoughtfully, "that I could cultivate some plants; if Lord Parandour would permit, if I were allowed to dig up the plants and if I were given suitable ground."

She sighed. There were too many 'ifs'.

"Ask him," advised Tomar. "He is open to ideas. I fought for my Lord against Parandour and I most certainly did not wish to be taken prisoner, but it may be that a larger domain, under one Lord and at peace, will improve the lives of most of the population."

They parted company and Tammina set off at once to seek the seeds that she wanted.

As she had been warned, they were not easy to find and it was days later that she delivered a box to the Sick House. It was marked for Master Tomar Shean and fastened with an official seal.

Official seals were not often seen at the Sick House, and the parcel caused some interest.

Tomar was also surprised. He opened it in private and smiled when he saw the labelled jar and the neatly written instructions for the use of its contents.

She was dedicated, careful and thorough, he thought. He wanted her to work with him. This particular lotion might not be effective – some problems were intractable – but her presence in the School of Medicine would, he was sure, be very effective. Next time he met her, he would introduce the idea.

Chapter 26

Before he had chance to see her again, Lord Parandour summoned him.

It was an unusual summons, being late evening and dark. The messenger was a guard whose orders were to escort him to the private rooms in the Residence.

The Great Lord was waiting with his son. He looked grim, his son desperate. The Lady Drusil was in labour and had been for many hours. The child was not in a good position and all efforts to change the way it lay had failed.

"She is dying!" exclaimed Roddori. "I have listened to her screams all day and still the child is not born. My father says that you can cut her and end the misery. Will you do so? Can you do so?"

Tomar took a deep breath.

"Lord, I can cut, but I cannot be sure that the outcome will be good. She may still die, and the child with her."

Roddori gave his father a contemptuous glance.

"I can end her pain. I can kill her," he said, "and myself when she is gone," and he walked out of the room.

Tomar stared at Lord Parandour.

"I will need Mistress Farsay," he said.

The words came reluctantly. He did not want this responsibility, but he could not refuse it; he did not want to involve the woman, but with her there was a better chance of success.

"Mistress Farsay?" Lord Parandour was for a moment uncertain. "Ah! The Witch! But will she come?"

Tomar nodded. "She will come."

"At this hour she will be in her room. You will need a guide."

Some minutes later Tomar knocked loudly on her door.

"Mistress Farsay, you are needed," he called.

Instinctively the guide backed away, though everyone knew that it was useless to move away from a witch's curse.

She opened the door covered with a wrap, barefooted and with her hair untied.

"Good evening Master Shean," she said calmly. "Why I am needed?"

"Lady Drusil," he answered. "Her labour does not go well. He has asked me to cut her."

"Whom else would he ask? But he did not ask for me. I am not a Healer."

"*I* asked for you. *I* need you." He stretched out a pleading hand, but he did not touch her.

She did not take long to decide. He had come when she had called, and he had done as she had asked. She could not refuse him.

"I must dress first," she answered and shut the door.

She reappeared swiftly, clothed and shod with her hair twisted tightly into a knot. She bade the guide find a lamp for she needed to go to her workroom. He did so, but when they emerged from the house, the moon was bright and she sped away declaring that she would be faster without the lamp.

The guide followed. He cursed her roundly, but someone would pay dearly if any harm came to her, and he preferred to die in his bed.

Tomar waited. She knew her way and he did not; and he needed composure. He did not want to be breathless.

She *was* faster without the lamp, for she returned first bearing her basket. The jars within were sealed and firmly packed.

"Your knives?"

"Are waiting for me."

The guide arrived, and he stood aside to allow the man to lead them.

"I have what I need," she told him, "but I may alarm the Lady Drusil. She knows me only as Witch. And her husband. How does he feel about me?"

Tomar answered dryly that both were beyond care, but he sensed that she was still anxious.

Those round the bed had been told to expect them. They did not like it, but they stood aside and allowed a male Cutter and a Witch to approach.

Tammina saw the exhausted woman and was anxious no longer. She wanted to know what had been done already and questioned tactfully, but there was no need for caution. All were ready to tell of their efforts. They had done all that was possible.

"I have a potion that alleviates pain and will not harm the child," she measured the liquid as she spoke and began to dribble it slowly into Lady Drusil's mouth, "and Master Shean has cut a babe from its mother before. It is not easy, and may not be successful, but all else has been tried."

She talked as she tended her patient, and even Tomar found her explanation soothing.

She rubbed a cream into the swollen belly. This was the cream that she made for Commander Verryon's wife, she told them. It had the same active ingredients as the potion, but was applied to the skin. She had used it with some success on those injured in the battle at Telmarr castle. She did not know, but she hoped that it would numb the pain of the incision. Those who had never worked with a Cutter ought to stand at a distance in case their first sight of a Cutting caused nausea.

She spread a towel, placed others near to hand and called for more light before she took up a position by Lady Drusil's head.

Her preparation could not be faulted, but Tomar found it, and the presence of so many others, unnerving. He picked up his knife.

She sensed his hesitation, and she remembered her mother's oft repeated words. 'Healers must make decisions and they must take responsibility.'

She turned towards him. "Now!" she said firmly; and Tomar made the incision.

In some ways, he found it easier than before. The woman was quieter, but the child moved and caught a limb against the knife edge.

He cursed softly.

"It is but a scratch." Tammina's voice was comforting. "She is alive."

He heard a tiny cry. The highborn girl was not nearly as lusty as the peasant boy had been. It was a fleeting thought. He must mend the cut that he had made.

She helped him, leaving the care of the child to those with greater experience. She handed what was needed almost before he asked, and removed both waste and tools.

He turned to thank her, but saw only his tools neatly laid on a clean towel and the waste carefully deposited in a bin. She was taking a jar from her basket.

"To guard against infection", she announced as she spread the cream liberally on the wound, and she listed its contents. The precise method of preparation was in the third of her family books, and, no, it was not suitable for the baby's scratch. It was too strong. She would mix a little with some oil. So diluted, it would not damage tender skin.

Tomar packed his bag carefully. He felt bereft. There was none of the elation that they had shared so many months ago. She was grave, though she did have a smile for the cheerful girl holding the newborn to her ample bosom.

They were guided along a corridor and shown into a room warmed by a bright fire and furnished with comfortable seats. A servant stood ready to provide hot drink and food.

She sank gratefully into a chair and Tomar realised that he too was tired.

"Did you rise early today as usual?" he asked.

She nodded. "I had only a small stock of the potion that I used just now, so I gathered the ingredients this morning and prepared more. It is a long process."

He did not ask how she had known that it would be needed. He kept his knives clean and sharp; she replenished her stock when it ran low. The Healer who had followed them wanted to ask, but did not. She asked another question.

"The potion; it was very effective. Is the recipe in the books?"

Tammina shook her head.

"Not that precise recipe. There is one that uses similar ingredients, but it is weaker. My mother tried a different method of preparation. I helped her. I was encouraged to gather and to prepare, but I never saw her use that potion. I was present only when she dealt with minor ailments and injuries.

"She had used it at least once, for my cousin knew of it, but I found nothing written. Perhaps she had the paper with her when she died."

"I heard how she died, but why was she thought to be a witch?"

Tomar thought the question impertinent and surprised that it was answered. He did, however, listen with interest.

She spoke without emotion of the Padri who had used a lie to impress and later had maligned the woman who had healed him and knew his secret.

"I searched for her body, but found nothing. It seems that everything lost in Bosron Bay is washed onto a sandbank south of Lairmouth. She is there. I found her grave when we were returning from the campaign."

She finished as calmly as she had begun. There was no bitterness now. The vestige of a smile was given to the questioner.

"I did not mean to intrude." The anxiety was evident. "I wanted only to ask you to come when my daughter has her child. She is small, and she is worried. So am I, though I try to give her confidence. Will you come? Or give me the recipe for the potion?"

"I will come if I am able, or I will give you a small bottle ready prepared, but I have only used it in the last stages of labour. To give it earlier may harm the child. I do not know."

The woman was so profuse in her thanks that the servant ushered her out. He was respectful, but firm.

Tomar hoped that the servant would also leave, but he did not. It did not matter, for this was not the best moment to ask Mistress Farsay to work with him. She had leant back in her chair and closed her eyes.

The man enquired gently whether she desired more to drink, but there was no answer. He refilled Tomar's cup.

"The sofa will be more comfortable for the lady," he said. "I will fetch blankets, Master, and all other necessities. Lord Parandour has retired, but I have been informed that it is quite permissible for you both to stay, if you so wish."

Tomar did so wish and neither waited for an answer from the lady. She was so deeply asleep that she scarcely stirred when he lifted onto the sofa and removed her boots.

The servant returned with the blankets, followed by others bearing basins, buckets, jugs of water and a screen. They crept in, deposited their burdens and left without a word, closing the door silently behind them.

The man handed one blanket to Tomar and spread the other carefully over Tammina.

"I am pleased that you are staying, sir," he said. "It will be noisy in the town tonight. The Lord Roddori has seen his wife and child and has gone to start the bells a-ringing; and doubtless to celebrate the new life with his friends."

He moved to the window and pulled the hanging aside. "Without the tapestry you may be able to hear the bells. It is the tradition to start the ring at the church by the castle, where the Lords used to live."

Tomar nodded, overcome by the luxury of glazed lights in walls and the deference paid to him.

The bells were audible. They were faint with distance, but other churches began their peal and soon the night was filled with the joyous sound.

His heart lifted. Here at last was the elation! He turned towards the sofa as the servant let the tapestry fall. She had heard; he was sure of it. She smiled in her sleep.

"If there is nothing else, sir, I will leave."

There was nothing, but before he went the servant erected the screen and set two chairs beside the sofa. "It would not do for her to fall," he said. "Lord Parandour would not be pleased. He is very fond of her."

Tomar stirred the fire and removed his boots, but he took a moment to gaze again on the sleeping girl before he lay down to sleep, for he too was very fond of her.

In the morning, they went together to see their patient. Lady Drusil lay quietly, her colour only slightly better than when they had last seen her. Her eyes were closed and Tammina noticed the wetness on her eyelids.

"Are you in pain?" she asked softly.

The eyes opened briefly. "No, not pain. I am not comfortable, but it is not pain."

"Is it not?" questioned Tammina when she saw the great wound that crossed the poor girl's belly. It was too early for any sign of infection, but her body was dreadfully swollen.

"It looks to me sufficiently sore to be called pain. I have brought something that will help." She placed a flask and a small cup on the table.

"You may take it as you please, but do not take more than three cups full in one day. As you are not feeding your daughter yourself there is no need to restrict the dose beyond that."

She smiled. "Have you seen your daughter? She is a perfect child and she is thriving."

The large blue eyes opened again. "Yes, I have seen her and she is beautiful, but she is a girl and I cannot have another child. I cannot give my husband the son he wants." The voice was despairing and a tear ran down the pale cheek.

Tammina wiped it away.

"Yes, I can see that that is a matter for regret," she said with robust sympathy, "but it has been known for a woman to bear as many as six daughters and no sons. That is chance, or Namier's will. It is the fault of neither the woman, nor the man. Your daughter will learn and she may rule as wisely as any man."

The eyes opened wide in surprise.

"Oh, yes! Such things need to be learnt. No one is born knowing them. Ask your husband. His father is still teaching him, and both are still learning."

Tomar had poured a cup from the flask and he offered it. It was accepted with gratitude.

"You are kind – and skilled. Who taught you to cut?"

"My father was a butcher," answered Tomar. "He taught me accuracy and I was persuaded to cut by Healers, from my own village – and from elsewhere."

"My father was a fisherman," said Tammina. "Perhaps he regretted that his only child was a daughter, but he was a loving father. It was my mother who taught me to care for people," – Tammina thought of her mother, weeping for her dead love, but still rejoicing in the sun and the beauty of the land, "- and to value life."

They left her then. Her grief was her own, and she must learn to manage it as best she could.

Lord Parandour was in the sitting room.

"My son is sleeping," he said. "He celebrated until the bells ceased ringing last night, but he is grateful to you. He loves his wife. How is she? May I see her?"

"She is very weak. It will be some time before she is able to leave her bed," Tomar answered, "but she is alive. You may see her, but do not stay long."

Parandour nodded and moved towards the door, but Tammina stopped him.

"There is one problem. She does not complain of the pain that she must be suffering, but she is disappointed and distressed, because she has borne a daughter and cannot have another child."

She pleaded with him then. She had never pleaded before.

"Reassure her. Tell her that it is her *life* that is important, and her daughter's life. Tell her that a woman may rule just as well as a man."

"Women do not rule," he answered, frowning. "My lands are not ready for a woman to rule."

Tammina stiffened and prickled like a startled spineback.

"Then make them so!" she spat at him angrily. "You use women! You have used me. Namier's Power, can you not think of a good use for your own granddaughter!"

She turned her back on him and Tomar went towards her with arm outstretched.

"Mistress Farsay is right," he said mildly. "She sees. You know that, Lord, and have used it. That is why she is a superlative Healer. Your daughter-in-law will recover from the birth, but she may die of grief or by her own hand, if she is not reassured that her suffering has been worthwhile."

Lord Parandour stared at them with annoyance. He did not like to be instructed by his – his -. He sought for the right word. They were not slaves, nor mere labourers. They were his subjects, but they were valuable subjects, whose cooperation and whose work, he wanted.

"Very well," he said. "I will say nothing against her."

Tammina turned to face him. "Have you seen your granddaughter?" she asked, and when he shook his head, she said simply, "Then you must. Come," and led him from the room.

Tomar waited by the window. He was not needed. She could manage the Great Lord and would do better alone.

She did. When he returned, Lord Parandour looked bewildered and Tammina was confident and smiling.

"She is so small," he said.

"All newborn infants are small. She is feeding well and will grow fast. Go, tell Lady Drusil what a fine child she has borne," she said and waved him to the door.

"What a hopeful race we are," she continued. "There is so much pain and suffering in our world and yet we are so pleased when another child is born."

"I was relieved rather than pleased," answered Tomar honestly, "especially when we managed to stop the bleeding." He held out a hand in acknowledgement of the shared effort.

"And when we heard the child cry," she reaffirmed taking his hand.

"That too." He nodded. "He is grateful. Do you know that I am working for him? He is intending to expand the work of the Sick House and found a School of Medicine. It will be on a new site, close to a source of clean water. He has a Cutter and a Healer as figure-heads, but I –."

He hesitated. This was the moment; to ask and to tell her. He stood tall and continued proudly, "I am the director. I am planning the experiments and teaching; increasing and passing on my skills. We need a Healer, a young and enthusiastic Healer, in a similar role. Will you work with me?"

"But I -," she began and he interrupted firmly.

"Do not say that you are not a Healer. You are a fine Healer. I know that you struck someone once in anger, but you do not have to be perfect to be a Healer. You struck someone, *once*. It is past. Healing is in your blood, and in a School of Medicine you, like me, can both increase your knowledge and pass it on to others. Spread it wide and alleviate some of the pain and suffering in our world."

She looked down at her hand, still in his.

His long slender fingers were like Jael's. He was like Jael, but, then again, he was not at all like Jael. She smiled and nodded.

"Yes. I will work with you."

Tomar lifted her hand to his lips and kissed her fingers. "I am glad," he said.

She did not pull her hand away, and she seemed not to have noticed that his other arm was around her waist. This was another moment.

"And will you marry me, Mistress Farsay?"

She was startled and she did not answer immediately, but she did become aware of his arm about her and the closeness of his body.

There was no revulsion, no unease, only a sense of belonging. Did she want to belong to a man? Did she want to belong to Tomar? She considered.

"Yes, Master Shean," she said at last. "I will marry you," and she smiled at him.

At last, she smiled at him and all he desired was in her smile.

He gave a long sigh and would have kissed her on the lips, but the door opened and Lord Parandour appeared, so he did not. Instead he said again, but with more intensity, "I am glad."

Lord Parandour shut the door quietly behind him and regarded his subjects.

She had her back to him, but he could see that she had changed. The tension had gone, and the wariness. That air of 'otherness' that had set her apart, had vanished. His Witch had flown.

He knew a moment of regret, but it was only a moment. She would re-emerge as the Healer she had always been. She and Shean would lead his School of Healing. It would bring health to his people, and fame to his land.

The King of Cendara in Irrok, he would hear of it. He had four young sons already, and every one a Prince. There would be a husband for his granddaughter; a husband who would bring his title with him. She would be a Princess and her lands – his lands – would become a Princedom.

The Great Lord of Bosron let out a small sigh of pleasure.

Tammina turned and he studied her face. Her smile was serene.

Yes, his Witch had flown, but he had no more use for a witch. He walked forward to give them his blessing.

"I, too, am glad," he said.

Epilogue

Master Jared Shean rode happily along the broad track by the river. It was a fine afternoon and the sun glinted on the water. He had eaten well and had concluded a very satisfactory arrangement with his host. He gazed, as always, on the School of Medicine as he passed. The Great Lord Jared Parandour had founded it, but his ancestors had made it famous throughout Erion.

It was a source of pride in one way, and a drawback in another. One could not hide one's origins if everyone knew that Tomar Shean, the man who had made Cutters into respected professionals, had started life as a butcher. Fortunately no one knew how his wife, the Healer, had started life, and he frequently hinted that she had been nobly born, and her skills had been acquired tending the sick on her father's estate.

He skirted a copse of trees and smiled as his house came into view. It was in a splendid position on a small rise overlooking the river. The first dwelling had been built of wood and parts of it still remained at the back of the house, but the frontage was now enlarged and built of stone. Two wings had been added, but they were in proportion with the facade and made the house substantial but not ostentatious.

The track was a public thoroughfare, but a thick hedge guarded his land from the passers-by. He rode to its end and surveyed the farm that adjoined his land. Soon it would be his.

He had long coveted it, but had not dared to approach the highborn owner. Now the owner had approached him and they had agreed a price – a very reasonable price in his view. To be sure there was the small matter of the marriage of his daughter to the younger son, but that too had advantages. He was pleased with the arrangement.

Unfortunately, when he told his family of his splendid bargain, Linneath was not impressed, especially when she discovered that he could not describe the young man in question, for he had not met him.

"You have promised me to a man you have not even seen!" she exclaimed indignantly. "I do not consider that the fine looks of his elder brother have anything to do with the matter at all. Siblings differ. Look at Darl and I! He has fair hair, a large nose and a stocky figure. I am dark and slender and have neat features. This younger son may be fat and ugly and equally as superior in his manner as his elder brother. He I have met; and did not like!"

Darl grinned.

"The younger one may be as different from his brother as you are from me. He may be taller, less superior and a better rider. You may like him."

"It is all very fine for you," she retorted, whirling round to face him. "*You* will inherit enough land to apply for influential positions and to strut around the town in a short cloak; whereas *I* may be very unhappy."

"I do not wish you to be unhappy, Linnie," said her father. "You will not be *forced* into a marriage, but you should realise that the match will be advantageous for you also."

He began to enlarge upon that theme, but she interrupted.

"Oh, I am sure that you will not drag me to the ceremony, but you will persuade me by persistence, just as I was persuaded to ride with Geral Hostron yesterday, because he is the son of Mama's friend. He is *so* dull! Just like his mother."

She turned to her mother. "I do not know why you have such lacklustre friends, Mama," she declared in a decidedly disrespectful manner. "Why do you not have interesting friends with interesting sons?"

"Linneath!" exclaimed her father, using her full name, which he did only when he was angry. "Apologise to your mother at once!"

She coloured, but expressed no regrets. Instead she muttered sullenly, "But they *are* dull."

"Linneath," rebuked her mother sadly, and her father ordered her from the room. He took her to the servant's quarters in the old part of the house.

"Do not expect to be comfortable," he warned. "You owe your mother a very abject apology and, until you give it, you will be cold and hungry."

He locked her in a room and walked away.

Linnie was not pleased. She knew that she had been insolent and deserved to be punished, but the usual punishment was banishment to her bedroom or the schoolroom where at least there were books. She looked about her.

There was nothing here, not even a place to sit. The only chair was missing a leg and leaned drunkenly against an untidy heap of other discarded household items.

There were one or two pictures, and lacking any other occupation, she looked at them. All depicted plants, in leaf, flower or fruit; all were named and all had a use. She had seen many such. Everyone in the Shean family had, even those who had no inclination to study Healing.

One was different – a bunch of grapes with the inscription 'grapes – fermented to give alcohol, used for loosening the tongue.'

She laughed at that. Someone had had a sense of humour. No surprise that this drawing had been placed by itself, hung on a wall of cupboards. She opened them, one after another.

Some contained empty jars, some equipment which she recognised. How could she not? She was a Shean; and this had been a Healer's workroom.

She looked again at the picture and considered its position. It was not in the centre of the wall. There were two cupboards to one side and three to the other.

There must, she concluded, be a cupboard behind it; and there was, but it was locked. She stamped her foot in frustration. Where, in a room furnished with only a heap of rubbish, would she find the key?

She did not search; she did not know where to begin, but after a while the picture stirred her conscience and she lifted it up, intending to replace it – and found the key.

It was wrapped in fine cloth and pinned to the inside of the frame. It was easily removed and it fitted the lock, but it was rusted and would not turn.

She searched for some means of cleaning it, and found a torn sheet among the rubbish and a solid waxy material in one of the jars. She was not used to cleaning, and found it a dirty and unpleasant task. She did not manage to a produce a shine, but the surface gradually became smoother. It slipped more easily into the lock and eventually she managed to turn it and open the door.

Her elation turned to disappointment. The cupboard seemed to be empty! But why lock an empty cupboard and hide the key?

She looked again, more intently, and saw the tiny gap between base and sides.

There was no treasure beneath the false base, just a few sheets of paper. 'Recipes,' thought Linnie. 'Not worth filthy hands and a broken nail.'

Still, as she had nothing better to do, she lifted them out and began to read.

'Today Annia Helen Drusil, daughter of the Great Lord, was married to a Prince, third son of King Cendara of Irrok. Her grandfather, the first Great Lord, would have been proud.

I miss him still, though he has been dead for near three years. He understood me, and his son, Roddori, does not. He is ashamed and if he could, would wipe the Witch of Bellue from all memory. He has tried to remove all references from official records, but I do not know whether he has succeeded.

To do him justice, he did invite us to the celebration and it was a great occasion. Now it is night. We drank deeply, and Tomar sleeps but I cannot, so I have come to my workroom to think.

Roddori remembers that I was Witch, but none else has thought of me so for twenty years or more. It is twenty five since last I danced under the round moon.

I know now that Tomar watched that night and worried that I might burn myself. He knew the flames were real, but he has never asked that I tell him my secrets, and I have never offered.

Now I will write them down, but I shall hide my words, for now is not the time to make all known. Later, perhaps, there will a time, but knowledge can be dangerous – that is how it all began.'

Linnie put down the sheet. This was interesting. She arranged the torn sheet on the dusty floor before she sat down and started to read again.

She learnt of poison spines, profligate men and dangerous knowledge. She learned of revenge and derision, of sacrifice and subtlety, of shrewdness and of fear.

She read that chalk paste whitened limbs, but irritated skin, that a red variety of lova grew in the north and so too did a tree whose potentially useful blossoms attracted hornets. The Witch's life was told and her secrets were revealed.

It was dated and signed, 'Tammina Farsay Shean, Witch of Bellue.'

Linnie turned the last page and found more writing and another, later, date.

'We have returned to the north many times, but never to Telmarr's domain at the right time of year to find red lovas or the 'hornet tree' in bloom.

Whoever reads this, may be moved to do that for me; but take care. The oil from red lovas may be better than ale for extraction of ingredients, but it takes fire easily so stay alert. The blossoms from the tree do cause unconsciousness, but vapour is difficult to direct and control and in large quantities it may be harmful. I regret that now I do not have time to experiment.

As to this document, use your judgement. If you feel the time is right, show it to all of Eastland; if you do not, hide it, as I have hidden it, for another age.

Tammina Farsay Shean'

Linnie re-read a few paragraphs and laughed; she hugged herself in delight. Since her earliest days, her several-greats grandmother had been held up as a model of decorum and sobriety; and here she admitted, almost revelled in the fact, that she was the Witch of Bellue!

She had not been evil, that was plain, but neither had she been the staid and forbidding creature who stared down from the wall in the entrance to the School.

"Perhaps,' mused Linnie, 'Tomar was also different from the severe man in his portrait. They did have five children!"

She stroked the signature with her fingers.

"Dear Great – however many – grandmother, what shall I do? Find your red lovas and your hornet tree, certainly; but how? How do I persuade Father to allow me to travel north? Namier's moon! It will be difficult! I must be very apologetic, and meek, and humble, and probably volunteer to ride with the tedious Geral and marry Fidel Mayenjon as he wishes. But it must be done."

She started by closing the cupboard, hanging the picture in its place and hiding the written pages in her bodice. She began to practice her penitent expression – she had need of it frequently – but it was banished suddenly by a broad smile. She had had a splendid idea!

Aunt Jenna Shean, her Naming Sponsor, lived in the north. She was elderly and a visit, now that Linneath was eighteen, could almost be considered a duty. Linnie rarely felt dutiful, but she was good at appearing so. Such a visit, she would argue, had best be made soon, before marriage, for *afterwards* it might be more difficult.

A suitable expression to accompany that observation required thought.

Master Shean accompanied his offspring and their guide, one Dontor Baldron, to the docks. They did not think it either necessary or desirable; for he had given all three detailed instructions and comprehensive warnings on several occasions.

He began to repeat them as soon as the carriage reached the road.

Master Baldron, who had accompanied many young people on their travels, was well used to parent's anxieties, but none of his standard reassurances were voiced. Linneath spoke before he could, pleading with her father not to frighten her more and threatening to run home if he did.

"And I do *so* want to visit Aunt Jenna, and all your arrangements will be wasted if I run back to Mama."

No more concerns were expressed. Instead Master Baldron was able to listen to calming phrases issuing from a parent's mouth. He concealed his amusement, and they boarded the ship and waved farewell to Bosron without further strictures.

"Linneath Shean!" exclaimed Darl as they stood together on the deck, "You are a wicked liar! You are not in the least inclined to run home! I do not know how you persuaded Father to allow us to come on this journey in the first place. He certainly would not have permitted it had Fidel Mayenjon been at home; but he, like us, is travelling and apparently is in no hurry to return."

"Perhaps his father has not told him of his plans, or perhaps he has and Fidel likes them as little as I do. How can one love a man called Fidel? Every second son is called Fidel and they are all *so* dull!"

Darl laughed at her vehemence.

"You are wrong. Some elder sons are called Fidel and not all are dull; just as you are not always right!"

He ceased laughing and returned to his original theme.

"I admit that Father's warnings have been exceptionally tedious, but playing the timid miss to stop them was dangerous. Master Baldron may think you fearful and allow us no freedom at all!"

"I considered that before I spoke," declared his sister complacently. "So I have spoken to him and he does not think me afraid. Also, he is used to worried parents," – a trace of doubt entered her voice as she continued – "and their 'over-confident offspring'. That was what he said. *You* must have appeared too rash."

Unsurprisingly this remark initiated a lively argument that lasted until the two unseasoned sailors decided first that they were hungry, then that they were not, and both retired to their cabins to lie down.

Darl was not surprised that his sister recovered from sea-sickness as swiftly as he did for she was a robust girl, but he was surprised at her interest in their mentor's educational talks.

She gazed out at the barely visible coastline of Bellue and listened with apparent interest to a lengthy discourse on how it had changed. The fort still stood, but to the east some of the northern shore had been undermined by the waves and fallen away, and closer to Bosron the sea had shed its burden and broadened the beaches beneath the cliffs.

At the first port of call, she ignored the lure of the stalls and the cries of the vendors and spent hours studying a viaduct. To be sure, it was an historic one, built by Parandour to commemorate his victories, but it did not warrant more than a brief visit. Also the purchase of a shawl, however fine, could have been made without showing *quite* so much interest in old pictures of the area.

His comment that they were sadly inaccurate, the sea being far too close, elicited a stern correction and she began to lecture him on the manner in which the coastline had changed.

Angry that he had not had time to sample more than one of the various shellfish on offer, he interrupted his sister rudely and a serious quarrel ensued.

The discord lasted until they reached Felten. Neither sibling was happy to be at odds with one another, but neither was prepared to offer the first conciliatory word. Master Baldron did not attempt to mediate. Young men settled arguments physically and did not bear grudges, but females were different. He was not accustomed to dealing with them and left ill alone for fear of making it worse.

Darl left the ship as soon as they docked at Felten. He left his baggage in his cabin and went in search of the fish market and the local delicacies. The stalls were found easily enough, but the choice was overwhelming.

Standing uncertainly in front of a large selection of smoked fish, he was joined by another, more knowledgeable, young man who advised him on what to buy. He made his purchase and he made a friend.

Linnie was at first unimpressed. She had been left in the unwilling care of a seaman whilst Master Baldron searched for the carriage that was supposed to meet them. Standing in such poor company on a windy quay and surrounded by baggage had soured her temper.

Darl did not notice.

"This is Jon," he announced cheerfully. "He knows about fish. There is so much to tempt, that I could not make up my mind; but his choice is excellent!"

He offered her a damp bag and invited her to taste.

"I do not think your sister will want to eat here," interposed the young man before Linnie could make her own indignant refusal, "but the smoked ray may be safely transported to your lodgings for her to enjoy in private."

He doffed his hat, bowed deeply and gave a friendly smile. The proffered package was well wrapped and dry. Linnie's frown disappeared.

Master Baldron returned some minutes later to find the three young people chatting happily. The seaman, whom he had hoped would assist with the baggage, had disappeared as soon as Darl had returned, but fortunately Jon was willing to carry a bag.

"Rather too willing," thought the guide, seeing the new arrival take up a place by Linnie's side, "and too charming; but he is well dressed and impeccably mannered."

He was also concerned by the fact that the young man was staying at the same hostelry and travelling in the same direction as they were, but a discreet enquiry revealed that he was a man of quality, with relatives in Felten. He had been there for several weeks and his travelling arrangements had been made some time ago.

Master Baldron relaxed. There seemed no reason to suppose that the new acquaintance was out to steal either the purse of one charge, or the heart of the other. He was further reassured when he overheard the young gentleman making enquiries of his own. It showed wisdom to ascertain the background of those whom one met along the way.

They spent several days in Felten for it was an old port of great importance in the north. Darl was disappointed that his new friend left before they did, but was consoled by the knowledge that he too was intending to visit the birthplace of the famous Tomar Shean and the site of Parandour's last battle.

Linnie missed Jon almost as much as did her brother, but she admitted only that he rode well and was not as dull as Geral. His company had made a pleasant change from that of Master Baldron whose discourses on Felten's history could be tedious. She was obliged to listen attentively though. He was an observant man and it would not do if he suspected that her prime interest was in the Witch of Bellue. She was glad when they moved on to Aunt Jenna's house.

It was a small house with no stables. The horses and carriage were accommodated at the village inn where Master Baldron also stayed. He had been saved from the ordeal of sharing a room with Darl by Jenna Shean. She commented quietly that this was not Bosron. Strangers and their doings were noted and even the wildest of young persons would come to little harm in the neighbourhood.

Darl was delighted with the freedom he was given.

"It is true," he owned to his sister, "that there is little social life here, but I am not questioned about whom I met and what we talked of, immediately I return from a ride. And that horse I borrow is a fine animal."

Linnie smiled. "Aunt Jenna does not need to ask. She hears. She was pleased that you discussed the breeds of buffalo with the farmer whose name I cannot remember, and amused that you dismounted to walk the shepherdess through the woods."

She glanced briefly at her brother's scarlet cheeks before changing the subject.

"For myself, I think it worth the journey simply to see these portraits." She waved a hand at the array on the wall. "They may not have been painted by distinguished artists, but they are all so full of life. I am not ashamed to own these people as my ancestors."

Darl agreed gratefully and they spent a full half hour contrasting the stern faces displayed in the School of Medicine with these friendly, informal pictures of Tomar and Tammina Shean.

"She was certainly dutiful and dedicated," concluded Linnie, "but I believe that this artist found her good company. I am sure that there is laughter in those eyes."

Aunt Jenna was also good company and, for a widow of advancing years, unexpectedly adventurous. She would, she announced, travel with them to Telmarr Castle. It was years since she had last seen it; or indeed seen anything other than the road to Felten. She would pay her own way, naturally. She would not be a burden on their father's purse.

As they had been housed and fed at her expense for near a week this was not a prime consideration, but it was possible that the journey would be slower in her company.

It was not. She brought but one bag and she rode for most of the way, declaring that one was able to see so much more from a horse than from a carriage. For the most part, they travelled at a gentle pace, but even Darl acknowledged that her sturdy mount was urged to a very smart canter when speed was required.

There was an inn not far from the battle site and it was there that they encountered Jon once more.

Linnie was pleased. If the two young men kept company, it would, she reasoned, be easier to explore alone and search for the red lovas and the hornet tree that she so wanted to find. Master Baldron and her aunt were of her parent's generation and she had rarely had any difficulty in escaping their attention when she had wished to do so. Obviously she had chosen a suitable hour and had never 'disappeared' for any great length of time, but older people generally assumed that young ladies were abed or safely occupied with household duties and did not ask awkward questions. Her brother, on the other hand, frequently did ask awkward questions and usually at the most inopportune moments.

Jon had visited the most important places already, but he did not seem averse to revisiting them in company and Aunt Jenna made no objection. She had consulted Master Baldron and had been intrigued by one of his disclosures, but she said nothing to anyone.

The visits to the impressive Telmarr Castle, the battle field and the walk by the Aishe occupied most of the next few days. Linnie enjoyed them. She heard many stories about the Witch of Bellue, all reputed to have been handed down from ancestors who had taken part in the battle or witnessed the Witch's dance on the night she changed the river's course. They reinforced Linnie's resolve, but she had no opportunity to explore alone. An early morning expedition was her last resort.

Only the kitchens of the inn were busy on the morning that she slipped out and she did not encounter anyone, but the grooms were already about their business in the stables so she abandoned all thoughts of taking a horse.

It was as well, she thought, as she walked. It was some way to the hill, and a lone female rider might attract attention, whereas a lone female on foot was not unusual. Also she carried a packet containing the precious letter. It would have been a greater encumbrance on horseback.

With more forethought, she might have copied the most important passages and left the original in the hiding place where it had lain so long, but she had not considered the matter; and had she done so she would probably have come to the conclusion that it was as safe with her as it had ever been.

It was a steep climb and she was tired and disappointed long before she reached the summit of the hill. There were fewer trees than she had expected and brown lovas grew in terraces on the slopes. Now they were cultivated here, as they had been for years in the south. That meant that red lovas would have been rooted out.

She hugged the packet to her chest. She must not be despondent. She must persist as Tammina Shean had surely done.

Despite her resolve, after more than half an hour searching beneath the trees, she was despondent and so near to tears that she almost stood on the single red fruit that lay among the leaves.

She stopped so suddenly that she stumbled and fell, but she did not care, for there, hidden beneath the more vigorous growth, was the bush she sought.

She pulled a drawing from her precious package and knelt to compare the leaves and fruit. It was a poor specimen, with weak growth and small, sparse fruit, but it was a red lova. She had found one thing that she sought!

She was still on her knees when she heard the first rumble – dull and slow, as a distant roll of thunder. Instinctively she tucked the drawing back into its packet to protect it from the expected rain, but a moment later she laughed at her precaution. The sky was cloudless and the season for thunder had passed.

She ceased laughing and frowned. What had caused the noise?

There was no enlightenment from her surroundings, so she gathered some of the fruits and broke off one or two shoots. If red lovas did prove to be useful, it would be necessary to propagate more plants. Pleased with her success, she stood up and went in search of the hornet tree.

She stopped after a short distance, feeling suddenly dizzy. The world had seemed to tilt.

"I ought to eat," she thought, and sat down. In her bag was some bread and cheese that she had secreted at dinner last evening, but had forgotten in her excitement. Now she realised that she was hungry.

She had eaten more than half her food before another rumble disturbed her. It was louder this time and she stood up and looked about her.

The branches of the trees higher up the hill were moving, but there was no wind. The world seemed to tilt again, and this time she recognised that it was not dizziness. The ground had moved!

She knew of groundshakes – every child was taught about them, but they did not happen in Bosron. They happened in other lands, or occasionally in Salima's mountains. She was not in the mountains, but they were near. She stood very still and concentrated on watching and listening.

The birds were not singing. They were calling in alarm and flocks of them rose above the swaying trees. There were no farm animals near, but there were animal sounds – high pitched squeals and deep throated roars that she did not recognise.

A rabbit scampered in front of her. It was followed by others and also by a fox and a wild boar. They were not chasing food; they were running, running from the uncertain ground and the tilting trees and seeking safety.

She did not run, but like the animals, she went downwards. She knew no reason for her choice, but her instinct, like that of the wild things, led to lower ground. A moment later, she knew that it was right for stones began to tumble down the slope.

She heard the scream of an animal, but she did not turn. Her own name was called almost at the same moment. She did not recognise the voice – it was harsh with urgency – but she ran towards it.

She ran through the falling stones and stumbled on the uncertain ground. She fell sideways and looking up was horrified to see a much larger stone, almost a boulder, bounding down the hill towards her. There was no time to gain her feet. She covered her head with her arms and rolled.

"Linnie! Linnie!" The voice was despairing.

She raised her head. The boulder had passed without touching her, but she had dropped her bag and the precious packet and both were slipping downwards out of reach.

"Linnie! Namier be praised, you are safe!"

Jon lifted her to her feet and held her close, pulling her away from the mass of debris that followed the boulder. She did not struggle, but she turned her head away.

"My papers!" she cried, but she saw that it was too late. She did not need Jon to tell her that they were lost. She watched sadly as they tumbled among the soil and stones, the broken branches and the uprooted clods of grass.

"*You* are safe," Jon was saying, "and you are more valuable than a few papers."

He did not ask what they were, he hurried her downwards calling to Darl that he had found her and she was safe.

Her brother scolded when they met and shook her hard, but briefly, for they needed to hasten away. He took her hand though, and held it as they ran and she knew that he was not angry. He had been anxious and was relieved to find her.

She had not been anxious; she had scarce had time to think of her own safety and it had not occurred to her that others might be in danger. Now she wondered about her Aunt and Master Baldron, but had no breath to ask.

She saw the stream of people before they reached the road and amongst the walkers was a cart. Aunt Jenna, surrounded by baggage, was standing in it anxiously scanning the turbulent countryside for her charges and Master Baldron was at the horse's head.

He too was anxious, but the groom and driver needed his help to manage the horse. All others had broken free and galloped away after the first shake, and this frightened creature wanted to follow them.

Linnie would not have owned it, but she was glad to stop running and wait for the cart to reach them. She was not glad to find that at some point she had hurt her ankle. Fear had made her unaware of it, but now that they had ceased their headlong rush, the pain became evident.

She stood on one foot and moved the other carefully. It was not broken, she concluded, but when she put it to the ground she knew that she could not walk far.

Darl was waving reassurance to Aunt Jenna and did not notice her discomfort, but Jon did.

"Are you hurt?" he asked and slipped his arm around her in support before she answered.

"My ankle," she replied, wishing that his concern did not give her so much pleasure. "I do not think I will be able to walk far."

"You will not have to," he said and picked her up.

Much to his disgust he needed Darl's help to lift her into the cart, but he made sure that it was he who lifted the injured limb and laid it gently on the luggage opposite.

"We have your bag," Aunt Jenna declared complacently.

Despite the panic all around her when the first shake had been felt, Aunt Jenna had insisted upon all their belongings being packed. She was aware that the fine shirts and coats would be stuffed hastily into convenient spaces, but that was not important. Nothing would be left for the inevitable looters.

Linnie's eyes followed her aunt's pointing finger, but her casual glance sharpened into interest when Jon thanked her. His voice betrayed his feelings and they were not entirely grateful.

His bag was of good leather, as was her own, and like hers initials were embossed discreetly into the hide.

F G M

She read them aloud, slowly, and looked at him.

"Why are you called Jon?" she asked.

"When a boy is named Fidel Gerharst, as so many are, he chooses another name, with fewer connotations."

Linnie stared at him suspiciously, but he turned and spoke to her aunt. He knew that there was space for him in the cart, but he was well able to walk and many on the road, fleeing from the shake, were less able. Would she object if he gave his place to one such?

She did not, and an elderly woman carrying a large bundle and balancing a stew pan on her head, gratefully accepted a ride.

Darl did not take his seat either. He handed up a young woman, big with child, and lifted onto the willing laps a wooden cradle that her man was carrying in addition to several heavy sacks.

"You are most kind, sir," she said and apologised for the weight of the cradle. "He would not leave it," she explained, looking lovingly down at the young man. "He made it from the trunk of a great tree, and spent much time making it smooth. The babe is due soon and he wanted our child to have a cradle, no matter what else we had to leave behind."

Her eyes filled with tears as she spoke, and the old woman patted her hand.

"A good man is worth all the goods in Erion," she said.

"Indeed that is so," agreed Aunt Jenna emphatically.

Linnie, who had not taken long to link the initial M and the taken name Jon with Mayenjon, glared at her.

"You knew!" she whispered venomously.

Aunt Jenna nodded and replied quietly,

"I could not permit either of you to become friendly with anyone whose parentage I did not know."

Linnie allowed that, but she did not think that Jon's identity should have been kept from her, and when her aunt murmured that she had left it to the young man to announce himself, Linnie turned her baleful glare on him.

Darl had not interpreted the initials as swiftly as his sister had done, but immediately he understood the situation he dropped tactfully back.

"I did not intend to deceive you, Mistress Shean. We met by chance and I did not know who you were until I heard Master Baldron say your name."

Jon looked up at her appealingly, "I ought to have told you, but I did not find the right opportunity. When is there a good moment to tell a young lady, whom you have met by chance and have come to admire, that you are the man her father has chosen for her?"

Linnie stared at him doubtfully. Did he admire her? She knew that she was pretty, but that was not an admirable quality. She answered his question instead of fretting about his choice of word. It was a robust reply, but delivered with hint of laughter.

"Indeed I do not know, but it is certainly not when she is sitting with a sore ankle in a crowded cart and fleeing from a ground shake!"

He gave her a swift smile, but his thoughts were on a small child who seemed determined to run under the horse's feet and who at that moment broke free of his mother's hand.

Linnie watched him run to the rescue and swing the child in a high arc. It squealed in delight and he repeated the action.

"Sir, she will tire you out," protested the mother, but Jon shook his head.

"I will tire her first, I think, for I am not carrying my belongings; and when she is sleepy she can ride on the cart for a while."

Linnie smiled her assent. If she were able to walk, she would be happy to do so, and a child on her lap was not an onerous undertaking.

She heard a familiar song and looked for her brother. He was singing the rhyme that they had sung as children when they were tired and did not want to walk. Several little ones were about him, holding hands and chanting.

"They are good men," said the old woman.

"No more than is right," commented Aunt Jenna, but the curt words were softened with a smile. "We would be a sad race if we did not help one another in times of trial; besides," she added proudly, "we are Sheans, and the Shean family have a tradition of service to others."

Her passengers nodded. They had seen the labels on the baggage and everyone had heard of the Shean family and the School of Medicine in Bosron.

Linnie looked down on the two young men and her heart filled with love for them both. Jon was not a Shean, but he would be part of the family when they married; and was worthy of such a place.

Perhaps it was as well that she had lost the papers. Her ancestor would be for ever associated with good, with the School of Medicine and the care of the sick; and the Witch of Bellue would become a legend, a magical creature who had served the Great Lord with fire and spells and curses, and vanished when her work was done.

As she thought of Tammina Shean, Linnie recalled the portraits. The stern face that gazed down on all who entered the School of Medicine would not want to be remembered as a witch; and the lady who smiled on her aunt's house, though she had written of her actions in a nostalgic moment, would not care one way or another.

Linnie had laughed with her brother at some of the wilder tales about the Witch of Bellue and she was sure that Tammina Shean, wherever her spirit roamed, would do so too.